Worthy of Legend

Books by Roseanna M. White

LADIES OF THE MANOR

The Lost Heiress
The Reluctant Duchess
A Lady Unrivaled

SHADOWS OVER ENGLAND

A Name Unknown
A Song Unheard
An Hour Unspent

THE CODEBREAKERS

The Number of Love
On Wings of Devotion
A Portrait of Loyalty

Dreams of Savannah

THE SECRETS OF THE ISLES

The Nature of a Lady
To Treasure an Heiress
Worthy of Legend

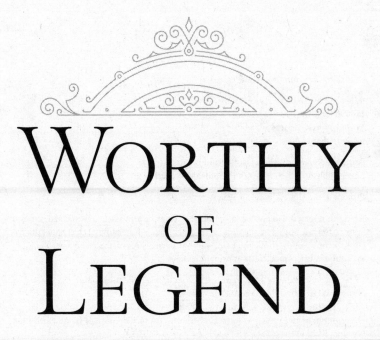

WORTHY
OF
LEGEND

ROSEANNA M. WHITE

BETHANYHOUSE
a division of Baker Publishing Group
Minneapolis, Minnesota

© 2022 by Roseanna M. White

Published by Bethany House Publishers
11400 Hampshire Avenue South
Minneapolis, Minnesota 55438
www.bethanyhouse.com

Bethany House Publishers is a division of
Baker Publishing Group, Grand Rapids, Michigan

Printed in the United States of America

Library of Congress Cataloging-in-Publication Data
Names: White, Roseanna M., author.
Title: Worthy of legend / Roseanna M. White.
Description: Minneapolis, Minnesota: Bethany House, a division of Baker Publishing Group, [2022] | Series: Secrets of the Isles; 3
Identifiers: LCCN 2022010981 | ISBN 9780764237201 (paperback) | ISBN 9780764240898 | ISBN 9781493439140 (ebook)
Subjects: LCGFT: Novels.
Classification: LCC PS3623.H578785 W67 2022 | DDC 813/.6—dc23
LC record available at https://lccn.loc.gov/2022010981

Scripture quotations are from the King James Version of the Bible.

This is a work of historical reconstruction; the appearances of certain historical figures are therefore inevitable. All other characters, however, are products of the author's imagination, and any resemblance to actual persons, living or dead, is coincidental.

Cover design by Jennifer Parker
Cover photography by Todd Hafermann Photography, Inc.

Author is represented by The Steve Laube Agency.

Baker Publishing Group publications use paper produced from sustainable forestry practices and post-consumer waste whenever possible.

22 23 24 25 26 27 28   7 6 5 4 3 2 1

To Rowyn,
for always building me a library in your game worlds,
even though you don't share my love of books;
for laughing at all my jokes and coming out to share
with me all the ones you hear online;
for rising to the challenge
and taking life's curveballs in stride.

Since your diagnosis, I'm keenly aware
that each day with you is a gift from God.
Mama loves you more than you'll ever know.
I love seeing the young man you're becoming . . .
but resign yourself now to always being my boy-o,
no matter how much taller than me you grow.

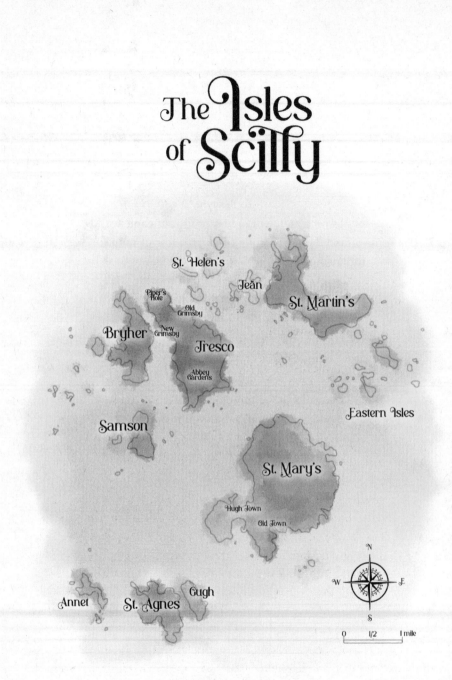

The Isles of Scilly

St. Helen's

Jean

St. Martin's

Piper's Hole

Old Grimsby

New Grimsby

Bryher

Tresco

Abbey Gardens

Eastern Isles

Samson

St. Mary's

Hugh Town

Old Town

N

W · E

S

0   1/2   1 mile

Annet   St. Agnes   Cugh

Cornwall due East 28 miles >

Prologue

The sea was vengeance. The sea was justice. The sea was the hand of the Almighty, stretched out to slap and strike. Elizabeth Mucknell turned her eyes from the tumultuous crash of the waves, bundle clutched to her chest and feet feeling for the next crag of rock beneath the thin soles of her slippers.

If John ever knew what she held in her hands, his fate would be sealed. She'd lose him to the waters, just as the last person to hold it had lost his entire domain. He mustn't know. He must never find out. If he did . . .

Tears lashed at her eyes as the wind lashed at her face. She scanned the dark horizon one more time, satisfied at last that no one had followed her. Then she turned and made her way through the dusk, toward the hiding place she'd stumbled across two years ago.

Praise the Lord that she'd found it first. That *she* had been the one to reach her hand into that crevasse and pull out the artifact. If John had beaten her to it . . . well, her husband was many things. But *noble* wasn't one of them. She daren't imagine what would have befallen him had he set his gaze on this living legend and seen only the silver or gold it could bring him. The fame. The fortune.

She blinked the tears from her eyes, though still they burned. She loved John. Loved him because he was hers and she was his. Loved him because the Lord had knit them together and made them one. Loved him because she'd sworn to. She loved him because hidden under the cutthroat ambition and the cruel streak and the drunkenness was a heart that just craved acceptance and approval, as they all did. She loved him because he would move heaven and earth for her . . . even when she begged him not to try it.

How many times had he said he did it all for her? The piracy, the mutiny, the murder?

How did he not realize how it broke her heart each and every time she heard it? How could he not understand the terrible burden he placed on her soul with those words?

Only the moon lit her path as she navigated over the granite, toward that opening too small to rightly be termed a cave. There were legends about it, here on the islands. Legends about the artifact she'd found too. Legends that, praise God, had led her here first.

She'd known the moment her finger touched metal that she must protect him from it. She must keep him, at all costs, from discovering what she had. Otherwise, the same curse from heaven that had swallowed Lyonesse would swallow him too. She'd lose him to the waters. Forever gone. Swept away. Drowned.

John, my John. The words sing-songed through her mind the same way they'd been doing for decades. Because despite it all, she loved him. It was a burden, but one she gladly bore for his sake. Perhaps if she prayed hard enough, if she interceded enough, as Trevelyan had done for his people, then God would have mercy on him. Perhaps someone else would reach his stubborn heart for the Lord—little Eben, perhaps, with his heart of gold.

Lizza, my Lizza. She heard his echoing song in her heart, and it made her smile into the darkness. Her husband may be, as Mother had declared twenty years ago, a drunken, ambitious fool, but he loved her. His first thought was always for her. He took her with him everywhere he dared—not like so many other seafaring men who just looked in each port for a new woman to warm their bed.

And he even brought Eben, his cabin boy, home for her to dote on. She a woman with no child, he a child with no mother.

John had his strengths. His good qualities. He was brave, he was clever, he was loyal—to those he deemed worthy.

Her fingers went tight around the leather wrapping she held. Would he be angry if he discovered what she'd been hiding from him all this time? So angry that he'd toss her aside? *Nay.* He loved her more than silver or gold or legend. Didn't he?

Regardless, it was done now. Tomorrow she would leave Tresco. Now that Charles was back on his rightful throne, these waters wouldn't yield the bounty they once had. No more preying on East Indiamen. If John was to continue to make his fortune with piracy, he'd have to go somewhere else with the king's commission.

The Caribbean, he said. But he didn't know enough about it to know if it was safe for her to come, and the journey would be so long. He'd said, sorrow in his eyes, that they'd better not risk it, not yet. She ought to return to London. Stay with her sister, or use some of the silver he'd put away to buy a tidy little house of her own.

Her teeth clenched. Her sister, yes. Spend his stolen, bloodstained silver, *never*. She hadn't said it, but he knew her answer to his suggestion. It was why his eyes had flashed, why he'd slammed his tankard onto the table too forcefully. *"I only did any of it for you!"* he'd roared. *"Will you turn your nose up at all I've provided?"*

It wasn't how she'd meant to spend their last evening together before he left.

There it was. She stopped, stood for a moment, just stared at the black streak in the rock, darker than the night around it. The moonlight glinted off lighter bits, and she sucked in a breath. John's mark. He'd carved it there, into the granite, marking it as another possible place to store what pieces of booty he didn't see fit to turn over to the prince. She dropped to her knees and felt around inside, but it was empty.

Her breath heaved out in a rush. Good. He'd have no reason to check it again, then. And if he found treasure in the Caribbean, he wouldn't come back to the Isles of Scilly to stash it; he'd bring it to London. This crevice, where the artifact had been at home for centuries already, would be its home again without worry.

She slid the leather-wrapped treasure, long and slender, back into its place and scrambled to her feet. And she stared at it, then out at the sea.

Her fingers curled into her palms. "You won't have him," she told the vengeful waters. "Not if I have anything to say about it."

The waters laughed upon the rocks.

1

Lady Emily Scofield had become an expert over the years at blending into shadows. Or wallpaper. Or furniture—she could hide herself quite effectively beside a nice armoire. And crowds—crowds were the best camouflage of all.

She tilted her head down a few degrees, so that her wide-brimmed hat would not only shade her face but also keep the beacon of her scarlet hair out of view of the cluster of gentlemen standing in a knot outside the telegraph and post office. And she kept moving slowly, haphazardly, just like all the other tourists ambling along the cobblestone street of Hugh Town. As if she were just one more of the carefree throng.

The note she meant to send to her mother in London weighed a stone in her pocket. Why bother, anyway? It wasn't worth the risk. If she pushed through that crowd of trustees from the British Museum, one of them might recognize her and she'd lose her anonymity. Point her out to her father or, worse, her brother. Then they'd remember she was here, and they'd remember her betrayal, and she'd pay for it a thousand times over.

No, better to let them forget her.

They were good at that. And she at encouraging it. Being forgotten by the Scofield men was a far better alternative to being thought of by them.

Her brother's thoughts inevitably left her with scars—emotional ones, if not physical ones.

Her father shifted in the crowd, coming more fully into sight. He was laughing, booming out his mirth at something one of the other gentlemen said. Light covering darkness, that's what his laugh was. A mask. To look at him, hear him, one would never guess that he had no heart in his chest.

No, that was unfair. He *had* a heart. It was just that he'd never granted her a place in it.

Two more steps, three, and then she was past them. She wanted to let her shoulders sag, but that wouldn't do. She had to keep walking like every other visiting lady on St. Mary's, shoulders square and posture impeccable.

Emily was good at the mask too. And in order for it to be effective, to ensure she blended in with the crowd of her peers, she had to make certain it didn't slip for even a moment.

She had no idea where she meant to go now that her actual errand had been circumvented, so she kept trailing the half-dozen white-clad ladies she'd made herself look a part of. They had the posh and polished accents of London educations, and she caught a few wisps of conversation here and there that made her think they'd been in Town just a few days ago. This soiree and that ball and whether Lord So-and-So would be hosting a house party over Christmas again.

She hadn't at all minded missing most of the Season this year. In London, she had endless acquaintances but few true friends. And it was impossible to ignore, there, the truth of her part in the Scofield family—just a box to be ticked off. *Lovely daughter, check.* And then foisted onto the most advantageous potential husband. Father hadn't decided yet what match would best suit him. But he would. Soon. She'd heard him grumbling not two months ago to her mother that he tired of wasting good silver on the hats and shoes and gowns necessary for her.

What he'd meant was that he was tired of wasting time and energy on *her*.

The gaggle of women was leading her to the quay, she realized a minute later. Emily checked the watch pinned to her sash. How long could that knot of men stay tied up in front of the telegraph office? If she turned back now, would they be gone?

Better to give it a few minutes more.

The ferry was just tying up, which meant a new passel of holiday-goers was debarking. How many, she wondered, were here just for the day, and how many had cottages let in their name or rooms at the hotel ready to receive them?

Her gaze drifted to the two yachts anchored in the deeper waters. She hadn't been brave enough, in this last week since the British Museum's team had shown up, to ask around to see where they were all staying. Perhaps on the yachts—heaven knew they had room enough.

"But I don't *want* to go home yet, Mama!" A small lad's whining voice snatched her attention. She looked over to see a sunny-haired boy of perhaps six tugging on the hand of a woman who didn't look to be quite of the London-society ilk but who wore last year's fashions well.

The woman chuckled. "I know you don't, Charlie. But with the amount they gave us for those rooms, we can holiday for weeks more on the mainland. You wanted to explore Land's End, didn't you?"

Or maybe they *weren't* staying on the yachts—at least not all of them. Emily sighed. She didn't much care where Lord Wilhelm or Mr. Scott were staying. But she needed to find out where Nigel and Father were. Otherwise, how could she continue to avoid them?

She checked her watch again. If she dawdled much longer, Briggs would grow worried and come in search of her. Emily had assured her maid she needn't interrupt her letter writing to accompany her—the post office was just a few doors down from

13

their flat above the hat shop, after all. But she'd already been gone twenty minutes.

Lifting her gaze, she scanned the newly arrived visitors for another likely group she could tag along behind, back into town.

There—two gentlemen, but they looked like the family sort. There was a woman between them dressed in the pinnacle of fashion, ushering two older girls along. The eldest of the girls looked to be only a few years younger than Emily, and the younger had a mahogany tint to her hair. Emily could blend in well enough with them. She would simply look like the eldest of three, or perhaps a cousin or friend.

As the family strode along the planks of the ferry's dock, Emily fell in behind them, which meant she couldn't help but catch snippets of their conversation.

". . . I *live* on the seashore, Mary. I have no need to *holiday* at one."

The mother of the group let out a gusty sigh. "Really, Ambrose, it isn't at all the same. You can't exactly bathe in the waters in North Yorkshire, can you?"

The younger of the girls caught the man's hand. "I'd try it! Let's do, Uncle. Next time we visit you there."

The man—Ambrose—chuckled. "You'd catch your death, then I'd never hear the end of it from your mother."

The other man—the girls' father, from the looks of him—tugged lightly on the girl's braid. "Which is his only concern, of course. He'd feed you both to the sharks without a wince if your mother wouldn't whine about it."

As the girls squealed a protest, the first man let out a snort of laughter. "Watch yourself, Ram, or I'll decide to spend Christmas with you after all, to punish you."

Christmas. Emily let a few more feet come between them, so that the wind snatched their conversation from her before she could hear it. The holiday was still four months away—but where would she be then? She couldn't go home. Not until either Father relented or she apologized to Nigel.

Her throat went tight, and she lifted her chin. She wouldn't. Couldn't. It may have taken her twenty years, but she'd finally stood her ground, and if she backed down now, he'd never learn. Never change. And he *must*. If her brother continued on this path, it would be his end. She knew it would. He was worse even than their father in his dealings, thinking he could walk all over whomever he pleased and just pay them off when they objected.

He had to stop. And if he wouldn't of his own volition, then he had to *be* stopped.

Why would he listen to her, though? He never had before.

Father God, help me to reach him—*them*, she amended when the telegraph office came into view again. Surely Mother, at least, would soften. Surely. She wouldn't remain silent forever . . . would she? Eventually one of these wires Emily sent every other day, or one of the letters she penned twice a week, would be answered. Mother still loved her. Mother would take her side. Mother would . . .

Do whatever Father told her to do. Just like she always had.

"'Scuse me!"

Emily leaped out of the way just in time to avoid being run over by a massive cart full of steamer trunks and hat boxes. She backed up as far as she could, which was farther than she'd anticipated, given that a narrow alley was behind her.

A narrow alley with an awning stretched between the buildings, closing it in. It wasn't exactly dark. Certainly wasn't threatening. But those facts, which she went so far as to mutter under her breath, didn't keep her palms from going damp or her breath from tangling up in her chest.

The walls were bending toward each other, closing in on her, threatening to topple. She squeezed her eyes shut and rested one hand on the summer-warm stone of the nearest building. Proof to herself that it wasn't moving. And that it was *stone*, a building, not that stupid wardrobe. *You're not five, Emily. You're not locked in anywhere. Chin up. Stiff upper lip. Move on.*

The pep talk didn't calm her racing heart, but the familiar words convinced her to open her eyes again and focus her gaze on the brilliant sunshine just a step away.

The cart of trunks and boxes had lumbered its way past, so Emily dragged a breath into her stubborn lungs and moved back into the street. Much as she tried, she could never explain to anyone that when she took one step away from close, dark spaces, it made her feel as though an elephant had been moved from her shoulders.

The gents had moved on from the telegraph office, praise the Lord. She was able to slip inside, give a polite smile to the man behind the counter, and send her wire to Mother without any more close calls.

And it was probably her imagination that the chap looked at her with pity. For all he knew, she wasn't even waiting or hoping for a reply from the many messages she sent.

She'd just stepped out into the street again and set her sights on the hat shop when familiar voices brought her feet to a halt and inspired her to look around. If Oliver Tremayne was here, then chances were good that her best friend, Beth, his little sister, was too. She hadn't expected them today. Yesterday evening when Beth sailed her back to St. Mary's from the Tremayne family home on the island of Tresco, they'd said Emily would join them again on Tuesday. Tomorrow.

She spotted Oliver's dark head, and though a blond one was beside him, it wasn't petite, energetic Beth. Emily drew in another fortifying breath. Lord Telford. A fine enough fellow, to be sure . . . if one liked being in the company of just *fellows*. Which Emily most decidedly did not. Because, granted, the only fellows she ever had the opportunity to be with until this summer were her brother's friends or their father's peers, all of whom seemed bent on reminding her that she was nothing but a marriage pawn—whose ideas were worthless, whose purpose was to be pretty, and who could otherwise be either ignored or insulted at will.

These gentlemen were a different sort, but still. A few examples of different gentlemen were not enough to overcome her deep-seated impulse to avoid being caught alone by them.

There was no help for it, though. Oliver was even now lifting a hand in greeting and calling out, "Lady Emily, hello! We've been sent to fetch you and the Howe sisters."

Oh good—they weren't only looking for *her*. Emily scanned the space behind them, but the fashion-forward figures of Lady Abbie and Lady Millicent were nowhere to be seen. Emily must have been their first stop. She pasted a smile onto her face. "Has something come up?"

Lord Telford's lips twitched in that way they did—the way that said he was trying, for some reason, not to smile, even though he wanted to. "So says Mr. Gibson. He's called a family meeting and won't breathe a word about why until everyone has gathered—everyone involved in the search for pirate treasure included, not just actual family."

Emily glanced at Oliver, but he offered no more insight into what his maternal grandfather had to tell them. He was scanning the space behind her. "Briggs with you?"

"She's in the flat."

Oliver's gaze went toward the windows above the hat shop at that pronouncement. Telford's did not. He was still looking over her shoulder, and it seemed something had seized his attention— and not in a good way. His face went as hard as Scillonian granite. "Close ranks," he muttered to Oliver. Not that he waited for Beth's brother to sort out what he meant—he grabbed him by the arm, and the two of them shifted around her.

She had no idea what they were about until she realized they were now completely blocking her from the view of passersby. And just in time. A moment later, a chill went up her spine when she heard Nigel's laugh. Her back stiffened, and she dipped her head, just in case he peered around the gentlemen's shoulders.

Father would simply ignore her—it was his usual way with her. But Nigel . . . she could never tell what Nigel might do. Sometimes it suited him to follow their father's example, but other times he delighted in calling her out, forcing her along on whatever business he was about. So he'd have someone to berate, as best as she could tell. Or just so that he could leave her wherever he took her, alone and vulnerable, no doubt in the hopes that she'd never be seen again and he'd finally be rid of her.

She'd had to find her own way home from so many unfamiliar parts of London that at this point she knew the city as well as she knew the family manor. And she'd learned never to go anywhere without a reticule filled with change enough for the Tube or cab fare.

This time, though, Nigel didn't seem to spot her. A sigh of relief eased out once he was gone around the corner, and she offered Telford a more sincere smile. "Thank you."

Telford motioned her toward the hat shop. "*Some* of us know how to be good brothers."

Her own lips played his twitching game, and she pressed them together to avoid grinning, which would only invite a scowl from him. To hear his sister Libby tell the tale, Bram Sinclair, Earl of Telford, thought being a big brother meant protecting his sister even from the experiences she craved and seeking her safety even when it would make her miserable. The prime example being that he'd tried to arrange a marriage she didn't want with a man she didn't like—Telford's best friend, Lord Sheridan.

But his heart was in the right place, at least. And once he saw that Oliver Tremayne would make Libby happy and Lord Sheridan would not, he'd relented. Which was a good thing, since Sheridan had tumbled head over heels in love with Beth the moment they met, more or less. Emily would go so far as to say that Telford and Oliver were becoming quite good friends at this point, even.

She spun on her heel and hurried toward the back entrance and the flight of stairs that would lead her to the flat she and Briggs had been calling home for the last month. Both Libby and Beth may complain about their brothers not being understanding enough, but when it came down to it, her friends had no idea what a lousy brother was like. Theirs, whatever their faults, loved them.

What must that *be like?* she'd wondered over the years, especially after becoming friends with Beth at finishing school. When she heard her talking about all the teasing and fun and memories she and her brothers had . . .

Emily had always resorted to silence at those stories. What could she possibly share in return? *"When I was five and my brother thirteen, he said we were going to play hide-and-seek with the nurse. He led me into a wardrobe and then laughed as he locked me in. Oh, just a joke, you'll say. But he left me there for over twenty-four hours. I screamed until I was hoarse, but no one could hear me in that part of the manor house. I cried until I was so dehydrated I had no more tears. And he never did tell anyone where I was. They found me the next afternoon because of the smell coming from the wardrobe."*

Her fingers curled into her palm in the remembered shame, even as she reached with the other hand to unlock the door, praying the gentlemen waiting below didn't notice the way she trembled. Was it any wonder she hated small, dark spaces after that?

She'd learned that day what she meant to her father, though. *Nothing.* He hadn't been relieved that she'd been found—only disgusted at the mess she'd made of herself. He'd berated her for getting into the situation, as if she'd locked *herself* in that wardrobe, despite such a thing being impossible with the way the lock was fitted. When she'd told him it had been Nigel, Father had slapped her and told her not to blame her brother for her own mistakes.

And that was the story of Lady Emily Scofield's family life, in a nutshell. Nigel could do no wrong, and her only important task was to keep from shaming her father.

"There you are, my lady!" Briggs surged forward, relief upon her countenance, the moment Emily opened the door. "I was about to go in search of you. I was beginning to fear you'd stumbled into your brother."

A fear Emily knew so well that she had no difficulty covering it up with an empty smile. "Nearly, but I avoided them at first, and then Lord Telford and Mr. Tremayne saved me from a second encounter."

She waved a hand toward the door. "They're waiting below. Apparently Mr. Gibson has something new to show us."

Briggs nodded but didn't immediately reach for their hats. "Shall I come with you, my lady, or do the grocery shopping as originally planned?"

"Oh." Emily darted a glance to the small kitchen Briggs had been putting to use daily. She'd never had to think of such things before, truth be told. She knew how to run a household, but that just meant empowering a servant to take care of all those details, not making direct decisions about them herself. She felt her brows knit. "We've enough to get through another day or two, haven't we?"

"I believe so, my lady."

"Then you should come, of course." Briggs seemed to enjoy the company to be found at the Tremayne home on Tresco. And if by chance the Howe sisters didn't want to return at the same time as Emily later, Briggs's company would ensure she wasn't left alone with any of the gentlemen, if someone other than Beth volunteered to sail her back to St. Mary's.

Briggs nodded and gathered up her hat, reticule, and wrap.

Emily kept her blank smile in place. She'd gotten to know more about her lady's maid in this last month than in the entire term she'd been in service up until now—and the knowing made her stomach go tight with dread. Beth had looked at her as though she were half monster when she realized Emily had no idea about any bits of Briggs's personal life, but it was self-preservation.

Her maids never lasted long. Oh, they always seemed happy enough to serve her while Nigel was away, off gallivanting about the globe in search of fame. But within months of his return, they always resigned. Always.

One didn't have to be a genius at mathematics to realize that one plus one equaled two in those cases. Emily didn't know exactly what he did . . . but something. Clearly. She'd tried to get an explanation from her last two maids, but neither would say. Did he threaten them? Harass them?

Were she braver, she would ask Briggs point-blank whether Nigel had ever hurt her in any way. With Libby, he'd shoved her, bruised her arm. With Beth, he'd arranged a rather complicated failure of a stone to try to crush her—cruel in the worst, but also distant. He hadn't struck her, hadn't done direct violence. So what sort would he turn on her maids?

And did it really matter? The point was that he'd likely done *something*, which meant that Briggs wouldn't be with her much longer. Which, in turn, meant that if Emily got to know her, came to rely on her for more than the duties any hireling could perform, it would only mean another chip out of her heart when she finally left.

But Beth couldn't understand that. How could she? The Tremaynes had only one family in their employ, and the Dawes had been serving them absolutely forever and always would. Beth couldn't fathom maids coming and going like the tides whenever a brother snarled at them—or perhaps struck them?

Briggs looked up at her now, her smile cheerful but every bit as blank as Emily's, her freckled nose and warm brown hair all but screaming that, at least before she was hired by the Scofields, she was all brightness and innocence.

What would it be like to be friends with her? Like Libby was with Mabena Moon? Like Beth was with Senara Dawe?

Don't be a fool, Emily. She'd already asked too much of Thomasina Briggs by having her leverage her connections with the other servants in the Scofields' employ to spy on Emily's father and brother. Briggs would never want to be her *friend*.

It would have to be enough to have her as an ally.

"Ready, then?" Briggs tied her hat into place even as she asked.

Emily could only nod. And pray, as she led the way back to the waiting gentlemen, that somehow, at the end of all this, she wasn't left absolutely alone.

2

Bram Sinclair, Earl of Telford, despised a bully. Oh, if one were to ask his sisters, they'd say he *was* one—but they didn't know the meaning of the word. Perhaps his concern for them made him a trifle . . . overprotective. But that was different. He never had anything but their best interests in mind.

Unlike a certain Nigel Scofield. Bram kept his gaze darting hither and yon in search of the reprobate as they strolled through the streets of Hugh Town. They were on their way to the cottage on the garrison wall that was technically his sister's rental, but which Sheridan's sisters were currently occupying. Libby had been staying on Tresco instead, with her maid's family. Which suited Bram fine—having his sister so much closer was only a good thing, what with Scofield on the loose.

And he had no need to worry about Lady Abbie and Lady Millicent. They were more Sheridan's mothers than sisters, and they could intimidate the lichen off a stone if they glared at it enough. If Scofield showed up at *their* door, they'd probably have him begging for mercy within five minutes.

But Scofield's own sister was another matter entirely. Lady Emily obviously had been bullied by Nigel more than anyone else had, and though Bram didn't know the details, he didn't have to. He'd seen the way she cowered away from Nigel every time he came near, and the war in her eyes when Beth Tremayne blithely suggested she take their side against him.

Lady Emily Scofield needed *someone* to protect her, to champion her, especially now that her father and brother were on the islands. And Bram seemed to be the only one available for the job. Which was fine—he had plenty of practice, both with fending off bullies and nursing back to health the puppies they tended to kick.

Not that he would liken the lady to a puppy. Aloud, anyway. Though there *was* something about her eyes that put him in mind of the sad little creature he'd rescued from the village when he was a lad.

And bother, but he missed his dogs. A walk just wasn't the same without a faithful hound panting at his side.

"You can let up on the scowling, you know," Tremayne said softly as they topped the hill. His voice all but dripped amusement. "I don't think he's going to leap from behind the wall and attack."

"Never can tell with that sort of chap." Bram scanned the wall at the suggestion, though the only heads he saw popping over the top were a couple of children squealing with laughter. "These islands are too blighted small. He could pop up *anywhere*."

Tremayne lifted a brow. "I don't think you can really blame it on the islands."

He wasn't, not really. The Isles of Scilly, though stuck firmly in the last century, had a charm he couldn't honestly deny. It was no wonder Libby had come to love them just as much as she did Oliver Tremayne and his family. But he didn't like the feeling that with the Scofield men here, they couldn't afford to let their guard down for even a minute. There was nowhere to hide, nowhere outside their reach. "Then again, maybe I *want* him to pop up. I still owe him a sock in the nose."

Tremayne snorted a laugh. It turned to a longer chuckle as they neared the holiday cottage and the sound of frantic yipping greeted them. "Someone hears you."

Bram let a grin spread to the corners of his mouth. He found great joy in poking Lady Abbie with the tease that her pug liked him better than her. An exaggeration, of course—Lancelot knew to whom he belonged. But Bram needed *something* to hold over Abbie's head now and then.

The cottage door opened, and the dog shot out, curly tail wagging wildly. Chuckling along with Tremayne, Bram crouched down so he could greet his canine friend. "Hello there, Lance. Hello. Yes, I missed you too. I'll just take you home with me, shall I? Abbie won't mind."

"Ha!" Lady Abbie had stepped outside, dressed in one of her usual concoctions of lace and ribbon and whatnot that would make his older sister Edith drool in jealousy and Libby wrinkle her nose in distaste. "Did you just come to kidnap my dog, Bram? Where's Theo?"

Bram scooped the wriggling pup into his arms and stood again. "He and Beth took a picnic lunch to the cairn fields. But Old Man Gibson is calling a meeting, so we thought we'd better fetch you all."

Oliver nodded along with his explanation. "He wouldn't tell us what he's found, but he seemed excited. Can you come?"

Abbie cast a frown over her shoulder. "*I* can. But Millicent is planning to spend the afternoon on Gugh."

Bram scratched Lancelot behind the ears and breathed a laugh. "Harassing Vandermeer?"

She met his gaze, hers twinkling with silent laughter. "What else?" She turned back to the tiny interior of the cottage Libby had let for her holiday—though how his sister could have been so blissfully comfortable in the cramped quarters, Bram didn't know. Sheridan's sisters at least had the good sense to complain about the lodgings. "Perhaps we can lure her into giving the American a reprieve."

Bram grinned. "Tell her we may learn something to which he won't have access. That will convince her to join us instead."

"Good thinking." Abbie moved back inside, and though Bram could have listened to every word she exchanged with Millicent, he happened to glance to his right and caught the strained look on Lady Emily's face.

She always wore an expression like that when mention was made of the competition between Sheridan and her father, or Sheridan and Vandermeer, or anything else so much as hinting at the cutthroat side of the antiquities trade.

Understandable—Bram wasn't exactly fond of that aspect himself. Then again, he'd never felt any particular draw to that world, unlike his best friend. He instead contented himself with watching Sheridan and his sisters dart about England and the world, scrambling to be the first to uncover whatever random artifact they were set on finding, and chuckling over their outrage when someone else—say, Donald Vandermeer—beat them to the punch. All from the comfort of his own modern, fully updated, *not*-bursting-with-dirt-encrusted-nonsense home.

He slid a bit closer to Lady Emily when Lancelot provided him with an excuse by leaning that way. The pug thought it his right and privilege to receive a pat of greeting from each human he saw, after all.

And the redhead had now become well-enough acquainted with him to know his demands. She smiled a bit and reached over to stroke the pup's head. "Good day to you, good sir."

Lancelot's pink tongue lolled happily out of his mouth, making Bram stifle another laugh. "All fine manners, this one. Better, I suppose, than some of the humans around."

Lady Emily sighed and didn't meet his eye.

She never did, really, unless they were in a crowd of friends and he spoke up. *Then* she had no problem looking over at him, and if he happened to return the attention, she didn't jerk her gaze away. Why was it different when they were speaking directly? He'd think it just him if she weren't the same with Sheridan and Oliver too. And if someone was bashful around Oliver Tremayne, that was saying something indeed. His soon-to-be brother-in-law could get granite to bare its soul to him, Bram was sure.

He'd never claimed to be a charmer, and heaven knew if young ladies ever batted their lashes at him, it was more because of his title than his sparkling personality. And generally speaking, he didn't much care whether said young ladies in general liked him or not.

But he didn't want to be lumped in with blighters like Nigel Scofield in anyone's mind, much less in the mind of the man's sister.

Abbie emerged again a moment later with Millicent—whose eyes were sparkling with a glee that one might term maniacal if one didn't have any sense of self-preservation. Bram had learned long ago that pointing out Millicent's cutthroat tendencies to her meant said tendencies would turn right back on you. He opted instead for a smile and offered an elbow for whichever lady wanted to take it.

Millicent did. Abbie and Oliver led the way, Emily and Briggs fell into place behind them, and Bram held Millicent back so they could bring up the rear. It was best to keep Lady Emily surrounded, so her brother couldn't catch her unawares.

Millicent leaned close as they walked back along the familiar streets of Hugh Town. "What is it Mr. Gibson has found? Something to drive the museum chaps mad with jealousy, I hope?"

Bram breathed a laugh. "I've no idea. He wouldn't say."

"I do adore Mr. Gibson. And Mrs. Tremayne too. Quite a family my brother and your sister are marrying into, isn't it?"

"Indeed." He hadn't let himself think so at first. It was his duty, after all, to first look for any base qualities in the man Libby had fallen in love with, so that he could be sure he hadn't been pursuing her for the wrong reasons and would end up breaking her heart. But Oliver Tremayne was as true as they came, and his family the absolute best sort.

Libby would be happy here, with them. And Sheridan would be in bliss, having the adventure-seeking Beth by his side for all his expeditions and excavations. Which meant that Bram would be able to rest easy at home, knowing all those he loved were content.

Millicent poked him in the side, and when he looked down at

her, he found her eyes twinkling. "Now we have only to settle *you* with someone worthy of you," she murmured.

This time his laugh emerged as a snort. "Well, there are no more Tremayne siblings. Shall I propose to Mamm-wynn?"

Millicent laughed and patted his arm. "I don't think you could manage her. No, dearest, you need someone who will let you protect them, not someone who's constantly proving she knows things you can't. Ignoring the small issue of her being ninety-five."

Bram's lips twitched. Millicent and Abbie had both been telling him and Sheridan what they needed in wives for the last decade. And now that they had their brother safely engaged, Bram would be their focus. Just one more thing for them to arrange and take over and organize. "I think there have been betrothals enough for one summer."

She sniffed and lifted her chin in that way she had—the one that said his innocuous words had been viewed as a gauntlet, and she'd just picked it up. "We shall see, Bram. We shall see."

Heaven help him.

Fitzwilliam Gibson lived in a cottage typical of Tresco—which meant it was rather small to be hosting the number of people currently crammed into it. Bram left the seats to the ladies and leaned against the wall, smiling a hello to Sheridan when he and Beth came belatedly through the door, looking windblown and out of breath.

And utterly happy with their fingers woven together. Sheridan used their joined hands to tug Beth over toward Bram. "What's it all about, then? I mean—a summons!"

Bram shrugged and turned his gaze from his best friend's bright eyes to Beth's maternal grandfather's wide smile. "Your guess is as good as mine, old boy. Perhaps better."

Beth didn't seem to mind that the other ladies—including not only Mamm-wynn and Libby and Lady Emily, but also Libby's former maid Mabena Moon and Beth's housekeeper's daughter, Senara, and Lady Emily's maid, Briggs—had taken all the seats. She looked quite content as she leaned there beside Sheridan and Bram. "One never can tell with Tas-gwyn."

"Best thing about him." Sheridan grinned.

"All right, then, we're all here." Mr. Gibson positioned himself in the center of the room and turned in a quick circle, showing his grin to them all. "Excellent. Everyone comfortable? Adelle?"

Mamm-wynn rewarded him with a smile. "Perfect, Fitz. If on the edge of my seat in suspense. What are you up to now?"

If anything, his grin went more mischievous. "Well. I have to say, I was quite inspired by the fact that our Beth found such secrets in my very foundation. I'd always known that the great pirate admiral John Mucknell had once called my humble cottage home. But I'd never dreamed he'd left anything behind here until you found all those maps and letters, Bethy."

Beth tilted her head. "I never had either."

"Well, it got me to thinking." He tapped a finger to his temple. "If he'd left all that, there could be more about. So I've been looking. Everywhere, absolutely everywhere."

Mamm-wynn lifted her white brows. "That does explain the plaster dust."

Gibson waved that away. "I've torn nearly the whole house apart over the last two months, in bits and pieces. Always putting it back together, mind. But here's the point—I *did* find something more, just last week."

"Last week—and you're only just now telling us?" Beth took a step away from the wall, practically vibrating with energy. Bram would wonder how Sheridan ever intended to keep up with her, except that he was a ball of electricity himself, all but quivering with anticipation like a puppy at Gibson's pronouncement.

Gibson made a calming motion with his hand. "Now, dearover, I would have told you the very minute if I thought it had any bearing on the hunt for Mucknell's hoard itself. But it doesn't. Not really, though she does mention it a few times."

"She?" Libby tilted her head and studied her soon-to-be grand-father. "You must mean—"

"Elizabeth! Mucknell, that is." Sheridan pumped a fist in the air. "No other *she* it could be."

"What did you find?" Beth surged forward now, toward her grandfather. "More of her letters to her husband? We had his to her already, but only some of hers to him, which . . . of course." She sucked in a breath. "*She* must have been the one to stash them. How could it have been him, given the ones from his time in Portugal and Spain? He never returned here after that. He'd sent them to her. And no doubt left the map."

Gibson's head bobbed along in agreement. "Exactly. All that you've found—she must have hidden it all after he left the Scillies. And she hid a bit more too."

The old man spun toward the tea table against the wall, and even Bram straightened as he reached for a small lidded chest sitting there. He wasn't nearly as fascinated by the whole pirate-treasure thing as Sher was, but he had to admit it had made for a more entertaining summer than the Season in London would have provided.

Gibson opened the box with a creak of hinges and pulled out a leather-bound book that looked as though it had seen better days. The edges of the paper were yellow, crumbling, and ragged.

Oliver edged closer too. "A book?"

"A diary." Gibson offered it to his grandson. "Careful now, lad. It's fragile. I thought to show you all the original, but I've made a few copies for everyone to read through, so we didn't put undue stress on the old one." He flexed his hand as if still feeling the strain of the writing.

Perhaps he did, depending on how full those pages were with text. How long must it have taken to transcribe "a few copies"? Days, possibly.

While Oliver carefully opened the original, Gibson turned back to the chest and pulled out a stack of more modern-looking notebooks. "Here we are. One for Lady Emily . . ." He handed her a copy with a warm smile, and she murmured her thanks as she accepted it. "One for my dear Libby . . ." A copy went into Bram's sister's hands and was received with equal gratitude. "One for Sheridan, lest he steal someone else's . . ." This copy he delivered with a wink. Sheridan flashed an unrepentant grin. "And I only had the knuckles for one more thus far, though I plan to get another finished soon. So this one is for Lord Telford."

For him? Bram jolted a bit, knowing his brows came crashing down in confusion even as he reached for the bound pages that Gibson held out.

Oliver looked amused. And perhaps *be*mused. "I see how your own grandchildren rate."

Gibson chuckled. "I imagined you'd not argue with sharing a copy with Libby. And Mabena can, too, until I get another finished. Beth and Sheridan will enjoy putting their heads together. But Lady Emily will be on St. Mary's, so she needs one of her own—and if the Howe sisters could share with her until I get another copied . . . ?"

Millicent had been eyeing up the copy in Bram's hand but smiled with some grace at that. "That does make sense, as we're the three on St. Mary's."

"And if Telford simply leaves his copy in the library when he's sleeping the morning away, that'll make it available to someone else." Gibson's nod said he was quite proud of having sorted the copies as he had.

Frankly, Bram would probably leave his copy in the library in general. He wasn't nearly as fascinated by this whole search as the others—but he wasn't about to rebuff the old man's gift. He ran a hand over the new pages. They felt no different from those of any other notebook he'd had as a schoolboy, or which Sheridan left littering every surface of whatever house he was staying in, be it his own or Telford Hall. Though the volume that Oliver was gently closing again surely gave a whole different sensation.

Sheridan was already flipping eagerly through his copy, mumbling

30

random words he presumably saw within. "Prayer . . . hopes . . . fear . . . Oh, this is interesting. 'The waters will devour him, as they did those of Lyonesse who were ruled by greed.'" Sheridan looked up, first at Beth and then over at Bram.

Bram leaned back again, running the pad of his thumb over the edges of the pages. Lyonesse, admittedly, was more interesting to him than pirate treasure. Because Lyonesse meant Sir Tristan.

And Sir Tristan wasn't just the hero of the tragic tale of love potions gone awry with the Irish princess Isolde that Wagner's terrible opera had made famous anew. Tristan was a knight of the Round Table.

Of course, Sher knew that would intrigue Bram, hence the look.

He pretended not to see it. This whole collection of people didn't need to know that he'd never quite outgrown his fascination with Arthurian legends. It was one thing for a lad of twelve to be ready to go off gallivanting in search of the "once and future king" supposedly just sleeping away the centuries until it was time to rise and rule England once again. It was quite another for a twenty-six-year-old earl to admit that he still camped under the stars near Cadbury Castle every Midsummer night, hoping to catch a glimpse of the king and his knights sallying forth to inspect the land, as the stories said they did every year.

No, not *hoping*. Not *expecting*. He wasn't that ridiculous. Just . . . *wanting*. For some reason he'd never cared to peel back the layers of himself enough to identify why.

His fingers twitched on the cover, itching to flip the pages until he saw that mention of the kingdom of Lyonesse. Maybe he *wouldn't* just leave his copy in the library.

"I made every attempt to keep the lines and pages uniform, for easy reference," Gibson was saying. "Ignore spacing between words and the like, that isn't a quirk of the original, just me trying to match Mrs. Mucknell's hand and failing. But if you'll all turn to page twenty-seven, you'll see why I've called everyone here. Lines ten through seventeen."

Bram flipped the notebook open and saw that Gibson had numbered each page in the bottom outside corner, as well as numbering each line in groups of five. Though it took him back to his school days of translating Greek and Latin, he couldn't argue line numbers made it much easier to reference in conversation. His gaze fell immediately on the lines Gibson indicated.

> *I cannot believe the stories were true. More, I cannot believe that I—a nobody, wife of a pirate—am the one to have put my hand to the actual artifact. How many centuries has it lain there, untouched, hidden? Nay, not only hidden but secreted away. Because, the stories say, it is a symbol of nobility and honor, and the people of Lyonesse had none.*
>
> *Why, Lord, would you show this precious thing to me? When you know well my husband, though he has many strengths, cannot claim nobility and honor either? I must keep this from him at all costs. But how?*

"Artifact?" Sher was vibrating again, bouncing on the balls of his feet in his eagerness.

Bram stuffed down a grin. It was true that Sheridan got just as excited over a random pottery shard unearthed from his own garden, but that was part of what made him Sheridan. And what made him such good company. Bram had always tended more toward the serious—he needed someone full of mirth and light in his life, and there was no one the world over as bright and joyful as the Marquess of Sheridan.

For some reason he also didn't care to examine too closely, his gaze drifted to Lady Emily. She, too, could do with some sunshine in her life. Did Beth give that to her, as Sher did to Bram? Maybe. He hoped so. Hoped she had *someone* to brighten the days for her.

But as she sat, head bent over the pages she was sharing with Briggs and Senara, he had to wonder if perhaps she didn't. If perhaps that was what kept her hiding in the shadows all day long.

If she simply didn't have anyone to shine the light into her corner for her.

Well, blast. Bram could protect her, show her what a brother was supposed to be like. But he was no shiner-of-light.

Gibson eased himself to a seat on an old wooden stool. "Intriguing, isn't it? I've no idea what artifact she's speaking of, but if it's linked to Lyonesse . . . You'll want to turn to page forty-three too. The other time she mentions this artifact she's found."

Bram obediently flipped the pages. And nearly choked at the words that leaped off the page at him.

If John knew I had something of King Arthur's—it doesn't bear thinking about. He would try to sell it to the highest bidder and likely get himself killed in the process. I must protect him from this artifact at all costs.

King Arthur—it actually said *King Arthur*, right there on the page. Not just Lyonesse and Tristan and a link to the Round Table, but *King Arthur* himself. An artifact directly linked to him, that had belonged to him—or that Elizabeth Mucknell believed had, at any rate. What were they talking about here? The Holy Grail? Excalibur? A piece of the Round Table itself? Or it could be his lance, his shield, his helmet, one of the lesser swords or daggers. There were virtually endless possibilities.

Bram was definitely *not* leaving his copy of this diary in the library during his own waking hours.

"Fancy that! Well, it puts one in mind—Telly, do you remember?" Sheridan spun to him, face alight, as usual. "Of course you do. When we were . . . what, thirteen? Fourteen?" He pivoted back to Beth. "Jolly good fun. We went to Cadbury Castle on Midsummer Eve—that's close to Telford Hall, you know. Next-door neighbors, really. Well, not *really*. But the same neighborhood." Sheridan waved a hand in the air.

Abbie laughed. "Oh, I recall now! The two of you thought you'd catch Arthur and his knights on their annual sortie, wasn't it?"

"There's a local legend, I believe." Millicent turned to generally face the others. "Local to Cadbury. That Arthur is buried in the castle there, and that every year at midnight on the solstice, he ventures forth from the crypt." She chuckled. Indulgent, like the big sister she was. "Our boys were convinced they'd see him if they could only stay awake."

Sheridan chuckled. "Failed at that. Well, I did. No doubt the fault of the sugar I ingested in the hours before that eventually sent me crashing down. You remember, Telly?"

"You facedown and drooling as the knights galloped by, you mean?" He winked. "Hard to forget. You missed all the fun." That had been his story the next morning, when Sheridan finally regained consciousness—that it had happened exactly like they'd hoped, and he'd missed the whole thing.

There had, of course, been no nighttime riders, ghostly nor fleshly, with armor glinting in the moonlight. But there had been a pearly white moon and endless stars and night birds and insects serenading him, along with the occasional snatch of music from the annual Midsummer Ball going on at the castle proper, where his parents were dancing. Bram had been enamored. Not just with tales of nobility and honor, but with the peace of a quiet night. It had been his first time staying up until the dawn painted its glory over the horizon. But certainly not his last. After school, when his time was more his own, he'd made it his habit to stay up to greet the dawn whenever the weather allowed. To breathe in the crisp morning air and watch the mist rise and see the sun shoot it through with gold.

To know that if there *were* secret forays, they'd happen in those dark, starlit hours. And if there *was* a hope that defied reason, it would surely come with the first kiss of dawn.

Bram hadn't found Arthur that night. But he'd found a bit of himself.

Sheridan was chuckling at the old joke. "Regardless, though. You're the expert here. On Arthur, I mean. Well, that is, if you remember it all. Years ago, I know."

34

Bram cleared his throat, lest a self-deprecating laugh slip out. He'd let Sheridan think the fancy had evaporated with childhood, but in truth . . . Well, in truth his private library wasn't brimming with classics or history texts on Druids or Vikings, like Sher's was, nor was it filled with scientific treatises, like his sister's.

No, Bram's shelves were still filled with tales of chivalry. With Arthur and Merlin and Guinevere and Camelot. With the Round Table. With legends of honor and nobility and everything the world today seemed to lack.

He couldn't very well just admit it. But he could tilt his head to the side and say, "I *think* I recall enough to be useful."

3

Thomasina Briggs did her best to stay at the edges of the room as the conversation spun around her, keeping out of the way of all the lords and ladies. Usually she simply would have stuck to the sides of the other domestics—Mabena Moon and Senara Dawe. But neither Mabena nor Senara were interested, it seemed, in *not* mixing with the others. Which made sense if one considered that Mr. Gibson was Mabena's grandfather as surely as he was the Tremaynes', and Senara had grown up here too.

But Tommie was under no delusions. She did not belong in this group, not as anything more than a companion for Lady Emily on their travels to and from the islands. She was not a member of the treasure hunt, not really. She was not a friend.

Definitely not a friend.

She tucked herself into a corner and let her hand drop to her pocket. Her fingers found the outline of the envelope she'd been carrying there for the last six weeks. It was sealed, but she didn't need to reread it to know exactly what words she'd chosen to pen before she accompanied Lady Emily to the Isles of Scilly from London.

My lady,
I thank you for the opportunity you've afforded me over
the last eighteen months to serve you, both in your country

*home and in your London house. I am now offering you my
resignation, as the circumstances that propelled me to seek a
position in service have been reversed. I pray all the best on
you and your family. Please consider this resignation effective
immediately, though I do apologize for any inconvenience it
causes you to leave you without an attendant.*

Truth and lies mixed, that's what the letter was. Was she grateful
for the opportunity? She had been—at first. It was a prime position,
and one she honestly hadn't expected to land, given how little experience she'd had as a lady's maid. Oh, she'd done a few coiffures
and the like for a lady in her hometown, but Mrs. Walton hadn't
exactly been a society matron, just the wife of a wealthy merchant.
Tommie hadn't expected her reference to go far.

She'd needed *something*, though, after her brother stopped sending funds home. Something to support Mam and the two sisters still
at home. And being a lady's maid certainly sounded more pleasant
than being a scullery maid—hence why she hadn't expected to get
the position when she applied.

She'd thought it a gift from God when she'd been hired.

How very wrong she'd been.

She shook that off. She'd get away soon enough. It was truth
she'd penned when she said the circumstances had reversed. Oh,
not that Maddox had started sending money again—her brother
had always been about as dependable as sunshine in an English
autumn. But Mam had remarried, and Mr. Merton had no need of
the salary Tommie made. He owned a mill and did quite well for
himself. Mam and the girls would never go hungry. And he'd even,
bless him, invited Tommie to come home and enjoy a bit of leisure.
Enter their little Welsh town's small society. Find a good husband,
start a family of her own. She'd thanked him and told him she
expected to be home by the end of summer.

Yet here she was, with the resignation letter still in her pocket and

August nearly at an end. With Lady Emily still at her side instead of Mam or Meredith or Cecily.

With Nigel Scofield haunting the islands now.

She'd leave soon. *Very* soon. Certainly before Lady Emily's brother could determine where they were staying and come to pay them a visit. She just hadn't been able to bring herself to resign when Lady Emily found herself at odds with her family. When, for the first time since she began serving her, she looked at Tommie like a person and not just a piece of furniture.

It had nothing at all to do with the fear of going home, of her mother looking into her eyes and somehow knowing what had happened. Of pasting a smile on her face in her own little society and wondering if she dared to try to deceive some nice Welsh lad into marrying her when she ought to be tossed aside instead, like the rubbish she often felt she was.

"Well." Mrs. Tremayne stood, gathering her shawl around her shoulders. She held out a hand toward Mr. Gibson. "We should discuss this more over tea. Mrs. Dawe should have it ready for us by the time we get home. Join us, Fitz? It's lemon cake today."

The old gent grinned. "Well now, I can't turn down lemon cake."

Tommie breathed a quiet sigh of relief and led the way out of Mr. Gibson's front door. The Tremayne house was larger, which meant it was easier to stay in her proper place. She'd slip into the kitchen and finally be able to breathe, with no one for company but the Dawes and Ainsley and Collins—the lords' valets. She could joke and laugh and enjoy her own slice of lemon cake without worrying about whether she was invisible enough or what Lady Emily needed or whether her face was devoid of all expression.

"A blank slate," Mrs. Walton had advised her. *"That is what a good lady's maid must be, Thomasina. Ready to receive her mistress's instruction without any opinion of her own beyond what the lady requires."*

Tommie had nodded and even written down all the advice Mrs. Walton had to offer. So eager to make a good impression. To land the position. So naïve, ready to think it all a grand adventure. And she'd thought she'd enjoy it, even the pretense of having no life of her own. It was just like playacting, after all, and she'd always enjoyed the little shows she and the other children had put on at school. She'd simply pretend she was one of Shakespeare's players, enacting a role.

No one had told her living it day in and day out would wear away at who she really was.

She curled her fingers into her palm and told herself the same thing she'd been telling herself for months. *You're still you, Tommie. Underneath it all.* Her tenure in the Scofield house couldn't have completely stripped her of her real identity. No. No, it would be good to go back to Brecon once this business was over, to see her old friends and assure herself that Mam enjoyed being Mrs. Merton. To smile with Meredith and Cecily over the new dresses their stepfather had given them—they'd written to her in such detail about their new wardrobes that she'd joked about how they'd penned books instead of letters. To just be Tommie again.

No one would ever have to know what being Briggs had cost her.

For now, she tilted up her face to receive the warm Cornish sunshine, not caring a bit whether it added a few more freckles to her nose. The noise from all the ladies and gents behind her reminded her to step aside, to let them lead the way back through Old Grimsby and to the lovely house the Tremaynes called home.

They emerged in a gaggle, laughing and talking and striking out through the village. First Mrs. Tremayne and Mr. Gibson, then Lady Elizabeth and Oliver Tremayne, Lord Telford and Lord Sheridan and Miss Tremayne and Lady Emily all in a bunch, the Howe sisters, Mabena and Senara and Collins and Ainsley.

Tommie shook her head at the flock of them, a smile teasing her lips. She wasn't quite sure how they'd all fit into Mr. Gibson's cottage, honestly. But she was more than happy to let them all walk ahead of her and to bring up the rear.

"Were you all in Old Man Gibson's house? It's a wonder it didn't burst at the seams."

Tommie turned at the voice, her smile not knowing whether to bloom full or retreat. In the month and a half she'd been in the isles with Lady Emily, she'd met Oliver Tremayne's best friend more than once . . . and *never* knew whether to smile or retreat. The sight of Enyon Thorne always made her heart beat too fast, and she didn't know if she should revel in it or run far and fast in the opposite direction.

He was a good man—she tried to tell herself that. He wouldn't be Mr. Tremayne's best friend otherwise. But that didn't change anything, not really. If anything, it made her racing heart even more pointless.

Today, Enyon Thorne had an armload full of empty boxes and an expression of pure amusement on his handsome face. He'd have been taking items over to St. Mary's for the shop his mother ran there for the tourists, she knew. She saw him both on St. Mary's and on Tresco, helping with the summer business. Then he'd be off to the flower fields he and his father tended—their winter business, though it required attention year-round. "Good afternoon, Mr. Thorne."

He gave her a look of mock frustration. "Now what have I told you about that? It's Enyon. There are so many Thornes running about the islands that you'll have me confused with my father or brother or cousins if you insist on the surname."

It was what she called him in her mind, to be sure. And really, they were of similar society, so it wasn't out of place to call him by his first name. Still, it felt odd, knowing he was the best friend of Mr. Tremayne, who was engaged to Lady Elizabeth Sinclair.

Societies mixed in the strangest ways around here.

But she offered a shrug and a grin, praying it looked easy and unconcerned. "Habit," she said with a nod toward the flock of ladies and gents.

Enyon shifted the boxes a bit and shook his head. "Still can't believe the high company Ollie and Beth are keeping these days."

He about fumbled the boxes, so Tommie took the top two off his stack. They were awkward but certainly not heavy, otherwise she would have called for Collins and Ainsley to lend a hand. "What did you take over for the tourists today?"

Enyon chuckled. "Rubbish, as my tas would say. Some driftwood sculptures, baubles made from sea glass and sand. That sort of thing."

Charming, in her estimation. But then, she was a tourist here, who his mam was aiming for with that "rubbish." Not that she had the coin to spend on any of it—she'd been putting it all aside to pay her way home.

"So, what was everyone doing at Mr. Gibson's?" Enyon asked after a few more steps. "Did he have a new tale to try out on you? If so, I imagine he'll tell it later at the pub. I'll be sure to be there."

Having heard plenty of Mr. Gibson's fantastical stories over the last few weeks, Tommie chuckled. "No, not today. At least not his usual fare. He'd been hunting for more evidence of the Mucknells in his house and found a diary belonging to Elizabeth Mucknell." She didn't mind telling him this latest bit of information, knowing well that Mr. Tremayne had kept his best friend at least generally up to date on their treasure hunt.

Enyon whistled and shook his head. "We all thought it was just another of his tales, all these years, saying his house had been the pirate's. Makes you wonder what other stories of his have their roots in the truth." He laughed at the thought.

She did, too, she couldn't help it. "Clearly next a dragon will swoop down and blast the Roundhead fleet into the sea with one fiery breath."

"Obviously." He sent her a grin and then nodded toward a cottage up ahead—his parents', if she recalled correctly. "I'll drop the boxes there."

She followed him to the door so she could hand him the boxes she carried, casting a glance at the rest of the group. Her chest went tight. What was she thinking, letting herself get pulled away from them like this? She couldn't walk alone with Enyon into the Thorne house, that would be stupid. She should shove these boxes back at him— drop them to the ground—something. And then hurry to catch up.

But Enyon merely set his empty boxes just inside the door, reached to add hers to his stack, and then shut the door again and nodded back toward the group. "Shall we? Mrs. Dawe sent a note round this morning telling me she was making my favorite lemon cake for tea and that I was to join you all."

Her breath came out more shakily than she cared to admit, and she prayed he didn't notice it. Covered it with another lie of a smile. "She's the most thoughtful lady, isn't she?"

"And the best cook in all the Scillies," Enyon agreed, though he made a show of casting a glance over his shoulder. "Though don't let Mam or my sister hear me saying so."

"Your secret—if it is one—is safe with me." She let her arms, now empty, swing at her sides while they walked up the hill. The rest of the group hadn't gotten more than a handful of steps ahead, and catching up took only seconds.

See there, Tommie? Your fears were ridiculous.

They'd walked a minute more before her attention was drawn to the right when a door slammed, and the boulder of a man called Casek Wearne charged into the street toward them, bellowing, "Benna! Come and tell Mam she's wrong, will you?"

Mabena Moon peeled off from the group, smirking at her fiancé. "Are you daft, dearovim? You want me to argue with my future mother-in-law?"

"She'll only listen to you on the matter."

"'The matter,'" Enyon whispered to Tommie, steering her clear of the scowling headmaster and Mabena both, "is his twin brother, Cador. Their mam is insisting he be invited home for the wedding next month, but there's bad blood there. Cador was engaged to Benna years ago but tossed her over for a rich girl from London. Turned out well enough for Benna and Caz, but . . ."

Tommie winced on their behalf. She'd heard the story of the heartbreak that had sent Mabena to the mainland, and how it had landed her in Lady Elizabeth's employ. And she'd seen much of the romance unfold between the newly returned Mabena and Casek, who'd been waiting all these years for his chance with her. Still—she knew *she* wouldn't fancy having Cador at her wedding, if she were in their shoes.

But then, her own mam had always chided her for holding a grudge. "Do you think he'd come, even if they did invite him?"

Enyon snorted. "If it meant parading his wife around and boasting about all his literary glory, he probably would. Though to hear Caz tell it, his first book of poetry has been a complete flop, and his fancy wife was disowned by her father when she married Cador."

"Well, they'll have the last laugh either way, then, won't they?" She nodded toward Casek and Mabena, who looked at each other with complete adoration, even as they bantered over Mrs. Wearne's stubbornness. "They've come out the winners."

"That they have." Enyon sighed. "It's strange, you know? When we were lads, it was Cador we liked better. We ran all over the islands with him, while Ollie and Casek were constantly at odds. Now, no one much likes Cad anymore—he all but declared he was too good for the likes of us mere Scillonians. And Caz and Ollie are about to become cousins and are actually getting along."

"Strange indeed, what changes over time." Of its own will, her gaze flicked to the back of Lady Emily. If one didn't know her, one would see only a picture-perfect young lady of society—her day dress impeccable, her hair pinned up in a graceful sweep of red curls, her laugh sterling. Exactly what she was expected to be. Well mannered. Pretty. Without a thought for anyone but herself.

That was honestly all Tommie thought she was, until they came here. She'd either changed, too, or just hadn't ever shown Tommie her true colors until now. Because since coming to the Isles of Scilly, she'd suddenly grown a backbone and stood up for herself—stood up to her father and brother.

Maybe it was new. Or maybe . . . maybe lady's maids weren't the only ones taught to be a blank slate.

Maybe it was a lesson drilled into the ladies too.

4

The late-summer air danced, warm and golden, around Emily as she stretched to a more comfortable position on the sun-baked rock she had staked out as her morning reading place. For a moment, she tilted her face up toward the endless blue sky, away from the pages she had open in her lap. For a moment, she let her imagination take her back two hundred fifty years, to when Elizabeth Mucknell may have sat on this selfsame rock under this selfsame sky . . . and mourned for her husband even before his death.

It was her third time through the diary in the last two days. The entries were sporadic at best and only covered the years that Elizabeth Mucknell had lived in the Scillies—a few at the start of the Civil War, when her husband had first come here to pledge his loyalty to the exiled royal family. And then again after a brief span of time in Ireland.

A few years, with entries only every few months. These were clearly the musings of a woman trying to come to grips with her own life and the hand she was dealt. They were as much prayers as simple recordings, her own thoughts and her beseeching of the Almighty woven together in a beautiful tapestry.

44

Emily drew in a long breath and read again the passage she'd just finished.

> *I nearly lost my temper last eve, Lord. How many times has John said that exact same thing? That it's for me, it's all for me. How does he not understand? How does he not see the burden he places on me with such a claim?*

How indeed? Emily lowered the notebook to rest against her chest and let her eyes slide closed for a minute. Mucknell was Cockney born and bred, a man of common stock who rose in the ranks of the merchant fleet of the East India Company over many years of hard work. He wasn't a man who had a family name to live up to or a legacy to preserve—just a man trying to build one. When he'd stolen the *John*, flagship of the Company, and brought it here to the Scillies, he'd branded himself as an outlaw in the eyes of those currently in authority under Cromwell—and a hero to the Royalists who were hunkered here in the islands, where there wasn't enough food to feed the entire exiled court. And so he'd stolen more. Food, ammunition, coin. Whatever the East Indiamen sailing through the waters had on board. He and the fleet of similar pirates he ended up commanding.

On the surface, no one would equate her family with the Mucknells. Her father was the eighth in their line of earls; they could trace their lineage back centuries. Yet when he said, over and again, that Emily must remember she was a Scofield, that everything he did was for their family, *this* was how she'd always felt. Exactly as Elizabeth Mucknell described.

He placed such a terrible burden upon them. Not just the usual expectations—that Emily must be the epitome of a proper young lady, that she must be pretty, that she must be articulate, that she must always be careful of their family's reputation. Those she could handle.

But the dark side she'd begun to see more and more fully this summer—the people he cheated, the deals he reneged on, the back-handed way he dealt with anyone he deemed not an equal, all in the name of protecting their family—that she couldn't bear.

Pressing the open notebook to her chest in a bid for her heart to stop aching, she dragged in an unsteady breath. Being a Scofield was a burden under which she feared she'd break. But she'd never met anyone else who understood that.

Not until she read Elizabeth Mucknell's diary. Emily opened her eyes, lifted the pages written in Mr. Gibson's steady, masculine, frill-less hand, and kept reading.

> *I bit my tongue because I know my temper would only fan the flames of his. I bit back anger, but I cannot stop the pain that bathes my soul when I consider his. That is my true concern, Father God. My husband's soul.*
>
> *I had a letter from my sister, and she berated me yet again for my choice in husband, for staying with him even now, when he's become what she calls a traitor. I cannot think him that, not when he has remained loyal to the sovereign that God himself ordained. But I cannot argue with her other charges—that he is a thief and quite possibly a murderer. My own husband—my dear John—taking lives as if they mean nothing!*
>
> *Lord, you know how it hurts to consider. You know how many times over the years I've struggled to beat back the bitterness, the anger, the fear. Oh, the fear. That he will never see. He will never understand. That all my love will fail to show him the way to you, Father.*
>
> *Show me, please. Show me how to love him better. Show me how to show you to him.*

Tears stung Emily's eyes. Not just at the tender heart that a woman had poured out onto the page over two centuries ago . . . but at the sting of her own conscience.

Did she love her father like that? Enough to beg the Lord to use her somehow—to show her some way to reach him?

Did she love her *brother* like that?

"Well, well, well. If it isn't my dearest darling sister."

She snapped upright, warm rock and blue sky forgotten in the shock of her thoughts seemingly having summoned Nigel. And he wasn't even sneaking up behind her, giving her a hope of hiding the journal—he was striding for her head-on, that half-sneer on his face as his gaze raked over her, cataloguing everything he'd berate her for.

At least there were none of his friends or the trustees behind him. Audiences always made him more determined to point out her every flaw. To give them something to laugh over together, she supposed.

She let the journal fall closed, careful to keep her actions slow, casual. Just a book with a blank cover. Nothing to interest him.

Except his gaze fell on it anyway, and that nasty glint came into his eye. The one that immediately reminded her of why *she* had never kept a journal or diary. She'd tried it once, at age ten, and he'd stolen it before the ink of her first entry had dried.

"Good morning, Nigel." She strove for a calm tone, a welcoming one even. Praying his attention would return to her face instead of the notebook in her hands.

No such luck. "Taken up writing again, Emily? As if you have thoughts worth putting down?"

She could imagine a brother delivering such a question as a tease, with a good-natured laugh. She could imagine one immediately assuring her that *of course* she had worthwhile thoughts. But no, Nigel's chuckle was cold, amused with his own supposed wit, nothing more.

That prickle in her conscience dug deeper. Was he really so cruel, or was she simply seeing it that way because she expected to?

Her fingers tightened around the edges of the notebook, but she forced a smile to her lips. She didn't know how to take even first steps toward reconciliation with him. But she couldn't just sit here in silence like a ninny. "One never knows when even silly thoughts may brighten someone's day. Shall I read you some?"

He would dismiss the offer—when had he *ever* sought anything she offered? But she'd hoped he would just wave it away and spin off again, like he'd done so many times in the drawing room at home.

Instead, he closed the remaining space between them and reached for the book.

"Nigel!" She kept her hands firmly around it, feeling ten years old all over again. "Don't!"

He jammed his knee into hers, making it twist oddly against the rock. The unexpected pain made her grip loosen as a hiss escaped her lips. In the next second, he was chuckling, the notebook in his hands, from a step away.

Blast him. Blast *her* for never seeing his next move. And now what was she supposed to do, other than pray he didn't realize what he held? Though her hands shook, she tried for casual again. "Since when are you so eager to take an interest in something of mine?"

"Since I saw you yesterday with this same book, and since I saw that Sinclair girl with a matching one too." He angled away, flipping it open and thumbing through the pages. "What is it? Masculine hand—coarse, at that."

She had no idea what answer to give that would make him lose interest, so she pressed her lips together and pushed off her rock. Her knee pulsed for a few beats but then calmed. Momentary pain, not damage. "Haven't you enough to do on Gugh without worrying over my reading material?"

Something flashed over his face, too quickly gone for her to identify it. Resentment? Vulnerability? Maybe he regretted that Father and his museum friends had taken over the expedition that had previously been his alone. Maybe he felt pushed aside, now that they were here.

That she could commiserate with, if it were true. Perhaps that was a place where they could meet and identify and—

"Wait—John? Piracy?" Nigel's eyes went disturbingly wide as

he looked to her again. And his face went so, so hard. Calculating. "Is this Elizabeth Mucknell's diary?"

Her throat was dry and tight. She could deny it, but he could read as well as any of them. He'd clearly seen the words that verified it. She shrugged. "Possibly. Well, a copy of it. A working theory, anyway. But it has no treasure maps or anything else pertaining to Mucknell's hoard, so it's nothing to excite you."

"I'll be the judge of that, shall I?" He spun toward the path that would lead away from this grassy knoll that she'd let herself think secluded, toward the village. Her notebook still in his hands.

She clambered after him. "Nigel! That is not yours, nor is it mine. I was only borrowing it. You can't just take it!" She felt like a child again, screaming, *"Give it back, give it back!"* while he summarily ignored her. She would never get through to him like that. Her only hope was maturity and compassion. "Give it back!"

Drat it all. Old habits.

She reached for his arm, fisted her hand in his sleeve. Thinking only to slow him, to make him face her. To give herself the chance to make a more reasonable-sounding plea.

He spun more quickly than she'd anticipated, his arm swinging up with force enough not only to knock her hand away but to make her lose her balance in the sand. Made all the worse when something crashed into the side of her head.

She stumbled, fell, tumbled a few steps back down the sandy path. It took her a long moment and a hand to her ringing ear to realize that he'd struck her. Actually struck her—with his hand or the book, she wasn't sure which.

The tears that stung her eyes weren't from the pain. That would vanish soon enough.

Her brother had struck her. He'd never done such a thing before. Grabbed her by the arm and hauled her somewhere she didn't want to go, yes. Insulted her, always. Torn her down verbally, without fail.

But *violence*? Gentlemen didn't behave so. They didn't . . . he . . . she . . .

He'd vanished over the crest of the hill, probably striding back toward Hugh Town without a care, glad to have knocked the pest off his arm. With her copy of the journal in his hands.

"No." It was more a whisper than a shout. She pushed herself back to her feet and rushed after him. "Nigel!"

He was already moving among other holiday-goers converging on the paths back into the town, though. Short of making a scene that would get her labeled hysterical and leave him unscathed, she had no idea what to do. Still, she hurried after him. If she could catch him somewhere, perhaps she stood a chance of reclaiming the journal.

Five minutes later, that hope was dashed. She spun in a circle on the corner of Porthcressa Road and Church Street, unable to spot him in the crowds. Had he gone toward the hotel? The post office? The quay?

And those annoying tears were doing more than stinging her eyes now.

Such a simple task—reading a journal, sharing it with the Howe sisters—and she'd failed. She'd let it slip into the hands of her brother, who had appointed himself their adversary. How was she to look her friends in the eye and admit what had happened? How could she ask the aging Mr. Gibson if he could put his aching hand to another copy for them?

"My lady? Whatever is the matter?"

Emily spun to face the voice and found Briggs but a step away, with two market baskets looped over her arm. Still empty, which meant she was only now leaving their flat for the errands she'd been planning to run this morning. Emily had imagined herself passing the entire morning wandering the shore, reading and exploring and praying.

But her own empty hands mocked her. She held them up, evidence against herself. "He took it. The journal. Nigel saw me and . . ."

Some small part of her must have hoped that Briggs would say it was no great loss, that she shouldn't worry herself over it. A lie, of course, but an attempt at consolation. But no. Her maid's face washed pale, making her freckles stand out in contrast, and her eyes went wide with horror. "No. My lady, he—he'll see that there's another artifact. Something linked to Arthur."

And what could be more alluring for any Englishman in the world of antiquities than to be the one to uncover some long-lost Arthurian object? He would do anything—*anything*—to beat them to it.

She lifted a hand to where he'd struck her. The spot didn't ache—but her heart did. And Elizabeth Mucknell's penned words ran in her own mind. *It would destroy him.*

The fog cleared from her mind, and she drew in a breath, drew up her spine. "I must get word to the others. And to Mother—to let her know that Nigel may well be seeking information on King Arthur, and to beg her to keep him from it, for his own good." Whatever this item was, Elizabeth Mucknell knew it would destroy her husband, and the search for it could destroy Emily's father and brother too.

Briggs nodded. "We can send a note with Enyon Thorne to the Tremaynes—I just saw him making a delivery to his mother. I'm certain he'd wait to take a note with him before he goes back to Tresco."

Emily made a dash for the millinery and the flat they rented above it. "You stall him, if you would. I'll pen a note." And one to send to Mother. She couldn't be certain that her mother wouldn't fail to respond as she'd been doing, but perhaps, if she could impress upon her that it really was for Nigel's benefit . . . perhaps then she would listen.

She had no idea if the words she scribbled onto the pages even made sense, but she couldn't escape the feeling of urgency and so she didn't allow herself to second-guess her word choices. Soon she was hurrying back down the stairs, foisting the note for Beth and her family into Briggs's hand and then darting toward the post office.

She would post the letter and send a short telegram, too, telling her mother it was coming and begging her to pay attention.

"Morning, my lady." The postmaster greeted her with that sad little smile he'd been giving her of late. The one that said, *Poor thing, ignored by her family*. Well, she wouldn't be. Not for long. Not now.

She slid the letter onto the workbench and opened her pocketbook to draw out the necessary coins. "And a telegram too."

Given that she'd already put a few pounds in Briggs's care for the groceries, she hadn't much left of the pocket money with which she'd arrived on the isles. A stop at the bank would be in order in the next day or two as well, but for now she drew out what she would need for this errand and penned the telegram.

When she exited onto the street again, she saw Briggs waiting for her, that worry still in her eyes despite the small smile on her lips. "Mr. Thorne assured me he would get the message to Mr. Tremayne right away."

"That was good of him," Emily said, though she was far from eager for her friends to realize how she'd failed them. She sighed and tried not to let it sag her shoulders too much. "I suppose I might as well tag along for the rest of the shopping. The only thing waiting at the flat is that children's book on Arthurian legend that we've already looked through once."

Briggs nodded, and they aimed themselves toward the end of the street with the grocer and the fresh produce he'd have from the local farmers, as well as Polmers' bakery for bread. Briggs had borrowed a few recipes from Mrs. Dawe and proven herself quite skilled at fixing the fresh fish that was for sale each day. They hadn't been dining on crème brûlée or soufflé while they'd been here, but Emily hardly missed the fare their French chef served. There was something lovely about the simpler foods they could prepare themselves.

A seagull cried overhead, snapping her from those easy thoughts. Reminding her of Nigel's mocking laughter as he took her best hope away from her.

Briggs sighed. "It'll be all right, my lady. The journal is so cryptic— he won't discover anything in her words. And if he does, then we will have first. How could we not with Lord Sheridan and Miss Tremayne both on the case?"

She did have the most remarkable friends. Emily mustered a smile. "If there is anything to be found, they will find it."

"What do you suppose it is? The artifact she refers to, I mean. The Holy Grail?"

"I can't think so." Emily shook her head, wishing she better remembered the old legends, wishing she had something useful to offer. "King Arthur never actually had the Grail, did he? This sounds like something he himself had. One of his swords or knives or helmets, perhaps. Or the Round Table." She smiled again at the thought of Elizabeth Mucknell hiding that from her husband.

Briggs chuckled too. "Maybe Mrs. Mucknell was serving her husband on it for years, and he never even noticed. Just like a man, wouldn't it be?" She nodded toward the shop with crates of fresh vegetables on display outside it.

Emily grinned and let the bright colors of the produce pull her in. She picked up a plump peach and held it up to her nose to inhale the sweet scent. Smiled and tucked it into the empty basket Briggs had handed her, along with three more. "Whatever it was, it must have been clearly associated with King Arthur, if she had no doubt about its provenance. There are only so many artifacts that would so obviously be his."

Briggs reached for some salad greens, but she sneaked a look at Emily. "Do you hope it is? That we find it?"

Emily didn't even hesitate in her reach toward a few plump tomatoes. "Honestly—no. High-value artifacts are nothing but trouble. They invite theft and betrayal. I'm just glad that Mr. Gibson has the diary—a glimpse into the heart and soul of a woman that history remembers only as a footnote. It's her husband who gained infamy, but now . . . now we can know *her*. An ordinary woman who clearly loved in the most extraordinary way. That matters." She looked up, hoping to see understanding in Briggs's gaze instead of scoffing.

Her maid stared at her as if she'd never seen her before—but maybe that was a good thing. After a moment, Briggs nodded and added a cucumber to her basket. "That's a lovely perspective, my lady."

Emily sighed. "But not at all what my brother will be thinking and hoping for. He'll see the word *artifact* and start envisioning something as grand as the Grail or Excalibur, without question."

When neither of them reached for more produce, Emily led the way to the shopkeeper, and they paid for what they'd selected. As they struck off for the bakery next, she said, "All Father and Nigel ever cared about are the finds that will lead to fame and fortune—lost cities and pharaohs' tombs and pirate gold. The things that tour the museums and get one mentioned in all the newspapers." She shook her head. "I always preferred the things stored away in the archives rather than the ones out on display. Less important, perhaps, yet more *real*. Those are what really tell us about the people who came before us."

Briggs opened the door to the bakery, and the fragrance of yeast and flour and sugar wafted out to greet them. Emily's stomach gurgled in response. They'd had a lunch of cold sandwiches, but perhaps supper could involve a few of the Polmers' famed sweet rolls after their fish and salad. "You've been in the archives? Of the British Museum?"

Emily nodded. "Several years ago. I wandered about for hours." Because Nigel had said he wanted to show her something and then had left her there, locked in, overnight. No doubt he'd intended it to frighten her—and no doubt he'd bribed the security guards, who should have discovered her within an hour, to take an evening off or just ignore her.

But the joke had been on him that time. Far from being frightened or reliving the wardrobe experience, she'd enjoyed every moment and had been rather sorry when she heard the lock being turned the next morning. It had marked the first time in her life when she'd gotten to explore history on her own terms, looking at what she wanted, for however long she wanted—at least outside of their own house, though she'd certainly explored every crevice of that over the years, too, peeking into suits of armor and trying to heft swords. Studying the artifacts Father kept for himself when he wasn't around to scold her for it. But even his private collection was nothing compared to the museum's.

And she'd come back out into the sunshine fully convinced that her father and brother had it all wrong. They thought that the important things were the ones made of precious metals or jewels, the stories of kings and conquests.

It was the everyday, though, that made the world go round. The farmers and millers and fishermen. The wives who paced the towers until their husbands came home, the mothers who spent priceless daylight hours stitching their love into christening gowns and knitting blankets to hold the newborns who may or may not live beyond their first breath. The world was such a harsh place—but its every shadow was offset with the light of joy. That's what the archives had shown her. That for every king fighting for his crown were a hundred thousand people never seen, never remembered, who made it possible. Who kept the harvests coming and who lived and laughed and loved without caring who ruled over them.

It gave her hope. Hope that she, who had been told all her life that her only role was to be what they told her to be, could live too.

Elizabeth Mucknell had issued her a new challenge in her diary, though. She'd made her wonder if she really understood what love was. Made her question whether its truest form wasn't in giving it to those who deserved it—or weeping over how one's own family didn't seem to know how to give it at all—but in loving each person however they needed, whether they loved one back or not.

She'd never loved anyone like that. But what would change if she could?

While she woolgathered, Briggs had purchased their bread and sweet rolls and rejoined Emily with a glance at her list. "I believe fish is all that remains."

Emily nodded. "Either afterward or tomorrow, I need to go to the bank as well. We've almost used up our pocket money."

A flock of children raced by when they stepped out onto the street, clearly engaged in a game of some kind, given the laughter. Briggs smiled at them, making her face light up and a bit of the worry leave her eyes. She never smiled like that at Emily. It made her look younger, though. Cheerful. It gave a glimpse of who she must actually be.

If so, the real Thomasina Briggs certainly seemed like a fine young woman to get to know. Better by far than the cut-out version she usually showed her.

Did she dare try to bridge the gap? It was a risk. Briggs could rebuff her efforts. And Emily knew herself well enough to realize that, once rebuffed, she rarely had the heart to make a second attempt at a friendship.

You're being pathetic, Emily. What did she possibly have to lose? They weren't friends now, and their relationship could hardly get any chillier. A rebuff would be no worse than continuing as they'd always been.

She cleared her throat. "Have you any younger siblings? Or cousins?"

Briggs watched the little ones a moment more before turning to Emily. Her expression bespoke a mild confusion, but she didn't hesitate. "I've an older brother and two younger sisters—Meredith and Cecily. Mere is eighteen, and Cecily will be sixteen at Christmas."

Her face had gone back to its usual placid expression, but she couldn't quite hide the warmth in her voice. She clearly loved her siblings. Like Beth loved her brothers, Oliver and Morgan. Like Libby and Bram. The pang in her own chest might be jealousy, but mostly she thought it was sorrow. A grief over what she'd never known with Nigel and likely never would. "You must miss them."

Briggs nodded, and for a long moment Emily thought she would say no more. Then she surprised her by adding, "Dearly. But they write to me all the time, and they're happy. Our mam has just re-married, and so—"

"What?" Emily came to an abrupt halt there in the middle of the street. "When did she marry?" That *just* certainly made it sound like it was in the last year and a half, but Emily knew for a fact that Briggs hadn't taken any time off, not more than the day or two offered her on holidays. Not enough time to travel home to . . . Wales, wasn't it? Certainly not enough to enjoy her mother's wedding festivities.

Perhaps Briggs heard all her silent questions. She sighed. "In May. It was a quiet affair, she didn't expect me to come for it. And I couldn't have—not with all the balls your mother had scheduled for you in London."

Emily just stared at her companion. Trying to see beyond Briggs her maid to Tommie, whose mother had just gotten remarried and who had two sisters she adored. "Your family is far more important than a few balls." It was the truth.

But it made Briggs's brows lift. "If I'd left, your mother would have sacked me."

She was right. But even so. Emily blustered out a sigh. "Well, you must visit them soon—you'll want to assure yourself that your mother's happy and well, and to see your sisters. And heaven knows you've earned a holiday after all . . . this." She waved a hand at the islands at large and then shuffled into a walk again. She'd earned more than a holiday—she'd earned a raise and a bonus and anything else Emily could think to give her.

Of course, the problem was that while Emily paid Briggs out of her own funds—Mother thought it important that she learn how to manage money as preparation for running her own household someday—those funds were provided by Father. And he'd probably have something to say about a large bonus going to her lady's maid for no reason she could disclose to him.

And for that matter, should she even be accepting her father's money, when she was none too sure he'd gained it honestly? But what choice did she have?

Elizabeth Mucknell had planted all sorts of moral questions in her mind that she'd never pondered before.

"Thank you, my lady. I've been thinking a trip home would be just the thing."

Emily nodded, smiled, even while another bolt of maybe-jealousy struck. She couldn't return home until she mended her relationship with Nigel—which meant telling him he'd been right and she'd been wrong to side with the Tremaynes, and promising to do whatever he asked of her in the future. And she wasn't honestly sure she *wanted* to go home, knowing now that home could mean warmth and love and joy, not just obligation and expectation and dictation.

She didn't want to go home—but where did that leave her? She couldn't stay here above Mrs. Gilligan's hat shop for the rest of her life.

They had to sidle through a crowd of ferry passengers as they made their way toward the fish shop, so they didn't try to talk anymore, but Emily spent the time compiling a list of other questions she'd ask Briggs when the opportunity arose. Questions Beth would say she should have known the answers to already. What was her favorite thing about Wales? What had happened to her father? Where was the brother she'd mentioned? Did she know and like her mother's new husband? What sort of books did she like to read?

The more questions she came up with, the more that skipped their way onto her mental list. If Briggs answered them, they'd be friends before the week was out. Mother would be horrified, but she didn't need to know. And how would she? It wasn't as though she'd replied to a single letter or telegram in the last six weeks. She *couldn't* know anything other than what Emily told her. And she clearly didn't care about any of that either.

Stop. She indulged in a moment of squeezing her eyes shut while Briggs haggled over the fish, but only so that she would *not* indulge in that familiar self-pity.

It didn't matter if Mother cared. Well, it did. Of course it did. But it couldn't affect how Emily loved *her*. She had to love her mother for her own sake, the way she needed to be loved. She needed to love her enough to try to understand her.

What would make a woman turn her back on her own child just because her husband said to? Did she really care so little—or was she perhaps afraid to cross Father?

And him—what drove him to be the way he was? Why did he think so much rested on what he accomplished, on what he discovered, on what he could sell? Had his own father made him feel he had to achieve the heights of fame in order to be worthy of the Scofield name? Was it a perpetual cycle that she and Nigel had simply been born into?

And her brother . . . *O Lord, I will definitely need your help with loving him. I don't think I can do it on my own power.* He had to have a kernel of goodness somewhere inside, didn't he? He, too, was made in the image of God. There must be some kindness, some compassion hidden away.

Mother and Father loved him, after all. He must have *some* lovable quality.

And that thought made her ears ring with jealousy again. She eased out a breath and watched Briggs hand over the last of their pound notes. Emily would definitely need to wire for more before Friday, when she was due to pay her maid's wages.

"My lady! Turn quickly."

At Briggs's urgent murmur and accompanying tug on her arm, Emily obediently spun toward the fishmonger, tilting her head down so her hat shielded her face, as usual. But then she dared a peek out from under the brim to see which of her family it was.

Father strode up from the quay with the rich American, Vandermeer, beside him.

She let her head find its usual angle and turned a bit toward him.

Briggs grabbed her arm again. "My lady—what are you doing?"

That was a good question. It had been their explicit goal since the museum trustees and staff arrived last week to avoid them all, especially Father and Nigel.

But Nigel had already found her, had already taken the only advantage they currently had over them. She had to know what he found in those pages, but how would she if she continued to avoid them all?

And even more importantly . . . how could she love her father properly if she hid from him? And how could she complain that he didn't love *her* properly if she never showed him who she was? If she always did the easy thing, the quiet thing, and never spoke up?

She shook free of Briggs's hand and, before better reason could assert itself, while this strange, intoxicating surge of determination still filled her, she stepped out into the road. She even lifted a hand and put on the smile she always *wished* she wanted to give him. Perhaps if she took the action, the feeling would follow. "Father! Good afternoon, Father!"

For three blissful seconds she felt only the thrill of *trying*, of deciding to be a better daughter, of going out on a limb.

Then her father's furious gaze slashed through her, and she wished she'd just kept her head down like always.

5

She was a madwoman, that was what. Tommie shoved the wrapped fish into her basket and had to suppress the sudden urge to run in the opposite direction. What was Lady Emily *thinking*? They were trying to avoid her family, not *call* to them!

Granted, it was only Lord Scofield and the American at the moment, but one never knew when Master Nigel might come out of the very woodwork. Hadn't he proven that to his sister once already today? Tommie didn't dare to chide her, nor to take her arm and drag her into the fish market like she wanted to do. It wouldn't have mattered anyway—it was too late. She'd already stolen the attention not only of Lord Scofield but also of Mr. Vandermeer, and there was no undoing it now.

They would just have to figure out how to mitigate the damage, that was all. Tommie kept her face blank, her spine straight but shoulders bent enough to look deferential, and her gaze fastened securely to the middle distance. In other words, she made herself completely invisible, which was exactly what she needed just now.

And indeed, neither of the gents, as they came to a halt before Lady Emily, even spared Tommie a glance. Perfect.

"This is your daughter?" Mr. Vandermeer was saying even as they stopped, the words sounding strange in his Yankee accent—but even with that, his surprise and pleasure came through. He chuckled. "Scofield, you old dog—you led me to believe your daughter was still in short dresses. And here she is all along, an absolute paradigm of beauty!" He slid a gaze down Lady Emily as he spoke. There was nothing rude about it, somehow, just appreciative. No doubt the sort of look the lady got at every ball she attended.

Still. He meant it—of course. Lady Emily *was* a paradigm of beauty, so he *ought* to appreciate her. But there was something calculating in his eyes, something that made Tommie bristle on Emily's behalf.

The lady barely even glanced at Vandermeer. She was too busy trying to smile at her father, for some reason.

Vandermeer's attention didn't go unnoticed by Scofield, though. He looked from his daughter to his guest and then let out a laugh of his own and slapped the American on the back. "She still is in short dresses in my mind, I'm afraid. You know how fathers are. But come, come. My dear, allow me to make introductions." He reached for Emily's hand and tugged her forward. "This is Donald Vandermeer, of the Manhattan Vandermeers—you've heard me mention his family. Mr. Vandermeer, allow me to present my daughter, Lady Emily Scofield. Emily has been in the islands these weeks visiting friends."

Vandermeer took Lady Emily's hand, his sparkling eyes never leaving her face as he bent over it. "How do you do, my lady?"

Lady Emily murmured the appropriate reply, but Tommie paid little attention to her choice of words. Not given the thoughts flying through Lord Scofield's eyes fast enough to give her whiplash. She hadn't a hope of decoding them all, but she saw enough to note the instant recognition and know what it meant.

Scofield had just decided that his daughter could be useful. Which meant that he would use her.

The surge of protectiveness nearly knocked Tommie over, and even though she kept her feet, she couldn't keep her breath. Eighteen months she'd served Lady Emily, and never had she pitied her. Never had she really felt any loyalty or desire to put herself in harm's way for her employer's sake. Never had she felt more than a vague sense of obligation to her.

In this moment, however, the only thing that kept her from leaping between Lady Emily and her father—with all the ferocity she'd have used had it been her own sister being shoved at a man—was the sure knowledge that she would only make things worse if she tried it.

She held her place, bit her tongue. But it took all her self-restraint. Because never, in those same eighteen months, had she ever seen Lord Scofield pay his daughter even a minute's attention. He never met her gaze, he never exchanged a word with her that wasn't required, he never really acknowledged her existence beyond mumbling about the expenses of outfitting a daughter for the Season. She had heard him more than once simply instruct Lady Scofield in how to "manage Emily" while Emily was standing right there. Now, all of a sudden, she was "my dear"?

It had to sting. No, worse, it had to slice Lady Emily clean through. But she wouldn't show it. She merely reclaimed her hand and turned to her father as if she did so every day. "Father, I'm so glad I ran into you. I was hoping we could spend some time together while we're both here. Tea, perhaps? It's been ages since just the two of us have spent any time together."

Lord Scofield's eye twitched, but he smiled. "Of course, my dear. That would be delightful."

Tommie forced herself to breathe. She still didn't know what Emily was really angling for, but she'd certainly played it well if it really was her sudden—if baffling—desire to get him alone. She'd framed it all in such a way that he couldn't very well say no without looking like an ogre before his guest.

"Vandermeer!" A voice, unfamiliar but educated, came from the direction of the village and had that gentleman's head turning toward it. Probably a museum trustee, from the looks of him—a portly gent in an expensive linen suit. He was waving a hand and picking his way along the cobblestones as if he expected one to leap up and bite his foot. "A moment, if you please!"

Vandermeer nodded, directing it to the two Scofields with a bright smile. "If you'll excuse me for just a moment, my lord. My lady." He strode away.

And just like that, Scofield shifted, turned his back to the other gents, and grabbed Lady Emily by the elbow—not gently, either, from the looks of it. "You have some nerve," he said, voice low and taut. "Coming here for the purpose of undermining your family, shaming us all with your affiliations—and now hailing me as if I will waste a moment on you while you're being so rebellious?"

Tommie inched closer, though she still didn't know what she could do to help.

Emily's complexion, always fair as cream, now washed pale as a ghost. "Father, if we could just *talk*—"

"Do you mean to apologize to your brother? Make up somehow for your betrayal—as if that's possible?"

"But I didn't—"

"I thought not." He released her abruptly, gaze flashing down to her baskets. "Well, if appealing to your family obligations won't move you, I suppose we'll just resort to the next step, shall we?" He straightened his spine, tugged down his waistcoat, and glared at her. "You'll not get another pence from me until you see reason."

Tommie's hands went tight on the basket handle. He was cutting her off? Cutting *them* off. Not just emotionally, but physically as well.

And they'd just spent their last cash on these groceries that wouldn't last but a few days. Tommie's mouth went dry.

Emily swallowed, too, and stood straight, though her lips quivered. "It isn't your money I want, Father. It's the chance to get to know you."

He snorted. "Now you're talking nonsense." He leaned closer, but no one who saw his face could think it was anything but a threat. "Perhaps going hungry for a few days will bring you to your senses. You know how to find me when you're ready to be reasonable." He spun on his heel and stalked after Vandermeer.

Be reasonable? Knuckle under, he meant. Kowtow to Nigel. Apologize for doing the right thing and swear never to do it again.

Tommie grabbed at Lady Emily's basket just as her fingers let the handle go. The lady was staring after her father, dazed. "I thought . . . if I could just love him. But I have to know him first. If he would just talk to me for an hour . . ."

That's what it had all been about? Tommie set down both their baskets and rested a hand on the lady's forearm. "You tried." And it was admirable—if foolhardy. And sad. So sad, that a sweet young woman had to try so hard to win her father's love.

Tommie may not have grown up with manor houses and servants, but she'd had that, at least. The sure knowledge that Tad would do anything for them while he had the breath to do it.

Lady Emily shook her head slowly. "That's why I got involved in all this to begin with, you know. When Beth wrote to me—I thought finally I'd have something to get his attention. Finally, *finally* I'd really be part of the family."

"I know." Tommie rubbed her hand up and down Emily's forearm. It was a warm day, but her skin was cold. "My lady—it isn't you. It's him. *Them.*"

"But *I* am the only one I can change. So I have to try, don't I?" She turned, bent down to pick up her basket, blinked away the sheen of tears. But she just stared at the fruit and vegetables, then looked up at Tommie. She didn't have to say it—that they'd just spent her last money, that this basket of food wouldn't provide for long.

Tommie swallowed, though her throat was dry. "I know." Other than what she'd put aside for her train ticket home, she didn't have any money either. If it came to eating or traveling—but then, wouldn't it be smarter to go home, if it came to that? Relieve Lady Emily of the responsibility of feeding *her?*

Facing her mother and sisters, risking that they'd see in a glance all that had brought her back to them. How could she both yearn for a thing and fear it so deeply? She pushed thoughts of her own life back down, into the pocket with her resignation, tucked away. Neat and tidy.

Emily. She would focus on Emily. And the fact that Lord Scofield had just told his daughter he'd rather let her starve than spend an hour in her company. Tommie reached out again, this time settling her fingers over Emily's. "I'm sorry, my lady."

Still looking a bit dazed, Emily nodded. "So am I."

Had Bram ever mentioned that he hated bullies? He *hated* bullies. Hands jammed in his pockets to keep them in line, he clenched his teeth and held completely still in the shadows until Lady Emily and Briggs meandered away. A bag dangled from his wrist, the slim book inside all that the bookshop on St. Mary's had to offer on Arthurian legend. He'd been thinking, five minutes ago, that it hadn't even been worth the trip.

Now he was quite glad he'd come over with Oliver, despite the paltry book offerings. And even more glad that he'd followed the familiar head of red hair when he'd spotted it. He'd meant to catch up and ask them if they'd looked over the copy of the diary yet, engage in some easy, idle chitchat until Oliver finished his own errands and returned to the *Adelle*, which was anchored in the quay. But Lady Emily had looked so lost in her thoughts that he'd just tucked himself into the shadows instead, meaning to let them go by again without a word.

Then her father had come. And Vandermeer. And while manners said he should have retreated, he'd opted instead for eavesdropping, and he wasn't the least bit sorry. In fact, he was fairly certain Oliver would say God himself had led him to that very spot in that very moment. So that he could hear that awful sham of a conversation.

What kind of father acted that way? Cut off his own daughter and said outright that he wanted her to go hungry? When she'd done absolutely nothing wrong?

All right, so Bram had told Oliver he would do the same if he and Libby got married—but he'd only been testing him. Making sure he wasn't after Libby's dowry. He would never actually *do* it.

And he wasn't about to let Scofield get away with it. He couldn't mention it to Lady Emily—she would likely be mortified if she realized he'd overheard her conversation with her father and seen him rebuff her attempt at reconciliation. And he had a feeling confronting Scofield wouldn't be the best tack either, though it would be satisfying.

He cast another glare toward the village into which Scofield had vanished and aimed himself toward the quay. He'd liked Scofield, once upon a time. They were members of the same club in London and had played a few games of squash here and there. Sheridan had even had him over to dine once, in his eternal quest to endear himself to all the trustees of the British Museum in the hopes of someday being one of them. Bram had thought him an intelligent, interesting fellow. He'd thought him like his *own* father. Had, in fact, enjoyed those hours spent with him because it felt a bit like he had Father back.

How could he have been so wrong?

There was the barb, as it pertained to him. The real barb was how he treated his daughter, of course, but that only accounted for the anger in his chest, not the disappointment. No, the disappointment was because Bram had ascribed to Lord Scofield the same noble spirit and deep heart that had characterized the late Lord Telford—and Scofield had none of it.

Bram clenched his hand inside his pocket. He'd never been much given to prayer before spending so much time around people—well, Oliver—who talked about it incessantly, but just now he found himself offering a rather strange plea to the Lord. *Help* me *live up to the noble spirit and deep heart of the late Lord Telford. Help me to be like my own father—not hers. Never like hers.*

He scanned the dock, but Oliver wasn't back yet, so there was no point in scrambling aboard the *Adelle*. Bram leaned against one of the massive wooden posts instead and drew out the slim book he'd just bought. Perhaps King Arthur and Merlin would take his mind off Scofield for a few minutes.

He had this same book at home—he was fairly certain he had *all* the books on Arthur at home. This one had been good enough that he deemed it worth buying again now, but it certainly didn't have all the information they'd need. It was more a primer about the legend than a detailed study. Not enough to account for all the information he had swimming around in his head.

Could he convince them all that he just had an excellent memory and wasn't still obsessed with the story? Unlikely. He *did* have an excellent memory, it was true, but it wasn't something he flaunted, for everyone to expect it of him.

Perhaps he could follow Sheridan's example, though. Inspired, he slipped the book back into its bag and reached into his jacket pocket, where he'd stuffed the letter from Mother he'd barely had time to open before Oliver invited him to come to St. Mary's.

The letter was, as usual, three pages longer than it really needed to be. She had to tell him every little detail of her recent days with Edith—the eldest of the three siblings—and how perfect her new grandchild was. Bram would read those details more slowly later, since he really did want to know, but right now he skimmed it all until he saw the words he'd been waiting for.

Yes, there it was, on the last page. Edith and little Devon were doing brilliantly, the nursemaid had things well in hand, and Mother would soon be departing. She intended to stop for a day or two at Telford Hall to exchange her summer wardrobe for her autumn one, and then she would be coming to Cornwall. She was most eager to meet the Tremaynes. . . .

Perfect. He would simply send her a wire asking her to bring some of his books with her. Not all of them—that would look far too telling. But the best of them. And he'd send another note to Telford Hall asking them to box up the titles he wanted. That would work. It would take a couple of weeks, but no longer than it would take for the little bookshop here to order the titles in for him.

And these would be *his*. The ones with his markers and notes in them.

"Well, hello there. Lord Telmond, isn't it?"

Bram folded the letter and looked up, though he didn't need to see the man ambling his way to recognize the flat American vowels. He smirked. "Nearly. And you're . . . what is it? Van Groot?"

Vandermeer smirked right back and held out a hand. "Close enough. You're Sheridan's friend?"

He tilted it up at the end like a question, but they both knew it wasn't, just as they both knew they knew each other's names. Bram nodded.

Vandermeer did, too, and slung his hands into his pockets as he looked out over the water. "I don't recall seeing you with him on any of his other expeditions—just those sisters of his, and his valet."

Bram granted that with a dip of his chin. "What I lack in the desire to pursue archaeology, I make up for in sanity."

A bark of laughter burst from Vandermeer's lips before he schooled his features again. Though his eyes still sparkled. "You just haven't been bitten by the bug yet, clearly."

"And I carry a swatter around with me at all times to ensure that I never am." But he could appreciate that the American at least had a sense of humor. He reached into the bag with the book and pulled out a smaller sack he'd slid inside. "Chocolate drop?"

When he held it out, Vandermeer chose one with admirable care. "Thanks. I'm surprised you all are still here, since you were only granted the right to excavate that one small section of Gugh."

Bram selected a piece of chocolate for himself and popped it into his mouth. "You mean the section that actually had something hidden in it? Yes, shame, that. We should all run home in dismay—except that we're not here just for an excavation. My sister's engaged to a local chap." He probably knew that, too, honestly. From Millicent's complaints about him, Bram had gathered that Vandermeer did his research and did it well.

"The vicar, yes. I've heard it mentioned here and there." Vandermeer sucked for a moment on the chocolate and made an impressed face. "Quite good, really. Where did you get them? I haven't seen a confectioner's shop."

"The sweet shop itself is on Tresco, but they sell some of their sweets in Polmers' bakery too." Bram weighed the bag for a moment in his hand and then slid it back into the larger one.

Vandermeer nodded. "I'll have to stop by later." He surveyed the water for another moment, then said, "You know, I've been wondering. Scofield—the younger one. What am I supposed to call him, anyway?"

Bram moved his chocolate to the other cheek. "Our favorite title so far is 'odious,' I believe."

Another chuckle slipped out. "Don't get along, I take it?"

Bram lifted his brows. "Call me biased, but I have trouble liking homicidal maniacs. He threatened my sister and tried to kill Sheridan's fiancée."

Vandermeer gave him a look that said he was being dramatic. "If that were true, he'd have been arrested."

A smile that probably looked every bit as condescending as it felt pulled up his lips. "Ah, Americans. So naïve you all are. Or—no, we'll call it 'idealistic' instead of 'naïve.' To be polite." He made a show of leaning closer. "We Brits are all politeness and manners, you know."

This time Vandermeer's laugh rang out long and full. "I like you, Telby."

"Then I can die happy." He folded his arms over his chest. "Was that your question about the younger Scofield? What to call him?"

Vandermeer settled again, though he was still grinning. "No. I was going to ask what the argument was between him and Sheridan, but I believe you answered it. I'd noticed that the antagonism there went well beyond the friendly rivalry I've long had with him and his sisters."

To hear Millicent talk, it wasn't so friendly. But then again, *she* was probably being dramatic. Sheridan had certainly never spoken of the American like he did Nigel Scofield. And it hadn't escaped Bram's notice that Sher's was the one name Vandermeer got right. That must indicate respect.

"You know," Vandermeer went on, "the younger Scofield came back to the yacht last week fuming about how the only thing in that trunk you all excavated was a bunch of moldy books and rusty rubbish. Which I found very curious indeed. The pirate admiral wasn't exactly famous for his love of literature. And not stupid enough to bury something that would rot and rust."

Blast. They knew it was a risk, trying to pull the wool over Nigel Scofield's eyes. But they had to at least buy themselves some time, hence Sheridan indicating his *own* sea chest full of artifacts he'd been collecting was the one they'd just dug up.

Bram fished another chocolate from the bag within the bag and tossed it in his mouth with a shrug. "A very logical deduction. I shall point it out to the vice admiral and the pirate prince both, so that next time they bury their booty, they choose the items with more care."

Vandermeer grinned at him. "What was really in it? Come on, you can tell me. I won't breathe a word to the Scofields."

That much Bram might grant him—maybe. He seemed the sort to enter into an alliance only so long as it benefited him. If he could find what he wanted *without* the Scofields, then he'd bid them adieu and proceed on his own.

Bram cocked his head to the side. "Interesting."

"What?"

"You don't *look* like a fisherman—and there are plenty of them about. But there you are, fishing."

The American chuckled again. "Can't blame a fellow for trying."

Why had he even put the chocolates away? Bram drew the bag out again and offered it once more to Vandermeer, who thanked him with a nod. Bram nodded back. "What's your interest in this pirate hoard, anyway? Even if Mucknell hid away everything he was ever rumored to, it's not a Viking king's burial chamber or anything. Just a bit of random gold. I mean, Sher has the excuse of being interested in anything having to do with Prince Rupert, whose daughter married into his own family. But you?" Bram gave him a look. "I haven't puzzled you out yet, Van Gogh. What's brought you into all this?"

Vandermeer grinned. "Isn't a pirate story enough of a draw?"

For a man who dedicated his life to finding hidden relics that could rewrite history? A man who apparently had a fortune even greater than Sheridan's, made from the sugar and rum trade in the Caribbean in centuries past? "No."

The American opened his mouth, no doubt ready to offer a simple disagreement. Then he paused, pursed his lips, drew in a long breath. And let his head rock back and forth. "Actually, Mucknell ties in with my own family history."

"Oh?" They'd wondered as much. Mucknell had, after all, disappeared and presumably died in the Caribbean—around the same time when the Vandermeers were making their fortune in the Dutch West Indies.

"It was one of my great-greats who killed him." He positioned himself against the post opposite Bram's with a shrug. "He apparently tried to rob one of our ships taking rum to America. It didn't go well for him—or so the story goes."

"Hm." That made as much sense as any other theory they'd come up with. And if being friends with Sher had taught him anything, it was that it only took the smallest connection with one's own family history for these antiquity hounds to go tearing off in pursuit of something. "You believe the story, I assume."

"No reason not to. And there are a few details that make it credible—for instance, Mucknell's dying words were recorded as being, '*Tell Lizza I love her.*'" Vandermeer spread his arms wide, as if to say, *See? Aren't you impressed?*

He was. Not that he'd admit it. But how, unless it were true, would that long-dead Vandermeer have known Mucknell called his wife Lizza? And really, why lie about it? "And did he ever find a way to tell her?" As if he didn't already know the answer.

Vandermeer chuckled. "My great-greats weren't known for their selflessness. No, they never crossed the pond to deliver that message."

"I suppose that's why you're here now, to deliver it to her memory. Has nothing at all to do with wondering what he may have more successfully stolen." Not that, as he'd already decided, the pirate hoard was all that big to someone like the American. But combined with that family history—well, Sheridan was proof that a fellow could chase such a lark just for the fun of it, wasn't he?

Vandermeer certainly was a cheerful chap. He was grinning again. "I never claimed to be known for my selflessness either."

Bram snorted a laugh. "I suppose I ought to at least credit you with self-awareness." He jiggled his bag of chocolates around until he found the perfect piece to next enjoy.

"One of my many virtues." But his grin faded as he shot a glance up the hill toward Hugh Town. "Say—have you met Scofield's daughter? Lady Emily?"

Bram slid the chocolate into his mouth. And fastened his gaze on Vandermeer. "I have."

"I just did too. Lovely young lady, isn't she?"

"She is." Bram lowered the bag of candy. He'd been about to offer another one but didn't. "And you met her last week—or could have done. She was there on Gugh that morning."

Vandermeer swung his head back to face Bram. "No, she wasn't."

"Yes. She was."

He actually reached up and scratched his head, a perfect caricature of bemusement. "She couldn't have been. Why wouldn't her father have greeted her?"

Bram lifted his brows. Apparently, he'd have to spell it out for him. "Because she was there with *us*."

Amusement replaced the confusion. "Why would she have been there with *you*?"

It was rather annoying, really, that he liked this chap so much. "Because we're better company than what you're currently keeping."

Another flashing grin. "Perhaps I'll start keeping company with you all instead, then. I'm sure I'd be most graciously received, don't you think?"

Millicent might have an apoplexy—which, granted, would be entertaining. So long as it wasn't a real one. Bram snorted a laugh. "Certainly, Van Horn. Come on over to Tresco anytime."

"Perhaps I will." It was subtle, that shift from amusement to challenge. But it was there, and Bram didn't miss it. "Could be worthwhile, if it means a chance to get to know Lady Emily a bit better. I had no idea the Scofields' daughter was of age—and so lovely."

He definitely wasn't getting any more of Bram's chocolate. Because, yes, Lady Emily was lovely—but Vandermeer hadn't even noticed her a week ago on Gugh. He'd certainly never had a conversation with her to know that she was sweet and compassionate and more than a little lost right now. And never mind the fact that he was twice her age.

The real issue here was that he was clearly only interested in her *because* she was Scofield's daughter. Beauty, a dowry, and connections—that's what she'd mean to Vandermeer.

It was the way society worked. But it would break her. It would be one more boot to the puppy's ribs, to be pawned off to the highest bidder who just wanted to add her to his art collection.

No. Bram wasn't going to let that happen. He'd made himself a royal heel just to be sure his own sister didn't make a match that would end up hurting her, and he'd do the same for Lady Emily, if it came down to it. Because she who'd just gone out on a limb to try to reach her father—she had a heart far too good to go unprotected.

"Oh, heaven help me." Vandermeer shoved his hands back into his pockets again and sighed. His gaze was once more fastened on the road to the village, though this time he was tracking someone. "Millie's on the warpath."

Bram glanced that way and grinned at the sight of Sheridan's sister. He'd never been so happy to see her striding his way with that expression on her face that said she was ready to take over and fix everything, whether it really needed fixing or not. "You know, a bit of friendly advice—because I really do like you, Vandergraff. If you keep calling her that, one of these days she's going to box your ears. It's Millicent, never Millie. And Abbie, never Abigail."

Vandermeer's grin returned, and this time it was impish. "I can handle an ear-boxing. It's worth it to see her so riled." He held up a hand in greeting as she drew near. "Millie! Good afternoon!"

She put on a smile, but it was the sort that barely masked the warrior glint in her eye. It would prove entertaining to watch, given that Bram was on the sidelines and not in her line of fire this time. But even so, he was glad to spot Oliver trailing along in her wake. They could make their escape if shrapnel started to fly.

"Donald, darling." She reached out and grabbed his hand, and even from where Bram stood, he could see that she dug her nails in. She was wearing gloves, so it probably didn't hurt, but still. He'd get the picture. "Still haven't outgrown your tendency to harass the children, I see."

Vandermeer sighed. "Look, Millie, perhaps your brother was only a lad that first time I tried to wheedle information out of him. But he's a grown man now—as is Telforth here. If they can't stand up to a little friendly inquiry, then they shouldn't be playing with the big boys."

Millicent batted her lashes. "I do so love those crass American-isms of yours. They make certain I never forget where you come from . . . and where you don't."

Vandermeer rolled his eyes. "Oh yes, a dagger through my heart. Point out yet again that I come from a line of merchants instead of royalty or whatever. I'm devastated."

Bram couldn't resist a poke. "Don't worry, Millicent, it's a lack he intends to remedy by marrying a noblewoman. He's set his sights on Lady Emily."

Vandermeer flashed him an annoyed glare. Oliver widened his eyes in obvious concern.

Millicent's smile went so sweet that only a fool would fail to look for the poison in it. "Has he? Well, from what I'm given to understand, she *is* in need of a more dependable father figure. Being twice her age, Donald darling, you would seem a fine solution."

He winced. "That was low, Millie. I'm only a year older than *you*."

"But I'm not chasing after someone barely out of short pants, am I?" She tugged him a step away. "Though if this is the course you've set, I will be happy to offer you some direction, having got to know Lady Emily quite well recently."

Vandermeer groaned.

Bram took pity and dug out a few more chocolate drops. "Here. You're going to need these."

The American accepted them on his way by, though he still sent Bram an exaggerated glare. "I'm going to pay you back for this, you know."

"Oh, the chocolate is my gift to you. No need to pay it back." He offered a mock salute.

Millicent winked at him before arrowing her gaze into Vandermeer again. "And while I'm dispensing matchmaking wisdom, I'm also very happy to tell you anything you need to know about our activities here, so that you don't feel the need to try to wheedle it from my brother or his little friends. Though, sadly, we have been all but idle since your delightful group arrived, relegated to sightseeing and bird watching with Lady Elizabeth Sinclair . . ."

Oliver slid into the place beside Bram, his gaze on the back of the departing two as Millicent all but dragged Vandermeer away. "Should I pity him or be concerned that he sought you out?"

Bram was still trying to shrug off that "little friends" bit. Sometimes Sher's sisters were just infuriating. But useful too. He had to grant them that. Millicent would probably have the American going off on ten different tangents, convinced he'd ferreted out a clue she hadn't meant to let drop.

But she never spoke a word awry. Not that Bram had ever heard.

She was pure calculation, that one. "I think . . . pity. Definitely pity. He's really not a bad fellow, if one ignores his current alliances."

"Mm." Oliver frowned at him. "You didn't bring chocolate with you."

"Picked it up at Polmers'."

"Don't you still have a pound of it at home?"

Now he was starting to sound like Mother. "That wouldn't help me now, would it?"

His companion shook his head and turned toward the *Adelle*. "I'm baffled at how you have any teeth left. And don't weigh as much as an elephant."

He brushed his teeth obsessively and spent most of the night-time hours walking—but why destroy the mystique? "I am clearly made from the bones and blood of gods, impervious to your mortal failings."

Oliver snorted and leaped onto the deck of his sailboat. "I suppose that explains why your sister is so divine, anyway."

Bram had never met any other vicar who would joke about such things—but then, they all knew it was just a joke. He'd also never met anyone so devout as Oliver Tremayne. Bram jumped down, though he then stole one last look at the retreating American. "Since you pray with every breath, add that to your list, will you? His interest in Lady Emily, I mean. It has to be motivated by her family connections and her looks, nothing more. But that's not what she needs."

"No, it definitely isn't." Oliver, face sober, nodded as he unhitched their line. "I'll be praying." Then he lifted a brow. "You could too, you know."

Bram sighed. He wasn't ready to admit it out loud—but he'd been thinking the same thing. Lady Emily could use all the prayers she could get.

6

The stars were putting on quite a show tonight, shining with a brilliance he never saw in London. They were spectacular in Somerset, but somehow it still felt different here, with the sounds of the surf providing a backdrop. Could sound somehow amplify vision? Bram tilted his head back to take in the galaxies even as he kept walking along the cobbled streets of Old Grimsby. It certainly seemed like it. That the ocean made the stars brighter. He'd follow the road down to the shore and then walk it instead. Maybe the crashing surf and summer-warm wind would help his thoughts clarify.

"Bram!" His sister's voice came in a stage whisper even as a door creaked and her familiar steps hurried over to him.

He held up and greeted her with a questioning look. He hadn't even realized he was walking past the Moon house, but there it was. Why was Libby up at two in the morning, though? "Everything all right?" He, too, spoke in a whisper, keenly aware of all the sleeping people behind the doors and windows of the cottages.

The moonlight traced her smile. "Couldn't sleep." She was wrapping a shawl around her shoulders as she moved to his side. No doubt the purple one that Mamm-wynn had given her, though it looked colorless in the night.

He offered her an elbow. "You can tell me why once we're away from the houses."

She nodded and tucked her hand into the crook of his arm. They'd walked like this countless times over the years, but just now—blame the starlight and ocean sounds—he felt decidedly sentimental at the feel of her hand against his arm. It was Oliver Tremayne she usually walked with now. And when Bram left in a few weeks, would she even come with him, or would she convince Mother that the wedding ought to be this autumn, here on Tresco? Maybe his baby sister would never really leave the islands again, other than a visit here and there. Maybe these strolls with her on his arm were all but over.

He drew in a deep breath, let it out, and hoped it would blend into the wind and not worry her more. He loved his older sister, Edith. And when they were all children, he'd preferred her company to Libby's, since Lib was the baby and a lad of eight couldn't be caught doing baby things—obviously.

But now? Libby was the one who held the soft spot in his heart. She was so . . . different from anyone else. It frustrated him at times, true. But he'd also realized at some point in the last five years that he needed to protect that about her. Protect *her* from the world that would try with all its might to make her conform.

It was why he bought her sketchbooks and pencils and water-colors, microscopes and slides, and every book on naturalism they could find. He wasn't just humoring her, like she probably thought. He wanted to see her flourish and grow. Thrive.

She was thriving here. He knew that. Still, he'd miss her fiercely when he went home and she made hers here in the Isles of Scilly. What was he going to do with himself if he wasn't scolding her for lying in the dirt examining beetles or teasing her for belting out opera every time she put her eye to her microscope? It was going to be far too quiet at Telford Hall. Too . . . empty.

They stepped from street to sand, and Bram took the excuse to cover her hand with his under the guise of steadying her. When really it was to steady *him.* "There. Now you can tell me why you're awake at the haunting hour instead of dreaming about orange blossoms—or whatever their Latin name is."

"*Citrus sinensis.*" He could hear the grin in her voice. Though then she sighed. "When do you think Mama will arrive? Did she give a date?"

Ah. He gave her fingers a squeeze and released them. "She didn't. You know how she is when it comes to leaving Edith and the children. It's one excuse after another to stay just one more day."

Libby chuckled, but it sounded strained. "I'm not at all sad to be here instead of there. That always drives me mad."

"I don't know why, given how splendidly you and E have always got along," he said dryly.

He could *hear* her rolling her eyes. And he couldn't blame her. If Edith had chanted that constant litany of *"Can't you just be proper for one day in your life?"* nonsense at him every day for the last decade, he'd have taken to hiding in the garden to escape her too.

But Mother was different. She'd always indulged Libby's quirks. "You don't need to be nervous about her coming, you know. Oliver will take her elbow and look into her soul, Mamm-wynn will present her with a shawl that perfectly captures her personality, and she'll be swearing they're the best family in all of England within five minutes, just like Sheridan's sisters are."

"I know." But she didn't sound like she knew. She leaned into his arm as they reached firmer sand and turned to follow it. "It's just . . . I keep remembering something Mabena said at the start of the summer. That Mama will love him, just as everyone does. She just wouldn't love him for *me.* I don't know what I'll do if she disapproves, Bram. I can't imagine getting married without her blessing—but I also can't even consider *not* marrying him. I love him so much."

Which he'd been able to tell from the moment he first saw them together, before he was entirely certain that Oliver loved her just as much and for all the right reasons. "She won't disapprove. Come now—we all know that I'm the ogre in the family, not Mother. And he's won *me* over, hasn't he?"

She laughed and, when their steps brought them closer, rested her head briefly on his shoulder before lifting it again when her foot sank into softer sand. "There's no man in the world like him. He really is wonderful, isn't he?"

He really was—it was annoying. "If you expect me to write ballads about him, you obviously have me confused with someone else."

She rewarded him with another laugh. The sea provided accompaniment, and the wind wrapped around it and whisked it away.

Sometimes he wished nights like this would go on forever. The days were never so soft and quiet, so peaceful. And when could two people really have a conversation like this in the sunshine? No, moon and starlight were made for the meeting of hearts.

Listen to him—he probably *could* write a ballad.

They walked in silence for a little ways before she turned her face toward him. "Bram . . . what are you going to do? After this, I mean. When I marry, and Sheridan has Beth now, and . . ."

He must be utterly transparent. "You think getting married will mean I stop pestering you? You greatly underestimate my determination."

She shook her head. "I'm serious. Obviously you'll visit us here and still visit Sheridan, too, and Edith, but that still leaves a lot of time at Telford Hall with only Mama for company—and you know she's been wanting to travel more. Will you just go with her?"

Tagging along with his mother when he wasn't imposing on a sister or his best friend? My, she did paint a life of excitement for him, didn't she? He sighed. "It's my job to worry for you, Lib, not the other way around."

"You obviously don't know how this love thing works." She bumped her shoulder into his. "Maybe you just need a wife. I imagine

Lottie Wight would volunteer, even if it meant tossing aside her rich beau and his titled cousin. I can talk to her for you before she leaves on Sunday, you know. . . ."

He gave an exaggerated shudder, having met her friend from boarding school before. It had taken days for his ears to stop ringing from her constant chatter. "Generous of you, but no."

Libby laughed. "All right. My next question, then—how long are you going to let everyone muddle along in this new quest before you admit you know everything there is to know about King Arthur and share the information that could help us?"

Totally, utterly transparent. At least to those who had always lived in the same house as he did. He gave her a mock stern face. "I don't know what you're talking about. I long ago outgrew that childish fascination with the most noble king ever to rule our land and the legacy of honor and chivalry that he instituted, which the world today could certainly use more of."

She pressed her lips together, but the grin still peeked through. "Mm-hmm."

He huffed. "If you must know, I've been plotting how best to share what I know without looking a complete buffoon. I already sent a note to Mother, asking her to bring a few books that I've instructed Landsem to pack."

Libby, however, didn't look appeased. "That could be weeks from now! Are you really going to let us flounder until then, content with what we can find in those tiny little storybooks while Nigel Scofield is off trying to solve the mystery too? These books don't even mention Lyonesse!"

He *had* been content to do just that, until Enyon Thorne had caught up with him and Oliver and passed them the note from Emily. But the fact that Scofield would be on the hunt for whatever this mysterious "artifact" was too . . . that made it considerably more urgent that they decode the diary and find it first. "I was considering writing it all out in a false hand, staining the paper with tea to make it look old, and burying it—then cleverly pointing Sheridan and Beth to it. They can discover it all and take the credit for it, and my secret will be saved. What do you think?"

"I think," she said on a laugh, "that Sheridan's absurdity has rubbed off on you."

He sighed. "Probably wouldn't fool them anyway. I suppose I'll have to claim I have a memory like a steel trap and that I just remember it all from my school days and that research paper I wrote on the legend."

"Or you could admit you enjoy the stories. There's no shame in that."

Wasn't there? Then why did it make him antsy even to consider admitting it? He was a grown man, for heaven's sake. An earl, a peer of the realm. The other lords would likely laugh him out of Parliament if they knew he spent so much of his spare time reading about Merlin and the Sword in the Stone and everything he could dig up on each of the twelve central knights to sit at the Round Table.

One *could* argue that it was better to spend one's time immersed in tales of chivalry than sitting in a gaming hell, losing the family fortune at tables far less Round. And it wasn't as though he was in danger of turning into a Don Quixote and declaring war on any windmills.

Probably. Although if he grew bored enough without Sheridan and Libby . . .

"What's that?" Libby drifted to a halt and pointed out to sea. Or, more specifically, to a dark form emerging from the night.

Bram stopped, too, and frowned at it. "'Here be dragons'? Or perhaps I've been listening to Mr. Gibson too much." He blinked, then sucked in a breath as the shadow tracked through the moonlight. "Boat. No—*yacht*."

Libby backed up a step. "Why would they risk sailing these channels in the dark? Don't they know how dangerous it can be? Beth was telling me about the nasty currents that can grab you if you get even a bit off course—and there are all the shoals and sandbars and—are they coming *here*?"

They certainly seemed to be. Well, not to this very beach, but to Tresco. He muttered a choice word under his breath and tugged Libby into a jog. "They'd only try it if they thought it worth the risk."

Neither of them had to elucidate who "they" were. It could only be the Scofields, possibly with Vandermeer, since it was the *Victoria* they were sailing, from the looks of it.

"The treasure." Libby had never been one for strenuous exercise, but she had no trouble keeping up just now. "Do you think they know where it is?"

He couldn't imagine they did. Who would think to look for pirate treasure in the record cupboard of a church? But still. "I don't know. It could have something to do with the journal instead. Regardless, I don't intend to just let them stumble across what we've already found or the notes we've taken. Sher and Beth would be heartbroken."

"*He* would be, you mean. She would be furious."

"You have a point. Let's save him from tears and her from murder, shall we?"

Though they'd entered the beach from the main road through the village, Bram chose a shortcut up the bank now, which required a bit steeper climb but delivered them far faster to Grimsby. He didn't intend to make a scene and wake up any of the neighbors if the yacht kept on sailing or if its occupants were clearly aimed in an altogether wrong direction. But if they neared either the Tremayne house or St. Nicholas's church . . . Well, he didn't really know what he'd do. But something.

Times like this, a chap could go for a suit of armor. He felt altogether too vulnerable in only his shirtsleeves.

Libby stayed close to his heels. "Should we wake Oliver? And Sheridan? Perhaps the valets?"

Should they? He'd much rather come up with some brilliant plan all on his own. But there was a reason Arthur put together a council of knights and didn't just rely on his own wisdom. "I'll wake them. You wake Beth and perhaps Moon. They're every bit as terrifying as the men."

She made a sound that crossed a laugh with a gasp. "I'll have Mabena fetch Casek—if we want terrifying, I mean."

"Good thinking." He nodded as she peeled off toward the Moon residence and he kept jogging toward the Tremaynes'.

Just for the fun of it, he ticked them all off mentally as he went. Him and Collins, Sheridan and Ainsley, Moon and Libby and Beth, Senara and Mr. and Mrs. Dawe, Casek and Oliver. He grinned into the night. That made twelve. A perfect Round Table.

Scofield and Vandermeer didn't stand a chance. What thieves wouldn't turn tail and run when they saw a dozen valiant knights standing against them? Even if said knights were as many women as men and wore nightclothes instead of armor.

Of course, they were missing the king and queen. The *knights* of the Round Table numbered twelve, but that wasn't counting Arthur and Guinevere.

He skidded to a halt halfway up the flagstone path when he saw the front door to the Tremayne house was open and a bleary-eyed Mr. Gibson stood there with Mamm-wynn.

Well, there were the king and queen. He ought to have known they'd show up whenever a whiff of adventure was to be found. The Tremayne matriarch seemed to have a sixth sense about such things.

Gibson, however, grunted. "I'm too old for this midnight nonsense, Adelle. Why can't we leave it to the young pups?" He waved a hand at Bram.

Mamm-wynn just smiled. She had that vague look in her eyes, the one that seemed to come at the oddest times, just when they most needed insight.

Maybe Libby was right—maybe God really was mysterious and powerful enough to whisper in Adelle Tremayne's ear. And maybe He really was concerned enough with their well-being to do so.

"I've already roused the others," Mamm-wynn said as Bram

joined them. "They ought to be out any moment. Where do you think, Bram? Here or the church?"

She was asking *him*? "You're the one who seems to hear directly from the Almighty, Mamm-wynn. You tell me."

One of those uncanny, all-seeing smiles of hers sent a shiver up his spine as she reached for his hand. "You can believe, you know," she whispered. "No one whose opinion matters will think it makes you weak."

Bram's breath caught. "Uncanny, I tell you."

She chuckled and squeezed his fingers. "Where, Bram?"

They didn't have time to waste, surely, arguing over who ought to make the call. If she was deferring to him, then . . . well, he'd better get to thinking.

He still didn't know if it was Scofield or Vandermeer or both on the yacht. On the one hand, Nigel had just stolen Emily's copy of the journal, but it was too vague to have pointed him here for any real leads. And it was the *Victoria*, not the second yacht owned by one of the other trustees—he'd been able to tell that even in the darkness by counting the masts. Which meant Vandermeer was likely involved.

He had his doubts that Nigel had gone directly to the American with his new acquisition. He'd want to keep it to himself, along with any glory it may gain him. But Bram had just been talking to Vandermeer that afternoon. Vandermeer, who had asked him about the chest they'd unearthed, yes. But he had very little information about it—that was undoubtedly what was eating at him. He knew only what Nigel Scofield had told him.

And Nigel thought he'd seen the chest here, in the front parlor, where Sheridan's trunk of Prince Rupert artifacts had played the role of buried pirate treasure. It would be gutsy—foolhardy, even—to try to sneak into a house that was fully occupied in the middle of the night.

But when else could they hope to do so? The house was never empty during the day. If they intended to sneak in, this was the time they'd do it.

Bram nodded. "Here. Parlor."

"Oh good." Mamm-wynn clapped her hands together and laughed. "This will be great fun. Fitz, you position everyone in the room in the absolute most intimidating order—I'll man the knob to the gaslights. We'll go for the full theatrical effect. Curtain rising, players in place."

Bram's lips twitched. He did like her style. "Should we leave the door unlocked, then?"

She shot him an amused look. "It's Tresco, dearovim. We *always* leave the doors unlocked. It would be odd if we didn't."

Noises were coming from within the house, but Bram hung back at the door to wait for Libby and company to appear, which they did a minute later. She and Mabena Moon, and yes, the enormous shadow that could only mean Casek Wearne.

Gibson had better leave that one standing for the full effect of his height and breadth.

He greeted them with a nod and ushered them in, easing the door shut behind them. "Parlor. We've decided they mean to sneak in for another look at Sheridan's trunk. Mamm-wynn was waiting for me at the door."

"Of course she was." Libby moved in that direction. "Did she already wake the others?"

"Naturally. I think they've all assembled."

Someone had a small electric torch they'd turned on—the curtains were drawn, so that was probably safe enough—and was using it to direct everyone to the various chairs and sofas. Gibson took definite glee in positioning Casek Wearne in the center of the room, flanked on either side by the next-tallest men, who happened to be Collins and Bram.

Bram shot his valet a crooked smile. "Hope you didn't mean to sleep tonight."

Collins shrugged. "I can always sleep late. My employer never rises till luncheon anyway."

There was a fair amount of whispering and shuffling before the light-holder—Oliver, perhaps?—switched off the torch and they all fell silent. Then came the tense waiting. Minute after minute ticking by on the old mantel clock, probably allowing the same questions and doubts to chase through everyone else's mind that filled his own.

What if no one came? What if they went to the church instead, or somewhere else entirely? Bram could have been wrong. And Vandermeer wasn't stupid. This, however, would be stupid.

They wouldn't come. Why would they? Fourteen people had simply gathered in this room in the middle of the night for no reason at all. No one would dare to break in here.

But if not, then why had Mamm-wynn been awake? Why had she roused everyone else? Her odd insights had never been wrong before—but then, she'd put the final decision to Bram.

Blast it all. Was this what those knights-errant had felt when setting off for a quest to battle a beast who was little more than rumor? Did they fear finding nothing even more than they feared finding a monster?

At least Lady Emily wasn't here to see it if they were in fact startling at shadows.

On the other hand, it would be a shame that she wasn't here to be a part if it proved an adventure.

Casek sneezed. Bram passed him a handkerchief. Another interminable minute ticked by.

His nerves were just about to the breaking point when a noise came from outside. Quiet, but a noise nonetheless, and something bigger than the feral cats Bram had tried to charm with bits of left-over dinner. Footsteps. Careful, human footsteps.

Then came the creaking of the front door. The soft sound of the latch catching again. Slow, cautious steps, and what might have been a low whisper for direction.

His every muscle went taut. They were here—he and Mamm-wynn had been right. God really had whispered to her.

Had He also helped Bram piece it together? Had He led him and Libby to that particular stretch of beach at that particular moment to see the *Victoria* sailing their way? And if He had, then had He also truly led him to follow Lady Emily along the road through Hugh Town earlier?

If so, it seemed the Lord was far more involved in their lives than his own vicar had ever led him to believe. He and Mr. Gregory may have to have a chat one of these days.

The steps moved to and then through the parlor door, which had been left half-open, just like it always was.

Light suddenly flooded the room. Even though he'd been braced for it, Bram winced and blinked against the onslaught. Still, he saw their faces in that first moment—the shock on them, the incredulity.

Vandermeer and Nigel Scofield stood immobile. Caught, and the realization of it striking them like a blow. Bram could only imagine what they must be thinking as their eyes flew around the room, taking in the veritable crowd of captors. Panic had to be mounting. They must be debating whether to run away or try to fight.

Nigel spat out a string of incendiary words and tore from the room, back into the hallway, and straight for the door.

No one chased after him. Perhaps because Vandermeer's very different response was baffling enough to hold them all in thrall.

He surveyed the room, seeming to catalogue each and every one of them. And then he chuckled, held up his hands, and rocked back on his heels. "I surrender. And while I'm at it—is it too late to switch sides? You all seem to have an edge my previous allies are decidedly lacking."

Sheridan stepped forward, arms folded across his chest. He may have looked more intimidating had the back of his hair not been standing straight up in a cowlick. "What makes you think we'd ever want you on our side? You just broke into the Tremaynes' home."

Vandermeer turned one of his upheld hands into a raised finger. "I did no *breaking*, Sheridan. I merely *entered*. Upon your friend's invitation."

When he motioned with that finger toward Bram, Bram lifted his brows. "I beg your pardon?"

Vandermeer grinned. "You said to come on over to Tresco anytime. I took you at your word."

Cheeky. Bram nearly wished it didn't make him like the man even more.

"With what intent, exactly?" Beth elbowed her way past Oliver, who was trying to keep himself between their uninvited guest and both his sister and Libby.

Vandermeer raised his hands a little higher. "The hope of assuaging my curiosity. Nothing more. I swear it. I didn't mean to take anything, I merely wanted to see what was in the chest."

For some reason, Bram believed him. He glanced over at Sheridan, who glanced at him just then too. Bram inclined his head half an inch.

Sheridan blustered out a breath in a way that clearly said, *If this is the wrong call, it's all your fault.* And he lowered his arms. "Fine. There it is." He motioned to the trunk that his sisters had brought with them from Sheridan Castle.

Vandermeer hesitated a moment when Casek cracked his knuckles. But when the giant merely grinned and said, "Go ahead, Yank. I won't stop you," he edged his way around the three of them in the center of the room and made for the trunk against the wall.

Bram turned to watch, as did Collins and Casek. By his reckoning, it ought to take Vandermeer about ten seconds to realize what Nigel Scofield never had—that the items in that trunk were definitely *not* from the sea chest buried on Gugh.

It took him five. Bram hadn't given him enough credit. Vandermeer breathed a laugh and leaned down to pick up one of the teardrop-shaped grenades that Rupert of the Rhine had developed—an inactive one. Probably. He hoped. Sher wouldn't have one in there that could randomly go off, would he?

Bram glanced at his best friend, but Sheridan didn't look concerned. Just smug. Good.

Vandermeer shook his head. "This is your Rupert collection, Sheridan."

"Is it?" He did a fair impression of sounding surprised, really. "Well, fancy that."

It didn't seem to douse Vandermeer's curiosity any. He was turning over the grenade with a look of fascination on his face. "Where did you find this? A friend of mine has quite a collection of antique weaponry and has been trying to track one of these down for ages."

"Preston, you mean? I—" Sheridan cleared his throat when Beth elbowed him in the ribs. "Right. Irrelevant. That is . . ." He frowned and looked down at Beth. "Frankly, I have no idea where we go from here. Darling? My mind's still sleep-clouded."

It was because Beth smiled softly up at Sher instead of rolling her eyes that Bram hadn't felt the need to put *her* through an inquisition to prove herself worthy of Sheridan's affections. It had taken her a few weeks to warm up to him, but then she'd clearly seen that Sher was unlike anyone else in the world.

She tucked her hand into the crook of his arm and turned to Vandermeer. "You asked if it was too late to switch sides. I don't know if you were serious, but if so, you'll have to prove yourself."

"A quest?" Vandermeer bent down to exchange the grenade for a book. Probably a rare first edition of some obscure text that only he and Sheridan even cared about. "Excellent. Make it one that'll keep me occupied for a while, will you? Things have been rather dull on Gugh."

"I daresay your first task is simply to convince us that you really do want to become our ally—and why." Beth had a way of arching her brows in challenge that Bram quite admired. It was sure to keep Sheridan on his toes.

And it had Vandermeer rising back up from his crouch too. He glanced around the room again. Perhaps he was noting how ridiculous they all looked in dressing gowns and pajamas, with cowlicks and sleep-swollen eyes—or perhaps he was seeing the truth of them. That all these people had come just because they were asked. They were that devoted to one another. That true.

That honorable.

Vandermeer tapped the spine of the book against his palm. "I've always prided myself on being a step ahead of my rivals. I do my research, and I do it thoroughly. But this time . . ." He shook his head. "You all have an edge, and that intrigues me. You're loyal to one another, and that inspires me. And frankly, I just can't trust someone who digs out the wrong side of a cairn's burial chamber and thinks *this* is pirate treasure."

Sheridan didn't look impressed. "So basically, you want to be on the winning side. Is that it?"

"Not exactly noble." Bram folded his arms over his chest, though it didn't look nearly as impressive as when Casek Wearne did the same a second later.

Vandermeer shrugged. "Perhaps it isn't noble. But don't I get points for being truthful? Enough to at least move me to the next round in the quest?" He donned a crooked smile. "I could save a damsel. Lady Emily seems to be locked in her family's tower, meta-phorically speaking. She's your friend, isn't she, Miss Tremayne? I'll set her free. Surely that'll prove my mettle."

Bram nearly surged forward, though thankfully Casek's enor-mous arm was blocking his path just enough to stop him. A good thing, since he had no idea what he would say as an objection. *No, I've already claimed that quest, go and find another?* They'd all laugh at him. Or start planning a triple wedding—which would be a huge overreaction. He wanted to protect her, help her, not pledge his undying devotion.

Beth pursed her lips. And, praise the Lord, shook her head. "I believe Em has to slay her own dragons. No, Mr. Vandermeer. Your quest is going to be far more difficult. And the first step is for you to leave." She held out an arm and pointed to the door. "Go back to your yacht and your trustees and your camp on Gugh. Consider it all. Take stock. And then wait for our instructions."

Vandermeer sighed. But he also handed the book to Sheridan and nodded. "Fair enough." He surveyed the room again, his gaze pausing on Mr. Gibson and Mamm-wynn, to whom he offered a respectful nod. "Forgive me for intruding. And thank you for your good grace in receiving me so warmly despite my utter lack of manners in coming as I did."

Mr. Gibson folded his arms and harumphed. But Mamm-wynn studied him long and hard. After a moment, she offered a small, nearly sad smile. "You're not all bad, sir. But you're not all good either. Perhaps you ought to make some effort to evaluate which parts of you are which before you join us again."

Bram nearly laughed at the look on the American's face at that one, but to his credit, he didn't say anything. Just nodded, bowed to the room at large, and strode out of the parlor. A moment later, the sound of the opening and shutting of the front door reached them.

Everyone seemed to let out their pent-up breaths all at once, and three different conversations sprang up. Bram slid toward Sheridan, who was rubbing at the hair sticking straight up on the back of his head and asking, "So what, exactly, will those next instructions be, darling?"

Beth's laugh sounded exhausted. "I have no idea. We'll come up with something. But I didn't want to just dismiss him. If we *can* lure him to our side, it could prove useful." She greeted Bram with a nod.

"Not Emily, though." Sheridan yawned and sent Bram a good-natured scowl, likely because he *wasn't* yawning, or showing any evidence of his sleep having been interrupted.

Beth's look went dark. "Definitely not Emily. I don't know why he'd even mention that."

Bram cleared his throat. "He met her on St. Mary's today, which was the first time he realized she's Scofield's daughter. His interest was immediate."

And she may need more rescuing than even Beth knew, if Lord Scofield went through with his threat. Bram would have to keep an eye on the situation somehow. He wasn't exactly certain how he'd know when she was in need of a helping hand. After all, when Libby had arrived in the islands, it had been with pocket money enough to see her through for months, and the same was likely true of Lady

Emily. But he would be paying attention, waiting for the first sign of struggle. Praying, in the meantime—since that was a pastime he was becoming more familiar with.

Beth muttered something he didn't catch, then sent him back half a step with the force of the look she leveled on him. She even went so far as to raise a finger and point it at his chest. "Another antiquities hunter is the very last thing she needs in her life. Don't let him convince her father to arrange a match."

Sheridan frowned. "How's Telly supposed to stop him?"

Bram patted his friend's shoulder. It was only because he was so sleep-addled that he had to ask. "Isn't he adorable when he's tired?"

Sheridan swatted his hand away, but Beth laughed. "He's always adorable." She stretched up to kiss his cheek, which seemed to mollify him. A bit. "Scofield has never seen Emily as anything but another pawn on his chessboard, darling. So if he knows Vandermeer is interested, the only way to stave him off will be to present him with a better option for an alliance—say, an English lord. Only one of which do we have in our presence who is not already spoken for."

"Ah." Sheridan blinked, flushed. But also grinned and slid an arm around Beth. "You do have a point there. About me being spoken for, I mean. Although—" He turned his gaze on Bram. No doubt he was trying to see if Bram minded Beth's dictate. And no doubt even in his exhausted state, he could see that he wasn't the least bit put out. "Well. Just keep in mind that she's not one of your puppies, will you?"

"I'm aware." As if he could be otherwise. Were she a puppy, she wouldn't run from him every time he got near.

7

Whoever would have thought that hunger and guilt could be such close companions? Emily prayed no one could hear the rumbling of her stomach as they tidied up the stack of books and piles of notes on the library table at Beth's house. She'd skipped breakfast, and dinner last night had been small—she hadn't had much choice. They had to make their supplies stretch as far as they could. The produce wouldn't last long, and they certainly didn't want to waste anything.

Which meant she was keenly aware, as she closed a tome on medieval England that hadn't so much as mentioned Arthur, that she was here today in part because she knew they'd feed her lunch. Which was a terrible reason to come and see her friends.

And further, it made her think for the first time about how much entertaining her and Briggs was costing the Tremaynes, who already had extra mouths to feed, what with Lords Telford and Sheridan and their valets staying here.

Hadn't Beth confessed years ago that her family was strapped? It had been a stretch for them to send her to finishing school. They'd spent so much on the medical expenses of her eldest brother that they'd been forced to live quite frugally. Emily had no idea if their situation had improved any—it wasn't exactly a polite thing to ask—but what if it hadn't?

Here she was relying on them to feed her, and for all she knew, doing so could be pushing them into debt.

It wasn't fun, having to think about such things. But it was a good life lesson. That was what she'd been telling herself for the past two days as she plotted out how to stretch the sweet rolls, loaf of bread, and basket of fish and vegetables as far as they could possibly go. She just hadn't realized how guilty it would make her feel to be counting down the minutes until her next meal.

Perhaps she shouldn't eat as much as usual in case it *was* putting a strain on the Tremaynes' account books. And it would probably be a good idea to exercise some restraint anyway, so that her stomach would get used to smaller meals.

Or would that just result in waste, given that Mrs. Dawe had already prepared the food? What did they do with the leftovers?

Oh, she was giving herself a headache.

"Em? Are you all right?"

Emily looked up to find Beth at her elbow, a concerned look on her face. As if she needed to be worrying about Emily when they had so many larger concerns. She summoned up a smile. "Quite. I still just can't believe that my brother broke into your home the other night with Mr. Vandermeer."

That *should* have been what was occupying her thoughts—along with worries over what he was deducing from the journal he'd stolen—rather than her stomach. What kind of friend was she, to be wondering if they'd have sandwiches or soup or both when she should be apologizing again over practically handing their advantage to Nigel, not to mention for her brother's trespassing?

Beth's smile looked sincere—and impish. Which told Emily that she really wasn't as upset about Nigel's perfidy as she ought to be.

"I admit, it was rather entertaining to watch your brother run out of here like the hounds of Hades were on his heels." Beth chuckled and capped the fountain pen she'd been using.

"That *would* have been quite the sight." Emily had never seen Nigel run from anything. Usually he was the aggressor, the one making others run away. But even so. "It makes me uneasy, though. We really can't know if Vandermeer is trustworthy. What if he tells Father and Nigel that it was Sheridan's trunk and not Mucknell's? They could come back and try to find the real thing."

"I know." Looking serious now, Beth glanced over the table. "We spent yesterday trying to decide what to do with the treasure. Cataloguing it is obviously the first step, so that we'll know if anything ever goes missing."

Emily shook her head. "Nigel wouldn't be content to take just a piece or two, Beth. He'd take it all."

"Which is why the second step is to hide it better. We were discussing breaking it up into batches and hiding each one in a different location. So that if he finds one part, he won't find everything. What do you think?"

She thought that in addition to being too aware of her stomach, she was also too aware of the letter in her pocket from Father. She knew well he hadn't changed his mind about his ultimatum. She'd tried wiring the bank yesterday just to see if he'd been bluffing and had promptly received a message back saying her funds were frozen at the request of the primary account holder. So why had he asked to meet with her?

Probably to try to get information from her. And quite possibly because Vandermeer had already told him that they had, in fact, found actual treasure and not just old books and the like. She nodded. "I think it's a good idea to split it up. And it may also be a good idea if no one person knows where it all is. That way, if Father or Nigel corner one of us, we can't tell them everything."

Beth gave her a confused look. "None of us is going to spill the secrets, Em."

"Well, not on *purpose*. Without being under duress."

"It isn't as though they'd torture it out of us."

She said it like it was a joke to even consider such an idea, but when Emily blinked she saw that wardrobe and felt the dark walls of it closing in on her. "Don't put anything past them. He tried to kill you—why assume he's above torture?"

Words that ought never to have to be spoken about one's own brother. Words that seemed too fantastical to be necessary. But they were as true as they were sobering, and Beth clearly recognized it. Her grey eyes went stormy. "You're right. We won't underestimate him. I promise."

"Good." Not knowing what else to tidy, Emily folded her hands and waited for Beth to decide when to lead the way out of the library. Though really, she hated seeing that look in her friend's eyes. A young lady so newly engaged to a handsome marquess ought to be all laughter and sunshine, not considering whether a madman was going to try to hurt her again. Emily scoured her brain in search of something to bring the light back to her eyes. And she knew the moment she found it too. "We also ought to make a treasure map of our own—or even several of them. So that we don't misplace any of it."

As she expected, that brought Beth's smile back to her mouth. "Oh, that's a perfect idea! And will be so much fun. Come on, let's see if the fellows are ready for luncheon yet, and we'll tell them the plan."

Lunch! Emily told herself not to weep with joy at the word, though she did honestly feel a surge of elation that surprised her. Were her emotions really so tied to her stomach? She certainly hoped not, or Father would be able to offer her a pudding tonight and reduce her to a blubbering mess.

She needed to tell Beth about the invitation. And she would—but perhaps after their dispositions were all mellowed with one of Mrs. Dawe's delightful meals.

Beth sent another probing look over her shoulder as they moved toward the dining room. "Are you certain that's all that's bothering you? You don't seem yourself."

She was blessed to have a friend who knew her so well . . . even if

98

it did make it truly difficult to hide things from her that absolutely must stay hidden. If Beth knew about her sudden lack of money, then she would do what any good friend would and offer to help, regardless of whether she could truly afford to do so or not. She'd probably say it out loud, too, and then Lord Sheridan would know and probably offer to cover the costs to spare the Tremaynes, and then Lord Telford would feel obligated to chip in and . . .

No. No, she'd rather spend a few days hungry than throw herself on the mercy of her friends. That's what Father had said, after all—*go hungry for a few days*. He wouldn't act this way forever. He'd relent, and she'd have learned a valuable lesson about frugality and waste, and no one would have to know that he loved her so little that he'd . . . he'd . . .

"Em?" Beth's voice sounded frantic. Beth's hand felt insistent as it tugged on hers. But Beth's face had gone all blurry.

Emily blinked and then blinked again to clear the embarrassing tears. She sniffed, forced a laugh, and dashed at her eyes with her free hand. "Sorry! I'm being silly. Emotional. But I'm quite fine, I promise. Just a bit overwhelmed by it all."

And she *still* hadn't gotten so much as a word from Mother. Even when the subject had been for Nigel's good. What if she just never replied to anything?

Bother, now the tears were coming in earnest and there was no dashing them away. What a ninny she was. Beth must be embarrassed to even know her—she would certainly never crumble like this over a simple lack of letters.

"Oh, Em." Beth's arms closed around her, and she held her tight. "This isn't fair to you. None of it. You shouldn't be in this situation, pitted against your own family."

She'd never had a sister, but this was what she'd always imagined it would be like. Someone to understand her and just *be* with her. Emily clung on and let the tears have their way for just a minute, to get them out of her system. "I'm sorry. I don't mean to be so weak. It's just—why can't they love me?"

The sob that choked her probably made that question unintelligible—at least she hoped so. But no, given the way Beth held her all the closer, she'd understood every word.

She shouldn't have given it voice . . . but it was the truest question she'd ever asked. Why couldn't they love her? Was it her? But she was *trying*—she was trying so hard to be the sort of daughter and sister they could love. She was trying to love them as God did, to see them through His eyes.

Why were her attempts being met with such slaps, then? The very day she tried to reach out in love to her father, he'd delivered this latest blow—not even coincidentally, but in *response* to it. And Nigel had stolen directly from her hands and then promptly tried to break into her best friend's house, and Mother couldn't even be bothered to acknowledge her telegrams.

Even Elizabeth Mucknell didn't have this pain. Perhaps her husband was a thief and a murderer and difficult to love, but he at least adored her. She had that comfort.

But then, Elizabeth Mucknell had clearly been a woman of such strong character that it made sense she'd be so loved. She was probably like Beth, who could stand firm in the face of a hurricane. Or Libby, who was unashamed to be who God had made her to be. She'd probably been beautiful and in firm control of her emotions and so devout that she'd certainly never questioned the Lord's leading like Emily was doing even now.

Not like Emily. Nothing like Emily. Not a burden on her friends, not cut off by the one who should be supporting her, not so weak that she didn't even trust herself to make the right choices when facing hardship.

She felt Beth shake her head. Was it in response to her thoughts—could she read them now? Or had Emily spoken aloud? No, she couldn't possibly speak around her gasps.

Then a hand landed on her shoulder, too large to be Beth's—and besides, Beth had her arms wrapped around Emily's back.

Which meant—obviously—that it was someone else. And not

even Mamm-wynn, given the size of that hand. One of the men. *Oh, Father God, please not one of the men!*

"We're going to pray, Emily." Oliver's voice. That relaxed her a little. Just a little. Of all the men to see her like this, the vicar would probably be the least ashamed for her.

He'd begun praying, but she couldn't even hear his words at first over the litany of her own silent ones. Over her sobs. Her gasps. But something about his voice calmed her a few degrees, and then a few more as he kept talking, and eventually some of the words seeped in.

". . . help her to see her worth . . . know that she is not alone . . . your peace and comfort . . . sustain her and provide for her . . ."

How did he know? A shudder coursed through her. She'd heard the others talking about Oliver Tremayne's insights, but she'd yet to experience them for herself. Now that she had—well, the only explanation was that the Lord told him how to pray. Exactly how to pray.

And that was enough to whisper the peace over her spirit that he'd asked for.

The Lord knew. The Lord saw her, no matter how dark and small the place in which she was locked. He saw her, and He cared enough to send someone to pray over her when she never would have asked for it.

Oliver squeezed her shoulder as he whispered an amen.

Emily blinked her eyes open, though the only thing she could see was Beth's shoulder, covered in a blue fabric that looked a few shades darker now than it had in the library, thanks to her tears.

She ought to feel like she couldn't look up, couldn't look either of the Tremaynes in the eye. But she didn't. She dragged in another shaking breath and pulled away.

Oliver must be standing behind her, because she couldn't see him. But he gave her shoulder another squeeze. "Whatever the enemy may whisper in your ear, know that you are a beloved child of God, Emily. And a welcome member of our family too—always."

Beth nodded along with that strong, fierce look of hers. "Always."

"Thank you." Paltry words, but all she could get out in the moment. And she meant them more than they could possibly know. She rubbed at her face. "I think I'd better tidy up."

Beth laughed softly. "Go ahead. I'll just get Sheridan talking and no one will even notice that we're a few minutes late eating."

Emily hurried away, feeling a bit lighter but a good deal puffier too. A cool, damp washcloth sounded heavenly right about now. Or at least a handkerchief to mop her face—she had one in her handbag, which was in the drawing room, where they'd started their day.

She turned toward the entryway rather than the dining room and came to an abrupt halt.

Lord Telford was there, leaning into the wall in a way that said he'd been there for quite some time. That he'd heard them in the corridor and had decided not to intrude and had just waited here, out of sight. He still looked drowsy, which made her wonder if he'd made an appearance yet at all today.

Maybe he was so drowsy he wouldn't even remember this encounter, with her looking a fright. Her face felt swollen, and she imagined it was red and blotchy too. Stray locks of hair fell before her eyes, from her burying her head in Beth's shoulder.

He didn't look quite that asleep, though. In fact, he looked entirely aware as he met her gaze without flinching.

He had eyes that mixed blue and green, like the sea around the islands. She'd never noticed that before—not surprising, since she'd never been this close to him and dared to meet his gaze. They were kind eyes. Blue and green and completely without judgment. But not the same sort that Oliver's were, somehow. They were a different sort. The kind that said he may not offer to pray with her, but he'd stand beside her, wherever she needed him to be, while she cried.

Clearly she was losing her sanity—imagining such emotions in his eyes just because he was leaning against a wall and not wincing in disgust at her.

Or maybe not. Because he reached into his pocket, pulled out a handkerchief—crisp and white and clean—and held it out to her. And then he smiled.

That was all. Just a handkerchief and a smile. But it soothed her as Oliver's prayer had done. She took the folded square of linen and gave him a smile of her own. It was small, but it was sincere. Then she stepped around him, rerouting to the downstairs lavatory without feeling the need to say a word, yet somehow feeling quite certain that he was a friend.

He and Oliver both, which meant Sheridan was too. Not just the girls, but the gentlemen. She could trust them. They wouldn't ridicule her or mock her or insult her, and they would never look at her as though she were nothing more than a piece of art to add to their collection, or a dowry they could add to their coffers.

Friends. She closed herself into the lavatory, dampened the handkerchief with cold water, and then dared to look in the mirror. She really did look a fright—splotchy and red and her hair a shambles. But it didn't matter. She had friends who accepted her even so. *Thank you, Lord.*

Because she knew they wouldn't mind, she took her time tidying herself up. The cold, wet cloth felt like bliss against her puffy skin, so she indulged in the balm of it for several long minutes. She waited for her breathing to regulate, the last of the hiccups and shuddering gasps evening out. She re-pinned her hair.

They'd all still be able to tell at a glance that she'd been crying—there was no hiding the red rims of her eyes. But they knew it anyway. Welcomed her anyway.

She drew in one last long breath and exited.

They were all gathered in the dining room when she entered, Beth and Mamm-wynn and Libby—who must have just arrived—in their seats, but the three gentlemen still on their feet. They didn't snap to attention or anything at her arrival, but Telford pulled out her usual chair for her, even though he kept his gaze on Sheridan, who was saying something about . . . something.

She sat and angled a smile up at him.

103

He looked down just in time to see it and sent her a wink that somehow felt friendly and warm instead of forward.

As Mrs. Dawe entered with a tureen of something that smelled delicious and Senara followed with a platter heaped with sandwiches, Emily realized the group was talking about how best to divvy up the treasure and where to hide all the smaller portions. Not surprisingly, Beth and Oliver had the most suggestions, given that they knew the islands inside and out. Though Libby had a fair number of thoughts as well, and Sheridan offered his opinions too.

Emily had nothing to add that could possibly be helpful, which was just as well because the soup proved every bit as scrumptious as it smelled. She didn't taste it until after Oliver had blessed it all, but then it was all she could do to greet the food outwardly with as much indifference as she would have done last week.

Their words were only noise for the first few bites. Mrs. Dawe may well be the best cook in the world. Emily had tucked away half of her sandwich and most of her soup before she really paid any more attention to the conversation.

They were talking about Nigel now. And her father. And whether Vandermeer had any actual intentions of defecting to their side.

"What we need," Sheridan declared as he slathered butter on a slice of fresh bread, "is to determine what this artifact of Lizza's is. Before anyone else, I mean. That is—Telly? List of possibilities?"

Lord Telford muttered something that sounded a bit like, "Right . . . yes. Moment," and put his silverware down so he could dig into his inner jacket pocket. He came up with a folded piece of paper, which he flipped across the table to Sheridan rather than reading himself.

His best friend leaped upon it like it was one of Mrs. Dawe's scones. "Ah! Knew it. That you could remember, I mean. Good man."

Beth, seated directly across from Emily, wore an indulgent smile that was aimed at Emily but inspired by her sweetheart, who had forgotten, it seemed, that there were others around the table who'd like to hear what was on the list too. "Dearovim? Care to share?"

"Oh." He grinned over at Beth. "Right. There are the expected ones—Excalibur, Holy Grail, Round Table—"

"I think we can assume that the Round Table isn't hidden in a sea cave." Oliver's smile, naturally, was directed to Libby. "We probably would have noticed something of that size over the centuries."

"Blades of all sorts, though. *Carnwennan*, his dagger. *Calwdvwlch* and *Chastiefol*, other swords of his. His scabbards—which, well, when you think about it . . . could be engraved, couldn't they? More easily than a sword?"

"Possibly." Beth leaned over to look at the list too. "Helmets, lances, spears . . . gracious, did they name *everything*?"

Telford snorted a laugh. "Except for his magic cloak of invisibility. I'm rooting for that one. It would come in handy."

"Never understood how those worked, without being themselves invisible." Sheridan flipped the paper over, though the back was blank. "Shield, helmet, blades . . . how do we know which one? Different sizes, though. Which means different possible hiding places."

"But Oliver's right that larger items like the Round Table would be hard to have kept hidden all this time, don't you think?" Libby glanced from her fiancé to her brother to Lord Sheridan. "It must be one of the smaller articles."

Beth let out a long breath. "We can compare this list to places Ollie and I know of in the islands and search them while we're hiding what we have already."

"Or—no." Sheridan frowned and set down his bread. "Hadn't thought that through, had we? Scofield will be too. Searching them all, I mean, for this new artifact. We had better not go hiding new things for him to find."

"Blast." Telford scrubbed a hand over his face. "I'm barely awake. What's your excuse for not realizing that sooner?"

Sheridan didn't look offended. He just grinned. "Well, thought it now, didn't I?"

A moment of silence fell, broken by Oliver saying contemplatively, "This artifact must be stored in some natural place that hasn't changed through the years—a cave or crevasse or burial chamber. But we can still make use of the places on our list that are manmade—in the Gardens, Beth's hiding places in the abandoned cottages on Samson, those sorts of places. He won't be checking there, since they wouldn't have been around in Elizabeth's day. Certainly not unchanged, at any rate."

"Perhaps we'll get lucky and he won't look at all. Maybe he'll simply dismiss the journal altogether, or get so bored with Lizza's musings about her husband's soul that he won't even notice those bits about an artifact." Hopeful as Beth's words were, her tone and expression both said she didn't believe it for a moment.

Emily sighed. She would have liked to hope the same, but Nigel was nothing if not skilled at plucking useful information out of thin air.

Lord Telford, seated as always on her left, looked her way. "Have you heard from them, my lady, since he stole the journal from you? Your brother? Or your father, perhaps?"

The letter in her pocket felt scorching all of a sudden. She set down her spoon and cleared her throat. "Not about that. But . . ." She pulled out the letter and set it on the table. "Father has invited me to dine with him this evening at the hotel restaurant on St. Mary's. I don't imagine it has anything to do with the journal, but . . ."

Libby was frowning at the letter. "He sent it to you in the post?"

That *was* rather curious. Granted, she hadn't told him where she was staying, but he could have found it out. Mother knew—Emily had sent her the address first thing. She shrugged. "He did."

"To invite you to dinner." Beth set her spoon down too. "Well, you can't go. Not alone."

Oliver sighed. "Now, Beth—"

"Actually." This was the part that made Emily wince at her father's nerve. "He instructed me to bring you, Beth, to make it an

106

even four." *Four* meant that Nigel would be there too. "Not that I expect you to go. Or would even ask it of you. Or would let you. You should never have to share a meal with Nigel after what he did on Gugh, and I don't want you thinking you should come just because of the journal. He won't give voice to any of his thoughts about that, I'm certain."

"He's not that careless, I daresay." Beth huffed out a breath and looked at her brother, then her fiancé, then—oddly enough—Telford. "But you're *definitely* not going alone if Nigel's going to be there."

"I'll go." Telford, his plate clean, tossed his serviette to the table.

The others didn't seem to find it strange. They were nodding and murmuring about it being a fine solution, completely ignoring the fact that . . . well . . . it was quite a lot to ask of such a new friendship, wasn't it?

Emily shook her head and met his gaze. "You don't want to, my lord. My father—"

"I know your father quite well—or thought I did." He leaned back in his chair, all long limbs and ease. "Frankly, that's part of the reason I'd like to go. There are still a few details about all this that I'd like to sort out. For instance." He lifted a finger and ticked it between Libby and Beth. "It was Lord Scofield who let me know that Libby was here in the Scillies. Yet Nigel thought that Libby was Beth at that same time. He threatened her on the very same evening. Which indicates that your father and Nigel weren't on the same page at that point, where the treasure hunt here was concerned. So, when *did* your father become fully aware of what was going on?"

She had no answers about that. Frankly, she was stuck on his earlier statement. "You know my father? Outside of all this?"

"Sheridan's fault."

Her gaze flew to him.

Sheridan cleared his throat, his neck red. "Well. Ah . . . he's a trustee. As you all know. British Museum. It's no secret I've long hoped to earn a position on the board myself. Someday, I mean."

"And we're members of the same club, your father and I." Telford smirked at his friend. "I introduced Sher to him, Sher was ever so nice, and lo and behold, we're all chummy. Though clearly we never *knew* him. And your brother, throughout all this, was not even in London."

Sheridan snorted and tossed a playful glare at Beth. "He was in Okinawa. Learning *karate*."

Beth blew him a kiss.

Telford loosed a snort of his own. "I still owe him a sock in the nose."

"Not at dinner, old boy. Bad form."

Emily just stared from one of them to the other. All this time—a year or perhaps more—her father had known these two pleasant, kind, wealthy, titled men who were unattached. And he'd never once invited them home to try to introduce her.

Not that she wanted her father to arrange a match with either Sheridan or Telford. But—but it was baffling. He'd always made it perfectly clear that her sole value to him was in the alliance through marriage that she could someday make between the Scofields and a family of his choosing. Yet before her sat two of the most eligible bachelors in all of England—before Beth had snagged Sheridan, of course—and he'd never made even the slightest move.

Why? Did he not deem them son-in-law material? Perhaps they weren't easily manipulated. Or perhaps he thought *too* highly of them and couldn't fathom they'd be interested in *her*.

Emily picked up her spoon again but just stirred a curl of carrot through the broth with it.

"So, that's settled, then—I'll accompany Lady Emily to dinner with her father." Telford didn't sound at all reluctant. If anything, eager. Probably because he wanted answers. "We just need to work out how we're getting there and how I'll get back here again afterward."

"Theo and I will sail you over." Beth grinned at her fiancé. "There's a little place in Maypole with the best fish and chips in the Scillies. I've been thinking we ought to go sometime. We can have a seaside picnic and then wander the beaches while Telford is grilling the Scofields."

Sheridan beamed. "Perfect! Just don't let my sisters get wind of it or they'll invite themselves."

Emily smiled, well able to imagine that. Then she became aware of Telford's gaze resting on her again. She looked his way and found his brows raised.

"Is that all right?" he asked softly. "That I come with you?"

The question felt as tender as his earlier smile, and just as thoughtful as the handkerchief. What could Emily possibly do but nod?

8

Were Bram home at Telford Hall right now, there would be a spaniel sleeping at his feet and a wolfhound barking at a bird from his window and a boxer trying to get close enough to drool all over his otherwise impeccable evening suit. Were he home, he'd be able to exorcise these odd nerves by tousling a pair of silky ears or throwing a ball or laughing and shoving a muscular body away. But he wasn't home, which meant no dogs, and even Libby's cat wasn't currently in the house for him to steal away from her for a bit of feline solace.

He had no reason to be nervous. They'd be dining in a public place, and the Scofields were sure to be on their best behavior. And blast it all, this was *not*, as Sheridan had so gleefully tried to tell him it *was*, a "date." The very term rubbed him wrong. It implied that it was an event to write down on one's calendar and remember for eternity, like Midsummer Eve or Christmas. But he wasn't sneaking out to Cadbury Castle or plotting what outrageous gift he could bestow on Libby this year. He was only having dinner with Lady Emily and her duplicitous, untrustworthy family.

He was going as a friend, as a protector. Roles he was comfortable enough in that his nerves were ridiculous.

"My lord, if you don't stand still, I'm going to throttle you with

110

this bow tie instead of tying it—and it'll be purely accidental, I assure you."

Telford chuckled and blinked Collins into focus. "Sorry." He shoved his hands into his pockets and forced himself to stop shifting from foot to foot.

Collins grinned, but it turned strained in the next heartbeat, after he'd finished the bow. "I don't blame you for feeling antsy—this is a dangerous thing you're doing. Facing them like this, with only you and the lady."

"Nonsense. They won't dare do anything untoward in a hotel dining room." Not that he was about to admit the nerves were more over the lady than her unsavory relatives. And not even over the lady exactly, just the situation with her. With Sheridan insisting it was a date. With Beth giving him those wide eyes that said this was the perfect first step in their plan to make Lord Scofield think that Bram was a potential suitor, and a better one than Vandermeer.

"I wouldn't be so sure." Collins lowered his arms with a sigh. "Well, you look fine enough—though I do wish we had some armor to put on you instead of worsted wool. I don't trust those two as far as I can toss them."

Bram wasn't certain if he and Collins got along so well because they both spoke the same language, or if they spoke the same language from spending so many years together. "You'd make a good squire, but alas. I left all my best suits of armor at home."

"Bit unwieldly to try to pack." Collins offered a fleeting grin and turned back to the desk on which he'd set the pair of cuff links he'd chosen for tonight. He picked them up but then just held them instead of threading them through the cuffs of Bram's shirt.

Which meant Bram just stood there like an idiot with his wrists held out indefinitely. "Ahem?"

Collins pursed his lips. "You will be careful, won't you? I don't fancy having to look for another position."

Bram rolled his eyes. "Cuff links, Collins."

"I like it in Somerset."

He bit back a smile. "I'm not in any danger."

"I've finally taught the cook how to make meat pies just like Mum."

The smile won. "There's no danger, not really. And Sheridan and Miss Tremayne will be on the island too—and the Howe sisters. You know they could intimidate anyone into good behavior."

Collins folded his arms, cuff links still held prisoner in his fist. "Maybe Ainsley and I should come along. There's safety in numbers."

Bram shook his head and dropped one arm, flipping his other over so his palm was out instead of just his wrist. "I'm not bringing my valet along like a nursemaid. Give me the cuff links."

Collins looked ready to offer another convoluted argument, but Mrs. Dawe's voice drifted up through his open window, calling her husband in for his meal. Which meant Collins's meal, too, and Ainsley's.

Bram wiggled his fingers. "Cuff links. You go and eat."

His valet looked offended. "I can put them in for you first, my lord. I'm not *that* hungry."

"Now!" The order may have been more intimidating had he not ruined it with a laugh.

But he won, if one could call it that. Collins dropped the cuff links into his palm. "Ainsley will agree with me, you know. And Sheridan never dares to argue with Ainsley."

"Sheridan *delights* in arguing with Ainsley. It's just that he seldom wins."

Collins moved toward the door. "And he won't win this time, I daresay. I'll be back up to gloat about our being invited shortly." He flashed another grin. "I'll put the cuff links in then, if you don't throw them out the window first."

"You're lucky I don't lob them at your head." They were both chuckling when the door closed.

And it only took Bram thirty seconds to be ready to accept the open window's invitation and send the baubles flying. How did anyone ever button their own cuffs, anyway? He managed to get his left one in well enough, but it was just impossible to fasten the one on his right wrist.

The blighted jewel laughed at his every attempt and finally leaped out of his fingers and went dancing across the floor. Bram dropped to his knees just in time to watch it bounce onto the bottom shelf of the floor-to-ceiling bookcase that flanked the desk. "Think you can get away from me that easily, do you?" He had to crawl a few feet to be able to reach in and then feel around to see where it had rolled to.

There were only a few books on this lowest shelf, and a decorative box. All, he had to assume, were the belongings of Morgan Tremayne—the eldest brother of the two remaining siblings, who had passed away a few years ago after a lifelong health struggle. Bram had made every attempt to keep each item in the room exactly as it had been when he was shown to it, whenever possible. Obviously he slept in the bed, and he'd sat at the desk to attend to his correspondence. But he hadn't gone snooping through the shelves.

It hadn't seemed right. Not with knowing how much Oliver and Beth missed their brother. Not with knowing how he would feel if it were one of his sisters forever gone, with a stranger staying in her room, amidst her belongings.

But he couldn't exactly leave a diamond cuff link unfound just because it had the audacity to intrude upon Morgan Tremayne's bookshelf. Still, he felt around carefully, trying not to displace the books or box.

There—no. His fingers had found something about the same size and shape as his cuff link, but it couldn't be it. This thing was set into the wood, almost like . . . His finger slid under the oval, hooked it. Lifted it up.

Lifted the wood up with it—a part of the shelf's bottom. It just pulled up, as if it was on a hinge. It must *be* on a hinge, which made no sense at all, unless . . .

Bram's breath puffed out in surprise. And in admiration. Morgan Tremayne had a secret compartment in his bookshelf.

He ought to leave it alone—especially given his own self-imposed stance on leaving everything *else* in here alone. But everything else was normal and ordinary and expected. How was he supposed to just turn away from a secret compartment without investigating it?

To answer his own question, he relieved his knees and settled into a sitting position and reached into the hole. He was only human, after all.

He half expected to find it empty, but his fingers immediately met with the familiar feel of paper and a wax seal. A letter? He pulled it out.

A letter. But it wasn't addressed to Oliver or Beth or Mammwynn or anyone else by name. On the front was scrawled *To the Finder.*

Well. That would be him, wouldn't it? With only a moment's hesitation, Bram broke the seal and unfolded the sheet of paper, heart racing more than he cared to admit.

To the person who reached into a secret compartment and pulled out a rather odd bundle—salutations. This is Morgan Tremayne, writing to you from beyond the grave. I've a message for you, and it's as weighty as the world.

Bram blinked and looked up, wishing there were someone else here so he could share a smile. The Tremaynes were the strangest family. He was glad he'd been given the chance to know them. His gaze turned to the letter again.

God loves you. He has a purpose for you. Maybe you know that already, or maybe you'll scoff and shake your head. Maybe, if you know my brother Oliver, you'll have heard this already from him. But it's easier to ignore the person before you, however well-meaning he may be, than it is a ghost.

You don't dare to ignore me, do you? So instead, listen to the wisdom I've gleaned in my years here on earth. They're

114

shorter than perhaps they should have been, had the world been fair. But I've learned that it isn't the number of days or years that count—it's how we spend them. It isn't the distance we travel—it's what we do where we are. It isn't the adventure we stumble upon—it's the one we make.

Wherever you are today, right now, be there fully. Be with the people God has put in your path. Look every moment of every day for how you can let Him use you to touch another heart. We none of us ever know what day will be our last. But we can make certain every day is worthy of being so.

I sit in my wheelchair, confined to my room, and dream of the world I imagine is out there—but I don't need to slay dragons or discover fairy caves, and neither do you. We need only to be who God made us to be. If we do that, we'll change everything for someone. And that someone will do the same for someone else. And on and on it will go, because you were brave enough, noble enough to reach out.

Live the legacy, my friend. Walk worthy of His calling. Go forth boldly—and live.

Bram touched a finger to the word *dragons* and shook his head. They shouldn't know the things they did, any of the Tremaynes. Yet here he sat with a letter from a man who'd been gone from this earth for years, a letter written to a stranger and yet for *him*. Clearly for him.

He read it again, and then a third time, before he folded it up and slipped it into his inner pocket. He closed the compartment, found his cuff link, and managed to get it in without any more trouble. Then he stood, put on his evening coat, and turned to the door.

He had a quest to live out tonight, and he would live it fully. Smiling, he hurried out the door and down the stairs. They'd better leave before the valets could succeed in inviting themselves.

He found Sheridan, Beth, and Emily in the drawing room with Mamm-wynn, and they all seemed amenable to leaving then and

115

there. So, Emily fetched her maid and then they were on the streets of Grimsby, on their way to Beth's boat, the *Naiad*.

"You seem awfully chipper." Sher had ended up by Bram's side, the ladies leading the way. He was, as usual, grinning. "Excited for your date?"

"Ready to face down the evil sorcerer and slay a few dragons, anyway." He grinned back. "They won't be expecting me—it's going to be fun."

Sheridan chuckled and watched the ladies for a moment. "You know—I mean, it *would* be convenient."

Bram chuckled, too, but also shook his head. It *would* be convenient if they ended up married to ladies who were already friends. But Sher knew just as well as Bram did that their future wives would become friends regardless. There was no way Bram would ever choose a wife who didn't get along with Beth, since Sher had beaten him to the punch and chosen his bride first. It was simply one of the tests any future Lady Telford would have to pass, because their families would be holidaying together and visiting the other all the time. That wasn't up for negotiation. "Convenience isn't really the reason I'm looking for."

"She's pretty too. I mean, she's no Beth. But who is?"

She was prettier, in Bram's estimation—not that saying so would help his point. And not that he intended to get in a debate with Sheridan about whether any other girl was prettier than Beth, who he swore was the most beautiful woman ever to step foot on the planet. "Also not reason enough to break out the family jewels."

Sheridan grinned at him. "How about a pirate jewel? We've a few of those lying about."

He really had no choice but to give his friend a friendly shove in the shoulder. Even though that *would* be hilarious—Lady Emily showing up to a dinner with her father and Nigel wearing one of the jewels they coveted so. Would they even notice?

It nearly made him want to detour to the church and borrow a diadem or an emerald ring, just to find out. Nearly.

Instead, once they were all settled on the boat and Beth was navigating them out of the quay, Bram turned the conversation to King Arthur. It seemed a safer topic of conversation than the treasure they already had and needed to hide again, or the dinner to come. And Emily's face was getting a bit more strained with every foot they drew closer to St. Mary's, so clearly she could use a distraction.

"You know, I've been thinking. About the King Arthur tales." It was a bit crowded on the *Naiad*, so he'd had no choice but to squeeze in beside Lady Emily. She was even now trying to convince a lock of brilliant red hair to stop blowing into her mouth as she turned to look at him. If nervousness were ranked on a scale of one to ten, he would guess her to be at around six right now. Perhaps he could lower it to a four.

Sheridan, seated across from him, lifted his brows. "What about them? Have you remembered more?"

He'd already added several tales to their repertoire, filling in the most crucial details he could think of that weren't in the storybooks they currently had available. "That's the thing—it doesn't really matter what *we* know about King Arthur, does it? It only matters what Elizabeth Mucknell could have found. So all those books we've come across over the years—if they're modern compilations, are they really even useful?"

Sher pursed his lips in concentration. "Well. I mean, they could be. Yes? Depending on what they've compiled. Historians rediscover things all the time—or put down oral histories." Sher shot a look at Beth and grinned.

That was just the thing Bram had been thinking of, actually—how the late Mrs. Tremayne and Morgan had been compiling stories and legends from the Isles of Scilly before she and Mr. Tremayne were tragically lost in a sudden storm at sea. "Exactly. But we don't need to know what historians in Northumberland or Cadbury have discovered—we need to know what the *local* legends are. About Lyonesse."

"Mother's stories," Beth murmured, gaze focused on the air as she considered it. She had only one hand on the tiller, the other resting on one of the lines. It looked, to all the world, like she wasn't paying a lick of attention to sailing them through the supposedly treacherous channels, but he knew better. She'd already proven herself an abler sailor than Bram could ever be.

Sheridan held a compass in his hand and motioned with it. "I've gone through them all several times, though. The only story about Lyonesse is the one of Tristan and Isolde—which had far more influences of Wagner's opera in it than I was hoping for. And was otherwise based on Tennyson."

Which was ridiculous. Those artists hadn't dug into any old legends or histories; they'd just revived the tales that had been languishing for several hundred years. Most of which weren't even based on English history, but on a French interpretation.

A lecture he'd bitten back several times already. If he got on a soapbox about how the French had distorted what was at its core the most Britannic of legends, they would all look at him as though he'd gone mad—or had turned into Sheridan.

Bram nodded in acknowledgment of Sher's observation about the handwritten stories they'd pulled out of the Tremayne attic nearly a month ago. "I was thinking about that. It's the only one that mentions Lyonesse as such—but if in fact the Isles of Scilly are the highest points remaining of the lost island of Lyonesse, then some of the more ancient tales *could* in fact be set there, and just not call it that."

Sheridan was nodding along. "Or!" He motioned so wildly with the compass that Bram sucked in a breath. He'd considered it a personal game for the last eighteen years to try to catch all the unfortunate objects that Sher tossed about in his enthusiasm. But they weren't usually on a boat, and he could only imagine Collins's objection if he dove overboard to try to rescue a flying compass.

Beth, thankfully, noted it too and reached out a steadying hand. "Dearovim! If you drop my compass, I'm going to send you into the drink again after it."

Sheridan obediently slipped the compass into his pocket so he could gesture more freely. "Or," he said again, grinning, "there could be stories yet to gather. I mean—think about it. It wasn't there at all, was it? The sinking of the kingdom of Lyonesse? That's a gaping lack, really."

It was. "But Elizabeth Mucknell's diary referenced it quite pointedly, which means the tales were told in the 1650s. What do you think our chances are of rediscovering them now?" Bram set his gaze on Beth, though he *really* wanted to look at Emily and see if the conversation had distracted her any from her anxiety. "Could they be recorded somewhere?"

"Or remembered. At least. That is—well, the neighbors couldn't have told *every* story, could they? In the single afternoon your mother and brother visited each one?" Sheridan clapped his hands together. "We really need to continue their work."

Beth was grinning along with Sher. "We do. We'll start with the Dawes, since they haven't even shared their family stories, and then begin asking some pointed questions. Tas-gwyn can help us too. His versions may be a bit fantastical, but he's good at remembering where he picked up the pieces—and knows well which parts he fabricated entirely."

Bram stole a glance at Lady Emily. She was watching Beth, a smile teasing the corners of her mouth. And yes, her eyes had relaxed a bit too. Good.

Although Briggs caught him looking. She didn't do anything so obvious as purse her lips, but her fingers went tight on the edge of the bench before she made a point of looking away.

He faced Sheridan again, even as he told himself he hadn't any reason at all to care if Lady Emily's maid saw he was looking at her. He was only acting as a friend.

"Well," Beth said a moment later, "we could begin tonight, Theo. Mr. Gale—the vicar on St. Mary's," she added, presumably for Bram and Sheridan's sake, "has always been an avid historian and particularly interested in the history of the priory in its early days.

We could pay him a visit after we've had our fish and chips. He'd like that—he's always telling us to drop in any time we're on St. Mary's."

"Perfect." Sheridan looked ready to jump in and swim to shore, he was so eager.

Bram chuckled under his breath and tried to control his smile, though it was a losing battle.

And since the sail only took half an hour, Sheridan didn't need to resort to swimming, regardless. Beth was soon dropping anchor in the quay in Hugh Town, and Bram was helping Emily and Briggs step up onto the dock. They all walked together into the village, though they bade one another farewell and broke into two groups once they reached the hat shop, promising to meet up again at the *Naiad* in three hours' time.

Lady Emily hesitated a moment at the base of the stairs that led to her flat. "Did you want to come up, my lord, and wait inside? I won't be long."

He certainly hoped not—they didn't have much time before her father expected her at the hotel. But he smiled. "Quite all right, my lady. The evening's fine—I'll just take a little stroll or perhaps poke about in the shops for a few minutes while you get ready."

Her smile, like so many of her features, looked ephemeral—like it might flit away at a moment's notice, given the slightest wind of opposition. Not that she struck him as weak. He could hear Mother in his head, chiding him for even suggesting that. No, she wasn't weak any more than his spaniel, Gallahad, had been weak when he'd followed Bram home from the village, limping, as a pup. Injured and mistreated wasn't the same as weak.

"Give me half an hour or so, then, and I'll be down."

He nodded and kept his smile in place until she and Briggs vanished. Once he heard their door open and shut again, proving them safely inside, he did as he'd said and turned to the thoroughfare.

Several of the shops were closed already for the day, but he spotted one door still propped open and meandered that way. It looked like a rather typical place aimed at tourists, selling a bunch of useless whatnots. But he *was* a tourist, so he looked about anyway.

And perhaps he hadn't given it quite enough credit. In addition to the expected postcards and seashells, there were some genuinely artistic pieces too. Framed photos from around the islands, driftwood sculptures, and a mirror framed in sea glass that he could well imagine his mother snatching up if it was still available by the time she arrived.

"To hear Mr. Gibson tell the tale, that one's an enchanted mirror, my lord. Look into it under moonlight, and it'll show you your future."

Bram spun around, smiling when he saw Enyon Thorne. This must be his mother's shop. "A convenient tale to tell, given that I imagine your mother closes up before nightfall."

Enyon chuckled. "Exactly so. One can't test the magic until one has purchased it."

"Clever." He turned back to study it again. It really would look perfect in his mother's dressing room. "You ought to have a tale of Gibson's to go along with each item. Will you ship it for me?"

"Absolutely." Enyon lifted it from its place and flashed the price tag at him.

Bram nodded and trailed him toward the till. "My mother will love it."

"No doubt—mine spent hours last winter creating the mosaic. It's one of her best, if I do say so." Enyon slid the mirror carefully onto the counter and pushed a few keys on the register. "Are Ollie and your sister here too? I'd thought to drop by this evening and lure him out for a row."

"No, just Beth and Sheridan. Libby wanted to sketch some of the night-blooming flowers in the Abbey Gardens this evening, so I imagine that's where Oliver will be found too." Bram pulled out his wallet and extracted a few pound notes to cover the cost and the shipping. "Shall I write the direction for you?"

Enyon pushed paper and pen over to him. "I'll get it crated up and on its way to the mainland tomorrow."

"No rush."

They chatted easily while they finished the transaction, by which time another couple had entered the shop, so Bram slid out with a nod.

The evening really was fine, the sky clear of clouds. Once he was back on Tresco, he'd change into more reasonable clothes and shoes and take another starlit walk.

For now, he strolled back and forth with Lady Emily's flat always in sight, so he saw the moment she stepped back onto the street, then ambled her way. She'd chosen a fancier gown tonight than she usually wore for dinner at the Tremaynes', this one beaded and dripping ivory lace. The green silk was a perfect complement to her complexion and hair, making her eyes stand out.

And he could hear his mother in his head again, telling him to compliment her. He bowed to Mother's wisdom with a smile. "You look absolutely stunning, my lady." He offered his elbow.

She took it with one hand even as she smoothed the other down her skirt. "Thank you. I—never mind." She forced a smile and squared her shoulders. "I won't bore you with my internal debates about what fashions will most please my father." Her chuckle sounded just as forced as her smile looked.

He led her down the street, toward the hotel. "If he has a shard of sense, he'll be proud to show you off tonight."

Her sigh blended with the breeze. "You're sweet to say so, my lord." *But that would be unlike him*, she might as well have added.

If he hadn't already decided he didn't like Scofield after all, seeing his daughter's anxiety at the thought of a dinner with him would have sealed it.

But that was, in large part, why he was here, wasn't it? To be a buffer. To try to instill in her, and in her father, too, the knowledge that some people saw her clearly—and that she had value worth seeing.

While they walked, he turned the conversation to Sheridan and

Beth, having a feeling that would be a safer topic for her than her own family. He couldn't quite bring himself to chat about weddings and all that nonsense, but guessing as to where they might end up traveling in the next few years proved an adequate way to fill the minutes of their walk. And soon enough the hotel came into view.

He didn't see the Scofields anywhere outside, but a glance at his pocket watch said they were exactly on time. Perhaps her father and brother were inside already. He led her through the doors, toward the maître d'. And then froze.

Lord Scofield was indeed already seated at an elegantly set table for four. But it wasn't Nigel beside him. It was Donald Vandermeer.

"Blast." Bram tugged her back a step, out of view of them, before they could be spotted.

"What is it?" Lady Emily's fingers dug into his arm just enough to shout her nerves.

He looked from the dining room to her. Her green eyes were wide, wary as she tried to see past him. And he finally thought to wonder whether she would even agree with Beth's pronouncement that she needed to be protected from Vandermeer. What if she liked him? Liked the idea of becoming his wife and moving an ocean away from her family? Bram didn't want to get in the way of what could turn out to make her happy. That would hardly be chivalrous.

So then. He wouldn't assume. "Vandermeer's in there with your father, not Nigel."

Her brows knit, but she didn't seem to be piecing together the obvious reason for his presence. "Well, that's odd."

"No, my lady, it really isn't." He covered her fingers where they still rested on his arm, much like he had Libby's the other night. "I spoke with him the other day—he means to court you. Is that what you want?"

"I beg your pardon?" She drew back a step, countless thoughts racing through her eyes. None of them looking particularly pleasant. "Why would he . . . ? No." She straightened her shoulders and lifted her chin. "If he's expressed such an interest, it's only because I'm a Scofield. And someone who wants an alliance with my father is the last thing I want."

"All right, then." He gave her a cheeky smile he usually reserved for Sher and Libby. "We'll give him a run for his flaunted money. Play along."

She stared at him for a moment before her lips parted again. "My lord, you needn't—"

"Don't rob me of my fun. Come." Not waiting for any other objections, he turned them back toward the dining room. "Our story is that our interest grew slowly the first few weeks you were here, but that I declared my intentions to court you two weeks ago or so. Perhaps we were inspired by Sher and Beth."

"Lord Telford. Really, he'll never believe it. Neither of them will."

"Of course they will . . . darling?" He pursed his lips. "No, that doesn't feel right. Let's go with 'sweetheart.' I *am* quite fond of my sweets, after all."

"You're being ridiculous." At least she sounded amused rather than horrified.

He sent her a wink as they moved into the entryway. "Mind yourself, or I'll decide to call you 'my little chocolate drop' instead."

There—she was laughing, which provided the perfect picture as he led her into view of the waiting gentlemen. He made sure to give her the warmest of smiles before he faced forward again and pretended to only then spot the other two.

Scofield and Vandermeer both stood, the elder looking utterly confounded as he glanced from Bram to his daughter.

Vandermeer, however, didn't seem confused at all. His eyes were absolutely sparking with challenge. "Well. Lord Tallcutt—I didn't realize you'd be joining us this evening."

Bram smiled. "I might say the same, Mr. Vandevoort, though it's good to see you again. How do you do?"

Scofield frowned between them. "Have you two not been properly introduced? Lord Telford—"

"They know each other's names, Father." Lady Emily spoke softly—frankly, Bram was surprised she spoke at all—but with an amused look at Bram. "They're being clever."

"Ah." That, it seemed, was all it took for Scofield to read the lay of the land. And by the glint in his eye, he rather liked the lay.

Might as well firm it up a bit more. Bram offered a smile to Lord Scofield. "I do hope you forgive my intrusion, my lord. Your daughter and I already had plans for this evening by the time she received your invitation, so we simply thought to combine them. I assured her you wouldn't mind. Didn't I, sweetheart?" He pulled out a chair for her, trying his best to look as doting as Sheridan did around Beth.

Vandermeer was fuming, so he must have pulled it off.

Lady Emily did a fair job of looking as though it wasn't news to her. "You did—though I was rather surprised at the insight. Father, why did you never mention that you knew Bram so well?"

He nearly blinked out of turn at the use of his given name—but she must have determined it was less risky than an endearment, and every bit as pointed. A young lady would never call him by his first name if they weren't intimates. "Well played," he murmured into her ear before taking his own seat.

Her smile was nearly bright enough to eclipse Vandermeer's scowl.

Nearly.

The end of the evening was at long last in sight, which lured Emily into relaxation. Too soon, however. Somehow, when she wasn't paying attention as they were making their way out of the dining room, she ended up by her father's side, Telford and Vandermeer both several steps away, behind another party that had come between them.

This was usually where Father would simply ignore her existence and stride off to his room or turn to wait for his guest, leaving her to drift away on her own. Her shoulders pulled taut again, waiting for that dismissal that never ceased to cut. That disappointment that inevitably surged.

Would she ever outgrow this deep-seated need for her parents' love? For their regard?

But instead of turning away, he cupped her elbow to lead her around another group of laughing guests. "That was unexpected," he murmured.

The very echo of her thoughts. Though she doubted he was talking about his own actions. "What was?"

He glanced over their shoulders. "Your arriving with Lord Telford."

Ah, yes. Totally inconceivable that she would have such a friend. Never mind that the courtship wasn't real—he *was* such a friend. It counted for something, didn't it? Not that she could convince her shoulders to relax any. "I was more surprised at Mr. Vandermeer's presence. I assumed when you issued the invitation that it would be Nigel with you."

"Your brother has returned to London to do some more research. Some new clue he said he found." From the offhanded way he delivered the news, Emily couldn't think he meant it as the blow that it was. He probably didn't realize this new clue was from something Nigel had stolen from Emily. He was too focused on the gentlemen now weaving their way toward them again. "This is quite a turn, though, isn't it? Quite a turn indeed."

One suitor just interested in her connections and the other there only because he was a good man and a friend? No, of far more concern was that news about Nigel. Much as she would like to be relieved that he'd left the islands, she couldn't be, given the reason.

What would he find in London? What information would he then have that they didn't? What if it helped him find Elizabeth Mucknell's mysterious Arthurian artifact before they could?

Telford arrived back at her side and seemed to see in a glance that something was wrong, given the concerned look he gave her.

It melted into another smile, though, when he wished her father and "Vanderwerf" a good evening. He steered her out into the star-lit night, waiting until they were out of sight of the hotel's front doors before he turned to her and said, "What did he do? Did he say something cruel?"

Emily shook her head, even as her chest warmed at his concern. "No. But he said Nigel has gone back to London to research 'a new clue.'"

"Blast." Though he could have shaken free of her now that they were out of sight, he didn't. In fact, he covered her fingers with his, where they rested against his arm. "That's not good. I don't suppose he had any helpful specifics?"

"I didn't press for details." Should she have? It probably would have seemed odd. She didn't imagine her father would think her suddenly on their side just because he bought her dinner. At least not so soon after his ultimatum.

"I would be surprised if he even knew, honestly." Telford turned them at the corner, back toward her flat. "Unless I'm mistaken, your brother is trying to prove himself, and hence being secretive. Or that's my best guess as to why he and your father were clearly not on the same page earlier in the summer, based on what I pried from him on the subject tonight."

Which hadn't been all that much, but Father had been so eager to impress both of the gentlemen that he'd played along at least a little with Telford's questioning. She looked up now at his profile, gilded by the moonlight, and nearly wished that hadn't been his main purpose in coming tonight, that he . . .

No, that was foolish. There was no point in wishing he hadn't just been playing a part. Even if she *was* suddenly aware of how chiseled his jaw was, and how tall he stood beside her. "I suppose we'll just have to wait until Nigel returns, then, to know what he's up to."

"And when he does, we'll have our quest for Vandermeer, won't we? We can task *him* with learning what your brother has discovered."

"Perfect. And in the meantime—thank you, my lord. For . . . everything."

"I assure you, my lady, it was no hardship." He had a beautiful smile, and he'd been bestowing it on her all evening. Which made her aware of how little she'd seen it before now. Usually he was the more serious half of the Telford-Sheridan duo, scowling more often than smiling.

But even so, he'd never been anything but kind to her. She suddenly remembered one of the first times she'd met him, the day Nigel had first tried to steal some of Mucknell's treasure from them—the day he'd forced Libby and Telford into Piper's Hole, thinking them the Tremaynes. He'd tried to force Emily in, too, but her phobia of dark places had overcome even her fear of her brother, and she'd refused to go in.

Nigel had thrown her to the ground in his frustration with her— but Lord Telford had helped her up. And he'd whispered in her ear, "*Well played.*" As if she'd put on the fear to have an excuse to stay out of the cave and lead help their way. As if he hadn't known perfectly well she'd been genuinely overcome.

"*Well played,*" he'd whispered again tonight when she felt like she was floundering.

That was, she was coming to see, typical of him. He always said things to make it seem as though she were stronger than she was. To hold her up. To turn her weaknesses around somehow.

Really, he was every bit as softhearted as Oliver and Sheridan. "Why do you pretend to be gruff so often?"

The question slipped out unbidden. Perhaps because she knew she could ask it without earning his ire.

And indeed he gave her another grin. "Who says I'm pretending?"

"I do."

He chuckled and turned them onto the street that would lead to her flat. "On the contrary. You usually see me during daylight hours, and I assure you, I really am in a terrible mood most of the time. I don't come into my own until sundown."

Emily laughed softly. "And I suppose all the sweets during the day are to try to sweeten your disposition?"

"You've found me out, my little chocolate drop."

Smiling, she shook her head. "At any rate—I appreciate what you're doing. Protecting me from my father's schemes."

"You don't need to thank me for that. As I said, it's no hardship."

Perhaps he meant it—because that was the sort of man he was. The sort who protected those who needed it. Who always took such care to preserve her dignity.

The sort she wouldn't mind spending a bit of extra time with, if the ruse demanded it.

And Father had seemed genuinely pleased with the situation. He'd clearly only invited her tonight to try to shove her at Vandermeer, not to try to sort things out between *them*. But now he'd think she had two potential suitors. He'd have to look at her a little differently, wouldn't he? See her through eyes other than Nigel's, which could only be a good thing.

Surely that meant he'd relent on the money. After all, he wouldn't want her going hungry if she was supposed to be charming a future husband.

Right?

9

MONDAY, 27 AUGUST

Tommie meandered into the Thornes' shop not because she had any money to spend but because, in fact, she had none—and that situation really had to change. On Saturday she'd drawn out the pound notes she'd set aside for a train ticket and used them to buy another week's worth of food, not telling Lady Emily where it came from. But the food would only see them through a few more days. Then they'd be right back where they'd been before *and* she'd have no way to take herself out of the situation.

Not that she regretted the choice, but . . . well, it was still a ridiculous position for an earl's daughter and her maid to be in, and she'd had enough of worrying over it. She wasn't about to suggest Lady Emily tell the Tremaynes about their predicament—she knew without asking why that wouldn't happen and could hardly blame her for protecting what dignity she had left. They already knew his lordship had told her not to come home until she'd settled things with Nigel, but admitting this latest turn of events was just asking too much of the lady's pride.

But Tommie was a healthy young woman, perfectly capable of working to earn a few extra shillings a week for some bread or beans. So work she would. Not that she'd mentioned her intentions.

Perhaps it was a long shot to think she might find a position in Enyon's mother's shop, and one that wouldn't interfere with her duties to Lady Emily, but when she'd stepped outside this morning, saying she needed a bit of fresh air, it was where her feet had taken her.

The door stood open, as it did any time the weather permitted, and Tommie drew in an appreciative breath as she stepped inside. It always smelled so lovely in here—some combination of herbs and flowers and salty sea air. She'd yet to identify the source of the fragrance, but she appreciated it.

"Good morning. Thomasina, isn't it?"

Tommie looked over with a smile for Mrs. Thorne, wondering where in the world the woman had heard her full first name. She certainly never went by it. "Tommie, yes. You're Enyon's mam, right?" She'd seen her around the islands but had yet to be introduced.

Mrs. Thorne nodded. She had the same dark hair as her son, but that wasn't saying much. It seemed ninety percent of the islanders boasted the same shade. They also shared a smile, though, and the eyes that tilted up in the corners when they did so. "I've been hoping you'd stop in sometime. I've heard all about you and your lady. Everyone on Tresco is still aflutter from so many lords and ladies spending the summer with us."

Tommie knew that in her own village only some of that fluttering would have been positive and had to assume the same was true in Grimsby. "I know they've all been enjoying their stay—well, the ones who've been here all summer. I can't speak for that crew that just arrived to excavate Gugh."

She was fishing, yes. But she couldn't imagine Mrs. Thorne would really blame her for it. The woman wrinkled her nose. "A different sort, those, aren't they? All highfalutin dictates and putting on airs, like they're better than every other tourist to step foot on the islands." She leaned across the workbench that held the cash register. "Would you believe they actually bribed people to leave the hotel and give them their rooms? And why? Just so they can tear up Gugh."

Tommie shook her head along with her hostess, though Lady Emily had said as much, about the hotel rooms. "Some people think money gives them the right to walk all over everyone else."

"Isn't that the truth. Biscuit?" Mrs. Thorne held out a tin of them.

Well. It would be rude to refuse. Tommie selected one with a grin. "Thank you." She took a nibble instead of shoving the thing into her mouth whole like she wanted to do and sent her gaze over the beautiful pieces on the shelves. "You have a lovely shop, Mrs. Thorne. I've thought so each time I've walked by. It's always been your daughter in here, though, whenever I've stepped in."

The lady chuckled. "We keep the whole family busy. Always more than enough work to go round."

Praise you, Lord. The perfect opening. "Well, if ever you need an extra hand, do let me know. With Lady Emily on Tresco with the Tremaynes so often, I've been all but useless. And my own mam taught me never to have idle hands, which means I've been at absolute loose ends."

"Oh, now. You ought to just enjoy the bit of holiday."

Tommie forced a chuckle. "I've had about all the holidaying I can suffer, truth be told. I'd be grateful for a few hours' honest work here and there."

The silence brought her gaze back around to Mrs. Thorne, who was studying her far too intently. Quietly, the older woman said, "I can't think your mistress would appreciate you leaving her side for other employment, Tommie. Even just a few hours of it."

She might, if it meant food in their cupboard. "She doesn't mind, I assure you, madame. I kept busy at first helping Mrs. Dawe, but now that her daughter's home, they haven't much need of me there."

Mrs. Thorne didn't look convinced, exactly, but she inclined her head to grant that point, anyway. "I haven't heard of anyone in need of another hand. Have you, Enny?"

"Have I what?"

Tommie whipped her head around just in time to see Enyon coming through the door with a heavy-looking crate in his arms. He smiled upon seeing her, even as his mother reiterated the question. At which his smile turned to another probing look—another trait these two Thornes apparently shared.

Tommie squirmed out from under it by peeking into the crate. Framed photographs, more driftwood. Lovely. "May I help you put these out?"

"Well, I never turn down help. But Mam's right, Thomasina, no one locally is looking for a shopgirl." He chuckled, though it sounded taut. "Don't you like being a lady's maid?"

"Not especially." The truth slipped out before she could stop it. She chased it with a sigh. "Though don't mention that to Lady Emily—it's no fault of hers. But . . ." Her resignation weighed heavy in her pocket as she snuck a glance at Enyon. He was watching her, just holding a piece of driftwood in his hands without placing it anywhere. "Honestly, I don't mean to go back to London with her when she leaves here. Not that I'd just abandon her now, when she's apart from her family."

"Really. Interesting." He set the driftwood on a shelf and reached for a photo. "You can't mean to just stay here, though, right? To be looking for work?"

There was a small hand mirror in the crate, adorned with shells and sea glass. Pretty. She'd pasted some broken tiles and bits of glass on a mirror much like this when she was a girl and had thought it the loveliest thing in the world, worthy of a princess from a fairy tale. And looking at this one provided her an excuse for not meeting Enyon's eyes. "I imagine I'll go home to Wales." She propped the mirror carefully against a decorative box, anchoring it up with a large whelk shell. "But there's no telling when that will be, so putting a bit extra away in the meantime wouldn't go amiss."

Enyon and his mother both nodded at that; no doubt every islander knew, just as her own neighbors at home had, that having a few extra pounds set aside before one left a position was never a bad thing.

"Tell you what," he said, "have lunch with me when we're finished here. I'll introduce you to a few people here on St. Mary's who know everything that goes on. They'll know if anyone's in need of an extra hand that wouldn't take you too far from Lady Emily."

Lunch with Enyon Thorne? Her stomach went tight. On the one hand, she'd be a fool to pass up a free meal, and his company was pleasant. Alluring, even.

But that was the problem. She couldn't let herself be lured in by anyone. If he wasn't as kind as he seemed, then it would prove her a fool. And if he was, then he deserved better than the likes of her.

But she was getting ahead of herself. She had no reason to think he was being anything but neighborly. He was, after all, the best friend of Oliver Tremayne, which probably meant he was merely trying to show kindness to the household of Beth Tremayne's best friend.

And that meal would mean one that Lady Emily didn't have to provide. She produced a smile, hoping her hesitation hadn't been too long. "That's kind of you. Thanks."

He winked and reached for another photo. "It isn't altogether selfless an offer, Thomasina. I like your company."

"I like your company."

Maybe she *hadn't* been getting ahead of herself. No man had ever said something like that to her. Her cheeks warmed, and a smile came unbidden to her mouth, even as any number of warning bells clanged in her mind.

Nothing good could come of this. If she were smart, she'd refuse him and march into every shop on her own. Make it clear she wanted no entanglements. No flirtatious statements. No warm gazes that produced warm cheeks.

Look where compliments and blushes had landed her before.

No. No, she had to keep her distance. She ought to retract her acceptance of the lunch invitation even now, and—

"You two go on, then," his mother said with a chuckle from her place at the register. "I'll take care of the rest."

Enyon made no objection. "Best not to argue with Mam, I've

learned. Shall we?" He offered an arm, just like the gents did for the ladies before every meal.

She swallowed past the tightness in her throat, knowing well that he wouldn't be treating her so if he knew how little she deserved the regard.

But the mask she'd learned to don could be used here too. She put it on—neutral smile, pleasant expression, empty heart—and tucked her hand lightly into the crook of his elbow. It was only lunch. And it was for a purpose.

She called out a polite "Nice to meet you, Mrs. Thorne!" over her shoulder and let him lead her from the shop.

"Fair warning," Enyon said once they were in the street. "I'm about to introduce you to the island gossips, which comes with its risks."

He said it lightly, but it made her supposedly empty heart stutter. She had nothing to fear, though. They had no way of knowing her secrets, not the real ones. The only fodder she could possibly be giving them was that she wasn't happy in her current employment. And what did it matter if that got around? As soon as Lady Emily left the islands, Tommie would be handing over that resignation anyway. "I come from a small village. Those are risks I know and accept." She prayed her tone had sounded as light as his. And added, because it was true, "I appreciate you doing this, Enyon."

"To be honest, I've been hoping for a chance to spend a bit of time with you."

She went stiff—purely reflexively—before she realized that his tone hadn't sounded flirtatious like it had before. It sounded heavy and grave, which meant that he couldn't have been wanting it just for the sake of her company. Which shouldn't have made disappointment arrow through the relief, should it?

She made herself relax again and turned her face toward his, brows lifted. "You sound serious."

He'd been watching her—perhaps because of the way she'd gone stiff?—but now checked over his shoulder, as if making certain there was no one nearby to overhear. The way he pitched his voice down only added to the feel of sobriety. "I am. Ever since that Scofield bloke left Beth to die on Gugh last month . . . Well, I haven't wanted to worry Ollie. But I've been worried *for* him, and his sister, and everyone else. A man who would do something like that—he isn't to be trusted, is he? Yet he's walking free."

"He's a gentleman." Far too often, that said it all. An earl's son could do what he pleased with very little thought to the consequences. Who would believe them if they dared to speak against Nigel Scofield?

"Well, so's Ollie! And we've got Telford and Sheridan in our corner now, too, don't we? I say it's time we bring him to justice." His dark eyes flashed, then banked down to a glow she could only name as concern when he focused them on her again. "And I've been thinking. A fellow who would behave like that with Beth, who would steal from his own sister, who would threaten Ollie and his Libby like he's done—well, that sort isn't likely to be kinder to those he deems beneath him than he is to his social equals. Got me wondering what he'd done elsewhere. At home. Or when he's been away. Whether we need to be telling the islanders to be on their guard."

It took all her strength not to let her fingers go tight on his arm. Beth and Emily had come to her a few weeks ago, yes, to leverage her connections with the other domestics in the Scofield house and get them information on what Nigel and his lordship were doing. But none of them had paused to ask what he'd already done—or was likely to do—to those normal, everyday people on the sidelines.

No one else had thought to wonder who else might get hurt during this treasure hunt of theirs.

Tommie drew in a long breath and let the question sink in. Really sink in, past her defenses. Past her pain. Past her assumptions.

A shudder chased through her. "I don't know." Her words emerged as a whisper, likely lost amidst the bustle of the thoroughfare. "I don't know what he's done to others." She'd never asked. Never wondered. Never looked.

But she could. Or could ask Dandy to, anyway, once Nigel left London again and it was safe to poke about. "I'll see what I can discover."

"I don't mean to go dredging up what's best left to settle, mind you." He looked forward now, but even so, she could see the tension around his mouth, his eyes. "But I don't fancy any more hurt befalling us here because of him. We've already lost Johnnie to this madness, and nearly Beth. It has to stop."

She'd never met the young man who had been killed by Nigel's associate in the sea cave, but she'd seen firsthand how precarious Beth Tremayne's situation had been. And she knew how all the staff in both of the Scofield houses avoided the young master whenever they could. But she'd never let it paint the full picture for her. She'd not had the capacity to wonder what other pain he'd left in his wake.

But Enyon was right—that wouldn't do. It wasn't good enough to simply watch him and know what he was up to now. They had to *stop* him.

She nodded. "You're right. The ladies and gents may be more focused on finding some new artifact, but we had better focus on him, before he has a chance to hurt anyone else."

Enyon nodded, too, looking determined. "Good. I'm glad to know I won't be doing it all alone." He made a show of brightening, smiling down at her. "Now, lunch. We'll go to Polmers'. They put sandwiches together for picnic-goers that are works of art. And if anyone in the Scillies knows of a position you could have for a few weeks, it would be Mrs. Polmer."

"Perfect."

Even more perfect was the enormous sandwich Mr. Polmer handed to her five minutes later—so big that it wouldn't look at all odd for her to eat only part of it and take the rest home for Lady Emily. The place was bustling, so Tommie wasn't sure how they were meant to get a word with the missus, but Enyon wasn't put off. Once he'd paid for their food, he simply led her back out, down the alley, and in again through the back door.

It was hot as the tropics in this part of the building, given the enormous oven, but it smelled even better than the front of the shop. A frazzled-looking woman of about sixty years looked up when they entered. She was up to her elbows in a huge mound of dough on her workbench. "Enny. What do you need? Didn't Kev help you out front?"

Enyon lifted his own sandwich but said, "Just wanted a word with you. Have you met my friend Thomasina Briggs?"

"Tommie," Tommie said, dipping her knees in a quick curtsy that made the woman grin.

"Seen her about. With one of the ladies, aren't you, dearover?" Mrs. Polmer kept on kneading the dough. "The ginger one."

"That's right. Lady Emily Scofield."

Mrs. Polmer nodded. "She favors the sourdough. And the sweet rolls."

"Everyone favors the sweet rolls," Enyon said on a laugh. "But listen. Thomasina is looking to pick up a few extra hours when her lady doesn't need her, if you know of any openings. I thought that perhaps, with the hotels all still booked thanks to the excavation, there might be more call than usual as we move into September."

Mrs. Polmer pursed her lips. "There's certainly been plenty of musing about the busy season lasting overlong this year, that's certain. I'll keep my ear out. If I hear anything, I can leave word at the millinery or the Thornes' for you, dearover."

Tommie smiled. "I do appreciate it, Mrs. Polmer. Thank you."

They escaped the heat of the kitchen a minute later, just in time to see the crowd of ferry passengers disperse.

All her hunger inspired by that beautiful sandwich evaporated when she caught sight of a familiar derby over dark red hair. Nigel Scofield was back on the islands.

Enyon must have spotted him, too, given the word he muttered. "Well. I'll let the Tremaynes and company know he's returned as soon as I go back to Tresco."

Tommie nodded. "And I'll alert Lady Emily."

"After lunch. I can't imagine taking the time to eat will make any difference."

She wasn't quite as certain, not until she saw Nigel stride directly to the hotel. Then she relaxed a bit. "All right."

Enyon led her to the garrison wall to eat their sandwiches. She didn't honestly expect her appetite to come back, but she found herself relaxing as Enyon turned the subject to easy, friendly topics while they ate. Her home in Wales, what it had been like for him growing up here in the Scillies, how his eldest sister lived just across the sandbar now from him, on Bryher, but the other two and his younger brother were still at home. Enyon, it seemed, had just a year ago rented a cottage of his own, the nearest one to Piper's Hole.

The mention of the sea cave sobered him a bit, though. He'd been the one to help recover the body of Johnnie Rosedew from the cave that spring, after he'd been killed because he got tangled up in this treasure hunt.

That thought was enough to turn her stomach too. It seemed everything led back to Nigel at this point. One way or another.

She folded the square of wax paper back around her sandwich— she'd eaten nearly half of it, anyway—and looked at the watch pinned to her bodice. "Oh, I'd better get back soon. Lady Emily will be wondering where I've gone."

"I'll walk with you. It's on my way to the quay."

She breathed a little easier, knowing she had someone strong and kind by her side for a few extra minutes, now that Nigel was back. Enyon wouldn't always be there, but she would take the assurance while she could.

As they strolled along the street, she couldn't help but think how normal they must look—just a young couple out for lunch, like so many others. No one would know that their purpose had been anything but carefree.

Even so, she'd enjoyed herself more than she had any right to. It was with a light heart that she climbed the stairs to their flat—at least until she stepped inside and Lady Emily bounced to her feet, her face pinched. "There you are! I was worried. I think I saw Nigel getting off the ferry, and I kept imagining the worst."

The lady's hands were trembling, though she hid them behind her back when Tommie looked at them. She frowned. "Sorry, my lady. I bumped into Enyon—Mr. Tremayne's friend—and he bought me lunch. I didn't mean to alarm you."

Emily donned a smile just as shaky as her hands. "It's all right. So long as you're all right."

Was it fear that had her trembling so? Nerves? Or . . . her eyes drifted to the small kitchen and the food they'd been rationing. Emily had said she'd eaten breakfast that morning before Tommie got up. She hadn't paused to examine the statement, but now that she looked at their supplies, she realized it couldn't possibly have been true.

They'd skipped supper last night, too, after sharing a large dinner with the Tremaynes after church yesterday. Which meant the lady hadn't had anything but water and tea for twenty-four hours.

She was in no danger of starving in that amount of time, it was true. But when had Lady Emily Scofield ever had to skip a meal before? Much less three of them? Her body wouldn't be used to it.

Tommie strode over to the table, grabbed a knife, and unwrapped the sandwich. "Have you seen the sandwiches the Polmers make? There was no way I could eat it all." She cut a clean swipe, eliminating her bite marks and leaving the untouched half. "I hope you haven't had lunch yet, my lady."

"Not yet." Emily flitted a few steps closer but seemed hesitant to draw too near. Her gaze darted to the sandwich but then decidedly away. "But that's yours, Briggs. Save it for your supper. I'll be quite content with a few slices of peach and some bread."

"There's still some left for me. If I even have room for it later." She smiled, trying to pretend she didn't know how hungry her employer must be. Trying not to look so touched at the thought that the earl's daughter before her would choose not to eat herself rather than take food she deemed Tommie's.

How could two siblings be so different? Nigel so deceitfully charming but cruel, Emily so seemingly distant but truly selfless?

The lady backed up another step and shook her head. Then looked her straight in the eye. "Actually, I've been thinking, Briggs, and . . . much as I regret having to make this decision, I think it's for the best. I'm letting you go."

Tommie set the knife back onto the table, that letter in her pocket suddenly weighing a stone. "I beg your pardon?"

Lady Emily's larynx bobbed with her swallow. "I'm no longer in need of your services. I'm terminating your employment." Her nostrils flared. She sliced a hand through the air that looked more defeated than decisive. "You're sacked."

Tommie planted her hands on her hips. "You can't sack me."

A spark entered the lady's eyes. "Yes, I can. I'm your employer."

"No, my employer pays me a wage, which you haven't done this month. Which means I'm here on a volunteer basis. You can't sack me—I'd have to resign."

The spark dulled to a low throb. "All right. Then I accept your resignation."

"You don't, because I'm not offering it."

"Tommie!" Emily huffed, looking more distraught than angry. She gestured wildly toward their empty cupboard. "I can't provide for you, I can't pay you—and I can't ask you to go hungry just because my father's trying to teach me some convoluted lesson about loyalty to a family that doesn't deserve it. Go *home*. See your mother, laugh with your sisters. You have no obligation to me."

No. No obligation. But she had an investment now. This was her fight too. Maybe it had been all along. Maybe she just hadn't realized it when she penned that note in her pocket. Maybe this was how she took back what that monster had stolen—by helping these good people, by seeking justice instead of trying to forget it all. By being a friend instead of just an employee.

Tommie lifted her chin. "I don't want to go home. I'm quite enjoying my time here. And I'm not hungry."

Emily shook her head. "You will be. Look." She pointed to their food. "That's one more meal, maybe two, if the vegetables keep, which I doubt."

"Three. Don't forget the sandwich."

"It's not enough." Emily sank into one of the kitchen chairs. "Not enough to outlast my father. I wired the bank again this morning while you were out, thinking maybe he'd have been pleased enough after the dinner on Friday that he'd have given me access again. But this time they said the account was closed. *Closed.* That doesn't sound like a lesson only meant to last another day or two."

No, it didn't. It sounded like a way to try to strong-arm his daughter into marrying whichever of the rich gents he decided would suit him best.

Tommie pulled out a chair, too, and pushed the sandwich in front of Emily. "Eat. This will all look better once you do."

"I don't see how." But the smell of the roast beef must have overcome her reservations. She pulled the sandwich closer.

"Well, we know we're not going to starve. The Tremaynes feed us every time we visit, and we go to Tresco every few days. So, this is hardly an emergency. We can always spend more time there."

Lady Emily took a dainty bite. "I don't want to put that sort of strain on them, though. Now that I realize how much it costs to feed us all . . . it's unfair to ask it of them. They've always lived very frugally."

Tommie opened her mouth to assure her that if it was a problem, the Tremaynes wouldn't have invited them all to join them—but then she closed it again. Because she honestly couldn't be certain of that. The Tremaynes were the sort of people who would be generous to their own detriment.

"All right. But let's at least assume that our current level of sharing meals with them isn't unduly burdensome. That still means meals every few days. And worst-case scenario, we could ask them for help. Even if the Tremaynes can't give it, the lords—"

"No." It sounded like a plea more than insistence. Emily set the sandwich down again and squeezed her eyes shut. "I'm sorry. I don't want to ask favors for myself, not unless it gets truly desperate—but I will for you. I'll ask to borrow train fare to get you home."

"Not interested." Tommie pushed to her feet again, hoping Emily would eat more if she wasn't being watched. Besides, she wanted to take stock of their supplies. "And I understand how difficult it would be for you to confess this to your friends. I do. I wouldn't ask you to humiliate yourself for me. In fact . . . I asked about positions in the shops while I was out—just a few hours here and there, when you can spare me. It could give us enough to eat on, anyway. Well, I mean, not that I've found anything yet, but I could."

They had half the small loaf of bread left. One tomato. A cucumber. A wedge of cheese. And the peach half-hidden behind the bread, which she'd thought Emily had eaten for breakfast.

Emily sniffed. "I cannot ask you to work to support me, Tommie. And I won't let you go hungry either. If you won't leave, then . . . well, I'll do what I must. My pride mustn't get in the way of your well-being."

"You're not asking; I volunteered." And Tommie wouldn't be the cause of yet another humiliation for Lady Emily. Better for her to work a few hours in a sweet little tourist shop than for the lady to grovel, wasn't it? "But we can't count on my securing other work, I grant you. So, then, here's the plan. You're going to eat that sandwich now because you haven't had anything since yesterday. According to Jeremiah Moon's big toe, we'll have rain tomorrow, so there will be no going to Tresco. We eat all this tomorrow. Midday. Wednesday we'll be on Tresco again so will have lunch with everyone. That means it will be Thursday before we're facing genuinely bare cupboards."

"Thursday." Emily said it like it was their execution date. It probably felt like it to her.

"Thursday. We have until then to come up with a solution, for me to find a few hours of work elsewhere, or for your father to change his mind." As unlikely as that third option seemed.

The lady sighed. "I think you mean we have until Thursday to pray. I know the Lord will provide—but if He will do that only through me humbling myself in this, then so be it. I'll throw myself on the mercy of Sheridan and Telford if I must."

Tommie pressed her lips together. She knew that the lady's friends would help. But even so, she didn't relish seeing her beg for it. For her own part, she'd be praying for another way.

10

WEDNESDAY, 29 AUGUST

Emily stared for a long moment at the treasure laid out before them, covering nearly every flat surface in the Tremaynes' dining room. By the time she'd arrived that morning, they'd already fetched the moaning, crumbling sea chest from the church and spread out its contents here. They'd spent the morning cleaning and cataloguing each piece, then dividing it all up in such a way that the most valuable items would be separated.

Should it have given her a thrill to see all the gold and silver? The jewels? Should she have wondered what it would feel like to wear that diadem or want to slide one of the rings onto her finger? She was looking at pirate treasure. Real, actual pirate treasure that had been buried on Gugh for centuries.

And all she could think about were more passages from Elizabeth Mucknell's diary. *How can he not understand that I don't want any of this bloodstained booty? How can he not understand that all I want is for him to turn from this path that leads to death and embrace the salvation of Christ?*

So many times over the years Father had accused her of not knowing what it meant to be a Scofield. Turned out he was right.

145

Scofields, it seemed, were a lot like John Mucknell—the bounty was all that mattered to them.

But Emily looked at this treasure and only saw trouble. She saw one more thing that had led her family down that same spiral of greed that had caught the pirate admiral. She saw something that stood between her and them.

She sighed and picked up one of the squares of sturdy cotton that Mamm-wynn had cut out last night. The sooner they hid it all away again, the better. And if no one else was going to start, she would. She laid out the cotton, scooped up a heavy gold necklace, some silver coins, and a few loose pearls, and set them in the middle of the square.

Her actions seemed to jar the others to follow suit.

"I'll put the catalogue of it all in the cupboard at St. Nicholas's, with the parish record books," Oliver said after a moment filled with jingling and scraping and thudding. "Unless someone has a better idea of where to keep it." He apparently thought "someone" was likely to be Beth since he looked over at her with a half-smile.

His sister grinned. "That sounds reasonable. So long as our map isn't in the same place."

Their map wasn't quite finished yet, when last Emily had peeked at it. Libby, stationed at the end of the table that got the best light from the window, was still putting the finishing touches on the watercolor. She'd been humming *Carmen* all morning while she painted first a bird's-eye view of the Isles of Scilly and then a series of marks and dashes and misdirections meant to lead them—but no one else—to the man-made hiding places they'd already designated for each parcel.

The map itself was a work of art. Emily had watched Libby for several minutes, envying her steady strokes and attention to detail. She'd even added a few whimsical touches that had made Emily smile—miniature plants where the Abbey Gardens stood, a bird perched on St. Martin's, and an old-fashioned-looking sea monster coming out of the waves at the line in the ocean where Beth had said the most dangerous current could be found.

Emily focused again on the treasure before her and folded the cotton around it. With a piece of the precut twine to tie it off, it looked like any other bit of nothing purchased from the market and wrapped for transport home.

Bother—her hands shook a bit as she tied it off. It seemed to come in waves. She'd be perfectly fine with an empty stomach for hours on end, then all of a sudden she'd start to feel weak and shaky. It would go away, though, just as it had this morning.

"You all right?"

But not, apparently, before Telford took note. He'd ended up beside her, groggy and silent until that very moment. She angled a concealing smile up at him. "I received your first three words of the day? I'm flattered, my lord."

His glare was about as intimidating as Libby's kitten, Darling, which was purring in his lap. "That's not an answer."

"I'm fine. Too much tea this morning, that's all." It was, subjectively, true. They had quite a supply of tea, so she'd had two cups before they left St. Mary's. Which, on an empty stomach, had proven too much indeed.

He stared at her, as if debating whether to believe her, and stroked Darling behind the ears. Then he sighed and turned to his own parcel, which he'd tied awkwardly. "Help?"

She had to chuckle when, right on cue, the twine came untied and the fabric flopped open. She pulled it over toward her and made short work of rewrapping it. "What's your excuse? Not *enough* tea?"

"Mm." He leaned back in his chair and closed his eyes. "Blighted mornings."

A ball of paper came soaring across the table and smacked Telford in the shoulder. Didn't even make him open his eyes, though Sheridan laughed. "You can only mutter that for two more minutes, Telly, you know. Then—well, it won't be morning anymore, will it?"

Telford blinked his eyes open. Reached slowly for his watch. Grunted. "Blighted noontime." He closed his eyes again.

Emily pushed their two parcels into the center of the table with the others. Ten in all. One of which would be stowed in the attic here, one at the church. The others to be scattered in other locations around the islands. Mr. Gibson's house. Their uncle Mark's. In each of the churches in the isles, an abandoned cottage on Samson, the Abbey Gardens.

She looked across the table at Beth. Whether the others were sad or glad to see it all go, she couldn't say. But Emily was ready to get on with it, and not only because she and the other ladies would be hiding several of them after they enjoyed a picnic lunch on Samson—the basket of food being the cover for the parcels.

Beth met her gaze and nodded. "All right, then. Gentlemen, have a lovely afternoon visiting all the churches. Libby, are you ready?"

"I will be by the time you fetch the basket from Mrs. Dawe. Just a few . . . more . . . details."

Emily pushed her chair back and stood, hands braced on the table. Though she froze when Telford's fingers touched hers. Her gaze flew to his face.

He was looking at her again. "Careful."

See? He was sweet even when he was morning grouchy. She smiled. "We will be. And the same for you, my lord."

He gave her a sleepy grin. "Hope he shows up. Sock him in the nose."

She wasn't about to ruin his dream by telling him that Nigel spent hours every day sparring. She'd simply pray Telford didn't, in fact, cross her brother's path this afternoon. Though there was no telling—in the two days since he'd returned, they'd spotted him absolutely everywhere, poking into every sea cave and crevasse to be found. All the Tremaynes' local friends were helping them note every place he went, so they could keep a list.

Their hope, until Vandermeer finished the "quest" they'd sent him in the post yesterday and got them information on what Nigel was searching for—*if* he got them information—was that by observing where he was looking, they'd at least be able to narrow down the artifact by size. Then the trick would be to find it first.

But at least they had the advantage of having the island locals on their side. If anyone knew where something could be hidden in the Scillies, it was Beth and Oliver Tremayne, not Nigel Scofield. He was a stranger here. That would work against him.

Emily gathered their parcels while Beth went for the empty basket and Libby finished up her map. A few minutes later, they'd stowed the treasure in the bottom, covered it with a serviette, and then let Mrs. Dawe heap more food on top than they could possibly eat in a single picnic.

Would anyone think anything of it if she took a scone home with her? She looked over at where Briggs—Tommie—sat shelling peas at the kitchen table. Emily had decided to simply act as though they truly were friends, since one could hardly call her an employee, given that she'd dismissed her. Only a friend would refuse to leave in such a situation, right?

Tommie grinned at her. "We've already sampled the fare, ladies. You'll enjoy it, I promise."

Beth tucked a checkered cloth over the mound of food. "As always. Has Mabena got back yet?"

Mrs. Dawe nodded. "She said to fetch her from the Wearnes' on your way by."

Emily sidled closer to Tommie. "Are you certain you don't want to come?"

Her maid—*friend*—waved her off. "I'm quite content right where I am, my lady."

She looked it, at that. Well then. Emily said her farewells, hoisted the heavy basket before Beth had the chance to do so, and started for the door.

Beth followed her with a laugh. "My, someone's eager. Libby! Emily's dragging me out the door, you'd better hurry."

With anyone else, Emily would have flushed and slowed down. Beth, however, deserved honesty. "I hate the thought of Nigel scouring the islands, for either this or the artifact. I'll feel so much better when the treasure, at least, is away from you all." She'd feel better still when they turned it all over to the Duke of Cornwall, which they'd likely have to do soon. He was, after all, the legal owner of everything salvaged in the Scillies. And once it was in his hands, she could be fairly certain Nigel wouldn't try to steal it again—given that the Duke of Cornwall was also known as the Prince of Wales.

But Prince George hadn't just dropped everything to come and see what they'd found, despite apparently being on a first-name basis with Ladies Abbie and Millicent, so in the meantime, they'd just have to safeguard it all for him.

Libby hurried from the dining room to meet them at the door, smiling. "Ready. Oh, I smell Mrs. Dawe's scones from here." She took an exaggerated sniff of the air above the basket. "Picnic first, right?"

At least Emily wasn't the only one eager for lunch.

Beth opened the door. "Picnic first."

Yesterday's rain had given way to a perfect late-summer day, and Emily soaked it in as they called for Mabena at the Wearne house and then strolled along the beach toward the quay. If one ignored the heaviness of the basket and the fact that she had absolutely no food left in her flat and that her dearest friends and her family were on opposite sides of a rather serious battle, then this would be the most enjoyable sort of outing.

Four friends, laughing along the shore. Three of them with weddings to plan. Joking about whether Beth would be able to lure Mrs. Dawe to follow her to Sheridan Castle, whether Libby's mother would agree to an autumn wedding in the Abbey Gardens, whether Cador Wearne would have the gall to accept the invitation Mabena had insisted they send.

Normal, lovely things. Things that tricked her into thinking, for just a moment, that her own life hadn't gone so horribly off the rails. She was just another young lady. Oblivious to hardship. Debating between two suitors—as if either were real. She smiled again as she remembered Telford's atrocious bow, his morning gruffness, and the kindness it couldn't hide. The way he'd touched her hand. How he looked straight into her eyes.

Oh bother. She wasn't supposed to be actually pining for him.

"What a picture. Four of the islands' loveliest ladies, all together."

They all froze, Emily nearly stumbling. No. No, no, no, no, *no*. What was Nigel doing here? Since he'd been prowling around Tresco in the rain yesterday, they'd deemed it highly unlikely he would return today. Why had he come back? Why was he here, today of all days, when they had treasure to hide from him?

She slammed her eyes shut, wished, prayed him away.

His arm draped over her shoulder in that way that always felt like an anchor. Because it always meant he was going to drag her somewhere she had no desire to go, and he was going to leave her there, and he was going to laugh about it while she tried to find her way home. And she hadn't any money left in her pocket to pay a local to ferry her back to St. Mary's or Tresco—and she had far too much gold in the basket on her arm for him not to notice the weight if he took it from her.

Father God, please. Please. Please, please, please.

"Nigel Scofield." It was Beth, of course, with enough of a snarl in her voice that Emily was inspired to open her eyes again. Her friend stood with her hands on her hips, not looking the slightest bit intimidated. "In broad daylight, no less—how very odd for a thief."

Nigel's chuckle may have sounded at ease to an untrained observer, who didn't feel his arm tightening around their neck. "*I* am not the one who stole a pirate chest from a museum-sanctioned dig. And it was Vandermeer who insisted on that midnight 'tour,' as he called it, of your parlor. I was only there to try to talk him out of it."

The basket weighed a ton. At least. Slowly, so as not to gain his notice, Emily repositioned it on her arm. "What do you want, Nigel?"

"Can't a fellow just spend a bit of time with his sister?" He squeezed a little more, making her bend her neck and tilt her head to try to relieve some of the pressure.

"You never have before."

"Ah! Listen to you." He released her so suddenly she nearly fell away from him, but then he pulled her in again. "As if I haven't taken you on *countless* adventures through the years."

She glanced at her three companions, who stood in a knot before them, clearly looking for an opening to save her. With a bit of luck, her eyes were shouting *Stay calm* and not *Do something drastic.* The last thing they needed was a scuffle that ended with the basket tumbling to the ground and spilling its contents.

She drew in a breath, slowly and steadily, so it could work its way past his arm. *Lord, please help us. Get us away from him. Please . . .*

A gust of wind blew in off the ocean, and another passage from the diary flitted through her mind and settled somewhere over her heart. *I do not know what is broken inside my husband, Lord. But I cannot mend it. That must fall to you. Mend his broken places, I beg you, so that he might be healed.*

It was as if the world went still—as if the sea stopped lapping the shore, the gulls stopped crying, the wind stopped trying to tease her hair from its pins.

He was broken. Her brother, whom she'd feared and hated all her life, was broken inside. She didn't know how it had happened or when, but it was undeniable.

And never once had she prayed that God catch him and mend him so that he could be whole. Happy. She'd only ever prayed that he'd stop making her miserable. That he be stopped, not that he be saved.

But God loved her brother. He loved him just as surely as He'd loved John Mucknell. As surely as He loved her or Beth or Libby or Mabena. He loved Nigel. And He wanted him to be whole. To be His.

The next breath she drew in tasted of honey. "What adventure were you going to take me on today?"

His arm eased off a little. It always did when she didn't fight. "I thought you'd like to join us on Gugh for a while, Emily."

Beth scoffed. "With you on Gugh—*that* always ends well."

Nigel pulled Emily back a step, away from the others. "I wasn't inviting you, Miss Tremayne. It's my sister whose presence has been requested. The American is quite eager to spend some time with you, sister dear . . . for some reason."

Vandermeer? Again? She may have doubted it, had Nigel not sounded so genuinely disgusted by the prospect.

But then, perhaps he had something to report already. It seemed unlikely that Nigel would have either slipped up or unburdened himself so quickly, but it was possible.

Beth had followed their single-step retreat. "And you're just his errand boy now? Oh, fitting. The rich American tugs the strings, and you dance along."

In general, Emily admired Beth's boldness, but how far did she really think she could push him before he snapped and they all paid the price? She widened her eyes and tried to send a silent warning.

From the way Libby bit her lip, *she* received it. And Mabena was edging around Beth like she was ready to tackle her cousin if necessary, to keep her from tackling Nigel. Beth herself, however, kept her focus on him.

"For that matter, why would you be helping him in *this*? Vandermeer is a decent chap and could make her happy. I didn't think you'd want that."

Nigel's laugh usually grated—just now, it stung. Because it acknowledged the truth of Beth's accusation. "Of *course* I want my sister to be happy. Why not seek it with . . . the American? Just think of all the adventures he could take her on. We'd probably never see her again, they'd be off gallivanting about so many places."

And there was Beth's answer. Emily shook her head. "Why do you hate me so?" She didn't mean to ask it, but it just slipped out. "You've always wanted to be rid of me . . . but why? What did I do?"

She expected him to deflect, to snap at her to shut up, to drag her toward whatever boat he'd used to get here.

Instead, he dropped his arm and turned to face her. "Because," he said, his voice strained, "you . . . *are*. And you always ruin everything.

Even this." His face was flushed, his eyes flashing as he swept a hand out toward Bryher. "I was supposed to be proving myself this summer, finally showing Father that I don't need him interfering with my every business decision. Instead, thanks to all of *you*"—this time his snarl encompassed them all—"he thinks me incapable of the simplest of tasks. And after that scene on Gugh, now all the trustees think I'm a fool. You've. Ruined. *Everything*."

Beth opened her mouth, but Emily shook her head. Perhaps a retort would feel satisfying in the moment, but Nigel was on the edge. She could see it in his eyes. One wrong word, and he could fly off the precipice of control. *Lord, calm him. Show him the better way. Help me, somehow, to love him as you do. To see him as you do.*

"You don't have anything to prove to them." The words emerged so quietly she couldn't be sure he'd even heard them. "Your value doesn't lie in their opinion of you."

Apparently, he did hear. He narrowed his eyes as if trying to find some hidden motivation in her statement.

Emily hitched the basket a bit higher onto her arm. "Nigel, you discovered an unknown Druid cairn! You speak four languages flawlessly and have mastered the Japanese fighting sports. You have dozens of friends, you can be entirely charming when you want to be, and you're one of the most intelligent people I know. If you feel you need accomplishments, you have them already."

Something shifted in his eyes. They still glinted with anger, but suddenly it wasn't directed at her, it seemed. "It's never enough, is it? It never will be. Even when I was just a lad, before you even came along—accomplishments were all that mattered."

To Father? To satisfy whatever demons chased him? Emily didn't know, but she shook her head. "It doesn't have to be that way. Because that's not how we're ultimately measured. God loves *you*, Nigel. Not what you discover or achieve."

His lip curled, no light chasing the shadows from his eyes. But one couldn't expect seeds to sprout up immediately. One could only plant them, water them, and pray the Lord would give an increase.

"You have clearly been spending too much time with that milksop of a vicar."

His gaze dropped to the basket on her arm.

She swore she could feel her friends' breath catch. See them all coil, ready to spring if necessary.

Please, God, she prayed again. But differently this time. *This treasure would only hurt him more, much like the artifact would. Protect him from it. From all of it.*

Nigel plucked the checkered cloth off the top of the basket and pulled out one of the scones nestled at the top. "I can detect these even over the sea. Are they as good as they smell?"

"Better." She gave him a small smile, a small nod. "Have it. We have more than we could possibly eat."

He took a bite then and there, laughing like a normal person when the light, flaky pastry crumbled around his mouth. "Delicious." Then he slanted a look at her. "Are you coming to Gugh or not?"

Her breath whooshed out. Never once had he given her a choice when he'd gotten it in his head to take her somewhere. She lifted the basket. "I'm afraid I already have plans. Perhaps Mr. Vandermeer could give me a bit more notice next time he issues an invitation?"

Nigel snorted in a way that made her wonder if he wouldn't, perhaps, enjoy disappointing the American that Father so wanted to please. "I'll deliver the message." He turned away, took one step, then said over his shoulder, "Father isn't going to like you declining the invitation. Don't say I didn't warn you."

No, he wouldn't. But what else could he possibly do?

11

Bram opted to roam the library of Mr. Gale, the vicar at St. Mary's, rather than take a seat with Sheridan and Oliver and the aging clergyman. The room wasn't all that large, but it was crammed full of books of every size, color, and topic. And the juxtaposition of titles was rather amusing. A book about the history of the circus alongside one about proper tooth care. A treatise on early church saints beside a novel set during the Battle of Hastings.

And a shelf dedicated to Lyonesse and any other stories that touched on it, hence the gentlemen's presence in Mr. Gale's amusing library tonight. He'd apparently been out paying a call of his own the other night when Beth and Sheridan attempted a visit but had invited them to come again whenever was convenient.

It had taken them all afternoon to dart around the islands, hiding their assigned bits of Mucknell treasure. Bram had been a bit grumpy about getting back in time for supper only to see that Lady Emily and Briggs had returned to St. Mary's already. He'd hoped to have a few minutes to spend with her when he was coherent so that he could subtly ask more questions to try to get at the truth of her shaky hands.

Her father had said a week ago that he wanted her to go hungry. Was that what was happening? She'd had a basket bursting with food that day . . . but all of it fresh produce. That wouldn't last long without cool storage. Did her flat have an icebox? Had she had pocket money enough for ice? He'd done his best to pay attention over the last week, but he hadn't seen nearly enough of her to have definitive answers on this score.

Why had she not stayed for supper if her resources were running thin? Maybe that meant she was fine, that it really had just been too much tea that morning.

But he couldn't get the question out of his head. And before they'd left for this visit with Mr. Gale, Mamm-wynn had given him the strangest look. What if the niggling wasn't just his own mind? What if it was God planting a concern?

If He'd led Bram to the fish market last Wednesday . . . if He'd led him and Libby to the beach just in time to spot the *Victoria* that night . . . why not also nudge him when Emily needed food?

Blast it all. This faith business was tricky. How was he to know what was God and what was his own mind? He'd had absolutely no practice discerning the difference over the years, and his own vicar preferred sermons on the most obscure Old Testament texts and on how unknowable the Lord was to anything actually helpful. But when each and every one of his friends had decided that matters of faith needed more attention, he would have to be a stubborn fool to refuse to look twice.

He slid a sloppily bound collection of papers from the shelf. It wasn't typeset and didn't look particularly old, though the paper had yellowed on the corners that stuck out randomly. The front cover—nothing but thin cardstock—had *On Lyonesse* scrawled across it in heavy ink, with *H. Gale* smaller at the bottom.

Bram glanced over at the vicar, who was coughing a bit as he lowered himself to a well-used armchair, a more tidily bound notebook in his hand. Apparently the old chap really had been collecting tales for decades. Not that he'd doubted it.

"This one ought to have some information you've not found otherwise yet, gentlemen." Mr. Gale reached for the spectacles lying on the table beside his chair and put them on, blinking a few times as the words presumably came into focus. "And that one Lord Telford has selected too. These two are my personal research, based on local oral accounts throughout Cornwall and a few obscure texts I came across in priories that I transcribed as best I could." His chuckle sounded raspy. "My Old English isn't perfect, I'm afraid, so there are a few places where I simply wrote out what the letters appeared to be. You'll have to puzzle through those on your own."

Sheridan shot Bram an amused look. "Old English, you say."

Bram sent his friend a glare, silently commanding him to keep his yap shut about Bram's proficiency with the language. It was far too closely linked to his intrigue with Arthurian tales for him to admit to publicly.

"We're grateful that you're willing to share your research with us," Oliver said before Sher could go spilling his secrets.

Mr. Gale chuckled again. "Willing? Goodness, lad, you know me. I'm thrilled anyone else cares!"

"I know exactly what you mean." And just as happily, Sheridan was easily distracted. "That is—Druids, you know. I've been researching them, and even my own sisters! Constantly changing the subject."

"Oh, but they're fascinating! Have you explored our cairnfields, my lord?"

On second thought, a seat sounded like just the thing. If Gale got Sheridan talking about Druids, they could be here all night. Bram settled into the remaining wingback and carefully turned to the first page of notes.

Across the top were the words *The Sinking of Lyonesse, Theory One*. He knew the basics, just from having been talking about it with the others and his own research into all things Round Table. That Lyonesse was a large island off the coast of Cornwall, ruled by a monarch of its own until England claimed it. Bram's own interest lay in that noble lineage of rulers, which had resulted in Sir Tristan, a rather gallant knight and the rightful heir to Lyonesse. Much like

Hamlet, though, his uncle had taken the throne instead. Tristan, too honorable to fight his own blood, ended up in Camelot.

He'd always been one of Bram's favorite knights—hence why he owned and had read three times the entire thirteen-volume set of *Prose Tristan*, as it was called, books detailing the impeccable character and many adventures of the prince-turned-knight. According to the *Prose*, Tristan had fallen in love with Isolde before his uncle ever decided to marry her. There had been no love potion involved, just his uncle's treachery. Tristan had been a knight of such strength and valor that he rivaled Lancelot. In fact, they had fulfilled one of Merlin's prophecies by dueling—though they'd come out of it as friends rather than injuring each other. It was then Lancelot's castle to which Tristan had run with Isolde, trying to save her from his uncle's vile ways.

All that was well before the sinking of Lyonesse, though. He read down through the page, lips pursed as he went.

This account placed the sinking firmly in the medieval era, centuries after Tristan had lived. There were no scientific theories about earthquakes or any other logical reason for the water level to have risen or the island to have sunk—though Libby insisted there must be one, if Lyonesse had indeed existed and now did not. This account was more a sort of Sodom-and-Gomorrah tale.

The people of Lyonesse had sunk into moral depravity. The story didn't detail what sort—just that their sins were so great that it stirred the wrath of the Almighty, and He sent punishment upon them in the form of a great wave that devoured the island whole, killing all the occupants. Wiping their stain off the face of the earth, as it were. The account ended by saying that fishermen still claimed to hear the tolling of submerged church bells around the Scillies, which had once been the highest points of the single great island and were now all that remained after the waters calmed.

Judgment—that was more the God he'd been taught about. Mysterious and firm and unrelenting. That wasn't the same God about whom Oliver preached, though. He spoke of a God who loved and forgave and offered mercy. Bram angled a gaze up at his sister's groom-to-be. He, too, was flipping through a book while Sheridan and Gale dissected the finer points of something Druid.

Bram tapped a finger to the page. "How do you reconcile this, Tremayne?"

"Hm?" Oliver looked up, slipping a finger in his page to mark it. "What am I reconciling?"

"The sinking of Lyonesse as heavenly judgment for their sins. Paints the picture of an angry, just God. Rather Old Testament. Where is the forgiveness?"

Oliver's lips twitched up. "Who's to say He didn't offer it? Over and again? That had they repented, the crisis would have been averted, like with Jonah and Nineveh?"

"So He takes the choice from them when they don't decide in time?" Bram flipped to the next page. *Focus on Trevelyan, Theory Two.* "We have limited opportunities, then, to turn from our wicked ways. That doesn't seem very merciful."

But Oliver's eyes laughed. "Well, we're all mortal, aren't we? We *will* die, and thereby run out of time. And whether it happens when we are ten or a hundred and ten, it is God who has those days numbered. We could *always* say He is the one who hands down our end, removing further opportunities. But . . ." Oliver closed the book over his finger and leaned forward, intent. "But I don't think that's looking at it quite right. That story aside, He has created a world of cause and effect. Actions and consequences. Sin comes with a set of consequences, but so does nature itself. Disasters simply *happen*, to the just and the unjust alike. The real proof of our mettle, I think, is how we react to them. Not whether we deserved them, but what we choose to do in their wake."

"Certainly, if we survive the tsunami." Bram skimmed the first few lines of the second tale, though he didn't really take them in. "But what of the innocents? The children? The cats and dogs? *They* hardly deserve such a fate, but they get swept up in it too."

Oliver chuckled. "Are you more concerned with the babes or the puppies?"

All right, perhaps he shouldn't have crammed them so close together. But he'd never quite forgiven his vicar for telling him when he was a lad of eight that his pets would not be allowed into heaven. Why would God have created such loyal creatures here on earth if He didn't intend to let them share in eternity? Heaven was said to have trees and lakes—seemed silly, if they were empty of animals. "I maintain that my dogs are better people than many people I know."

"Can't argue with you there." Which was why he liked Oliver so well. He may have as much theology as the next clergyman, but he didn't let it get in the way of being a well-humored chap. "As for why evil befalls innocents—that, my friend, is a question that has been pondered by far wiser minds than my own. I cannot give you a reason. Only the comfort of knowing that He gathers those innocents to himself, just as He does the faithful. And though we may mourn them, they are happier with Him than they could have been here."

It made him think of the letter from Morgan that he'd transferred to each new jacket as Collins pulled one out for him. Not that Morgan Tremayne had died as a child too young to have learned right from wrong—but he *had* learned. And had died too young. Had known all his life that it was coming for him . . . but still he'd chosen to embrace faith. And life. And adventure.

Not to mention that the fact that Oliver had lost his brother and parents all within such a short time meant he wasn't just speaking hypothetically. He knew pain. Loss. But he chose to believe they were better off.

Bram had been debating for days when and how to show Oliver the letter. Now seemed as good a time as any. Pursing his lips, he reached into his inner pocket and pulled it out. Extended it. "Speaking of being happier . . . you'll want to see this. I found it in a hidden compartment in the bookcase in my room when I was searching for a runaway cuff link."

It took only a moment for the implications of that to ignite a spark in Oliver's eye. Setting his book aside, he leaned across the distance between them and snatched the paper. "From Morgan?" Even as he asked it, he was unfolding the sheet and likely recognizing the hand.

Still, Bram nodded. "The envelope said 'To the Finder,' so I opened it."

Oliver's lips curved into a smile. "It's just like him to do something like that. Both to create a secret compartment and to fill it with something for a stranger. He wrote letters to all of us before he died, you know, and left them in Mamm-wynn's care. I haven't reread mine for months. I should get it out again."

For now, though, he read the one in his hand. Bram watched his smile ebb and flow, tinged always with that bittersweet expression that came of missing someone you loved so dearly. When he'd finished, he sat there staring at it for a long moment before refolding it and holding it back out.

Bram curled his fingers against the notebook to keep from reaching for it. "You can keep it. It's from your brother."

Oliver's eyes had that knowing gleam in them—the one that said he knew how much Bram wanted that letter back in his own pocket. "Yes, but it isn't for me. It's for you. I do appreciate you letting me read it, though. And I know Beth would appreciate seeing it, too, if you would share it with her as well."

"I will." He let his fingers reach now, take it again, slip it back into its happy home. "He was clearly a remarkable young man. It's no wonder you miss him so."

Oliver nodded, his eyes focused on nothing—or perhaps on the past. "He was. And I have asked myself countless times why God didn't heal him, didn't give us longer with him. But I think . . . I think perhaps Morgan is loving us even better from heaven than he could do on earth. He is reunited with our parents, and I have no doubt that the three of them, in all their worship of the Lord in the heavenly courts, continue to pray for us there as they did here." He blinked, refocused on Bram. "And perhaps that's what all the innocents who are called to heaven do."

"So that's the mercy behind these stories of divine punishments?"

Oliver shrugged. "You're assuming the ascribed reason is true. I would be more apt to say they're simply part of the tragic tale invented by storytellers centuries later to make a good story."

"Lizza Mucknell certainly thought it true." How many times in that diary had she said something about the sea swallowing people for their sins? Her greatest fear was that her husband would suffer the same fate as Lyonesse.

And he had, come to think of it. He'd vanished in the Caribbean. Perhaps not swallowed by the sea so much as slain by a Vandermeer, but it was the direct result of his seafaring . . . and his sins.

"She did. It makes for a compelling tale, you have to admit." Oliver opened his book again.

"If one likes tragedy and divine vengeance."

"Oh, but it isn't just the divine vengeance that has kept that legend alive, my lord!" Mr. Gale wagged a finger at Bram. Or perhaps at the notes he held. Apparently he and Sher had solved all the mysteries of the Druids already. "It's the role of nobility amidst depravity. You'll be quite interested in the account of Trevelyan, I think."

Bram returned his gaze to the page and its mention of that name. It sounded vaguely familiar. Elizabeth Mucknell had used it at some point, too, but only in a vague reference to "interceding like Trevelyan." Whatever she meant by that. "Who was he?"

"Local name, isn't it? To Cornwall, I mean?" Sheridan stood and came to look over Bram's shoulder. "There was someone or another with that name while we were in Penzance."

"Quite right. It's the Trevelyan families and their Vyvyan branch who told me the story of their ancestor. You'll note the coat of arms I sketched on the next page. It comes directly from the tale of Trevelyan—one of the few survivors of Lyonesse and, some say, its last governor."

Bram obligingly flipped the page to see the sketch the vicar had done of the family crest. Three horseshoes. "Was he somehow saved by his horse throwing a shoe?"

"Close." Mr. Gale picked up a pipe from the table, though there was no tobacco or matches at hand. He seemed more interested in gesturing with it than smoking it, anyway. "He was on the mainland for a hunt, riding his famed white horse—you'll also see a family crest there featuring the head of the white steed. Anyway, he paused for a rest under a tree but was awakened by the noise of a storm so terrible that he feared for his life. He jumped back on his horse and away they went, toward higher ground. The horse threw a shoe but still managed to get him to safety, and just in time. A terrible wave soon struck the coast, cutting away part of Cornwall . . . and all of Lyonesse aside from the peaks of the hills. The whole island gone in the course of one night, one storm."

Bram had flipped back to the first page of the story to follow along, though Sheridan now leaned over and tried to turn the page again. Having learned ages ago which battles to fight on this particular front, Bram relegated himself to simply holding it and let Sher flip at will. He looked over at their host, who clearly knew all about it anyway. "Where does the nobility come in?"

"Trevelyan, I expect," Sher answered. "Would have been why. He was spared, I mean. Right?"

"Exactly so." Mr. Gale hooked the unlit pipe in his mouth. At Bram's amused glance, he explained, "My physician said the pipe may be making my cough worse. Told me to stop smoking it—but I don't know what to do with my hands if I don't have it nearby."

Oliver had set aside the book he'd been paging through and now leaned back with a thoughtful look on his face. "There's a line in a manuscript we've come across that says Trevelyan interceded—for the people of Lyonesse, do you think?"

"P'haps," Mr. Gale said around the pipe, then used it to point again. "There were mixed stories about that—I've written them all out—but trying to find the kernel of truth in them all is a bit tricky. Assuming it's even there. Some say he was a descendant of Tristan himself, not just a governor but of the kingly line. Others say he wasn't a native of the island at all, but of a saintly mainland line, and he had tried but failed to bring civility and morality to them. Most agree that he had been spared by heaven—that the fate of the island came upon them that day particularly because he wasn't there. And that he was so crushed at his failure to save them that he never even returned to see what, if anything, had survived but instead settled in Cornwall."

Mr. Gale shrugged. "Others, though, say they found his boat where it had washed up into a tree and rode the wave out as it ebbed so that he could save any who hadn't been killed already. I fancy that one, personally. Much nobler."

Certainly more in line with chivalric tales, if one were going to claim he was of Tristan's line. "Did anyone give dates?" Bram asked.

Mr. Gale laughed. "A different one for each variation. Some place it during Tristan's day, and say it was he who was spared the fate when he was in Camelot, not Trevelyan at all. Others place it around 1099 or perhaps 1089—I couldn't quite make out the writing, and no one else seems to be able to either."

"The sinking isn't present in any Arthurian legends." When Sher angled the notebook toward himself, Bram gave up entirely and handed it to him before he decided to use Bram's head as an armrest. It had happened before. "That leads me to believe it wasn't during Tristan's day."

"This says a crime." Sheridan perched on the nearest thing at hand that resembled a chair—but was in fact another side table— and didn't even look up from the text. "That the people of Lyonesse committed, that is. But not what."

"That's the curious thing. Nothing mentions what. Not that I've been able to dig up."

"Fascinating."

His hands now empty, Bram rested his chin on one. "So the people did something horrendous. Trevelyan, of noble blood and with all the virtues that were assumed to go along with it at the time, pleaded with them to repent. And, if we're to believe our source, tried to intercede with God on their behalf." He shot a look at Oliver to see if he was interpreting that "intercede" correctly, that Trevelyan was thought to do on earth what Oliver hoped his own family was still doing from heaven.

Oliver nodded. "But they apparently didn't repent, if we're crediting the motivations. And so God sent a terrible storm."

"And a tidal wave or tsunami or the like—apparently enough of one that it never fully receded, since you now have a chain of small islands instead of one large one." Bram tapped a finger against his chin. "When was it resettled, then? As the Isles of Scilly?"

Their host chuckled. "Too many theories about that as well, especially if you ask the scientific community instead of storytellers. It wouldn't have been long, regardless. There are records and ruins on these islands from every era."

Sheridan rustled another page. "And some say it wasn't Lyonesse at all?" He tapped a sentence at the top of the page. "That it was closer to the mainland."

"Aye, but the mainland was farther out then, don't forget. The floodwaters stole part of Cornwall too. Or such is my theory. I've done more research on the question than most, and I'm fully convinced we're sitting on the remains of Tristan's kingdom."

Perhaps it was just because he *wanted* to be convinced, but Bram was inclined to agree. "I'm perfectly willing to accept you as the authority on the subject, Mr. Gale."

The old gent grinned at him. "Knew I liked you, my lord. You lads are welcome to borrow my collection, if you like. Too much to look through in just one evening, and while I'd certainly be happy to have you back anytime, it would be more convenient for you to take what you need."

"That's very generous of you, sir. Thank you." Oliver stood and walked over to the Lyonesse shelf. "You've proven yourself a veritable treasure trove of information."

Bram bit back a smile at the choice of words.

He was still thinking over all the stories and legends when he walked the beach under the stars that night. Tristan, Trevelyan, sinking islands, rising waters . . . and somehow, somewhere, an artifact. That was the part that still puzzled him. What was it Elizabeth Mucknell had found? And did Nigel Scofield really have any more of a clue than the rest of them?

She'd said it had been King Arthur's, but that she'd found it here on the islands. That surely meant it had arrived via Tristan. What had Arthur given to him?

He couldn't think of a single thing that legend said had been bestowed upon him, not that would be clearly identifiable as Arthur's. He could be forgetting something, though. He needed his books . . . and said a prayer that whatever information they needed would be in them and not only in whatever archives Nigel had accessed while he was in London.

A particularly ambitious wave hissed its way up the beach and soaked his shoes, but Bram didn't mind. He stood still for a moment and let it suck away some of the sand from under his feet. The sand would replace itself with the next wave, that's how it worked. Ebb and flow. Wax and wane. High tides and low.

Good and bad. Give and take. Joy and sorrow.

He drew in a long, salty breath and tilted his head back. The galaxies stretched out above him, like someone had flung a million diamonds out across the heavens. Had Tristan stood in this very place centuries ago? If so, it wouldn't have been beach at the time. It could have been a field, a farm—his family's palace, even. But he still would have been looking up at the same sky, the same stars. Perhaps he'd stood here, on what would have been a hill in his day, and dreamt of Isolde, the Irish princess who had stolen his heart.

It seemed the ancient tales of love were always bittersweet. There were no happy endings, not really. He lowered his head again to watch the moonlight dance on the waves. Hopefully his sister's story would be better with Oliver. And Sheridan's with Beth. They didn't have the entanglements of kingdoms to run and evil enchantresses, so there was that working in their favor.

His lips tugged up into a grin. By comparison, the Scofields and Vandermeer were altogether tame.

But that just made him think of Emily again, which spurred his feet back into motion. What could he do to make sure she was well? Slip money under her door? That would be the simplest means, despite it feeling terribly impersonal. But that could be good, really. He didn't want her to know it was him helping—then she'd realize he knew about her father. And if she wanted everyone to know about his ultimatum, she would have said something.

Money, then, or even a basket of food. Though the money would be easier to slip to her without anyone seeing what he was doing.

How was he going to manage that part at all? Blasted islands. Not only were they too small when it came to trying to avoid her family, they were surrounded by water, and he didn't have a boat of his own. He'd have to find an excuse for Oliver to take him back to St. Mary's tomorrow—or today, if one counted one's days by the clock instead of by when one slept and awoke.

Water and sand were squishing in his shoes and rubbing his ankles with every step, respectively. And Collins would then accuse him of being Sheridan, leaving sullied shoes all about for the valets to clean.

He turned to the nearest path from beach to village. It was time to go in anyway. Another hour and the sky would begin to lighten, the stars to fade. Fishermen would be whistling their way to their boats, ready to sail before the sun fully crested the horizon. Often he stayed out and talked to them, exchanging jokes and weather predictions and their thoughts on how the fish were running. Getting to know the people who would be his sister's neighbors, that was all.

He didn't feel up for it tonight, though, not with Emily still weighing on his mind. And Tristan. And Trevelyan. And—

Yip! Yip!

His foot paused on the first step from sand to cobblestone. His ears strained for the next little bark. There was no shortage of dogs on Tresco—other than in the Tremayne house—but that one had sounded close, and most people kept them indoors at night.

There, he heard it again. Not from someone's garden or coming through an open window, but from the tall grasses he'd just waded through. Bram crouched down and held his hands out, palms extended. He gave a low whistle. "Here, pup. Here."

Another yip, and a whimper to go along with it. Bram searched the grasses, wishing for a torch to help him tell what was plant and what might be animal, and finally caught sight of a little nose peeking out. He smiled but moved no closer. Not yet. "There you are. It's all right. Are you lost? Come on out, I won't hurt you."

The nose edged out a little farther, so that two small eyes joined it, and then a set of bedraggled ears in need of a good brushing. He couldn't resist a laugh but kept it low and even. "Hello there. Aren't you sweet? And tiny. You must be a baby, isn't that right? Come on, now." He rubbed his fingers together, though he had nothing to offer.

The puppy came to investigate, though, tail wagging. And ribs visible under his matted coat. Poor little thing. It couldn't be much past weaning age, if at all. "Where's your mum, little one?" Slowly, lightly, he ran his fingertips over the puppy's back. "And your littermates? Or were you the runt, perhaps? Hm?"

In lieu of an answer, the puppy rolled onto its back and panted happily up at him. Bram chuckled and gave its—his, apparently—belly an obliging rub. "Good boy. Are you all alone? Hungry? I bet Mrs. Dawe has a few morsels in the kitchen that would be just perfect for a growing pup like you. Want to come with me?"

The pup licked his hand.

"All right, then. I think perhaps you'd better let me carry you. My legs are a bit longer than yours, even taking into account that you have twice as many." He urged him back onto his paws and then scooped him up.

Tristan—because what other name could he possibly give him?—thanked him with a lick on the chin that made him laugh again. "All right, all right. I think it's safe to assume I'm not stealing you from anyone. You couldn't have got quite this thin or bedraggled in a day or two. But we'll ask about tomorrow, just in case."

He secured Tristan against him with one hand and used the other to stroke his head and keep him calm. His fur was light-colored, on the long side, absent true curl but with a bit of wave. Given that and the shape of his muzzle, Bram had to guess he was some sort of Labrador retriever or a mix that included it. That meant he'd be friendly. Faithful. And fearsome, too, when the situation demanded. As any good knight of the Round Table should be.

"Do you want to be a guard dog, Tristan? I know a lady who could use one."

He decided to take the next little yip as affirmation.

A few minutes later, he'd let himself into the Tremayne kitchen and set Tristan down so that he could light a lamp. The pup was sniffing hither and yon, tail wagging like the seagrass in the wind. Bram turned to the icebox—something he did most nights, to be honest. They'd had chicken for supper, and sure enough, Mrs. Dawe had tucked the remainder away. He pulled out the dish, set it on the table, and found a small plate to move a portion of it to.

Tristan gave a happy yip and tucked in the moment he put it on the floor.

Bram grinned. And then didn't. The puppy would soon be satiated and would quickly learn that he didn't have to fear for his next meal.

But Lady Emily couldn't say the same, and that just wouldn't do. With a resolute huff, he turned to inspect the rest of the larder. Mrs. Dawe wouldn't mind if he liberated enough to make a breakfast—and he'd restock her shelves himself as soon as the shops opened.

By the time Tristan licked the last of the chicken from his plate, Bram had filled a sack with the essentials and slid a few coins into the offering too. Then he scooped up the puppy again. "Come on, Tris. We're going in search of a fisherman."

12

Seagulls made excellent alarm clocks . . . even when one didn't particularly desire an alarm. Emily blinked her eyes open, noted the golden light of morning spilling through the window, and couldn't remember, for one blissfully long moment, why she'd been dreading the day and had wanted to sleep through as much of it as possible. Then it hit her.

Today would be their first full day without food.

It isn't an emergency. That's what Tommie kept saying, and what Emily repeated to herself now. They didn't need to eat every single day. A meal every other would be sufficient. And it wouldn't be for all that long. Father would relent. Or God would provide in some other way. Or Emily would simply swallow the last vestiges of her pride and confess to her friends how little her family loved her.

Drat. She tried to make it a policy never to cry before she even got out of bed, and yet here she lay with stinging eyes. How pathetic did that make her? Beth would never give way to such ridiculous emotions; she'd simply view it as an adventure and relish the chance to prove herself. Libby was far too practical and scientifically minded to be given to tears at all. Mabena Moon was more likely to leap from her bed and storm out like a tempest, ready to right all the wrongs herself.

171

"Chin up, Emily." She dragged in a deep breath that she told herself was fortifying and pushed to a sitting position. This was an opportunity, that was all. Either for the Lord to provide or for her to build her character.

She dug her fingers into the soft cotton of the sheet and stared at where the wall met the floor across from her. *Thank you, Lord, that we've already paid for this flat through the end of September. Thank you that we have friends who will take care of us, even when they don't know what they're doing. Thank you for all the years you supplied my needs when I didn't even stop to think about it. And thank you for showing me now how much I still have even when I lack some things, and how much I've always had.*

That was surely a lesson everyone should learn. She would never again take for granted the privileges of wealth. She would never again assume that just because she'd always had enough, that meant she always would—or even deserved to simply because she was a lady.

Tides could change in a twinkling of the eye.

She stood and reached for her wrapper, wanting its security more than the added warmth. Last night she'd told Tommie her goal of sleeping late and encouraged her to do the same, so the flat had that quiet quality that she'd experienced only rarely in her life, where the space seemed to echo with silence. It was lovely. She breathed it in and kept her footsteps silent as she padded into the main room. She would read her Bible. Perhaps write down her reflections, like Elizabeth Mucknell had done. Revisit for the twentieth time the new copy of the diary that Mr. Gibson had given her after Nigel's theft to see if anything new jumped out. Read one of the novels she'd brought with her. Once Tommie arose, they'd have a cup of tea.

She glanced around the cozy space as she entered, her gaze snagging on a square of white on the floor just inside the door. Paper, but she couldn't think what slip of it they could have dropped for it to land there.

Perhaps it was a note from their landlady. Mrs. Gilligan had slid one under their door on two other occasions—once to let them know she would be on the mainland for a few days and who to contact if they needed any assistance, and once to remind them of a concert in Maypole that they'd expressed interest in attending.

She took a step toward it, then stopped, a sudden fear rendering her motionless. Mrs. Gilligan had converted this space as a flat for her daughter and coming grandchild, who had just been born. It had been available for Emily to let only because the daughter had instead stayed on the mainland. But what if she'd just changed her mind? What if Mrs. Gilligan needed them to vacate the premises immediately? What if she was about to be not only without food, but without a roof over her head?

"Father God," she whispered into the room, eyes squeezing shut. But she couldn't even put words to the bone-deep plea.

For a long moment she stood like that. But ignorance of it wouldn't change the fact of whatever that piece of paper held. It was better to know. So, she peeled her eyes open again and strode over to the door. Bent, picked up the paper, and flipped it open.

She frowned at the script—not Mrs. Gilligan's simple, neat hand, but ornate calligraphy that looked nearly medieval, like the illuminated manuscripts she'd seen in the museum.

A small token of esteem for the ladies awaits thy fair hand on the other side of the portal.

There was no signature, just that odd sentence.

Emily lowered the note, staring at the door warily. It could be a trick. She wouldn't put it past Nigel to try to lure her outside with a gift and then . . . do something horrible. Or to have left something very un-gift-like at her door.

On the other hand, it could be something from Vandermeer, who'd have had no trouble discovering where she was staying. She wouldn't put it past the American to try something so overstated, since she'd refused his invitation to join him on Gugh yesterday.

Well, that would be harmless enough. And perhaps he'd left something she could sell or exchange for food.

That was enough to make her throw caution to the wind and open the door, gaze dropping immediately to the basket sitting there at the top step. She picked it up, stepped back inside with it, and flipped open the cover.

"Oh!" Not from Vandermeer—it couldn't be. How would he know that the sweetest gift in the world would be a loaf of bread, half a dozen eggs, a small jar of milk, and some cheese? It was far too mundane for him.

And yet the most extravagantly perfect thing. A sob caught in her throat, and she leaned on the door to close it, sliding to the floor so she could sift through the offering. Eggs had never looked so beautiful, their brown shells practically glowing. And the bread! She raised it to her nose and sniffed.

Then something shiny caught her eye, and she moved the cheese aside to reveal a handful of coins and two pound notes.

Footsteps sounded from the direction of the bedrooms. "My lady! What is it? Are you all right?"

She looked up through watery eyes to see Tommie rushing toward her, still in her nightdress, her fair brown hair in a frazzled braid.

Emily held up the bread and eggs. "Someone left us food. And money! We can buy more once the shops open."

Tommie dropped to the floor beside her. "Who could have known?"

Emily could only shake her head.

"It must have been one of the Tremaynes." Tommie took the bread from her and turned it over in her hands. "This looks like one of Mrs. Dawe's loaves."

She could tell one person's bread from another? Oh, what did it even matter? They could eat! "Perhaps Mamm-wynn heard the Lord's whisper and told someone to bring it." She blinked her eyes clear and laughed. "Let's find someone to sail us over. I bet if we surprise them, we'll see something telling in our benefactor's face, whoever it is."

Tommie grinned. "Oughtn't we to eat it first?"

"We could just take some bread and cheese with us." Because if it was Beth, or even Oliver, who'd somehow known and provided, then she needed to subtly let them know that their gift had been sent by God himself.

"All right." Tommie scrambled to her feet and held out a hand to help Emily do the same. They made quick work of putting the supplies in the kitchen, slicing enough bread and cheese to satisfy their stomachs, and hurrying into clothes and chignons. Soon they were all but skipping their way down to the quay, where there was always a local lounging about, ready to play tour guide or ferryman to another island for a few pence.

The wind tasted particularly sweet that morning as they sailed through it, and the water shone like emeralds and sapphires, with diamonds topping the waves. The circling birds were a symphony and a circus all at once, their acrobatics making her smile.

And then they were on Tresco, and the friendly local waved away the precious coins she held out, saying he'd been coming this direction anyway. And then she and Tommie were climbing the hill into Grimsby.

"When do you think they even came by?" she whispered as they passed by the first house. "There was nothing there last night when we locked up."

"And it's barely morning yet," Tommie agreed with a yawn that reminded Emily they hadn't taken the time for tea. "Which does narrow it down a bit. Or perhaps they'd only just left it, in which case we may be able to tell based on who looks as though they've been up and out already."

An excellent point. She wished she'd thought to inspect the *Adelle* and the *Naiad* when they were at the quay. Perhaps one of them would have looked more freshly sailed than the other . . . whatever that would mean.

They'd never arrived at the Tremayne house this early, but she'd stayed overnight with Beth enough times that she didn't feel entirely odd letting herself in through the back garden and toward the kitchen door. Some of the household may well be asleep yet, but Mrs. Dawe would be there without question.

It could even have been the Dawes, come to think of it. Mrs. Dawe had an eagle eye, and Senara the most nurturing spirit.

Tommie reached the door first, tapped a warning on the glass, but then turned the knob without waiting for a response. Emily followed behind her—and nearly plowed into her back when she came to an abrupt halt with a loud "Oh! Hello there!"

A happy, high bark sounded, pulling Emily to the side so she could see what in the world was going on.

A veritable party, that was what. Every single resident was sitting or standing or kneeling in the kitchen while a small golden puppy bounced back and forth from one adoring fan to another, wagging its tail madly all the while.

Emily slid quickly inside, nudging Tommie ahead to make room, and then shut the door behind her so the pup couldn't escape.

"Good morning! Look what Telford's found." Grinning, Beth slid over to her side, laughing when the dog chased her. She was still in her dressing gown, house slippers on her feet instead of shoes.

She hadn't been their benefactor, or else had changed back into her nightclothes and somehow uncombed her hair.

Emily smiled down at the puppy. "He's adorable. Or she?"

"He." Telford was sitting cross-legged on the floor beside a tub of filthy-looking water that had soaked his shirtfront too. "That, my lady, is Sir Tristan—your new guard dog. I found him whimpering in the seagrass last night before bed."

"Mine?" She hadn't had a dog of her own in years—and Poppy hadn't really started out as hers. Nigel had just grown annoyed with her and foisted her upon Emily. She bent down and extended a hand. Tristan waggled his way over and licked her palm. She couldn't help but laugh. "He's a little darling."

"Ferocious, you mean. Terrifying. He'll rip to shreds anyone who dares try to harm you. Isn't that right, Tris?"

Tristan ran clumsily over to Telford in that precious way puppies did when their paws were too big for the rest of them. Poor little thing, his ribs were visible under his damp fur.

From his seat at the table, Lord Sheridan snorted a laugh. "What did I tell you, darling? Only a matter of time. Before he found a pup or a pup him, that is."

Beth's slippers crossed in front of Emily as she made her way toward Sheridan. "I never doubted you. And it looks like he found him in the nick of time too. Though it's rather funny, isn't it? Your sister found a kitten in need of saving, my lord, and you a puppy."

Telford was tousling the puppy's ears, looking utterly content. And surprisingly coherent, given the hour. He glanced over at Emily. "You do like dogs, I hope."

He really meant for Tristan to be hers? Her chest went tight. She didn't have the means to take care of a dog just at the moment. And she could hardly let such a golden ball of joy, already malnourished, scrounge the alleyways for his meals, could she? No matter how dearly she wanted to cuddle him to her and call him her own. "Very much. Only, I don't know how to train one, and I probably—"

"Oh, I'll handle that part, if you can wait a few weeks to take full possession." Telford laughed and leaned away when Tristan made a licking lunge for his face. "I'll make a positively fearsome guard dog of him, one to rival even Abbie's Lancelot."

"Who he also trained." Sheridan's voice was all dry humor. "To give you an example, my lady. Of what sort of guard dog he creates."

The kind that was all wagging tails, lolling tongues, and joyful licks? Just the kind she wanted. A fuzzy companion, someone to love her blindly and be content simply to be with her. And surely, in a few more weeks, her current situation would have sorted itself out.

"This one will end up a good deal larger than Lance, I think. He's already nearly the same size and is still just a baby." Telford pulled the puppy into his lap and nudged at his lips, seemingly inspecting his teeth, though Emily hadn't a clue why. Did that tell him his age? His future size?

"I do like big dogs. Poppy—I had her when I was a girl—was enormous. She was a mastiff."

"Good." Tristan still in his arms, Telford stood. "Are you up for a walk, my lady? I think he could use one, before he makes a whole other kind of mess on Mrs. Dawe's floors. And we want him to get used to you as quickly as possible."

"Lovely." She stood, too, only then remembering that she'd meant to inspect the Tremaynes and Dawes for evidence of their having been out already. She glanced around.

Oliver leaned against the wall, dressed for the day but still looking rather drowsy, and with bare feet. And both of the Dawe ladies were up to their elbows in dough that they had no doubt begun earlier. Unlikely, then, that it had been them.

She looked again at Beth, but her friend's grin held nothing particularly secretive. And she very much looked like she'd just tumbled out of bed, likely when she heard the commotion of bathing the puppy.

"Ready?" Telford and the squirming Tristan were at her side.

Emily nodded. If the Lord wanted to provide mysteriously, that was fine too. She'd be grateful for the blessing. No need to dissect it. She opened the door and stepped outside. "Do we have a lead for him?"

"Not yet, nor a collar. I'll see about that later today. But I don't think he's going to run too far from us—and even if he tries, he's still weak from his ordeal." Telford bent down and placed the puppy on the ground.

Tristan took off to sniff some plants, tail still thrumming. It was only then that Emily thought to spin on Telford, eyes wide. "Wait—you're speaking, and it's before noon!"

Not only speaking, but laughing, too, his eyes gleaming instead of groggy. "All credit goes to Tristan. There's nothing quite like a puppy, is there?"

When he offered his elbow, she looped her arm through it. "Nothing in the world."

Tommie didn't mean to end up in the quiet sanctuary of St. Nicholas's church, but her feet had pulled her that way when she decided to take advantage of the beautiful morning and go for a walk. She'd slipped in through tall wooden doors, into the shadowed entryway, and then followed the slanting of colored light from the stained-glass windows to a pew. She had the time, given that Lady Emily was still out in the garden with the puppy after returning from her own walk.

The breath she drew in filled her with gratitude. The one she let out made her shoulders sag in relief. She leaned forward until she could rest her head against the wood of the pew in front of her. It was cool, solid, unmoving. Like so little in life had been lately.

A reminder of what God always was.

Thank you. They were paltry words, but the only ones she had. She'd thought . . . she honestly didn't know what she'd thought would happen. That they'd go hungry today. Perhaps even tomorrow. And that feeling her stomach tighten would quickly make Emily decide to just admit to her friends what her father had done—she'd thought it would be resolved soon, but not before they suffered a bit more.

She'd already been planning how to comfort the lady when it was time to admit defeat. She'd assure her the Tremaynes would be glad to help, and they couldn't possibly be as bad off as she seemed to fear. Tommie had made a point of paying attention over the last week, and Mrs. Dawe never cut any corners in her food preparation, as a good housekeeper would if she'd been given a tight budget to work with. And none of these fine, kind people would judge *her* for her father's behavior.

They certainly wouldn't see his opinion of her and decide to change their own. But that had to be part of Emily's fear. It had to be, because it was part of Tommie's.

That they'd see how little Nigel Scofield had decided she was worth and treat her the same way.

But the Lord had surprised her. Just for Emily's sake? Tommie didn't think so. She'd gone to bed last night nearly afraid to pray, had awoken in the middle of the night with that same terrible nightmare that it was happening all over again, that she could feel his hot breath, his hand clamped over her mouth. And she'd buried her face in her pillow and cried, "Lord, take it! Give me something better, if you really love me."

And then she'd awoken to bread and eggs and milk and cheese and money. An answer to Emily's prayer, most assuredly. But to hers too. Because it reminded her that He was bigger than her pain. Bigger than her troubles. Able to make manna fall from heaven in the middle of her desert.

"Ollie, that you?"

She sat upright at the voice, spinning on the hard wooden seat. The sunlight from outside cast the newcomer framed in the doorway in silhouette, but she still had no trouble recognizing Enyon. And her heart gave a little stutter—part joy and part a resurgence of that fear. How could she both want to be in his company and fear it? "I'm afraid not."

"Ah, Thomasina." He let the door fall shut behind him and came up the aisle, looking every bit as comfortable here as he had in his mam's shop, swiping his hat off his head as he came. "I saw the door closing a minute ago and made an assumption, but this is even better." He grinned and slid into the pew behind her.

Gracious. Shouldn't flirting not be allowed in church? She didn't know whether to smile back or look away. "I won't tell him you said so."

He chuckled. "I don't imagine he'd argue, given that he certainly prefers our lady's company above anyone's."

He seemed so at ease, so confident here in his world. So friendly. But how much of that would change if he knew what Nigel had done?

Yes, she understood all too well Lady Emily's fear that others' opinions would twist to reflect her father's. If they knew . . . if they knew how little value someone else had put on her—if this good, strong island man knew how little Tommie had been worth in the eyes of Nigel Scofield—then surely he'd see it too. Whatever defect she must have inside that made Nigel treat her that way. Whatever weakness, whatever ugliness, whatever failing. Given enough time, Enyon would see, and he would sneer, and that same look would flash through his eyes that had flashed through Nigel's.

He would know she was worthless.

She angled her gaze away. Flirting aside, he hadn't come here looking for her. He'd come seeking his best friend. "I believe he's at home, if you truly need him, helping to roll up all the rugs. Lord Telford found a puppy and brought him home."

Enyon laughed, and in light of the sound, it was hard to keep her gaze away from him. And impossible not to feel again the joy that had brought her here. "He's been threatening as much all summer. Ollie won't mind—he loves dogs. They've had them off and on all our lives, just happens they were in an 'off' stretch after good ol' Solomon died, then their parents and Morgan. I don't think he had the heart to take in one more creature he was sure to outlive."

The same reason her mam hadn't wanted another dog after Tad died. She nodded. "He says he means the pup for Lady Emily, though he currently seems the least likely guard dog I've ever met."

He leaned forward to rest his arms on the back of her pew. "And is that what has your eyes so bright today? The thought of a puppy?"

"No." She leaned back, and with him leaning forward, it meant their faces were but a foot apart. And he was looking at her as if seeing that light in her eyes gave him the greatest happiness. She pressed her nails into her palm, trying to convince herself to hold her tongue. And then gave up. Because this wasn't about her, nor about whether he had any reason to flirt with her. This was about the Lord's goodness, and she simply couldn't stay silent about it.

"No, I'm happy because the Lord is so faithful. I—we—Lady Emily's father cut her off. We were out of money, out of food. But someone brought us supplies this morning, and money for more, despite that we've said nothing to anyone. If ever I doubted that there were angels . . ."

Enyon straightened, his smile freezing and his eyes going wide. "You—but why did you say nothing? We'd all be happy to help, every one of us!"

"I know." Because he seemed more agitated than she'd have thought, she reached up and settled her fingers over his on the pew back. "It was hers to tell, I thought. Her pride that had already taken such a thrashing. And we knew help was only a sail away."

"Not even. You can go to Mam's shop anytime, she'd delight in helping." He moved his other hand atop hers, sandwiching her fingers between his. "That's really why you were asking after work."

A miscalculation, that hand on the pew. His fingers felt as heavy as an anchor dragging her down . . . and yet, at the same time, warm. Promising.

Oh, why did she have to be such a mass of contradiction inside? Why could she not simply enjoy the company of a kind young man, relish the handsomeness of his smile, dream of his deep eyes and the thick dark hair that was flattened amusingly from his cap?

She had to drop her gaze from his, but she forced herself to leave her fingers there, under his. To prove to herself that his touch was meant to give comfort, not to take anything from her. "Don't mention anything to anyone, will you? It would hurt Emily if they all knew how little her father thinks of her."

He pressed her fingers but then lifted his away. "You have my word. And since we're speaking of eating—my sister, the one who lives on Bryher? She's planning a family dinner for everyone in the next week or two. I thought . . . perhaps you'd like to join us?"

Her breath caught. He was inviting her to a family dinner? That seemed like a bit more than just flirting in church or buying her a sandwich from Polmers'. That indicated an interest deeper than just enjoying their random encounters.

That was the sort of thing that meant courtship. Secret-sharing. Confessing.

"Why?" She didn't mean to ask it, but the question slipped out. Why would he want that with her? She was nothing—nothing to grab anyone's attention. She never had been, and she certainly wasn't now.

But when Enyon Thorne settled that dark-eyed gaze of his on her face, it didn't feel anything like Nigel's gaze had. There was nothing demanding. Nothing selfish. Nothing dismissive.

His smile now was small and serious. "Growing up," he said softly, "I was always the lad most likely to be spooked by Mr. Gibson's ghost stories—a fact that Ollie and our other friends exploited time and again, mind you."

She let herself smile at that, though she had no idea how this was an answer to her question.

His eyes wandered the church, though it must be as familiar to him as everything else on the islands. Still, there was reverence on his face as he took it all in. "But I think one of the reasons Ollie and I always got on so well is that we both look for the unseen as much as the seen. It's what led him to the church. And despite his teasing, it's not just what makes me jump at noises in the night." He paused here to grin up at the cross behind the altar. "It's what makes me look for the sculpture in a piece of driftwood on the beach or an arrangement of colorful shells. My tas always calls it nonsense, but it isn't. It can't be."

"Beauty among the everyday?" Was that what he saw in her? Just a normal, common woman who he could accept the challenge of finding something pretty in?

But that didn't seem quite right, not when he looked back over at her as he did. "No, Thomasina. The extraordinary, the unexplainable that walks beside us if we only think to open our eyes. It's always there—we just have to look. We have to believe. Not just in fairies and ghosts and monsters, mind you—but in the possibilities of more than what most expect to see. What we *can* perceive if we accept that God is bigger than we are."

She nodded, because though she'd never much thought about

it, she could recognize the beauty of the ideas. She just still didn't know what it had to do with his invitation.

The corners of his mouth turned up a bit. "When I first met you, I thought, 'Now there's a bit of hidden treasure.' You were trying to be invisible behind Lady Emily, yet you were all sunshine and smiles in the kitchen. Brightness hidden in shadow. With a ghost story of your own in your eyes. I don't expect you to tell me all that put it there, certainly not yet. But I'd like the chance to earn your trust. So that if ever you do . . . well, you won't find a readier ear to hear it or a readier heart to believe it. Whatever haunts you, you needn't be haunted alone." His smile went lopsided. "I've plenty of experience with that."

"A ghost story of your own in your eyes . . . whatever haunts you . . ." She'd never thought of it in those terms, but it was true, wasn't it? Nigel hadn't just stolen; he'd killed something inside her and left a ghost in its place. A ghost of the Tommie who used to be. A ghost of all she once dreamed she could have.

But here was Enyon Thorne, seeing it—perhaps blurrily, as expected of a specter, but *seeing* it, and naming it, and offering to come alongside her. Was it foolish of her to want to let him? Or would it simply be cowardly to run away?

She dragged in a long breath. Any other day, she might have followed the instincts that said to run away, to protect herself, to keep any other man from ever having the opportunity to treat her as Nigel had done.

But it was today—the day God had already proven that He heard her cries, that He saw their needs. Maybe, just maybe, this was another answer to her prayer. Maybe He was asking her to believe in more than just His ability to send food to fill empty stomachs. Maybe He also could send understanding to fill broken hearts.

She made herself meet his gaze. Let herself feel the warmth of his words. Whispered out her own. "I'd love to meet the rest of your family. To share a meal with you. But it would depend on Lady

Emily and what our situation looks like at the time. I can't in good conscience go and enjoy a meal if she's hungry in our flat."

He must have known it was more than that, must have seen the battle before her words. His smile now was soft and patient. "Already thought of that—it's why I was looking for Ollie. He and Beth'll just invite the lady to dinner, to stay overnight even. She won't miss you, then, and she'll be well fed. Not that I knew the fed part would be such a necessity, except that I know you do the cooking when it's the two of you."

He'd even thought that part through? Taken such care to see to her concerns and responsibilities? Tommie let a smile build, let it bloom. And said, "Then . . . all right."

True, that knot of fear was still drawn tight in her stomach. But she wasn't going to let it win. Not today.

13

Bram let the frolicking, easily distracted puppy serve as his excuse for walking at a snail's pace along the coast, but really, it was about as fast as his legs would trudge. He'd snuck in a two-hour nap after lunch but otherwise had little choice but to deal with his exhaustion if he meant for it to remain undiscovered that he'd never gone to bed last night. As it was, he'd not quite made it back to the Tremayne house before Mrs. Dawe had arrived from her home next door. She'd come into the back garden just as he was reaching for the door, and he'd claimed he'd just been out with the puppy.

It wouldn't have been the first time he returned so late—or early, depending on one's viewpoint. Mrs. Dawe wouldn't have thought anything of it. But Tristan had decided to greet her rather noisily, announcing his presence to the neighborhood with a round of excited barking that had the entire household turning out. And in the light of day, Bram could see how filthy the puppy was, and he couldn't very well bring him into the house like that. So a bath had been in order, and then Lady Emily had arrived, probably to try to determine who had left a gift at her door . . . which he'd anticipated she would do. Hence why he'd already paid a St. Mary's local to ferry her to Tresco. He just hadn't expected her quite so soon.

And now here it was, twilight again, and he was running on those two measly hours of sleep. But no one would hear him complain. Not with how successful the entire operation had been. He'd simply go to bed at what everyone else would deem a reasonable hour tonight and be right as rain tomorrow.

"Fine evening, isn't it, my lord? Though Jeremiah Moon says there'll be rain tomorrow."

Bram turned to see Enyon Thorne striding up the beach at a mockingly fast clip, though he slowed to match him and Tristan when he drew even with them and smiled down at the puppy. "Is this the fierce guard dog in training?"

Tristan was busy playing tag with the surf. And barking at the sand crab that peeked out and then dashed back into its hole. Bram grinned. "Sir Tristan, indeed. Neither villain nor knave will dare approach Lady Emily with him around."

Enyon chuckled and kept his gaze on the pup. "I saw you, you know. Getting off Brick's boat this morning when all the other fishermen were still setting their nets. Coming from St. Mary's, were you?"

Bram held himself absolutely still, kept his face even. He knew plenty of gentlemen in London would be asking that question as an accusation or implication—hinting he'd been on St. Mary's for a visit of a certain sort.

But this was Enyon. Oliver's best friend. The one who they still teased for startling at the slightest noise after hearing one of Gibson's ghost stories, and who had been making moon eyes at Tommie Briggs.

He couldn't mean what it sounded like. So Bram said, "Why would you think that?"

Enyon sighed. "Thomasina told me this morning that they were out of food, and that some miraculously appeared on their doorstep before dawn today. Didn't take but a second to realize its appearance coincided with your predawn tour with Brick."

Well, blast. So much for his cleverness. He could deny it, but really, what was the point? And actually . . . Enyon could be the perfect ally in this. "You didn't tell her, did you?"

He shook his head. "She said something about it being an angel. It was too funny a picture to correct—you with a halo and wings." He held his hands at his sides and flapped them, pasting a ridiculously sweet look on his face.

Bram snorted a laugh. "If that's you applying for the position of co-angel, you're hired. You have a boat, don't you?"

Enyon settled. And grinned. "That's why I came to find you. I don't know how much you gave them, but if you're planning a second gift, I'd be happy to help with the delivery."

That would be far better than relying on finding a fisherman who didn't mind taking an hour out of his day. "I left them with breakfast and the means to buy another week's worth or so of supplies, if we account for them needing a ferry to Tresco several times too. Not that I want them to run out. So perhaps next Tuesday night or thereabouts? Or whichever night Jeremiah Moon's toe says the weather will cooperate."

Enyon nodded. "It's good of you. To see after them."

Bram shifted, not quite sure why compliments settled so poorly on his shoulders—especially when they were for something he hadn't wanted anyone to know he'd done. "It's nothing."

"Not to them."

"Yes, well . . ." For lack of a better response, he shrugged. "They don't deserve to pay for Lord Scofield's being a blighter." To dissuade Enyon from paying him any further compliments, he crouched down to get Tristan's attention and waved a twig that had washed ashore. He waited for the pup to follow it with his eyes and then tossed it. "Fetch, Tristan!"

Tristan leaped after it, sniffed it where it landed, and then dashed into the next wave.

Perhaps *not* a retriever in the mix . . .

"There was a family that summered here—just left last week— with a beautiful golden Labrador. She had a litter not long ago, and they were none too happy about it. Defiling her pure bloodlines with a local mutt or some rot. Bet he's one of those."

Bram shot to his feet. "You mean to say they left all the pups here, to fend for themselves?"

Enyon's lips went tight. "They had only the mother with them when they left. Honestly, I feared they'd drowned them. Might have done—could be that Sir Tristan just got away."

"Monsters." Were he not so tired, he may have tried to temper his reaction. But Enyon looked like he agreed, so why bother? "I'll have to look for the others."

"Ollie mentioned that you have a habit of taking in strays—or so your sister and Lord Sheridan have said. You can't keep them all, though."

There was more to the statement than dogs, he suspected. And Enyon was studying him like Brick had been studying the tide chart that morning. Why? Was he concerned that Bram was the sort to offer a rescue only when it was new and entertaining, and then forget about the needy in a week or a month?

Was he afraid he'd act that way with Emily?

Not that he knew why it was any of Enyon's concern—but even so, it didn't change the answer. "No, I don't keep them all, though I do have a kennel full. After I've tended them and trained them and taught them to trust again, if they've been mistreated, I find a home in need of a bit of laughter. You've seen Lady Abbie's pug?"

Enyon chuckled. "All the Scillies has. She doesn't go anywhere without him."

"He was the runt of a litter, and the lady who owned the dam had ordered him drowned. I saw her footman toss the wriggling sack into the Thames a couple years ago and fished it out." His hands shook with anger at the memory even now. He'd recognized the footman and knew the pug too—the lady was all the time crowing about her. Yet she'd tossed one of her princess's babies out like trash.

Not unlike a certain lord with his daughter, now that he thought about it. "Poor Lance was so tiny I had to feed him with a dropper for weeks. Lady Abbie's birthday was coming up, so I made a gift of him." His lips twitched. "She and the aforementioned lady had long been rivals. I thought it would be hilarious if she made a little prince out of the dog that wretch had rejected. Which she's done. Though otherwise, I'd planned to pretend to give him to my mother, so that I could keep him."

Tristan wagged his way back to Bram's feet and dropped to the sand, panting happily. It was usually obvious to whom a dog or cat ought to belong. Libby needed her Darling, for instance—not that she'd required Bram's help seeing that. Abbie her Lancelot. Several of the families in the village at home had received others to cheer their children after a hard winter or a bout of pneumonia that had kept a little one confined to the house too long.

And maybe that *was* what he was to do with Emily too. Show her that she was priceless. That just because her father didn't see her didn't mean she wasn't worth seeing. Restore the confidence that she should rightfully have, and then nudge her into the arms of someone worthy of her, who could make her truly happy.

That idea didn't settle nearly as well as giving Lancelot to Abbie had done. Which made him frown.

Enyon, on the other hand, seemed to be fighting back a grin. "So you keep some, too, then? How many do you have?"

"We've four of my father's hunting dogs still alive, though they're all more given to lounging about their kennel these days than running after any foxes. And I currently have three that are purely pets—a sadly low number." He grinned down at Tristan. "If he has any brothers or sisters running about, I've the room for them." Though he'd officially run out of the names of the twelve main knights of Arthur's court. He'd saved his favorites all these years, waiting for the perfect recipients.

Fortunately, some more modern variations of the legends named over a hundred knights, so he still had plenty to choose from. And some of the strays had been female, so they'd been Elaine and Enid and Guinevere.

Perhaps he'd find one of Tristan's sisters, so he could name her Isolde.

And clearly he was edging toward outright exhaustion if he was standing here in the sand thinking of puppy names while Enyon studied him. He glanced up at his human companion again and found his face had relaxed back into an easy smile.

"Well, if anyone mentions finding any other pups, I'll let them know you're happy to take them." He half turned as if to go but then paused. Drew in a breath. And faced Bram again. "Since we're sharing secrets—and you seem to be a night owl. Yes?"

That was no secret, not to the brother of a fisherman. He'd become a familiar face at the quay before dawn. "Firmly."

Enyon nodded. "Baffling. I'm a morning person myself. Don't do well with late nights, especially multiple ones in a row."

Clearly there was a point to his saying so, and presumably it had to do with a secret of his own, but Bram couldn't guess at what. "All right." He drew the syllables out, tilting them up at the end.

Enyon motioned toward Grimsby. "I'm not comfortable with that younger Scofield bloke running about my islands, so I've been warning everyone to be on their guard around him and have been keeping an ear out for rumblings. The pub seemed the likeliest place to overhear anything, but lips don't get loose until the families leave, and I'm about done myself by then, most nights."

A low hum rumbled in Bram's throat. He ought to have thought of such a thing himself. The sort of man who treated his own sister like Scofield did and went to such elaborate effort to pin Beth in a quickly filling pit was also the kind to think he could get away with anything else he pleased. In other words, the kind to cause trouble—and then simply cover it up.

But what exactly did Enyon mean for him to do? "I'm happy to help however I can, but . . . won't they all stop talking if I'm there? Being an 'incomer,' as you call me?"

Rather than leaping to offer assurances, Enyon tilted his head to the side. "It's possible. But you've proven yourself over the last few weeks. Making friends with the fishermen as you've done goes a long way, plus everyone adores your sister. If you started making a habit of going to the pub, they'd warm up to your being there soon enough. Just bring something as an excuse—Ollie said you were looking through Mr. Gale's research on Lyonesse, right? You could bring that. Ask about for stories to add to it, say you're compiling a book. Gents have the leisure for that, they'd believe it of you. Maybe recruit Mr. Gibson to be there now and then too."

The idea both excited and annoyed him. Excited, because it was a great idea for gathering any other local legends on Tristan and Trevelyan and artifacts related to Camelot. But annoyed, because this was really more Sheridan's sort of thing, and his best friend would never let him hear the end of it if he found out. Which he would. Because Bram would tell him. How could he not, when he'd need his advice on how to go about such a chore?

He felt his head nodding before realizing he'd given it the command. "All right. I can do that."

"Good!" Enyon rubbed a hand over his face. "That means I can get some sleep."

Ah, sleep. Ambrosia. "I can't begin tonight. I never actually got to bed this morning."

Enyon grinned and backed away a step. "I wouldn't think every night is necessary. Tomorrow or Saturday would be better for it anyway. And then—Tuesday night, early Wednesday morning? Weather permitting?"

Bram nodded. "I'll meet you at the quay. About four a.m.?"

"I'll be there." Enyon held out a hand. "Glad to sit beside you in the heavenly choir, my lord."

There was nothing to do but laugh and shake.

As Enyon left, Bram fished the slender lead he'd bought that day out of his pocket and hooked it to Tristan's new collar. Half the afternoon had been spent getting the pup used to these two new accessories, but he'd finally stopped trying to paw the collar off and bite the lead. Mostly.

"Ready to go back, boy?" He gave a gentle tug.

Tristan clambered back to his feet and tried to circle away from the lead, but finally he gave up and started up the sandy path ahead of Bram.

He passed Oliver and Libby, out for a twilight stroll, on his way back to the Tremayne house and offered them a grin and a quick tease about not staying out too long. Once back inside, he was relieved to find that Sheridan and Beth were engaged in a spirited debate about something that didn't interest him at all, making it perfectly natural for him to declare them too dull for his tastes and bid them good night. He told them he meant to read in his room.

He did not mean to read in his room. He meant to collapse and sleep for the next twelve hours. At least.

Yet after he'd dismissed Collins for the night and fallen onto his borrowed bed, his mind just wouldn't stop spinning, despite the weariness of his eyes and limbs. Everything kept circling through his thoughts.

Elizabeth Mucknell and her desire to see her husband saved from the doom that befell Lyonesse.

Tristan and Trevelyan and scores of people supposedly smote by an angry, just God.

An artifact entrusted somehow to them from King Arthur himself.

The look on Emily's face—buoyant and bright—as she slipped into the kitchen that morning. He'd never seen her smile so clear, so . . . beautiful.

The letter from Morgan Tremayne, sitting now on his bedside table, awaiting tomorrow's jacket pocket.

Bram scrubbed a hand over his face, Morgan's words scrolling over and again through his mind's eye. He'd said that God loved him, that He had a purpose for him. Words Oliver spoke all the time too. But how was that the same God that sent an angry tidal wave to destroy an entire kingdom? What sins had the people of Lyonesse committed that were so beyond redemption?

And even if he admitted, as Oliver had said, that what a story *said* was the motivation behind a natural disaster didn't make it so, his future brother-in-law certainly couldn't argue that God had done just that in the Bible. In some ways it seemed He was a God of contradictions. The just and the merciful. The loving and the vengeful. Yet if one were to go from the premise that God was perfect—which Oliver would say was the foundational truth, Bram felt sure—then somehow those seeming contradictions *weren't*.

Bram drew in a long breath and tried to ignore the sound of puppy claws on wooden floors, which meant Tristan wasn't still in his little basket-bed where he'd been put. It was easy enough, he supposed, to ascribe all those different things to an infinite God, a God who knew everything—how each person, each nation would act and react. What each situation demanded, and what the results would be if a different action were taken. Which meant that the same God who controlled the wind and the waves really could know what *Bram* needed too.

His breath leaked out. As the eldest son of an earl, and now an earl himself, so much of his life had simply been dictated. There were responsibilities and duties, people whose very livelihood and survival relied on him. He'd always considered that the only calling he really had in life—to live up to the precedent his father had set as Lord Telford.

But he wasn't just Lord Telford. He was also Bram Sinclair, and he had a feeling Morgan Tremayne would have said that it was Bram who the Lord was most interested in. Bram, who still had an obsession with tales of chivalry . . . because they represented all he wanted to be. Bram, who would do anything to protect his family. Bram, who craved just a taste of something . . . more. Something truly noble. Truly worthwhile.

Live the legacy, my friend. Walk worthy of His calling. Go forth boldly—and live.

He'd inherited a legacy, but that wasn't the one he wanted to be remembered for—to be just one more in a long line of earls. He wanted his legacy to be championing those who needed it, righting a few wrongs, charging boldly ahead to slay whatever dragons awaited him.

And perhaps, he granted, when Emily's bright smile from that morning came before his tired mind again, rescuing a fair damsel. Or, better still, helping her realize she could rescue herself.

14

It took Emily quite a few groggy moments to realize that the strange sensations tugging her from the haven of sleep were not the mermaid she'd been dreaming was pulling her into the water, but rather the wriggling form of a puppy nudging her, licking her face, and making little whimpering noises. She smiled even as she blinked away sleep and saw that the light coming in Beth's window was the pearly grey of predawn. Apparently Tristan didn't care what the clock said.

"All right," she whispered to the pup, setting him down and slipping carefully out of her borrowed bed, not wanting to wake Beth. She'd better take the dog out before he ruined his streak of three days without messing the Tremaynes' floors.

Telford had insisted last night that Tristan stay with her—to get used to her, he'd said. If he was awake before Beth took her and Tommie home this morning, she'd have to tease him about leaving her with a furry alarm clock. Not that she minded. She slipped as quickly as she could into her simplest day dress, grabbed her shawl, didn't even attempt to do anything to the hair still in its overnight braid, and hurried Tristan out to the back garden. She'd already told Tommie that she'd take care of herself as much as possible this morning, given that her friend had no idea what time she and the Thornes would make it back from supper on Bryher last night.

Tristan was quick about his business but then, with tail wagging, set off to explore every interesting smell to be found. Emily didn't mind that either. In fact, she simply stepped back into the kitchen long enough to grab his lead and then led him out of the garden and toward the bluff. If she was going to be awake for the sunrise, she might as well enjoy watching it over the water.

Her pace faltered, though, when she saw the silhouette of another figure on the bluff. Quick panic roared through her veins, then just as quickly subsided. She recognized the lanky form sitting there, arms propped on his raised knees, but it wasn't Nigel or Father or anyone else she wanted to avoid. It wasn't Oliver or Sheridan, who she'd be more likely to wave a hello to and then find another solitary place to watch the sunrise.

It was Telford. And though she didn't care to examine why, the thought of seeing his as her first human face of the day made her quicken her pace and brought a smile to her lips.

Only when Tristan let out a happy yip did she pause to consider that perhaps Telford wouldn't be quite so happy to have *his* solitude interrupted. And for that matter, what was he doing up this early? She slowed, hesitated, even though Tristan would have none of that and strained at the lead.

Telford turned at the bark and grinned, first at the puppy and then up at her. "Sorry—I should have warned you that we're still working on the overnight stretch."

"I don't mind." She couldn't help but smile back, her hesitation easing away in the face of his welcome. She sat down a few feet away, gaze on the horizon largely to keep herself from noting the way the wind had tousled his hair and how comfortable he looked in just shirtsleeves and waistcoat, his jacket and tie not yet on.

Or no. Taken off. It was yesterday's waistcoat. She'd noted how the blue threads brought out his eyes yesterday evening and . . . so much for not looking at him. She lifted a brow. "You haven't been to bed yet?"

He chuckled and motioned to the sky. "On a beautiful night like this? Then I'd have missed what promises to be a stunning sunrise and the four shooting stars I saw last night too."

When Tristan tugged on the lead, she dropped it so he could sniff at something just out of range, figuring he wouldn't dare run too far with Telford right there. "Do you always stay up so late?"

"Not always. No point in welcoming the dawn when it's raining—but if the weather's fair, then generally so, yes." He sounded perfectly content as he said it, as if he'd discovered some sort of secret in the night.

"I have the feeling you don't spend those midnight hours gambling and drinking as so many do, even when in London."

He made a face. "That would rather ruin the quiet that I so enjoy. No, my lady, I am drawn to the nighttime quiet of nature, not the raucous behavior that men like to hide in the dark."

So different from Nigel and his friends. They, too, were often out until dawn, but then he would come home laughing and stumbling and smelling of smoke and whiskey and cheap perfume, ready to collapse. Emily had only crossed his path in such a condition a handful of times, but it had been enough to teach her to avoid those homecomings.

She couldn't image her brother, or her father for that matter, sitting on a bluff before dawn with such peace on their faces, just soaking in the world. "And what thoughts keep you company amidst the nighttime quiet of nature?"

The other men in her life would have waved off the question or given her a non-answer like *Oh, this and that.* But Telford tilted his head to the side and drew in a long, contemplative breath that promised real words on its exhale.

"This particular night, as with quite a few previous ones, I was thinking of the juxtaposition of justice and mercy in the divine."

"So . . . light, easy thoughts." She drew her knees up to her chest, careful to keep her skirt covering her ankles, and smiled over at him.

ROSEANNA M. WHITE

Why, after these months together, did it still surprise and warm her when he smiled back? "Oliver already gave me his learned opinion on the subject, but the questions still niggle—hard not to, with the sinking of Lyonesse always on my mind." His smile had faded to a more serious expression, but he kept his gaze on her. "What think you, my lady? How am I to reconcile the just God who would destroy an entire kingdom with the loving God who would sacrifice His own Son for us?"

If he'd already spoken to Oliver about it, then he surely didn't expect any greater insights from her. No doubt Beth's brother had already questioned whether they ought to believe the motivation ascribed to God in the story . . . and Telford would have pointed out the similar occasions in the Bible itself, whose word they certainly should *not* doubt. She had no years of university study nor experience behind the pulpit to give him any better answer.

She had only her own life. Wrapping her arms around her knees, she said, "I know only this, Bram—the mercy of the Lord is always extended, His hand outstretched even in the fiercest storm. One has only to reach for it. But if one doesn't . . ."

"One finds justice instead." When Tristan tumbled onto his back beside Telford, the man grinned and gave the furry belly an obliging rub. "That was Lizza's fear, then. That her husband simply would not see the hand of mercy outstretched toward him, and so he would suffer justice in the form of a vengeful sea."

"A fear I know well when it comes to my own family." It slipped out in a whisper, blending with the wind through the seagrass.

Telford looked up at her again, gaze sharp now. "You would wish mercy for them? After the way they've treated you?"

She arched her brows, though she felt it lacked the boldness and challenge it did when Beth made the move. "For what do we ever need mercy except for the wrongs we've done? And what if the lessons that someone fails to learn at the hand of violence *could* be learned at the hand of mercy? Could it not inspire where fear fails to change?"

Somehow his silence rang of contemplation rather than dismissal. "You have a point. And I suppose if I am unwilling to extend mercy, then . . . perhaps I blind my own eyes to seeing where God extends it to me too."

Such weighty, true thoughts for so early in the morning. They settled slowly over her, resonating well with the understanding she'd already fought for. A nod was all she could think to offer, and the sea and wind spoke for them for several long minutes.

Then Telford pointed to where the sun was painting a spectacular wash of pink and purple and orange over the sky and water. "Would you like to meander a bit with me while it makes its appearance? Along the shoreline? Tristan looks as though he'd like the walk."

The puppy was indeed wriggling about, even as he tried to stay more or less in one place near them. He was such an adorable little thing, though already not so little as he'd been when Telford first rescued him. Two weeks could make a world of difference in the life of a baby animal—and it had made quite a one in her own as well. Food and money had shown up twice more, just when they needed it, and she was beginning to trust that it would keep doing so.

"Well, for Tristan's sake." And since the fiery dawn left no room for dishonesty with oneself, perhaps she agreed because she could think of nothing better than greeting the day beside Telford.

He stood before she could even unwrap her arms from her legs and held out a hand to help her up. And then, when she was on her feet, too, he wrapped her arm through his, just as he'd done when he was escorting her into the hotel dining room. Her heart gave a happy little sigh, and she accepted the lead he held out to her.

He led her down one of the paths cut through the seagrass to the beach. A fishing boat was gliding past as they gained the sand, and the sailors called out a greeting. Telford shouted one back, calling them by name.

She had to blink at that. She expected it of Oliver, but Lord Telford knew the fishermen's names? That took her by surprise. "You know them?"

"Had better, hadn't I? They'll be my sister's neighbors soon enough." That half-smile in place, he motioned to the boat. "Rigsby there was at the pub last night for a while and came over to tell me that he remembered his father telling a tale of Lyonesse. Thought they had it recorded in a family journal somewhere and promised to dig it out for me, if I wanted."

She'd known that he—and Sheridan and Oliver, sometimes—was making himself a regular at the pub with just that hope. But it was nice to hear it was working. "Do you think it'll offer any new perspectives?"

"Hard to say. He thought it had a mention of a magical something-or-another, so that would at least be interesting. And could be a firmer link to Arthurian legend."

They'd found precious few of those thus far. Certainly nothing to shed any light on what Elizabeth Mucknell could have found, or what Emily's brother had been searching for so tirelessly since his return from London.

But it was hard to be disappointed when the sun was peeking above the horizon like a blinding jewel, the sky was awash with colors never seen any other time of day, and her hand was resting against the arm of a man in whose company she felt not only safe, but welcome.

They stood in silence as the sun made its triumphal rise above the line of water, Tristan sniffing at seashells while they watched. Emily found herself as aware of the man beside her as the brilliant display of colors before her. When she'd first met Libby's brother, she never would have guessed that the fellow putting on such a show of grumpiness over his sister's relationship with Oliver Tremayne was the sort to wander the beach at night, counting shooting stars and waiting for the sunrise, musing about the nature of God. While she'd known from the first time he whispered *"Well played"* in her ear that he was an encourager at heart, she hadn't immediately pegged him as the sort to take in stray dogs and train them to be the friendliest of companions.

She certainly wouldn't have thought that she'd glance up just as he was glancing down and find herself wishing that he'd lean down and touch his lips to hers.

For a moment she thought he would. But then he just smiled and turned them away from the fully risen sun. Already those vibrant colors were fading to pastels, and Telford seemed to fade a bit too. "Shall we? You'll be wanting your tea and breakfast, and I need a few hours' sleep."

She nodded because what else could she do? Demand he kiss her instead? That he think of her as something more than a friend simply because she found she wanted him to? Ask him what it would take to make real the courting he pretended to do whenever her father or Vandermeer was around?

"Are you all right, Em?"

Em. Just like that, a bit of solace soothed over her runaway desires. Whether her foolish heart was getting ahead of itself or not, they *were* friends at least. Oliver was her friend because she was Beth's friend; Sheridan was her friend because he was Beth's fiancé. But Telford . . . he was *her* friend.

In answer to his question, she nodded. "Quite. Looks like it's going to be a beautiful day."

"Are you spending the day here or . . . ?"

"No, we're going back to St. Mary's. Tommie promised to help Mrs. Thorne in her shop for a bit today while her daughter takes a trip to Penzance for some supplies."

And Emily still hated to be away for more than a day, lest she miss a letter or telegram from Mother. Foolish, at this point, to even hope for it, but . . . but she *had* to.

Was he disappointed, or was it her imagination? "Too bad. I suppose I had better bid you farewell, then, since you'll be gone before I get up. Coming back tomorrow?"

They hadn't talked about it, but usually she spaced out her visits to Tresco so she didn't overstay her welcome. Not that the Tremaynes would ever say she did, but . . . "I don't know. Perhaps—or Wednesday."

"What do you do all by yourself on St. Mary's?"

Worry. Fret. Pray. Wait for a message that never arrived. "Well, I've copied out Lizza's journal again so that the Howe sisters have their own copy and we could spare Tas-gwyn's hand. I felt so bad that he had to make a second one for me. I've explored the island. And when Lottie and her family were still there, I spent a fair bit of time with them, since they were the ones who officially invited me to summer here."

She could feel his gaze boring into her. "But the Wights are gone. The Howe sisters are old enough to be your mother, and they are out harassing the team on Gugh as much as not. And while you and Briggs seem to have grown closer through all this, I happen to know she's been spending quite a bit of time with the Thornes. Don't you get lonely?"

Achingly so. "How do you happen to know that about Tommie and the Thornes?"

He narrowed his eyes at her. "Enyon stops by most every day, so I hear things. But you can't evade my question that easily."

Enyon stopped by—of course he did, because he was Oliver's best friend. But how strange it was, when one paused to consider, that Oliver was to marry the sister of this earl beside her, while Enyon was courting her own maid. Nowhere else she'd ever been did the lines between classes blur quite like they did here on Tresco.

"I don't mind the solitude. And I don't want to impose too much on—"

His laugh interrupted her. "You have *met* the Tremaynes, have you not? They don't view your presence as an imposition, they view it as a blessing. If anyone was imposing, it was me—and rather deliberately at the start. And even so they were nothing but graciously welcoming, and now we're planning who will holiday where, when. Trust me, Emily, you could move in and they would only rejoice."

They were too kind, that was all. "They've never had to suffer my company for more than a few days—"

"Suffer?" He drew her to an abrupt halt, scowling down at her.

"Who has filled your head with such nonsense? Your brother? Your father?"

She just pressed her lips together. She should have known better than to let such a sentence slip from her lips.

Telford huffed out a breath, shook his head, and covered her fingers with his, there on his arm. "Perhaps you ought to operate under the rule that if either of them said something, or otherwise impressed it upon you, that it is utterly false, and you ought to believe the opposite instead." He raised his hand again and pointed a finger at her nose. "Let's set the record straight here and now. You, Lady Emily Scofield, are an absolute delight, and no one in his or her right mind could possibly do anything other than crave your company. Do you understand?" He held still, finger in front of her face, waiting.

What could she possibly do but smile? "Certainly, my lord. I am a delight. My father and brother are mad. My friends crave my company." *Which means* you *crave my company.* He was probably just being nice, but still. Those words would warm her all the way home.

As did the way he touched that finger to the tip of her nose as he said, "Good. Then the day can proceed."

Whether or not he would ever care for her as she was beginning to wish he would, he *did* care for her, clearly. It was enough to keep her head happily muddled through breakfast and Tommie fixing her hair properly and during the half-hour sail back to St. Mary's. And when Beth suggested she come to them again the next day and that Tommie could come over with the Thornes, she found herself agreeing when she usually would have demurred.

Because maybe Telford was right. Maybe . . . maybe she wasn't giving her friends enough credit in thinking they couldn't really be so welcoming of her. And if that were the case, it was dreadfully unfair of her to ascribe to them motives and thoughts that belonged to her own family but not to theirs.

And when she put it *that* way, she knew for a fact she'd done them wrong by assuming them less hospitable than they truly were.

Even so, she had the rest of today stretching out before her and wasn't certain how she meant to fill it.

Not until a towering figure blocked her path up the street into Hugh Town. An iron hand curled around her elbow, and her father proclaimed, "You're coming with me. Now."

15

Emily needn't wonder long where he was taking her, given that he barked out the command of "Gugh!" to the captain the moment they stepped foot on the yacht. She could still see the muted outrage in Tommie's wide eyes when Father shoved her so hard she tumbled to the ground before he pulled Emily right back toward the quay and a small dinghy. Her last sight of her friend had been of Tommie running full-out into Hugh Town, though to what end she had no idea. Probably to find a Thorne, who would in turn alert the Tremaynes.

Alert her friends that her father had decided to spend some time with her. How amusing it would be, were it not so sad.

He'd dropped her elbow once the yacht was underway, apparently not thinking her mad enough to leap overboard and try to swim back to shore. Though it was tempting. Or would have been, had the destination of Gugh not offered some reassurance. That was where the museum team would be, and even if Nigel was in attendance today, no one would try anything threatening with the board watching.

Still, she took a step back when Father spun on her, leveling the full force of his thunderous gaze upon her, as he had done so rarely in her memory. "That will be enough of your avoidance. It is shameful how you've been putting off your own family for that pack of island rats."

Her mouth gaped open. "I beg your pardon?" The urge to fight had to have been borrowed from Beth—heaven knew she'd never dared it herself. "The Marquess of Sheridan and the Earl of Telford will be most interested in hearing your opinion of them, I'm certain."

He batted away those words with a snarl. "They aren't the ones I object to, as well you know. How many times have I told you not to sully yourself with a family like the Tremaynes? Hm? Every time that girl invited you to visit her here, every time I refused, did I not make it clear why? They are nothing. Rubbish. Scum."

Her cheeks burned hot. "*You* never told me anything. I was never even allowed in your hallowed presence. You always left Mother to deliver your rude refusals."

As usual, he didn't even seem to hear her. "Well, this willful behavior stops now. Perhaps I cannot stop you from seeing them without broadcasting for all my peers to see what a rebellious disaster of a daughter you are, but you will *not* refuse another invitation to join us when I issue one—do you understand? Mr. Vandermeer has been most distraught at your treatment of him."

"Ah. There we have it." It wasn't that he cared a whit what she did or didn't do, except that his precious American was displeased. "This is about Vandermeer, not me."

"*Do you understand?*"

Her nostrils flared as his question mingled in her ears with the same words uttered by a far different voice in a far different tone not an hour ago. Father, tearing her down, calling her a disaster. Telford, building her up, calling her worthy.

Her fingers curled around the rail. The angrier, more familiar voice was so much easier to believe—but not *right* to believe. And perhaps being a dutiful daughter didn't mean accepting whatever scathing coals he heaped upon her head. Elizabeth Mucknell, after all, was the picture of an adoring, obedient wife, but she never let her pirate husband dictate right and wrong to her. And she had a feeling Mucknell loved her all the more for it.

Maybe that was how to love her father better too. Maybe he would respond to spine as he never had to obeisance. Maybe if she could earn his respect, he would eventually listen to her.

He was looking at her as though she were a barnacle on his otherwise pristine hull. "I cannot fathom *why* he has taken a fancy to you, but you will not bring disgrace upon the Scofield name by scorning his attention before you even discover what his intentions may be."

"I don't care what his intentions are. I have no interest in Donald Vandermeer." She dug her fingernails into the polished wood. "And for that matter, how you can dare to say that the company I keep is a disgrace to the family name when you turn a blind eye to the sins of your son—"

"You will leave your brother out of this. That you would let your jealousy of him lead you to turn your back on your family is unforgivable."

Jealousy? The only thing she had ever been jealous of was their parents' regard, and she was beginning to wonder if she was better off for not having it. Father's attention, it seemed, carried with it far too much condemnation. She shook her head. "It has nothing to do with Nigel. I thought it did, I'll admit it. I thought that *he* was the problem. But I see now that it's been you all along. You taught him. You placed this enormous burden upon him. You shaped him into the selfish creature he has become."

His face turned red, he took a menacing step toward her, and he pitched his voice low. "How dare you?"

For a moment, she thought he might toss her over the rail and let the capricious currents carry her out to the Atlantic. But he wouldn't—that would look bad. She forced herself to lift her chin when she wanted to cower. "Why would I not dare? You've already taken absolutely everything from me. My family, your financial support . . . what more have I to lose?"

Rage stormed for another moment—and then snapped away,

covered by the calculation she expected of him. "You cannot understand the complexities of such matters, so allow me to spell it out for you. While either Lord Telford or Mr. Vandermeer would be a fine and advantageous match, we cannot assume that either will propose once they've spent more time with you—and yet neither will *before* spending time with you. So, you will do as you are told and you will entertain them both. Whoever proposes first you will accept, and a short betrothal—just long enough to avoid gossip—will follow, lest he change his mind. That is to be your sole focus. Not your vile little friends, not Mucknell's treasure. Your purpose is to marry one of them, nothing more."

He certainly knew how to strip the joy out of Telford's attentions to her. Gone was the warmth from that morning walk, the glow of knowing he valued her opinion and thought she mattered. The wind blew harsh and cold, tasting of autumn and chasing away that beautiful light of summer in her soul. "And what if *they* want more? My opinions, for instance, on Mucknell's treasure? Or the company of my 'vile little friends,' whom Lord Telford will soon call family?"

Father sneered. "I knew the moment I met his sister that she was unworthy of the burden of nobility. That she would choose to stay in a place such as this and marry a local rat—her brother ought to be saying good riddance to her." Already they were nearing St. Agnes and Gugh, and Father gripped her arm again, presumably to propel her toward the yacht's dinghy once more. "And as for you—don't delude yourself. They may ask your opinion, but only to be polite. They do not *want* it, so don't bore them with your inanities. Stick to being the pretty little mouse your mother raised you to be."

"Pretty little mouse." The phrase haunted her as she climbed down to the dinghy once the yacht had anchored in deeper waters, and while the servant rowed them to the shore. It echoed as Father marched her over Gugh's heather and granite, toward the collection of men and shovels and tents. It rattled as the trustees greeted her with absent deference and when her father turned her over nonetoo-subtly to the beaming Mr. Vandermeer.

"Lady Emily, how lovely to see you! You've just made the morning brighter."

"How do you do, Mr. Vandermeer?" *Pretty little mouse?* No. That wasn't what she wanted to be. It wasn't what she *would* be.

He chuckled, all light and mirth, and tucked her hand into the crook of his elbow. "Better now that there's a respite from the usual stuffy company. Come, let me show you around. You haven't seen our operations yet, have you?"

She shook her head, unable to help but note that having her hand on *his* arm made no warmth radiate through her, sparked no whispers of dreams. He was a handsome man, she could admit that—if a bit too old for her. Such things were overlooked often enough. She had no fewer than three acquaintances from finishing school who had married men even older than Vandermeer. But he wasn't . . . well, he wasn't blond, nor did he have eyes of that beautiful blue-green. He didn't smile at her as if he could see far more of her heart than even she knew, nor offer her a handkerchief the very moment she needed one, nor make it clear that she was not only accepted for who she was, but she also was appreciated for who she *could* be, if she were brave enough. He didn't inspire her to that bravery with the first words he spoke to her.

He wasn't Telford.

"Here's your brother's burial chamber." He waved a hand at the excavation still painstakingly underway—on the correct side now, the original hole Nigel had dug filled in to support the stone from that side. All evidence of Nigel's treachery with Beth, his attempt to let her drown in that pit, buried. Just like all his other crimes. Vandermeer laughed. "Well, not *his* burial chamber, but the one he discovered."

She told her lips to turn up. "You all have been busy. No pirate treasure, though?"

"As well you know." His eyes—a lovely brown, just not the color of the ocean—sparkled at her. "What about you? Stumbled upon anything interesting?"

Had Father paused to entertain *this* possibility? That Vandermeer wasn't interested in her at all and just wanted to pump her for information? Well, she had learned how to parry treasure-hungry men over the years, at least. "Lots of things. Pottery shards, what we think may have been a drinking cup, a seashell with the most interesting fossil—"

"Ugh." He made an exaggerated face and pointed them toward the tent under which tables were set up to examine any articles they brought from the earth. "You have clearly been around Lord Sheridan too long. His predilections have rubbed off on you."

"They didn't have to, actually." She paused at the table he clearly wanted to walk right by and surveyed the collection of items there. Broken pottery, what may have been an urn, beads, a few small bones. Treasures—just not the sort glinting with gold and gems. "I have always more appreciated the quiet items and the stories they whisper."

She reached for a curved piece of pottery, raising a brow in question at the man behind the table before picking it up. He nodded and smiled, so she lifted it, let the weight of it settle in her palm, ran a thumb over the pattern etched into it. "Who carved this? Who painted it? Was it a slave, commanded to create something to be buried with her chief? An artist, commissioned for the task because of his talent? Perhaps even a wife, pouring all her love into each design, hoping it would serve her husband well in his journey into the afterlife?"

"Hm." Vandermeer picked up another shard, of a slightly different color than hers, so not likely of the same piece. "Interesting questions, I grant you. But it's still just clay. Dirt, compressed and baked and glazed."

"The same can be said of the vases from the Ming Dynasty, yet I imagine you would part with quite a few of your Yankee dollars to buy one of those." She set the shard carefully back into its spot. "For that matter, what is a jewel but a compressed part of earth? What is gold but shiny earth? We are the ones who assign value."

A smile teased his lips. He put his piece down, too, and motioned her back out into the sunlight. "One cannot argue with the lady's logic. And yet I have a feeling you didn't come by these sentiments from your father." He glanced over his shoulder as he said it and steered her toward the shore, away from the excavation and all the other men.

She breathed a scoff of a laugh. "Hardly." She looked up at his profile, wondering again what he was really about. Well, she might do a bit of fishing of her own. "Have you had a chance yet to see the British Museum archives, sir?"

Intrigue flickered across his face. "I haven't. Though I've been through those of the Louvre. There are always such treasures hiding in those places! Have you been through them?"

She nodded and smoothed back a wisp of hair that had pulled free of both hat and pins. "Nigel locked me in one night, so I had it to myself for eight hours, where I could explore to my heart's content."

She paused, wondering how he would react to the statement about her brother. How he would react to her test.

He would laugh, apparently. "Sounds like a brotherly prank, all right—though clearly you enjoyed it."

"Much to his dismay. All manner of pottery shards and faded weaving to enjoy." She angled a look up at him. "If you're working with him, you really ought to know he's not a kind man. His 'pranks,' as you call them, frequently result in people getting injured or worse."

"I've already been warned." And he sounded none too worried. In fact, he looked the epitome of well-bred ease as he stopped once their feet hit sand, slung his hands into his trouser pockets, and tilted his head back to receive the sunlight with a happy breath. "Hence, I suppose, why my quest was spying on him. Am I allowed to report my findings to you, my lady, or do I need to sneak back over to Tresco and report to the entire council?"

The words sent a jolt through her. Did that mean he'd found the answers they needed? If so, then she couldn't imagine anyone would want to wait to hear it until they could all assemble. "I am happy to receive your report, sir."

He grinned up at the clouds. "Good. Well, let it be noted this wasn't much of a quest. No dragons, no evil sorcerers, nothing but a few pounds slipped into a servant's hand at the hotel. Your brother seems to think that the artifact in question is Ron—apparently that's a spear of King Arthur?" He shrugged. "Was never much for the legend, myself."

"Ron." She hadn't been familiar with many of Arthur's weapons until recently, she had to admit. But Lord Telford had provided them with a list of all the blades said to have been his. She hadn't been expecting Elizabeth Mucknell's artifact to be a spear, though. Wouldn't the long shaft make it difficult to hide? And weren't most spears' shafts wooden? That seemed less likely to have survived the centuries.

But she was no expert—and for all his faults, her brother *was*. He wouldn't be looking for it if he thought it unlikely to find. For that matter, they could be searching only for the spear's metal blade, she supposed.

Vandermeer lowered his head and looked over at her. "Am I allowed to suggest an addition to my own quest? Because there's an ace I was already keeping in my back pocket." His brows hiked, challenging. "Your friends may find it interesting—I know Sheridan would. But I don't hand over aces willy-nilly. So maybe this is more a return quest request—I need a show of faith, too, before I share my secrets."

Emily lifted her own brows. "A return quest request?" That was quite a mouthful, and she had to shake her head at the absurdity of it all. "I'll certainly give my friends the message about this 'other' information you say you possess." She took a step backward, putting some space between them. Not that she knew what she could do with the space. She was trapped here until someone delivered her back to St. Mary's. Though at least she had a few coins in her pocket now, thanks to her mysterious benefactor. If it came down to it, she could walk to St. Agnes if the tide was out and beg someone to ferry her back to the big island.

"Good. And now with that business out of the way . . ." He made a sweeping gesture up the beach. "Care to stroll with me? I intend to regale you with tales of all the adventures that paint me in a positive light and blatantly pass over any that don't. You can probably hear those from the Howe sisters anyway."

Despite herself, she smiled. "They've already done their regaling. I suppose it's only fair to hear your side."

He splayed a hand over his heart, an exaggerated crestfallen look on his face. "They've told tales on me already? No doubt the moment I arrived."

And if she wasn't mistaken, there was a flicker of something real behind the exaggeration too. Or perhaps it was a trick of the light. "More or less. Lady Millicent couldn't believe that 'the Dutchman' was threatening their search yet again."

"Ah, Millie. She—" he lifted a hand to shade his eyes as he gazed up the beach and then sighed—"is on her way. Ought to have expected as much. Well, what do you say, my lady? Make it easy on her and go to meet her, or walk the other way and make her chase us down before she rescues you from my clutches?"

Emily lifted a hand to shade her eyes as well and had to smile at the figures hurrying up the sand. Millicent and Abbie—and Tommie. That must have been where she ran. Not to the Thornes, who would have had to sail back to Tresco for help for her, but straight to the Howes. Clever girl. "I'd say whichever will keep us out of view of my father, frankly. I find I'm not in the mood for another of his lectures today."

He looked genuinely baffled. "What could he possibly have to lecture you about? He speaks of you as his perfect little darling—an impression I'm eager to uphold, mind you."

It was unladylike to let her complete surprise show on her face, but she didn't much care. "If he does, it's only because he imagines it's what you want to hear. I assure you, sir, that my father doesn't know me well enough to speak to either my strengths or my flaws. He has made a career of ignoring my existence."

His bafflement gave way to amusement. "Well, we *are* being blunt today, aren't we? Refreshing." He offered his elbow and nodded toward the approaching women. "I suppose that explains why he can't keep his facts straight on what you supposedly like and don't."

She set her fingers as lightly as possible against his forearm and was glad when he set a good pace toward their coming visitors. "And all the while he is baffled that you would be interested—if we're still being blunt."

"Why would he be baffled? You're beautiful, from a good family, and you understand the world I move in. Why not see if we suit each other on a personal level?"

He made it sound like any other business transaction. Examine the facts, see if the new piece will fit in the existing collection, debate whether it appeals. And perhaps that's what marriage was most of the time.

But her whole life had been nothing but transactional. Was it so wrong to wish for something more?

"That clearly didn't come out right. What I meant to say was that you're very appealing, my lady, and I would love the chance to get to know you better—and I cannot think why your father wouldn't see that. Perhaps you misunderstood him."

She sent him a look that must be every bit as scathing as it felt, given his wince.

"Obviously also the wrong thing to say. I'm charming, really I am! Despite all evidence to the contrary."

She let herself relax and chuckle at that, largely because Millicent, Abbie, and Tommie were closing in. "You are. But I'm not much interested in being charmed." She knew too well how deceptive it could be—Nigel, too, could be charming. And her father was always the life of the party.

Tommie broke into a run. "My lady! Are you all right?"

"All right?" Vandermeer released her hand but frowned. "What do they think, that I kidnapped you?"

Emily nodded her answer to Tommie even as she said, "Not you—but my father did, more or less. Put me forcibly on the yacht and knocked my poor maid to the ground to accomplish it."

"Are you quite serious?" He came to a halt, looking half-outraged and half-incredulous. "That nearly makes me regret all my hints that I'd like to spend more time with you. I didn't realize it would involve manhandling. Chalk that up to my pride, I suppose. No one's ever had to be *forced* into my company."

"It isn't your company, sir. It's the company you've been keeping." She nodded toward the hill and the swarm of men up on it. He'd know she meant her father and brother.

He held out his arms. "Happy to switch sides, as I said before. Perhaps they'll believe me now, after you tell them about Ron." Over his shoulder, he shouted, "Isn't that right, Millie?"

Lady Millicent was charging up the beach nearly as fast as Tommie. They both arrived, breathless, within a few seconds of each other. Millicent somehow made her gasp for air sound like an outraged huff. "I don't know what you expect me to agree with, Donald darling, but we both know I'd argue if you said the sky was blue."

He grinned over at her. "Because it really *is* cerulean today. To call it 'blue' is just far too vague. Imprecise."

"And imprecision is all but a falsehood." Her lips stayed straight, but her eyes smiled.

Tommie pressed close to Emily's side. "Are you certain you're all right? The way your father dragged you off . . ."

"I'm fine," she answered in a whisper. "He only wanted me to spend time with Vandermeer. Well, and to tell me how horrid I am."

Millicent dragged in another mouthful of air. "Well. We've come to rescue you, dearest. The Peppers' sloop is waiting in the harbor in St. Agnes. The tide is out, so we can walk over. Your father can't throw too big a tantrum if he sees us all walking together, and by the time he thinks to question it, we'll be back on St. Mary's."

Vandermeer was nodding along as if the plan was of his own making. "And usually Mr. Pepper just drops you off, so he won't assume you have a quick escape planned. Good thinking, Millie."

"Well, now I'm doubting myself."

He laughed and turned toward Abbie. "I keep telling you ladies I'm not the enemy. Allow me to prove myself a friend." He offered an elbow to Millicent with a wink. "For appearances."

Abbie halted her progress toward them and waited for them to catch up. Emily would have been happy to bring up the rear with Tommie, but apparently that didn't satisfy the sisters' protective instincts, because Millicent held Vandermeer back until they had passed them by.

How very funny it was—twenty years of her life she had felt alone in her family, forced to uphold the mask of the "honorable Scofields." But suddenly she had friends who not only believed the truth, but who went out of their way to help her. To protect her. To show her she was more than her father deemed her.

They strolled at a sedate pace, which was a good thing, given that her father stomped to the brow of the hill at one point and gazed down at them. But as soon as he did so, Vandermeer moved up to her side and said, "Laugh, my lady, and make it look convincing."

She obliged, and a moment later, Father ambled away, apparently convinced that the Howes were just dropping by for their usual espionage and that it was nothing to be concerned about. If he recognized Tommie, he apparently didn't question her presence.

Which meant that within a few minutes they were passing by the slanted standing stone called the Old Man and crossing the damp tombolo connecting Gugh to St. Agnes. It would take another few minutes to walk through the town, then onto Mr. Pepper's boat and back to the relative safety of St. Mary's. She would compose a note for her friends, telling them that her brother was searching for the spear called Ron, and send it to Tresco with the Thornes that afternoon.

Her shoulders eased as they followed Old Lane into the village proper. Her father wasn't chasing after her, and she hadn't even seen Nigel anywhere on Gugh. Really, the "rescue" was even a bit of an overreaction. Vandermeer was no threat, she was all but certain.

Abbie stepped around her to say something to her sister, leaving Emily and Tommie in the lead for a moment. Just a moment. But it happened to be at the same time a door opened in one of the houses, and a young woman stepped out, glanced up, saw her—and let the load of laundry in her arms fall to the ground, a strangled scream gurgling out.

Emily froze, clueless as to why their party should elicit such a reaction. The girl, shaking, reached for the door latch and struggled with it for a long moment before she managed to get it open. She was whimpering as she vanished inside.

Why? Emily had never seen the young woman before, but she was the one she'd been looking at, the one she'd reacted to.

"Keep moving, my lady," Tommie said quietly, prodding her onward. "You'll only gather more attention by standing there."

She moved, but she craned her head back to better note which house it was. Perhaps she could find out who lived there and why the sight of her would garner such a response. It wasn't as though her red hair—

Her hair. She lifted a hand to it, then touched her nose, her chin. Nigel's hair was only a shade or two darker. Her features were just feminine versions of his. They looked alike—so much alike that people who knew him always recognized her in a glance as his sister, which he hated.

What if it wasn't her that girl was reacting to at all, but her brother? She could all but guarantee that he'd come striding along that tombolo in the last month. He'd probably seen and spoken to every person in the village on St. Agnes. And what else?

Unable to catch her breath, Emily turned to Tommie. "What has he done?"

Her maid, her friend, didn't ask for any explanation of which "he" she meant, nor question her assumption that the girl's reaction had something to do with Nigel. Nostrils flaring, she simply shook her head.

Mechanically, Emily let the others urge her along the street. But she knew she'd be penning a second note as soon as she got back to her flat. The one to the Tremaynes, and another to her mother. Not a plea for communication this time—no, a demand. A demand to know whether Nigel was guilty of more than bullying and hiring others to do his dirty work. A demand to know if her brother could be capable of the worst kind of violence against a woman.

16

Tommie kept her fingers tucked into Enyon's as they walked up Old Lane on St. Agnes, the opposite direction from when she'd walked Lady Emily to the Peppers' sloop earlier that day. Now sunset was painting its colors over the sky, but Enyon said he wasn't concerned about having to sail home by moonlight.

She couldn't bring herself to be concerned about that either. Not with the vision of that poor, frightened girl haunting her through every hour that had passed. She'd recognized the fear on her face as surely as Lady Emily had and had made the same connection. But where Emily had gone silent, clearly trying to imagine what her brother had done, Tommie didn't have to guess. She knew.

Her fingers shook in Enyon's, and he gave them a squeeze. "Are you all right, Thomasina?"

She nodded, even though she wasn't, not really. "Are you sure you know who it was?" She'd told him which house the girl had been coming out of, but he'd shaken his head and said no young woman lived in that last cottage on Old Lane. She'd then described the girl herself—young, perhaps seventeen or eighteen, with hair black as midnight and skin clear as cream.

Enyon offered a small but confident smile. "There are only two families on St. Agnes with a daughter the right age, and the other has fairer hair. Ailla is the most likely candidate—and that's where her grandmother lives, so it makes sense. Old Mrs. Marrack has been ill the last few weeks, so it's reasonable that Ailla would have been gathering her laundry to do with her own family's."

Ailla. Had Nigel even bothered learning her name? Had he smiled at her, made her think he saw her as more than a common girl, lured her away from the safety of her family and friends?

Had he told her it was her own fault for smiling back?

Tommie's heart pounded. She had to make a concerted effort not to squeeze Enyon's hand too hard—but she couldn't. *Shouldn't,* anyway. Because there was no way they'd escape this meeting without him realizing what had happened to her. And no way this relationship that she'd blithely let develop would continue after he knew. No one wanted a girl who'd been stripped of her virtue. No one wanted a tarnished, broken soul.

"I hope it's nothing," she murmured. "That she was frightened because Emily looked like someone from a ghost story of Mr. Gibson's or something."

But she knew. She knew what Nigel had done to this poor girl, and she knew it was her own fault it had happened. If she had just said something, warned everyone to be on their guard . . .

She'd told Enyon only that she feared Nigel had hurt the girl. Perhaps he could imagine the *how*, but she'd given him no indication of *why* she feared it with such certainty. Perhaps she should have told him that afternoon, before he took her here. Perhaps she owed him that explanation, given that he was serious in his court. Perhaps it was cowardly of her to let him learn it simply by being there when she spoke with Ailla.

But she only had the strength to get through it once. If that made her a coward, then so be it.

Enyon turned them off Old Lane onto, of all things, New Lane. They seemed to be the only two named roads on the small island. It had amused her earlier, when she was simply hastening through the village so she could get to Gugh with the Howe ladies. Now she hadn't any room left in her spirit for amusement. Only for fear.

Fear that she was too late to help. Fear that Enyon would never again look at her as he'd been doing. Fear that this coming conversation would shatter her.

She couldn't turn from it, though, couldn't just pretend she hadn't seen that same fear in the girl's eyes.

This was Tommie's gauntlet. Her trial by fire. This was where she had to prove herself to be something more than what Nigel Scofield had made her. She had to face it, face what had happened, face the consequences of her own silence.

And if she lost everything all over again . . . well then, she'd just have to trust that the Lord could do more with her shattered than He could with her as she was now, barely holding together. That He meant her to be a mosaic instead of a whole.

A moment later, Enyon led her toward a little cottage, small but well-tended, with a riot of flowers blooming around the door and in boxes hanging from the windows. From somewhere nearby, children's laughter and squeals filled the twilight air. Enyon gave her fingers one more squeeze, offered one more sober smile, and knocked.

The door whooshed open after just a few heartbeats. A woman— somewhere between forty and fifty, Tommie guessed—smiled a broad welcome the moment she spotted him. "Enny! What an unexpected pleasure. How's your mam? I've been meaning to stop by her shop and see her."

"Oh, she's good as always. Sent you this." He lifted a basket full of fragrant bread rolls. "We heard Jack's mam has been poorly and thought you may be short on time."

"Bless you. Come in, come in." She stepped aside, taking the basket he handed her with an appreciative whiff. "Ailla, put the kettle on, dearover. Enny's here with his girl. Thomasina, isn't it?"

It made her start a bit to hear herself referred to as "Enny's girl"—

when had that happened? Did everyone think so? And if so, what would they say when he walked away? What would they think of her then?

And how did he have all the Scillonians calling her *Thomasina*?

She dredged up a smile and bobbed a quick curtsy, trying to catch a glimpse of Ailla without it being obvious. "Yes, Mrs. Marrack. Or Tommie, if you like. It's what everyone but Enyon has always called me."

She sent him a glance she hoped was teasing, and he grinned back at her. On Sunday, as they'd sailed over to Bryher together, she'd asked him why he never called her by her nickname. He'd shrugged and flushed and said that when Mrs. Dawe first mentioned "Tommie," he'd thought she was talking about one of the valets. Then when he'd met *her* and found her to be *"such a pretty thing"*—his very words—he just couldn't reconcile the name so had taken to thinking of her as Thomasina instead.

She'd never really cared for her full name. But then, she'd never heard it trip so warmly from his lips. Now she found she quite liked it.

Bad news, all of it. Much as she liked Enyon, much as he seemed different from any other man she'd ever met, much as he seemed to see those ghosts inside and invite her to believe in something greater . . . well, it couldn't end well, could it? He deserved better than her. And she didn't know if being able to tuck her fingers into his, now, was an indicator of being able to dream of a future. With him or anyone else.

Ailla stepped out of the kitchen, wiping her hands on her apron. "Kettle's on, Mam. Enny, Luke said to tell you next time we saw you that . . ." Her words tapered off when she spotted them.

Spotted *her*. Tommie hadn't been certain if the girl would even recognize her, given how complete her focus had seemed to be on Emily that morning, but clearly she did. Her face went pale, but she cleared her throat, forcing her smile back to her lips. "That, em, you owe him a sweet roll. Something about Casek and Mabena?"

Enyon chuckled. "He *would* remember that wager from five years ago. You've heard from him lately, then, I suppose?"

Mrs. Marrack nodded and passed the bread to her daughter, who slid it onto the table visible through the kitchen door. "He writes regularly, once a month, just like I told him he must if he didn't want his old mam charging onto the mainland and hunting him down in his fancy new position." To Tommie she added, "Luke's working for an import firm—he has an office and everything. Always had a head for numbers, that lad of mine."

Tommie's smile came a little easier at the clear pride in Mrs. Marrack's face. She was a handsome woman; it was no wonder she had such a lovely daughter. "I wish my brother had been as good at keeping his word to our mam. He scarcely remembers to write to her twice a year."

"That must break her heart. A mam can never stop thinking of her children. We want to share in their joy . . . just as we do in their pain." She flicked a gaze toward Ailla that Tommie would have missed had she not been watching for it.

She knew. That would make it easier. Tommie hadn't known how to get Ailla alone to question her outright or how to be subtle about her business if she couldn't. Nor had she known how to approach the family without Enyon by her side. They wouldn't slam a door in *his* face. She couldn't be certain the same applied to her. She was just an incomer, after all. One associated with the Scofields. Why should they trust her?

She'd decided that they *wouldn't* trust Briggs, Lady Emily's maid. But maybe they would trust Tommie, "Enny's girl," if she showed up by his side.

Enyon and Tommie followed the two Marrack women into their small front parlor, which reminded Tommie acutely of her own home. Each piece of furniture lovingly tended but faded with time and constant wear. He took the chair Mrs. Marrack indicated, one of the two flanking the fireplace, while the lady of the house took its twin.

Ailla sat on the sofa, stiff as the poker by Enyon's chair. Tommie eased to a seat beside Ailla. From this distance, she could see a yellowed bruise on her cheekbone, covered with powder and some sort of cream that had smudged off.

All her plans for how to start this conversation—none of which had felt right, anyway—flew from her mind. "He hurt you, didn't he? Nigel Scofield? I'm sorrier for that than I can say."

Ailla's head snapped around. Tommie had expected that same fear she'd shown earlier, but it was fire in her eyes now. Her mother was trying to stutter some claim about not knowing what she was talking about, but Ailla cut her off with, "You're *sorry*? You're one of them! I saw you with her this morning, with that monster's *sister*!"

Well, her instinct about that had been right, too, then, hadn't it? Tommie leaned close, ignoring both the fluttering matron and Enyon. "How do you think I know what he's done? I lived under the same roof as that monster, Ailla. I know what he did to you—I know because he did the same to me."

It wasn't a confession she'd ever made out loud, nor had she ever really wanted to. But face powders could only hide the bruise on her cheek. Ailla needed to know that she didn't have to hide the one on her spirit. That someone understood.

Enyon went stiff in his chair, but she ignored that, too, and kept her gaze on the girl.

Mrs. Marrack fluttered all the more. "Shh! Keep your voice down, Tommie." She darted an anxious look toward the door. "We can't let her father find out. He'd fly off the handle, do something foolish." She spun to Enyon. "You know he would! He'd charge into that camp with his hunting piece and shoot someone and be arrested and sent away, and then what?"

Enyon made some comforting gesture toward the mother, but Tommie didn't move her gaze from the daughter. Ailla's breaths came fast now, her eyes filling with tears. "I'm no fool," she whispered. "Nor the sort of girl who . . . I saw him in the village a few times, and he was charming, but I never was anything but polite.

Never. I certainly never . . . but then when I was coming home from my mamm-wynn's house one night, he was there, and . . ."

Tommie scooted closer and reached for her hand. "I know. It was no fault of yours, Ailla. Whatever he's said, or whatever lies have been parading through your mind and heart since, it's not true."

Words that were so easy to say to another, now that she knew there *was* another. Words no one had ever spoken to her, and which she wouldn't have believed if they had. Because it had *felt* like her fault. Like her sin. Like there must have been something defective in her, to make him treat her that way. She must have done something wrong.

But she could see it more clearly in Ailla. This pretty young island lass was not at fault.

Ailla squeezed her eyes closed, squeezed Tommie's fingers just as tightly, and sucked a breath in through her teeth. "I want him to pay. I want to march into the constable's office and tell him what happened . . . but I can't. I can't do that to my tas and mam. To my brother. Then everyone would know, and Tas couldn't hold his head up at the pub without being able to say he'd tried to set it to rights, and . . . and what's the point, anyway? He's the son of an *earl*. He'll never pay, not because of me."

"I understand. I do." Tommie covered their joined hands with her free one too. "And I can tell you this—if you make noise, if you involve the constable, I imagine the earl *will* make it go away, which would mean money for you, if you . . . find you need it."

Ailla's hands jerked. "I don't want his *money*."

"I know that—but it's the way of it in their world. It's all you'll get. There will be no apology, there will be no justice." It sickened her to say so, but she knew it was true. How many times had the servants shared gossip about the poor girls who this or that lord had to pay off? And it was the woman whose reputation and life were left in tatters, never the lord's. Oh no—and half the time, everyone talked as if the girl had just made it all up for blackmailing purposes.

"I'm sorry, Ailla. I should have said something, warned everyone, but I . . . I never paused to think he would treat anyone else this way. I thought it was just *me* he'd deemed so worthless." Guilt gnawed at her.

She should have spoken up. The very moment he arrived in the Scillies, she should have realized he posed a threat to others.

"It isn't your fault." Ailla's words came quieter now, and her fingers relaxed in Tommie's. "I just . . . I don't know what to do. I don't know how to talk to my friends, and I feel like a fraud every time I smile at my father. When I consider that there could be a child, I get this panic in my chest—and then the guilt. I keep searching my mind, trying to determine what I did wrong. How I should have left Mamm-wynn's earlier, before dark. I feel so . . ."

"I know." There were words for it, all of them ugly. None worth putting voice to. "I do, all of it. The way you feel as though everyone knows or should be able to just by looking at you—and then the *fear* that they do . . . and the terrible anger when they don't. That your life has been changed forever, and they just go on as if nothing happened."

"Yes. *Yes.*" Ailla leaned forward, a sob ripping from her chest, and rested her head on Tommie's shoulder.

She wrapped her arms around the girl—she must be around the same age as Meredith—and held her like she would have her own sister. Like she'd so desperately wished someone had known to do for her. Mrs. Marrack had surely already offered what solace she could, but she couldn't know exactly how she felt. And more, she'd be too concerned with how her husband would react and what the neighbors would think and how to protect her daughter. All reasonable fears, but they would get in the way of simply mourning with her.

Tempting as it was to look over her head and see what the other two were doing, Tommie kept her focus solely on Ailla—because this was about her, not her own worry over what Enyon thought.

Only when the girl's crying slowed and she sat up straight again did Tommie let herself look around. She found that Enyon was keeping watch at the door, and that Mrs. Marrack was arranging teacups on a tray, her own eyes red too.

Tommie smoothed a strand of ebony hair back from Ailla's wet cheeks. "There now. You can talk to me whenever you need to—I'm always either on St. Mary's or Tresco. Lady Emily and I are letting the flat over Mrs. Gilligan's shop, and occasionally I pop into Mrs. Thorne's to lend a hand. Or else we're at the Tremaynes'. I'd welcome you anytime at all—and you needn't fear Lady Emily either. She's no stranger to her brother's cruelty, though it takes a different form with her."

Ailla nodded and swiped at her eyes. "Thank you."

"If I may make a suggestion?" Enyon eased a step closer and waited for Ailla to look up and her mother to stop fiddling with cups and spoons. "You could consult with Ollie too—especially as concerns Jack, and how or if to tell him. You know he'll treat the situation with compassion and consideration . . . and Jack holds him in high esteem."

He glanced at Tommie, and she wondered if he meant the advice for her as well. *Talk to Ollie.* Him pawning off her troubles onto someone else's shoulders?

Oddly, Ailla looked not to her mother but to Tommie too. She gave her an encouraging nod, ignoring Enyon again. "Mr. Tremayne can be trusted," Tommie said, "and from what I've seen, he has an uncanny knack for speaking just the wisdom a person needs to hear when they're hurting."

Though Ailla nodded, she looked far from convinced. Her fingers gripped Tommie's again. "Would you . . . come with us?"

And admit not just to Enyon but to his best friend what that monster had done to her? She sucked in a long breath. She'd rather cover that wound over and pray that it would heal eventually if she ignored it long enough. She'd rather stew in her bitterness toward Nigel than let the uncanny Oliver Tremayne prod her into trying to forgive him.

But she knew that was foolish, even as she wanted to cling to it.

Knew that she wouldn't wish this eternal ache on Ailla. "Of course I will."

"All right, then. If you want to, Mam."

Mrs. Marrack sniffed and lifted her apron to dab at her eyes. "I could certainly use some advice on talking to your tas about it. And heaven knows Ollie's the only vicar in a hundred miles he'd consider listening to."

"Speaking of your husband, I believe I hear his baritone." Enyon thumbed toward the open window, through which a man's pitch-perfect voice drifted, belting out a sea shanty.

Ailla sprang to her feet. "Tell him I'm over at Beatrice's. He'll know something's wrong if he sees I've been crying." And with that she dashed up the stairs and presumably into her bedroom.

Her mother chuckled. "He won't think anything of *me* crying. Do it all the time. Here—have your tea."

Tommie accepted a cup because they could hardly scurry out and leave Mrs. Marrack to explain the fixed tray that sat untouched. But she barely tasted the tea or the biscuits. She smiled politely and murmured the right words when Mr. Marrack came in—a barrel-chested bull of a man who certainly seemed the type to want to teach Nigel Scofield a lesson with his fists or a gun. But she was relieved when, after half an hour, Enyon made their excuses and led her back out into the soft night.

The air was cool, promising autumn would soon be upon them. She wrapped her shawl tight around her shoulders and held it in place with crossed arms.

Protective, that. If she didn't give him a chance to take her hand or arm, then he had no chance to refuse to do so.

Enyon sighed and tucked his own hands into his pockets. "Thomasina . . ."

"Don't, Enyon. Not yet. Whatever you're going to say, I'm not ready to hear it." Because he would couch it in compassion—she knew he would. He would say he understood, and what a monster Nigel was, and he'd encourage her to go to Ollie, to seek solace for her soul. But then he would drift away. Maybe say he feared hurting her worse, or something else that would give him an excuse to go off and look for a girl with her virtue intact.

He drew in a long breath. "My words will keep—you just let me know when you're ready for them."

That was the moment—when she knew that their next conversation would be their last—that she realized she loved him. Loved the man who believed in the unbelievable, the boy who used to jump at ghost stories.

If only he wouldn't run from the ones inside her.

17

Bram had imagined himself in many situations—facing down dragons, opposite a dark knight in a joust, squaring off against evil sorceresses—but never in his wildest dreams had he thought that one of the greatest adventures of his life would involve him sitting in a quaint little pub on a tiny speck of an island with his future brother-in-law's grandfather at his side telling pirate stories. Yet here he was, at the same scarred table he'd claimed as his own a week ago, a single pint before him—half-drained at the two-hour mark—and a notebook on the table that he'd borrowed from Sheridan.

Most shocking of all: He was having a grand time, despite the serious reason Enyon had asked him to make himself a regular. He'd yet to hear any grumblings about Scofield, but he'd been hearing plenty of other tales. He clapped and hooted his approval along with everyone else when Gibson finished his latest outlandish story, smiling at the din that immediately took over from the hush that had fallen ten minutes before when someone shouted, "Gib's got another one!"

He'd thought that gentlemen were held in respect in the clubs in London to which they paid ridiculous amounts to belong. He'd thought it because they had liveried men to bow to him when he entered and offer to take his coat and hat, because the other gentlemen and lords greeted him with somber nods and knew his name and asked after his life. But he was now fully convinced that true respect was when one could get an entire pub to fall silent simply by saying, "Have I told you the one about the mermaid and the cursed pirate king?"

Bram leaned back in his chair and took another small sip of his ale, tossing his pen to the page in his notebook now covered in a scrawl nearly illegible. Sheridan had told him that he might as well record whatever stories the old man told, for the collection of them that he and Beth and Oliver were putting together. He'd grumbled about it, just to keep up appearances, but he didn't mind the task. Later he'd have to rewrite it, though, in a form that others could read.

Gibson laughed at something another old chap said and then turned back to Bram with a wink. "There you go, lad. I warmed them up for you."

Bram saluted him with his glass and then set it back down. "Much appreciated."

The pub's door swung open, and Hez Rigsby stepped in, along with a gust of cool air, damp from the evening's drizzle. The newcomer's gaze swung through the crowd and connected with Bram's. He grinned and held aloft an old, worn-looking book. "Found it, milord!"

Bram's smile grew. He'd sat here half the night last night, but Rigsby hadn't made another appearance. He'd known the fellow would return eventually, though, once he'd dug through his family's attic. "Excellent. Come and join me, Rigs." Much like he'd seen the locals do, he pushed out the chair across from him with his foot.

Rigsby exchanged a few greetings on his way, but eventually arrived at Bram's table and sat. Gibson and a few of his cohorts gathered around, too, having been trained, apparently, to always listen when a story was being exchanged. "Began to fear the missus had tossed out the lot of these," Rigsby said as he fished a pair of spectacles from his pocket. He positioned them carefully on his nose and hooked the earpieces into place. "But she found 'em this morning while I was on the water. Greeted me at the door with it this afternoon. I nearly ran it to the Tremaynes' then and there to show you."

Bram grinned. "You could have. Everyone's eager to see what you've found."

"Well, now." Rigsby opened the cover of the book, licked his thumb, and began turning pages. "Awful lot of folks around there these days. Never know what you young'uns may be up to on a given afternoon, so I says, 'Rigs, show a bit of patience. Tonight's soon enough, and you won't mind a trip to the pub, now, will you?' And I, being a wise advisor, decided to listen to myself."

Chuckling along with the rest of the audience, Bram granted the point with an inclined head and said in a stage whisper to Gibson, "I think that's a hint that I need to buy him a pint."

Gibson pushed away from the table. "I'll fetch it for you, Rigs. And put it on your tab, Telly."

"Perfect." No one in the world aside from Sheridan had ever called him *Telly*, but he wasn't about to argue with Mr. Gibson. Besides . . . it made him feel part of the family. He wondered, for one moment, what Father would say if he saw him now, here, slouching in an island pub with a scrawled-upon notebook before him, surrounded by island men of every generation, listening to island tales.

The question had no time to foment any true contemplation, though. Rigsby shouted, "Aha! Here it is," and turned the book around to face Bram.

It was handwritten, the ink rusted to brown and faded, and the scrawl wasn't nearly as easy to decipher as Elizabeth Mucknell's journal had been. But thanks to Sheridan, Bram was used to having old, illegible documents shoved at him and had become rather expert at decoding the handwriting of those from decades or centuries past. And at least this one wasn't written in Old or Middle English, which were always the ones Sher shoved at him, since he needed the translation help. Bram set about working through it.

"Aloud now, lad, come on. Don't keep us in suspense."

Bram grinned up at Gibson, who was returning with a pint in hand for Rigsby. "Give me a minute to decipher it first."

"You've had a minute. Come now, put that fancy education to use."

He chuckled. And relented. He'd have to skim over or correct as best he could a few parts where the text was too faded or blotted by time or mold, but they would surely expect nothing less. "All right. It's dated the second of February 1801 and begins, 'Mam was in one of her musing moods today and brought out the old story of Lyonesse. I'd heard the tale from other mouths often enough, but never from Mam. And I liked her version better. Perhaps she brought it with her from the mainland when she married Tas.'"

"Mam was a relative of the Vyvyans, you know," Rigsby said. "They love their stories of Trevelyan like no one else in the world."

Interesting. Mr. Gale's collection was the only place thus far he'd been able to find much mention of Trevelyan, but the vicar had confessed that he hadn't gotten as much information from the Vyvyans on it as he had hoped. Perhaps this account would be able to fill in some blanks in the story.

Bram went back to the page before him. "'Trevelyan, that noble governor of Lyonesse, had been struggling for years with his foolish people. He himself, a direct descendant of Sir Tristan, was as upright in character as he was in stature, and time and again he pled with the sinful citizens to give up their destructive ways and repent. Time and again he fell on his knees in the church that few others even attended and beseeched God to give him more time to reach them. Whene'er he was tempted to give up on them, he would look down to the gold on his hip, says Mam, and remember from whence he came. He would remember how his lot was to fight always for justice and mercy and truth and goodness, and that evil would not defeat it.'"

"That there." Gibson leaned over and tapped the page. "What the deuce is 'the gold on his hip,' Rigs?"

Rigsby shrugged. "Doesn't say, does it? Were I to guess, he didn't know, nor did his mam. Pocket watch, maybe? Inherited?"

Gibson scoffed. "There were no pocket watches yet in Trevelyan's day."

"Well, how'm I to know, then? Could be a blighted belt or a fancy what's-it for keys. That'd make sense, wouldn't it? Keys would remind him of his responsibilities."

"A chatelaine?" Bram let his head sway from side to side in thought. It *would* make a bit of sense . . . but if this was something passed down from Tristan and, perhaps, from King Arthur, then he wasn't convinced. There were no tales of keys and chatelaines in the *Prose Tristan* or any of the Arthurian tales he'd read. "Hard to say. Could be anything, really. A belt or buckler, the hilt of a dagger, or even something he kept in a money purse."

But not, so far as he could imagine, the spear or lance called Ron. One couldn't carry a spear on one's hip—and even if it was just the blade, it wouldn't be gold, would it?

Was it possible that Nigel Scofield was wrong? Dare they hope so? Though even if he was, that didn't mean he wouldn't find whatever it really was if he kept searching as thoroughly as he'd been doing.

"Boring, all." Gibson sighed. "Onward, then, before I come up with a better story than that for it."

Bram chuckled. "Onward. He continues, 'For never did he let that reminder out of his sight, that he was of Tristan's line, and his forebear had been so great a man that King Arthur himself had entrusted him with so precious a symbol of all that was good and noble.'" Now Bram paused, staring at the words.

King Arthur. It actually said it, right there on the page. His blood trilled in his veins, and he wished Sheridan were here to do a jig and shout.

Someone nudged his shoulder. "Go on, my lord."

"Right. 'But the people would not turn their hearts from their wicked ways. One day a message came for Trevelyan, bidding him come to the mainland. He obeyed, but alas, when he arrived he could find the sender nowhere, search as he might. After a fruitless day of riding hither and yon in search of the mysterious writer of the note, he gave up and decided to rest his noble steed and himself. But while he slept, a terrible storm set upon the land.'"

"Oh, we know this part!" someone else said, slapping the table. "The great storm what sunk the land."

"Hush, Lanyon."

"Aye, let him read."

Though he flashed a smile toward the two fishermen, Bram promptly returned his gaze to the page. "Let's see. ''Twas the shaking and moaning of the very land beneath him that woke Trevelyan from his slumber, but up he sprang with a terrible foreboding in his chest, and the metal at his hip singing a warning. Quickly did he heed it, jumping upon his white stallion and racing for higher ground. But all the while, his heart sank lower and lower. For he knew, deep in his soul, that the time of reckoning had come for his sinful people. And though God had spared him the same fate, he ached for them and spent that whole storm-tossed night in prayer, longing to be back on his island, helping whomever he could.'"

He would have liked to pause there for more than a moment and let it sink in, but his audience would have none of that, so he cleared his throat and kept reading. "'When dawn broke, it was a different world he saw. The waters had covered the place where he'd slept just a day before, and too well did he know what that meant for his home. Fast as lightning, he found a boat and sailed back to Lyonesse . . . only to find that Lyonesse was no more. All that remained were the very peaks of the hills, scattered about the seas that still rocked and churned, and from whose depths his soul could still hear the wailing of the lost.

"'But *all* was not lost. On those peaks were huddled the few—the few who had heeded his warnings, the few who had fallen to their knees, the few who were left of his kingdom. When questioned, they all claimed the same impossible thing—that minutes before the waters roared, they saw Trevelyan appear in their door, warning them to seek higher ground. And that all through the storm, when they stumbled and faltered, there he was again, leading them on. Even knowing he was on the mainland, they heralded him as their hero, claiming he'd led them with that symbol of nobility held aloft, lighting the way with its holy fire. But Trevelyan felt keenly where he had failed. So many souls lost forever, because they would not listen. Because they had scorned all things noble and good. And so, he took that precious reminder of light and nobility and buried it that day, offering it back to the Lord as a sacrifice. And so it remains to this very day, anchored in the Scillonian granite, Mam said, both a testament against us and a call to something better, buried in our very hearts.'"

Bram could scarcely breathe. Silence rang in his ears just as it had after Gibson's story, and though it slowly filled with whispers and rumbles, he couldn't make sense of any of them. He was too focused on the words.

This was it—it had to be. The story Elizabeth Mucknell had heard. A story with Trevelyan interceding, with some artifact, some "symbol" of nobility that had passed from Arthur's hand to Tristan's and from Tristan all the way down to him. A symbol he had then buried in the remains of Lyonesse—in the Scillies.

He had to show the others. He'd wake them all up if he must. His gaze flew to Rigsby's. "May I borrow this for a day or two, to copy it out?"

The fisherman smiled. "'Course you can, milord. It'd be an honor to have my family's stories put down in that book of yours. Take your time."

"Thank you." He ought to stay longer. Finish that ale. Laugh some more, listen some more. But he couldn't, not with a story like this begging to be shared with his friends. He stood. "I had better get back now, while the rain's let up. Thank you again, Rigsby. This will make a lovely addition to our collection."

Rigsby waved it off but looked rather pleased with himself. "Anytime, anytime. Have a good night, milord."

Gibson straightened too. "I'll say good-night too."

Bram settled his tab, tucked the two books and his pen under the shelter of his overcoat, and dashed out into the drizzle, Gibson at his side. While still in the light from the pub's windows, they exchanged a look. And grinned.

"Knew we'd find it sometime or another. And there it is." Gibson slapped a hand to his back. "Let's hurry. They'll all want to hear this, even if we have to wake them up to share it."

Rather than waste precious breath on agreement, Bram simply picked up the pace. They navigated with ease through the familiar streets of Grimsby and were soon back in the even more familiar entryway of the Tremayne house. Gibson let the door slam shut behind him. "I'll wake the children and Adelle. You see if Sheridan's still up."

Bram shrugged out of his damp coat, tossed his hat to a table, and strode toward the library. If anyone was still awake, that's where they'd be. And praise the Lord, a light shone from the partially closed door, and voices came from within.

He wasn't surprised to find Sheridan on the leather sofa with a book in hand, nor was it all that unexpected to find that Beth was leaning against him, another book in hers. What he hadn't dared to hope for but was delighted to discover was that Emily—who Beth had lured into staying over again tonight—was awake as well, seated in an armchair.

She looked up when he charged in and gave him a warm smile that mixed in his blood with that flame of discovery and chased away the chill of the night's rain. Perhaps he wasn't a knight returning from a quest, per se, but he felt like one as he brandished the book. "We've found it! The story Lizza Mucknell alluded to!"

"What? Let me see!" Sheridan sprang from the sofa as if he were more tiger than man and the book his prey.

But Bram found himself watching Emily's movements instead

of his best friend's. Sher's excitement he knew—and could parry in his sleep. A step to the side to avoid being bumped into, a quick instruction to turn to the page he'd marked with a slip of paper, and Sheridan would be happily lost for the next several minutes.

Emily, though. Her fascination unfolded far more quietly. She stood with all the grace she always exuded, and with the hesitation he'd come to expect of her. Moving slowly toward the table, she didn't leap toward Sheridan's side like Beth did or laughingly try to elbow him out of the way so she could get a peek. No, instead she moved softly to Bram's side.

A month ago—even a week or two ago—it would have been Beth's side she sought, to Beth she murmured her questions. But tonight it was Bram she stood beside, to him she said, "What is it? Does it answer any questions? Is Nigel on the right trail?"

She might as well have knighted him. Bram smiled down at her. "I don't know that he is. There are some answers there. Not all, but quite a few."

Oliver and Gibson joined them a minute later—Mamm-wynn had apparently declined the invitation and said she could be updated at a reasonable hour—so Bram retold the tale for everyone else. Sheridan followed along in the book, correcting his word choices here and there.

And unlike the group at the pub, his friends knew why the tale mattered so much, so there was no resumption of everyday murmurs at its close. No, the total silence was broken by three different conversations, all of them urgent.

Sher was the loudest. "Buried it, it says. Whatever it is, it's *buried*. Here in the Scillies. That's how Lizza found it, and she says she returned it to the same place."

"That hardly narrows it down." Beth had pulled out a chair at the table and slid the book her way while Sheridan was distracted.

And Sheridan was thoroughly distracted by whatever theory had set his eyes to glowing. He waved a finger in the air. "Of course it does! Where does one bury things in the Scillies?"

Gibson chuckled. "My foundation, apparently."

"No—well, yes, but not then. The cairns!" He declared it like it was obvious.

Bram felt his brows pull down. "They weren't Druids."

"Don't have to be." Pivoting on his heel, Sher lunged for some other book that was likely about Druids. Most of his books were. "They'd done the work, you know. Of digging. And building. Where else could they, here? I mean, granite."

Emily shifted uneasily beside him, which made his hands itch to reach for her. What would she do if he rested a palm against her back? Or took her fingers in his? "Sheridan, you can't be thinking—"

"Well! It's a place to start, isn't it, that your brother hasn't already covered? Searching beneath all the cairns?" Sheridan beamed, clearly oblivious to the way Emily had reacted in June when her brother tried to force her into Piper's Hole. Small, dark places were obviously not her cup of tea. But then, Sheridan wasn't with them at the time to have witnessed her panic.

Bram cleared his throat. "Sher, there's really no reason to assume that 'buried' demands burial chambers."

Not that such logic doused the excitement in Sheridan's eyes. "No reason not to either. Unless you have a better idea? And at the very least—well, it's not where Nigel's looking."

Blast it. It *was* at least a starting place. And what else could they do, upend every single square foot of every island in the chain? Keep following in Nigel's wake and re-searching what he'd already looked through? "Fine. But only the ones known in Mucknell's time. There's no point in exploring the more recently discovered ones."

Sheridan deflated, but only by a degree or two. "Granted. Though eventually I'll get to them all."

Beth chuckled. "You have the rest of our lives to explore them, dearovim. Any time we visit."

A lightning bolt shot through Bram, and it took him half a heart-beat to realize it was because Emily had gripped his arm. "You don't think . . . ? The one on Gugh—it's so near to where Mucknell had buried that chest."

And now he had an excuse to cover her hand with his opposite one. "Couldn't be. They didn't know of that one at the time, and the team would have found it already if this artifact were there."

Her grip eased a little, and she nodded. "You're right." She shifted her gaze to Beth or Sheridan or perhaps both. "Speaking of my father's dig—you should really decide if you want to get whatever that extra information was from Vandermeer."

Bram stiffened before he could think to temper his response. He hated the thought of her father absconding with her, yes—and hated it even more because it had meant delivering her directly to Vandermeer. She had *said* she had no interest, but he was a charming, persuasive fellow.

And to think Bram had shared his chocolate drops with him.

Beth nodded. "We should invite him to join us sometime. If he proves as much an ally as he seems, we could assign him a cairn or two. Or"—she added on a laugh when Sheridan spun on her and gave her a look of pure betrayal—"we could task him with continuing to keep an eye on everything at the museum dig. Regardless, I'd like to know what this 'ace' of his is."

"He made it sound important." Emily released her grip on Bram's arm and glided over to Beth's side.

His arm felt cold now. Bram crossed his arms over his chest to ward it off. "I still say we should send him on some other quest. Like recovering some other Mucknellian artifact from the Caribbean."

Oliver, still looking sleepy and having barely budged from his chair, sent him an amused look. "I thought you said he was a good enough fellow."

Good enough for someone else, certainly. But the chap had better take the hint and keep his distance from Emily. "Hence removing him from danger."

Oliver didn't look convinced.

Beth chuckled. "For now, Telford, let's just invite him to dinner and see what else he has to tell us. And start searching around the cairns."

Sheridan clapped his hands together once. "Well. Perfect. Let's all turn in, good night's sleep, all that. First thing tomorrow, I'll map them out. The cairns, that is. And we'll assign them. Divide and conquer, do you think, or safety in numbers?"

Oliver pushed himself to his feet, looking glad for the dismissal. "I say we hit the large, popular ones together—that way we can both cover all the cracks and crevices and also distract any other tourists. But we may want to divide and conquer on the countless smaller ones."

Everyone else agreed and began moving from the room. Bram considered staying here, reading over the text one more time, perhaps copying it out, but Sheridan planted his hands on Bram's back and pushed him toward the door. "You too, O Night Owl. Early start, you know. No growling bears allowed."

"Fine." He said it on a sigh, but really he didn't mind. This was one outing he didn't want to sleep through. Not to mention that the rain had picked up again, from the sounds of it, and staying inside the library wasn't nearly as alluring as a nighttime stroll.

Sheridan chuckled and moved to his side once they were in the corridor. "And I saw that, you know."

Double blast. He'd thought him too distracted to notice his reaction in there. "I don't know what you mean."

Sheridan's elbow collided with his side. "Jealousy."

He could deny it, but Sher knew him too well. So he put on his haughtiest look and said, "I am above such base emotions."

Naturally, his friend snorted a laugh and quietly taunted, "Vandermeer. Vandermeer, Vandermeer, Vandermeer."

Just to see him flinch again at the name, no doubt. He elbowed him back. "Your rival, not mine."

"Not for what matters." Sher nodded toward the ladies, who were already at the front door, bidding Gibson farewell.

Was it too much to ask to examine these stirring feelings for Emily on his own, without poking and prodding?

Clearly. He sent his friend a glare. "Your desire for convenience is clouding your eyes."

"Perfect vision, I'll have you know. And this is perfect too."

"*This* isn't anything." Yet. Perhaps he'd like it to be. And perhaps he'd explore how to make it so, sometime when she wasn't standing *right there*.

"Yet. Make a move, man. She could do with a good sweeping, I'd think. Off her feet, I mean."

The elbow hadn't done the trick, so Bram gave him a helpful shove in the arm. "Sheridan."

"Hm?"

"*Do* shut up."

Sher laughed and angled himself toward the corridor that would deliver him to his guest room. Though he spun, walking backward as he pointed once to himself, once to Bram, and then made a talking gesture with his fingers and thumb. "Tomorrow."

He rolled his eyes. But honestly, he felt a bit better about it all with the promise of a chat, just the two of them. Sher's perspective could be just what he needed to help him determine if this was genuine affection blooming in his heart or just his blighted sense of chivalry, overexcited at an excuse to be put to use.

Tomorrow. As for tonight . . . well, he might just work up a few plans of his own for what moves he ought to make.

18

She was utterly useless. Emily sat on one of the stones outside the Great Tomb of Porth Hellick Down on St. Mary's, trying to tell herself she was doing exactly as she'd been told and keeping other tourists away.

But it was seven o'clock in the morning, scarcely daylight. All was still damp and misty from last night's rain, and no other tourist in their right mind was out yet. Which meant that she was instead sitting here because she was a coward whose limbs had absolutely frozen at the entrance to the chamber. Alone and chilled and trying to ignore the water seeping through her shoes and her dress and the mackintosh she was sitting on.

It was highly unlikely they'd find anything here, anyway. To be sure, the site was huge, encompassing several different cairns, with at least a half-dozen grave entrances. If Sheridan's word could be trusted, it was the largest surviving cluster of cairn entrances to be found anywhere. Which meant that there usually was a steady stream of students and tourists and historians parading through it and had been for decades, if not for centuries.

If Elizabeth Mucknell had found and rehidden an artifact here, the chances of it then going unnoticed until now were slim indeed.

But they were going to leave no stone unturned—or unentered, as the case may be. So, it had made the most sense to begin here, at the most famous location in the Isles of Scilly. A theory that had sounded fine and reasonable in the comfort of the Tremayne dining room with a cup of steaming tea in her hand. Not quite so now.

She ought to just leave the others to the search and slink back to her flat, where it wasn't so glaringly obvious that she could be of no help in this.

No. She drew in a deep breath, pushed her insecurities away, and shut her eyes. She could do here the same thing she could at home: pray. For her friends, for this new hunt, for her family to see the path they were on before it led them to destruction, as it had the citizens of Lyonesse, John Mucknell, and so many others in history.

And for that poor girl on St. Agnes. Tommie said her name was Ailla and that she had spoken to her, but she'd gone mum when Emily pressed her for details. It didn't take a great imagination to think of why. Ailla had told Tommie what had happened, but that didn't give Tommie the right to tell Emily. She had said only, "He did to her what he did to me."

"What he did to me." Her brother had hurt Tommie, and this Ailla too. Not just rude comments, not just belittling them. He'd *hurt* them. And not, if she were to guess, simply by grabbing their arms too tightly and sending them tumbling. No, he must have—he must have violated them.

The very thought made her squeeze her eyes shut. Had he done the same to the two maids she'd had before Tommie? Had Emily been putting women in such terrible danger just by bringing them into her home?

Tears stung her eyes. For her friend. For the young ladies she hadn't known to try to protect. For that innocent island girl. For who knew how many other girls in all the places he'd been.

And for Nigel himself. Why must he be this way? *Why?* He could make better decisions. He could be a kinder man. He *could.* He was intelligent and charming and handsome and had the whole world at his fingertips. Why had he chosen this way instead of a better one? To hurt? To abuse? To destroy? How could he not see that he ought to heal, to encourage, to build instead?

And her parents—did they know? Had they covered up all his sins?

"Am I imposing? That's quite a serious look on your face."

She opened her eyes and saw Telford standing at her side, a soft smile on his lips. She blinked a few times to clear her eyes of the tears and spread the mackintosh out as far as it would go in invitation. The rock wasn't all that large, but he sat beside her anyway, their arms pressing together thanks to the limited space. She didn't mind. "Just thinking and wishing. That my brother was different. That *I* was different." Waving a hand at the tomb, she breathed a self-deprecating laugh. "I can't even join you all in there."

"We all have fears. Really, yours is a completely reasonable one. One never knows what could be hiding in the dark."

"It isn't the monsters in the dark that make me fear it." She bit her lip but then pressed on. "It's the monsters that create it to begin with."

Telford reached over and took her hand. That was all. Just a simple move, meant to impart comfort—and it did exactly that. Enough that, for the first time since she was five, she told the story. Nigel, telling her they were playing a game. Nigel, locking her in that dratted wardrobe in a closed-up wing of Scofield Hall. The endless hours in there alone, screaming, crying, making a mess of herself. The thirst. The desperation. How certain she'd been, at the tender age of five, that she was going to die in there. How over twenty-four hours passed before they found her.

And how her father had told her it was *her* fault. Not Nigel's. Never Nigel's. *Hers*.

She shook her head and stared off into the mist. "Father never gave me a scrap of his attention. Not after that. I don't honestly recall if he did before, just that afterward I could stand in front of him for what felt like an eternity, and he wouldn't even look up or acknowledge me."

Telford's thumb was moving up and down along hers, a rhythm of solace. "But you never stopped trying, did you?"

Her laugh probably sounded despairing to his ears. "How could I stop? They were my whole world, and yet they scarcely let me be a part of it."

"Ah, Em." He lifted her hand and pressed a kiss to her knuckles. "I think perhaps that was a blessing in disguise—because instead of turning out like them, you've turned out like *you*. As beautiful of heart and spirit as you are of face. Kinder than anyone I've ever known."

His gaze was latched on hers, those oceanic eyes tracing her features, and she could scarcely breathe. "Don't forget claustrophobic." She didn't know why she tacked that on, whether she meant to defuse some of the intensity or just earn a smile.

Either way, she failed. He neither pulled away nor laughed. Instead, he reached up with his other hand and brushed his fingers over her cheek. "I'm sorry for your fear. Sorrier still for the cause of it. But not at all sorry for who it's helped make you."

There was no audience, for this to be for their sake. And though she'd expect nothing less from him than encouragement, she'd certainly never seen him encourage any other friend in quite this way. Could that possibly mean . . . ?

"Hello, the cairn! If that isn't Sheridan's group there at this ridiculous hour in this weather, then I'm going to report you all as mad."

Telford's hand dropped from her cheek, and irritation flickered in his eyes. "Vandermeer. Shall we hide?"

Should the irritation have amused her so? She nodded to the figure emerging through the mist. "Too late, I think." And Bram didn't let go of her hand, nor leap up from the rock. Of course, Vandermeer *was* the audience he had begun the ruse for. But still.

Louder, Telford called, "Does being in Sheridan's party exclude us from madness? Because I'm not entirely certain just now. And what are you doing out on this miserable morning, sir?"

The American emerged, smiling, into the circle of the barrow. Though the smile flickered just a bit when his gaze dropped to their joined hands. "Looking for all of you. When I saw the *Adelle* in the quay, I hoped there would be a number of you here. A helpful fisherman said he saw the vicar and his friends walking toward Porth Hellick, and given that there is a cairn here and a Sheridan with you . . . well, two plus two and all that."

At least she wasn't the only one who couldn't help but smile—that telltale twitch was in the corner of Telford's mouth too. "Well," she said, "you've found us. What is it you need, sir?"

"This quest business." He meandered toward the mouth of the Great Tomb and yelled into it, "Sheridan, I'm stealing all your finds!" Then he turned back to them. "I can be quite patient as I await your judgment on whether I sufficiently passed the test, but here's the thing—I'm ready for some new company. So, I decided to employ a bit of my Yankee gumption and take a risk on trusting you all with *my* information." He patted his chest—or perhaps a pocket inside his jacket, given the crinkle of papers—and grinned. "I think you'll be pleased."

"Vandermeer!" Sheridan ducked out of the tomb, Beth and Oliver and Libby close behind him. "What are you doing here?"

He waved a hand toward Emily and Telford. "As I was just explaining to the gatekeepers, my liege—after completing the first stage of my quest, I decided to take it upon myself to present you with a token as the next phase, since you hadn't the sense to demand it yourself after I let a hint drop to Lady Emily that should have been downright tantalizing." He sent a wink to Emily that didn't make her feel anything like Bram's wink had.

Beth planted her hands on her hips. "Insulting your liege isn't usually best practice."

"You'll forgive me." Vandermeer reached into his jacket and pulled out a sheaf of folded papers, though a gust of wind whipped around them that had him pressing them back to his torso. "You may have learned that one of Lord Scofield's clerks vanished about a month ago?"

Sheridan nodded. "Right around the time he went chasing after false leads in Portugal, I believe."

Vandermeer grinned. "You?"

"Us. My valet, actually."

"The clerk was my doing. Not that he vanished. He simply accepted a better position in my firm. After, that is, he found this." He lifted the papers away again for a brief moment.

Sheridan was clearly hooked, his eyes on the sheaf. And frankly, Emily was intrigued too. She'd had a feeling all along, hadn't she, that Father's clerks could be a risk? She'd mentioned it to Beth, who had mentioned it to the others, and then she'd been proven right when Ainsley reported, via his cousin, that a clerk had defected.

Now they were finally to learn why. She caught herself tightening her fingers around Telford's and would have relaxed them again, but he held them back just as firmly.

"If you're waiting for us to beg, Vanderbosche . . ."

Vandermeer grinned at Telford. "Dramatic effect, my young friend. You can't begrudge me a little of it, can you? Which reminds me—you all are making me feel ancient. Where are your sisters, Sheridan?"

Sheridan looked as though he may resort to wrestling the papers from their guest. "Presumably still asleep in their cottage. Why? In need of a berating?"

"It does provide a certain element of entertainment. But all right, I won't push your patience any further." Another robust gust of wind tore up the hill, though, inspiring him to tuck the papers back in his jacket. "Not the best place to have these out, but he found a deposition. It wasn't grouped with the others from Mucknell's crew because this particular crewmember wasn't questioned until decades later. One Eben Franks."

Why did that sound familiar? The crew lists they'd found, perhaps? Or one of the lists of known Royalists? No, that wasn't it. She searched her mind for a moment, until she saw the name *Eben* in a familiar script in her memory and gasped. "His cabin boy!"

Elizabeth had mentioned him—how small he was, how sweet,

and how she'd welcomed him as a son whenever John brought him home. The lad had no parents and she no child, so the few months when it was possible, she'd enjoyed mothering him.

Vandermeer sighed. "So much for my dramatic reveal. How did you know that, my lady? His name wasn't on the crew manifest your father had sent to your friend, I happen to know."

Because he hadn't been part of the crew when the *John* belonged to the East India Company. He'd been a Scillonian lad who signed on after Mucknell had pledged his support to the crown here. Emily lifted her chin. "We have our sources, sir." Which Nigel had, too, but unless he and Vandermeer collaborated on this, then neither of them would have both.

"But we knew of no deposition," Sheridan added. "Was he arrested later in life? For piracy?"

"He was questioned but never charged—in part because he offered the Company information on where they may be able to recover some of their lost resources. Namely?"

"Mucknell's caches," Sheridan, Beth, and Oliver all said together.

Emily prickled at first, on behalf of Lizza and John. They'd taken the boy in and treated him as a son—why would he turn on them? But then she recalled he'd said it was decades later. Mucknell would have been dead, as was Prince Rupert's island bride. Rupert himself had embarked on a new career and a new life. And Elizabeth had already sworn off the use of any pirated loot. She could very well have given her blessing on that disclosure if she and Eben were still in communication.

Vandermeer was nodding. "Exactly. And that's what this is—a list of every place in the Scillies and Ireland where he saw his master bury his treasure. One of which, just for the record, was the north side of Gugh."

"And the others? Do any line up with ours?" Sheridan reached into his own pocket and pulled out the list they'd made over breakfast that morning of the cairns known at the time.

The wind snatched the paper out of his fingers the moment he unfolded it, earning a shout from Sheridan even as Telford leaped to his feet and grabbed it again. He'd dropped her hand in the effort but calmly wove their fingers again when he sat back down.

"Not a good place to compare, methinks," he said. "Perhaps we should have this discussion over some tea and Mrs. Dawe's cake of the day?"

It was, in essence, an invitation into their inner sanctum, even more so than the dinner invitation they'd planned to offer. Sheridan nodded and surged forward, Oliver tucked Libby's hand against his arm with a warm smile, and even Beth looked more intrigued than wary as she darted after her fiancé.

Emily let Telford help her to her feet and gather the mackintosh, making no objection when he then took her hand again. Perhaps it was for Vandermeer's benefit . . . but maybe not. Maybe it was simply for their own.

———————○———————

Bram had kept his station at Emily's side all through the lunch they ended up having with Vandermeer, but once the Howe sisters had arrived and commandeered the American's attention before afternoon tea, he'd deemed it safe to accept Sheridan's invitation to run a few errands with him. It would, after all, give them time for that promised chat.

He stepped out of the sweet shop now with a fresh bag of chocolate drops in one hand and one filled with lemon drops in the other. He looked down the street, his lips twitching when he saw Sheridan barely avoid a collision with a local—and the avoidance was thanks to the local's attention, not Sheridan's. His friend was, for perhaps the thousandth time in Bram's memory, trying to walk and read at the same time.

"You do know you could wait until you get back to the Tremaynes' to read that," he called out as soon as Sher was close enough to hear him over the normal din of a busy village road.

Sheridan looked up, blinked to clear his eyes, and grinned. "Well now—says who? Maybe it's imperative stuff."

Given that he was now only an arm's span away, Bram reached out and tipped the book up so he could read the title. Or rather, so he could see which flavor of Druid text it was today. Cairns. Of course. "Oh yes, the world would have stopped spinning had you not nearly plowed into poor Mrs. Gillis."

"Had I what?" Sher spun around, clearly looking for the woman in question so he could apologize.

Bram chuckled. "Don't worry, she avoided you—and with a smile. Here." He dropped the bag of lemon drops onto the still-open pages.

Sheridan blinked at it. "Why are you bribing me with lemon drops?"

"It's your consolation for missing tea."

Now he gave Bram full-on puppy eyes. "Why are we missing tea?"

Bram lifted his brows. "I thought you wanted to badger me about Emily. But if you prefer to just go back and have a crumpet with Vandermeer instead—"

"Hard choice. But when you put it that way . . ." He lifted the bag, then closed the book and tucked it under one arm before fishing out a candy. "Where shall I badger? Beach? Garden? Should ask Libby—where badgers best badger, I mean. She'd know."

Bram selected a chocolate with another chuckle. "She would, at that." He started them down the road. "Let's wander toward Cromwell's Castle." It seemed appropriate, to return to the place where he'd first seen Emily truly—where he'd seen her in her brother's grasp, clearly wanting to fight against him, and just as clearly not knowing how.

They walked in comfortable silence until the village was behind them. But the moment they were free of listening ears, Sheridan said, "I expect a ballad, you know. Given all those ancient tales you so admire. Or an epic, even. Detailing your love, I mean."

As if he'd ever been anything but rubbish at poetry, which Sheridan well knew. Bram snorted. "You should recall that my favorites were the *Prose*. Not poetry."

"But for Lady Emily?" Sher fished another lemon drop out and put it in his mouth.

She may be worthy of a ballad or two—but that made Bram no more capable of composing one, so he rolled his eyes. And then sighed. "It isn't just the convenience, you know."

"Mm." It was apparently all the insight Sher could work around the candy.

"There's something about her—the way she sees the world and her place in it. The way she's trying so hard to love her father and brother, even though they don't deserve it in the least. That takes a special kind of heart. To love where hatred would come so naturally and so deservedly."

Sheridan moved the sweet to his cheek. "Well, we knew she was special. Because she's Beth's best friend, I mean. Excellent taste. Beth has, that is. Well, and Emily too. To like Beth."

Bram let a breath of laughter puff out. Perhaps he would have objected to the love-addled Sheridan making this claim about Beth, if he weren't still so glad his best friend had found someone who appreciated him.

And it wasn't like Sher didn't know what he'd just done. He laughed, too, and rolled his eyes at himself. "Sorry. Em. Beautiful heart. Go on."

"I just . . . what if it's the situation? The chivalry that appeals to me? How do I know it's *real*?" Bram chewed the remainder of his chocolate drop so he had an excuse to reach for another.

"Hm." Sheridan sucked on his own candy for a moment, eyes focused on the tumbledown castle that had just come into view, or on the sea behind it, or on the question in general. "Well. When it's a puppy or a kitten or a parrot—"

Bram laughed and shoved him in the arm. "I have never taken in a parrot."

Sheridan sent him a consoling look. "Give yourself some time. Eventually, you know. It'll come up. Pirates and all."

"Right." He was still chuckling. "So when it's a puppy or a kitten or a parrot . . . ?"

"Canaries. Fish. Iguanas. Squirrels—wouldn't put it past you."

"Sheridan."

"Right." Sher grinned. "When it's an animal, you always save them. But you don't always keep them. Only certain ones, yes? So, how do you know? Which belong to you, I mean?"

It was similar to what Enyon had asked him, yet far more pointed—and to the point. But he'd never really paused to consider it before. He did so now as they meandered toward the tip of Tresco, the birds that Libby could have named so easily cartwheeling overhead, the sun sparkling down onto the turquoise water, the wind singing in their ears.

They'd bypassed the castle and settled to a damp seat on a few of the rocks at the water's edge before Bram had worked through his thoughts enough to answer. "I suppose in part it's that they fit in my world. They get along with the others."

"So, does she? Emily, I mean, with the others in your world?" Sheridan asked it with an amused quirk of his lips, clearly knowing the answer already.

"Obviously." She got along with Sheridan and Beth, with Libby. He couldn't imagine Mother doing anything but adoring her.

"Then what are the other parts?"

That was the side tripping him up. "I don't know. I just . . . *know*. I can't imagine them with anyone else. The thought of it hurts."

Sheridan snorted. "Vandermeer."

Bram winced. And then sighed. And then laughed. "Yes, all right. I clearly do *not* like the thought of her with someone else. But she isn't a puppy, Sher. The stakes are a bit higher."

"So then. The stories you so love, the chivalric ones. Imagine some adventures." Adventures were more Sheridan and Beth's language than his own, but the sweep of Sher's arms, encompassing not only the vista before them but the wide world, made his challenge clear. "Imagine yourself at—well, at the Midsummer Ball at Cadbury Castle. At my house for Christmas. In a ballroom in London during the Season. Can you imagine her with you? Or perhaps—well, even more telling. Can you imagine her *not*?"

Bram's gaze followed the flight of a gull while his mind obeyed Sheridan's command, reliving situations, events he'd been at many times, with no one at his side but Mother and Father or Libby or Sheridan himself.

Now when he imagined a crowded ballroom, he also imagined a beautiful redhead at his side. One with a gentle smile and eyes that were always looking for ways to do good. He imagined sweeping her onto a dance floor and feeling the swell of gratitude that she was there in his arms. He imagined gathering around the gaily lit tree at Sheridan Castle not only with Mother and Lib and Abbie and Millicent there, but with Oliver and Beth and Emily adding more light and laughter. He found himself wondering what gift he could wrap up for Em that would make her eyes go wide with joy, like Libby's had when he'd given her a microscope.

Still. "I suppose I simply distrust it because it *is* easy. Neat. Tidy. There should be dragons to slay, shouldn't there? Dark knights to vanquish. A few sorcerers to outsmart."

If nothing stood between them, was it really a proper romance?

"Telly." Sheridan smacked his shoulder and pointed out to sea.

No, not to sea. To the edge of Bryher just across the waterway and the too-familiar sailboat anchoring now off its shore. The one that Nigel had been using as he scoured each and every inch of the islands.

Perhaps Emily's family wasn't standing between them in a normal way, but they were still there, threatening to ruin everything.

"My lords! Could I impose upon you?"

They both scrambled to their feet at the vaguely familiar voice. It wasn't until Bram turned and spotted the face that went with it that he realized it was Enyon's mother. He strode toward her on the path, as did Sheridan. "Mrs. Thorne. How may we be of service?"

She held out a distinctive yellow paper. "This came for Lady Emily just an hour ago. Derrick ran it right over for her, but she wasn't at home, of course, being here. Asked if I would bring it to her. I could walk it to the house, but if you're going that way . . ."

A telegram for Emily? Bram increased his pace. "Certainly. We'll take it to her straightaway." He offered a smile as he reached out for it. "It was good of you to bring it—you didn't go out of your way, did you? Coming home this time of day?"

Mrs. Thorne waved that off. "It was no trouble. Usually I'd have sent it with Enny after his deliveries, but he had to make a trip to the mainland yesterday to get some photographs developed for us and won't be back until tomorrow. I don't mind the excuse to leave the shop for an afternoon once in a while, though. My girl can see to things."

Bram slid the paper into his inner pocket to protect it from the greedy wind. "I'm certain Lady Emily will appreciate it."

"No problem at all." Mrs. Thorne turned back toward the path. "Tell everyone I say hello, if you would."

They assured her of that and started off themselves toward the Tremayne house, the telegram scalding him through his shirt. If it was just from her friend Lottie Wight or something trivial like that, it would be such a letdown for her. She needed it to be from her mother. She needed it to be something positive. She needed it to be evidence that she was loved.

Upon arriving at the house, they followed the sounds of laughter and chatter to the back garden, where Vandermeer was regaling them all with some story just as outlandish as any from the *Prose Tristan*. Another jolt of jealousy speared him, lessened somewhat when Emily glanced up the moment they came within view and smiled at him.

She didn't smile at *Vandermeer* like that. Did she?

He only prayed she would keep smiling after reading whatever this wire said.

Under the cover of the continued laughter and interjected questions from Abbie and Millicent, Bram slipped to Emily's side, crouched down beside her chair, and pulled out the telegram.

Softly, he whispered, "Mrs. Thorne just brought this for you from St. Mary's. Said it just came in, and they hurried to get it to you."

He watched her freeze at the sight of the yellow paper, watched hope spark in her eyes, watched her bank it. "Oh. Thank you—and her."

She shouldn't have to bank it. Shouldn't have to *hope* that it was a kind word from her mother. That ought to have been something she could assume.

He would have stood again to give her privacy, but she opened the telegram and held it out so that he could read it as she did. An action that hit him directly in the stomach. It was what Libby might have done, or Mother, if they knew it was news of relevance to them all. But that Emily would include him so readily, before she had any idea who it was from or what it said?

It was as beautiful as any ballad could have been. It proved she trusted him, wanted him to be part of her life, at least in this much.

His gaze fell to the typed words.

Found letters and more STOP Do not anger your brother STOP More soon STOP Mother

"'Do not anger your brother?'" Emily's whisper was so quiet he could barely hear it over the louder conversation at the garden table. Her hand shook—and this time he knew it wasn't for want of food. "Even now, will she take his side?"

He wasn't sure what the "even now" referred to—and frankly, it didn't matter. The only thing that mattered was the tear spilling from his lady's eye, the heartbreak etched over her face.

He had no words to say, no way to make this right. All he could do was take her hand in his and raise it to his lips, press a long kiss to her fingers that he prayed would give some comfort.

But he knew exactly how those knights of old felt. Give him a suit of armor, a lance, and a target, and he would gladly gallop off in search of monsters, if it had a hope of bringing her joy. He would do anything to bring her joy.

Which was, he supposed, an answer to whether he could trust his feelings.

19

Tommie stood in their flat at the window overlooking the street, watching until Emily went out of sight, flanked between Ladies Abbie and Millicent. They all three looked stunning in their ball gowns, hair done up in elegant fashion, jewels gleaming at ears, neck, and wrists. But she knew Emily, at least, would have far preferred to be staying at home and playing with the puppy that Lord Telford had sent with them rather than going to the hotel for the ball the museum trustees were hosting, where her father and brother would be in attendance.

And Vandermeer—that was why Lord Scofield had sent the note round saying Emily must attend. It had been waiting for them when they returned from Tresco the other day, and rather than try to get out of it, Emily had merely made certain she would have a few allies present. Lords Telford and Sheridan had not received an invitation—a slight that anyone who realized they were in the islands would have been appalled at—but the Howe sisters had procured one somehow or another. And so, they went.

And now, here stood Tommie, alone in the flat but for Tristan, who was currently fast asleep on the rug. Her fingers slipped down the curtain with its cheerful print and fell uselessly to her side.

What was wrong with her? Usually the thought of an evening to herself would have thrilled her. She could read or write a letter to her sisters or flip through a ladies' magazine. She could knit or take a stroll with the pup or lounge in the bath for an hour.

She wanted none of it. No, what she wanted was the same thing she feared so much that her stomach had been in absolute knots for days: Enyon to show up at her door.

He'd left one note for her saying he had to make a quick run to the mainland and that he hoped that by the time he returned, she would be ready to see him. He'd said that he missed her and would be thinking of her while he was away. He'd sent another yesterday letting her know he was back and asking if she was ready to talk— that if she gave the word, he'd find her. He'd signed both of them *Yours, Enyon.*

But he wasn't. And even if he said he was willing to be, this would be always between them. They would both be aware each and every day of what he'd overlooked, what he'd forgiven, what another had taken. She wanted to let him assure her otherwise, but how could she ever believe it?

She knew. She knew what was missing inside her. She knew the fear and pain that reared up in the moments when she least wanted them to. She knew how that encounter with Nigel Scofield had changed her forever.

The knock at the door made Tristan leap up, barking. Tommie jumped and nearly shrieked. It wouldn't be Nigel—he'd be at the ball. But Enyon? Had she conjured him with her thoughts?

"Tommie? Are you in? I thought you could use a bit of company."

Senara Dawe. Tommie let out the breath she'd gasped in and shook her head at herself. "Coming!" She and Senara had been working side by side in the Tremayne kitchen any day that Tommie and Emily were on Tresco, so she'd gotten to know the older girl fairly well. At this point, she'd have called her a friend, even. She'd just never expected her to show up here on St. Mary's for an impromptu visit.

But having a cup of tea with Senara certainly sounded more appealing than standing at the window, waiting for Lady Emily to come home, so she hurried to the door and, after scooping up Tristan so he wouldn't escape, pulled it open with a smile.

The smile grew when Senara held up a bag. "I bring Mrs. Polmer's sweet rolls. You can't turn me away if I have these in hand, right?"

Tommie laughed and opened the door wide. "As if I would have regardless. Come in, please. Your timing is perfect—I was just trying to decide how I wanted to fill the evening and had no ideas."

"I rather expected you'd have more plans than you did free hours. That's how I always felt on those rare evenings when I wasn't needed." Senara tousled Tristan's ears on her way past and showed herself to the table while Tommie shut the door behind her. Senara's cheeks were pinkened from the wind and her hair in enough disarray to testify to her sail from Tresco, making her look effortlessly lovely. No doubt when she returned home, Ainsley would see her so and grow all the more smitten.

It wasn't jealousy, that pang in Tommie's chest. Not exactly. After all, she, too, had someone who'd been looking at her with warm, wishful eyes. It was just that she knew when next she saw him in the light of day, it would be different. And she didn't want it to be.

Mourning, that's what the pang was. Grief.

Senara took the puppy from her arms, set him on the floor, and then pushed Tommie toward one of the kitchen chairs. "Sit down, dearover, and talk to me. These last few days I've been seeing an entire ocean of feeling in those eyes of yours, and it's certain to brim over any minute. I thought you could use a listening ear."

"Oh." And so she'd sailed over here, sacrificing her own Friday evening? Brim over those feelings did, and Tommie had to forgo the chair and spin for the kettle to keep her tears from being observed. Though they were audible in her voice as she said, "That was kind of you."

Senara, however, didn't take one of the chairs either. She moved to the stove and lit it. "Kindness has nothing to do with it. If Enyon's done something to hurt you, I'll take him to task. Just tell me what I'm punishing him for."

The kettle full, Tommie turned off the tap. And spun back around, eyes wide. "He's done nothing—why would you think he has?"

Senara was giving her that look governesses were so good at. The one that said she would call you on any bluff.

But Tommie wasn't bluffing. Enyon had done nothing wrong. At all. He'd been a perfect gentleman, kind and good and so sweet with her.

Her guest held up a finger. "Simple maths, Tommie. The two of you went somewhere the other evening. Then off he went to the mainland and you're starting at shadows and gone all melancholy and contemplative. You've had a row, I expect."

Tommie was shaking her head before Senara even finished. "No. You have the wrong of it. He's not done a thing, and we didn't have a fight. The timing of his trip was purely coincidental."

Or perhaps not. Perhaps it was his way of giving her the time she'd asked for. But still, that spoke of his goodness and consideration, not his lack of it.

Senara's expression didn't change. "Then why these shadows I see in your eyes? I could have sworn . . ." Now she faltered, looked away. Hid her own expression behind taking the kettle from Tommie's hands and putting it on the lit stove.

Tommie frowned. "Could have sworn what?" What could make confident Senara falter so?

Her friend sighed. "You seemed to be struggling a bit as I've done. With . . . guilt. Shame."

She knew? How did she know? Or, no—what did she mean? "As you've done? But . . ." But how could there have been someone at her very elbow all these weeks who would have understood, and yet she'd missed it? She reached for Senara's hands with her own. "Who? The lord you used to work for? Is that why you left? Oh, please tell me it hadn't been going on all these years, I can't even imagine how that would destroy you!"

For a moment, Senara's gaze was blank. And then her eyes went wide and she pulled Tommie into a tight embrace. "Thomasina! You were *attacked*? Not by Enyon, though."

It had been months, nearly years, since anyone had pulled her in for a hug. But Senara folded her into her arms just like an older sister would have done, or Mam. Holding her tightly, not giving her any choice. It made her crumble a little more. "Nigel."

Senara muttered something in Cornish. Then, "Of course it was. That louse. You poor darling. But then—why are you feeling as you are? My guilt, it was deserved. I did willingly what I oughtn't to have. But this—it wasn't your fault."

"I know. Sort of." She squeezed her eyes shut and pressed her forehead against Senara's shoulder, willing those rebellious tears to stay back. "My head knows. But . . . but why? Why did he target me? There must be something wrong with me—"

"Rubbish! Utter rubbish, you have to know that. The wrong, the broken—it's in *him*, dearover, not in you."

She'd been trying to tell herself that ever since she comforted Ailla. Tried to believe the words she'd spoken so easily to another. But convincing her heart had proven impossible. "For the action, yes. I realize that. But what he took from me can't be got back. It's gone. Forever gone. My virtue—"

"Listen to me." Senara pulled away enough to frame Tommie's face between her hands and look her square in the eye. "Your virtue is your character, your chosen behavior—he hasn't touched that. No one can ever take that from you. There is, as my mam pointed out, a purpose to shame when we do something wrong, as I did. But when you feel it even though you've done nothing willfully, it is false, Tommie. It is shackles that will drag you down. Don't let it. That shame is not yours. That guilt is not yours."

More tears welled. Partly from gratitude. Partly from disbelief. "But how can I ever be anything but broken? It isn't fair to a man like Enyon, it isn't—"

"Enyon isn't going to judge you for someone else's sin." Senara wiped the tears from Tommie's cheeks for her. "And even if he did—because heaven knows plenty of people do—that would be his failing. Not yours. Your worth, Thomasina, rests on no one else's opinion of you. It doesn't rest even on you. It rests in the Lord. He sees your heart, your soul. And that is all the approval any of us needs."

He sees me. Wasn't that the very realization that had propelled her to St. Nicholas's the day Enyon found her there? Even though she was only a commoner, only a servant, abused by her master—God still saw her. Still loved her. Enough to care about every bruise on her spirit. Enough to send proof whenever she needed it. Enough to send a friend to speak truth to her heart.

Enough to put a man in her life worth taking a risk on? Maybe. Maybe.

"There now." Senara dropped her hands to Tommie's shoulders and used them to push her toward a chair, the puppy yipping his approval of that. "Sit. I'll make the tea, we'll drink some and enjoy those rolls, and you're going to tell me everything you want to and nothing you don't." She paused, caught Tommie's gaze again. "You're not alone, Tommie. However much it felt like it—you're not."

Words that brightened the evening far more than she ever would have thought they could.

Bram followed Oliver, Sheridan, and Enyon out into the evening, wondering when darkness had fallen so completely. They'd only intended to enjoy the fine weather with a sail, using the need to get Mr. Gale's library of Lyonesse books back to him as an excuse. But somehow dropping the books off at the vicarage on St. Mary's had turned into having a cup of tea with Mr. Gale, and a cup of tea had turned into bringing out a tin of biscuits, and Bram had pulled out his latest bag of toffee, and here they were, hours later.

Not that he particularly minded, and he didn't imagine the others did either. Libby, Beth, Mabena, and even Mamm-wynn had all been spending the evening at the Moons', working on the final wedding plans for Mabena and Casek, and Emily had been roped into attending that ball with Sheridan's sisters. So a nice gentlemen's outing had seemed in order. And had been rather fun, at that. Not that most of his friends in London would consider a night spent at a vicarage library with two clergymen, one Druid-obsessed lord, and an island farmer to be riveting entertainment, but they didn't know what they were missing.

Enyon especially seemed to be losing some steam now—and had been rather distracted all night, honestly—but Bram was just getting into prime condition. Which of course meant a whispered prod to the weary early riser. "I suppose we'd better get you home. We need to be back here before dawn tomorrow, you know. With our halos on."

Enyon yawned, even as something that looked strangely akin to conflict flashed in his eyes. "Knew I should have turned down that third cup. I'll never get to sleep in time to be up again."

Bram frowned at him. "You're not backing out of the heavenly choir, are you?"

"Hardly." But he sighed as he positioned his cap better on his head. "I just wish there were something more I could do. To show Thomasina that I care."

More? Hadn't he invited her to meet his whole family and basically declared for all the islands to see that she was his girl? What more was expected?

"What are you plotting back there?" Sheridan held up at the gate, grinning. "How Telly can best propose to Lady Emily? Has he been enlisting you to pry advice from Briggs?"

Enyon snorted a laugh, though Bram swore he could hear a shadow in it. "You've guessed it."

Well, he wasn't going to pry anything more from him now. That would have to wait for their sail in the morning. Bram shook his head. "Don't encourage him. For the last time, Sheridan, some of us can like a young lady without proposing within minutes."

Sheridan loosed a huff. "A gross exaggeration. As well you know.

That is, it took me at least a week. Given that she'd dubbed me a villain, I mean."

Oliver waved them onward, chuckling. "Pick up the pace, gentlemen. I still have a sermon to try to write tonight."

"Not finished yet?" Enyon clucked his tongue and moved up to Oliver's side. To be near his best friend, or to escape Bram's line of conversation? "You know what happens when you procrastinate, Ollie."

If he wasn't mistaken, Oliver muttered something that sounded suspiciously like "Dratted sermons" as he strode down the hill.

Bram fell easily into step beside Sheridan—his usual place, anyway—and chuckled. He would worry over Enyon later. "Our future brother-in-law is the strangest clergyman I've ever met."

"I know. Quite like that about him, really. I mean—he's saintly. But not stuffy. Well, when one actually looks at the saints of old—"

"Yes, we've already had that discussion." And would likely have it countless more times, which was fine. But at the moment, Bram's thoughts drifted elsewhere. Namely, to the telegram he'd just received that afternoon, saying that Mother would be arriving on the midday ferry on Monday. He'd stopped in at the hotel to reserve her a suite when they'd arrived, and the place had been swarming with the families of all the trustees, here for that blighted ball.

He'd still been able to get her a room, thankfully—all the summer holiday-goers had returned back to their lives elsewhere over the last couple weeks—but it was a good thing she hadn't arrived today or he wouldn't have been able to.

He hadn't felt the least bit slighted at not being invited to the ball, but he *had* wondered more than once if Lady Scofield had come. And if she planned to see her daughter or would keep ignoring her. He wondered for approximately the thousandth time that evening how Emily was faring.

"Frowning in the direction of the hotel won't help, you know. To see inside it, I mean. Though if you want to sneak in . . ."

"No." He chuckled at the thought. The last time he'd had to

sneak into a ball was when he was thirteen. And that, too, had been at Sheridan's prodding. "I'm just curious as to whether Emily's mother came."

Sher hissed out a breath. "Good question, that. Abbie and Millicent will let us know, I daresay. Along with every other detail. Wanted or not."

"You do have a point." They would report on absolutely everyone who came and didn't. Which meant that Bram was free to wonder instead about what Mother would think of the Scillies and the Tremaynes . . . and Emily. And what Emily would think of her. And why he was worrying so much about it all.

Blast. He was turning into Sheridan. If he didn't stop himself, he'd start composing lists of her virtues just in case he had to help along someone's opinion of her.

The music coming from the hotel was loud enough to reach them as they made the turn toward the quay and the *Adelle*.

"*There* you are! I've been out here for ages."

At least he wasn't the only one who jumped a bit at Vandermeer's voice coming out of the darkness. He stepped from the shadows into the moonlight, decked out in the finest evening wear, and glanced over his shoulder. "Here." He held out a slip of paper toward Sheridan. "I wired my new clerk for that clarification you asked for, and I had a reply this afternoon. I was going to just slip it to Lady Emily or your sisters, but the Scofield men were keeping too close an eye on Emily, and I wasn't quite convinced Abigail and Millie wouldn't burn it instead of giving it to you."

Sheridan chuckled and took it. "And you with it."

"One can't discount the possibility. But when I saw the *Adelle*, I figured you'd be coming back this way eventually and have been keeping an eye out."

Enyon's frown was gilded by the full moon. "You shouldn't have sought us out. You don't want the Scofields seeing you here with us."

"Don't worry, I made certain they were fully engaged before I made my escape. Though I'll probably be missed if I stay out here much longer." Vandermeer took a step back toward the hotel. "If you need any more clarifications, Sheridan, you know how to reach me."

"Mm." Sher was trying to angle the paper into the moonlight to read it now, but the light wasn't quite that good. "Cheerio. Good luck. Surviving my sisters, I mean."

Vandermeer disappeared with a laugh.

Bram shoved his hands into his pockets. He believed Vandermeer could hold his own against Abbie and Millicent. But he didn't much like the thought of the Scofield men keeping such a close eye on Emily.

If he'd been dressed for it, maybe he *would* have snuck in.

Even with a ballroom between them, Emily could feel the tension radiating off her brother. And as grateful as she was to Lady Abbie for trying to help, the tension had only increased since the lady had engaged what she'd described in a hushed whisper as their "emergency plan." She'd left Emily to Millicent's care an hour ago and cornered Nigel, engaging him in an animated discussion that he couldn't duck away from without being rude.

She was skilled, Emily had to grant her that. She'd managed to include an entire group in whatever conversation she'd chosen and kept turning to Nigel, presumably to seek his opinion and keep him involved. Normally, that was just the sort of attention that would have made her brother preen. These were, after all, the men he'd wanted to impress. Their father's peers, the trustees of the museum, men with the same interests and investments.

But his attention was not on Abbie or the group. It kept darting back over to Emily, and then around the room, as if searching for someone.

She shivered, though the ballroom was closely packed and too warm. It was never good when Nigel was focused on her. But what could she do? She was trapped in this room as surely as she'd been in the wardrobe. An hour into the ball, she'd tried to slip out and had been stopped by one of the servants she'd thought were just there to provide directions or assistance to any guests who needed it. No. As it turned out, they were there on her father's orders to "accompany" her if she left the main ballroom, even to visit the facilities. There would be no sneaking back to her flat, not unless she could give the slip to those guards.

If only Beth were here. They could devise a plan together to do just that, and have fun doing it.

Oh, who was she trying to fool? *Beth* might develop such a plan, but Emily would be the one shaking her head and saying it was too dangerous, that she'd only make her father angry if she slipped away, and was it really so terrible to stay at a ball for a few hours?

Nigel set off across the room, aimed directly for her, which answered that question. Yes. Yes, it was really so terrible.

Vandermeer slipped in between her and Millicent, making her wonder where he'd been for the last half hour. "One of you lovely ladies had better agree to dance with me or my reputation will be in absolute tatters. Who wants to bite the bullet?"

Millicent sighed. "Really, Donald, some of your Americanisms are properly atrocious. What makes you think talk of bullets is at all appropriate?"

"That's the problem with you Brits. You spend far too much time contemplating what's appropriate and not nearly enough on what's efficient."

Millicent made some catty reply, but the words were lost in Emily's ears. Nigel had reached them and curled his hand around her elbow. "Let's dance, sister dearest."

"Oh, I—was about to dance with Mr. Vandermeer."

Nigel was already tugging her toward the floor. "He can have the next one." Perhaps some would call that twitch of his mouth a smile.

She didn't. He knew how to smile, and he did it regularly to get his way. That was no smile, just like his posture wasn't perfectly upright—it was tense. Fear snapped through her, sizzling along her veins. Then it settled into something different. "Nigel? Are you all right?"

He turned a startled gaze on her as he clamped a hand to her waist, gripped her hand in his, and twirled her into the waltz. "Don't pretend to care, Emily."

"I'm not pretending." And, oddly, it was true. "You're my brother. And I don't like seeing you like this."

He snorted a dismissive laugh. And though he had kept looking her way when he had been across the room, now he looked over her shoulder. "Where was he?"

Though she wanted to frown, Mother's training was too well ingrained—one did not frown in a crowded ballroom. One kept a perfectly placid expression on one's face at all times. "Who?"

"Are you obtuse? Vandermeer. He vanished from the room for forty minutes."

The frown very nearly overcame Mother's eternal whisper in her ear. This was about *Vandermeer*? "How am I to know? Perhaps he'd eaten something that didn't agree with him."

That at least pulled his attention to her for a second, though he did nothing so human as laugh. "Don't pretend you aren't in league with him, all of you. Little traitor that you are." His fingers bit into her back, pressing painfully on a bone of her corset. "I've tried to warn Father, too—haven't convinced him yet, but I will. Once he gets over the mad idea that Vandermeer's going to take you off his hands, he'll see the truth. The Yank can't be trusted. He cares only for his own interests, not ours. Not like I do."

Emily smiled. "I do believe it's a miracle."

"What?" Now he looked at her again—like she was daft.

It only made her smile deepen. "We agree on something. That may be a first." At his arched brow, she added, "That Vandermeer cares only for his own interests."

Why could he not simply smile back, laugh, relax a bit? Instead, his eyes kept storming. "Don't think for a moment that interest is really you. He's just using you to get at the Tremaynes. He can't tolerate the thought that they know something he doesn't, and he'll do whatever he must to learn it. Even pretend affection for *you*."

As if that were the most unpalatable thing in the world. "I'm under no delusions about Vandermeer."

"That earl doesn't really care for you either, you know. It's only that you're there, and everyone else is pairing off. Convenient, that's all you are. He'll forget you the moment he sets foot back on the mainland."

He might as well have slapped her—which he well knew. She pressed her lips together, wondering for the millionth time why he chose to be so cruel. How he had grown so skilled at finding the thing she most feared, the thing she hadn't even admitted to herself, and poking that monster to life. "You know," she forced out, "some brothers *encourage* their sisters. Seek the best for them."

He let go of her waist, spun her when the music demanded it, and then reeled her back in. No one could ever say Nigel Scofield wasn't an expert on the dance floor. "Why would I encourage you when you've betrayed your family? You chose them over us."

Because *they* sought the good, the holy, the uplifting. Because they saw her as something more than a burden to be either suffered or tossed aside. Because they were the only ones in the world who had ever chosen *her* for anything. Why should she choose the flesh and blood that despised her over the friends who offered acceptance and love? "Who betrayed who first, Nigel?"

"They're not your family. They can't protect you forever, and you can't just stay holed up in some flat on an island for the rest of your days. You're a Scofield, much as we all wish you weren't. That comes with expectations, and it's high time you live up to them."

"Now you sound like Father." She didn't mean for it to come out so wearily, but he'd poked at another slumbering monster inside her.

She really *couldn't* stay here forever. She had only two more weeks paid for and then her lease would be up on her flat. What was she to do? She hadn't even let herself think of it. Would her benefactor know? Provide more money for another week or month or . . . ?

But she couldn't just rent that flat forever. Mrs. Gilligan's daughter would eventually come. Emily would get the boot.

She could just go and stay with Beth. What choice would she have? But Beth would soon marry Sheridan, and then they'd be off exploring the world together, and she could hardly tag along on their honeymoon.

Bother. Her eyes stung, but she blinked before her brother could see it.

He wasn't looking at her anyway. His eyes were following something else on the dance floor—Vandermeer, dancing with Millicent. Nigel leaned in a bit. "You can still redeem yourself, you know. Earn Father's regard. Make him proud to call you his daughter. All you have to do is find whatever Vandermeer's hiding from us. Leverage that attention he's paying you."

Father's regard, Father's pride—the very things she had sought all her life. The very things he refused to give her. "Regard that can be bought through a deception is not worth having."

"Your high-and-mighty morals won't keep food on the table or a roof over your head, Emily. You need us—you have no choice in that. We are your family. So, for once in your life, remember that and do what's expected of you."

The music hit its ending cadence, and Nigel twirled her again, so that she reached the extension of their arms just as the quintet played the final notes. Like every other couple, they applauded, bowed. And Emily strode off the dance floor.

She might be stuck here in this stuffy room until Father gave her permission to leave. She might spend the next hour praying yet again to be given the strength to love them.

But no one ever said she had to stand there and let her brother fill her heart with lies.

20

Night was fading into the soft light preceding dawn by the time Emily finally staggered up the stairs to her flat. Her feet were killing her. Her back ached. She could barely keep her eyes open. But somehow Father still had been laughing with his friends and calling for another round of champagne when he finally waved permission for her to leave.

All grace had been exhausted ages ago. She tugged her gloves off with her teeth so she could better fish around the minuscule beaded bag looped over her wrist for her key. She tried to be quiet. Tommie—and hopefully Tristan—was blissfully asleep inside. Were this months ago in London, Emily would have had little compunction about ringing for her to help her remove the elaborate evening gown and slide the pins from her hair. But it was here and now, and once she finally fumbled the key into the lock, she took care to turn it gently and to swing the door open slowly. She closed it behind her as softly as she could and tiptoed her way into their tiny front room.

No puppy came charging out with barks and wiggles, insisting on a trip outside, so she breathed a sigh of relief. Walking Tristan sounded like an Arthurian quest just now.

The shoes had to go. Now. That stretch of hallway back to her room looked as long as a track given the pinching of her toes, so she sat on the sofa, shook the beaded bag off her wrist and onto the end table, and then unbuckled the leather straps. When she was finally able to toe the shoes off, she swore her feet sobbed in relief.

And this was the most comfortable sofa in the world. How had she never noticed that before? Her breath came out in a long sigh as she leaned back against the cushions . . . and then gave in to gravity and slid down to rest her head against the pillow by the arm. She wouldn't stay here long. Just a moment.

Pins jabbed her scalp, so she tugged the offenders free while her mind spun through the last few hours. Abbie and Millicent had closed ranks around her again after that one waltz with Nigel, and Vandermeer had made frequent appearances, too, as if it were his duty to keep their trio laughing. Oh, she'd danced with a few of Father's colleagues and their sons—it was expected—and twice with Vandermeer himself.

That had been odd. She'd rather expected him to take the opportunity to flirt, but instead he had smirked and said, "Ran into Telford outside earlier. He looked for a moment as though he'd like to bully his way in to claim a dance with you. And I imagine you wouldn't have minded had he come in and seen you looking so lovely tonight, would you?"

That had been enough to keep her looking around the rest of the night, hoping he *would* storm in for her. And, yes, see her in her finest gown and think her beautiful. Whisk her into his arms. Dance with her, looking down into her eyes as if they were the only couple in the room.

Foolishness. She let the pins fall to the table . . . or perhaps to the floor . . . and draped her arm over her eyes. She'd seen the group of men from Tresco trekking up the hill while she was getting ready, the books they carried telling her they'd finally found the time to pay another visit to Mr. Gale. They'd been dressed in their normal attire, not the tuxedo required for a ball. There was no way Telford would force his way in—he was far too aware of social protocols, too much the gentleman. And even if he went home and changed and came back . . . why would he do that?

No. He wouldn't. Obviously. Because he hadn't. And that was fine. She didn't need him to see her in this particular gown of silk and lace. And she didn't . . . She should really get up and go to bed. Which she would do. Eventually. Perhaps.

Later.

She was in the middle of the most beautiful dream about dancing with Telford on a cloud above Tresco when something startled her awake. A noise. Something loud and crashing and—

"Wake up, you little twit!"

Rough hands grabbed her by the shoulders and jerked her upright so fast her head spun. She blinked, blinked again to try to clear the sleep from her eyes, but could still barely make out her brother's face through the blur. "Nigel?"

"I saw him whispering to you—tell me! Tell me where he's gone, what he's up to!" He shook her so hard her teeth clattered together and her neck snapped painfully to the side.

Furious, frantic barking added to the din in her head, and she prayed Tommie had Tristan safely closed into her room. He was no guard dog, certainly not yet. But he would try to be.

"Stop it!" She tried to shove his hands away, but her awkward fumbles accomplished nothing.

He jerked her to her feet, closed one hand around her neck, and slapped her hard across the cheek with the other. "Tell me!"

She choked out a cry of pain and clawed at the hand around her throat. Was the barking drawing nearer?

"Unhand her, you monster!"

Tommie—*no*. Emily tried to squeak out a protest, but it was too late. Her friend was already flying at them, something round and dark held above her head like a weapon. A frying pan? A bowl? Whatever it was, it never had a chance of hitting Nigel. He kicked out a foot, knocked the thing to the floor with a clatter, and then twisted and kicked again, his foot meeting flesh with a sickening crack.

"No!" Emily's scream was barely a whisper past the fingers he hadn't relaxed. She couldn't turn her head to see Tommie, but she heard her hit the floor with a thud and could just see her bare feet and the ruffled edge of her nightgown.

But Tristan was there, too, and he'd launched himself at Nigel's legs. She'd never heard from him the furious growl that tore from his throat as he latched onto her brother's ankle.

Did Nigel's fingers tighten? Was that why there was a sudden roar in her ears, or was he screaming in pain at the dog's bite? It sounded like a war cry filling the room, and surely it was a hallucination that Bram and Enyon were lunging through the door, their faces both masks of fury.

She couldn't have said exactly what happened next. Nigel pulled her or pushed her, she stumbled over her shoes and thought he would rip her throat out rather than let her fall, but then she was hitting the floor. There was scrabbling, shouting, something crashing, the tinkle of broken glass, and a wet nose nudging her face and the sound of whimpering. Then pounding steps out and away.

And Bram was on the floor beside her, kneeling, hands moving over her head and shoulders and back. A furry little body was there, too, alternately licking her face and trying to curl up against her. "Are you all right? Em, speak to me!"

She shook her head and pushed herself up a few inches, but when she tried to talk, her words dissolved into a fit of coughing.

Bram muttered something and pulled her against his chest, holding her tight even as Tristan pressed himself against them.

She let him hold her. It was a fine place to work on easing air back into her lungs and trying to swallow. "Tommie."

"I've got her. She's unconscious, but her pulse is strong," Enyon said from behind them. "Which room is hers, my lady? I'll go and make her comfortable, then call for my mam to come and tend her."

"On the right." It was all she could manage. She coughed again, letting her fingers curl into Bram's shirtfront.

He stroked a hand down her back. It was trembling. *He* was trembling. "He hurt you. God above, give me strength to keep from killing him. He *hurt* you. I thought—the way he had you by the throat . . ." A violent shudder tore through him. He held her tighter with one arm, reaching with the other for the eager puppy. "You did a good job, Tris. Good boy. You distracted him before he could do worse."

She relaxed her fingers from the cotton, splayed them out instead. His heart pounded under her palm. "He did. And I'm all right." She had to whisper it, and even that felt raspy, but it was true.

Bram buried his fingers in her hair, tilted her head back, away from him, and sent his gaze roaming across her face as if searching for a lie in her assurances.

That was when she realized that the light was still soft and grey and dim. It couldn't be more than ten or fifteen minutes after she had fallen asleep on the couch. Not yet dawn. "What are you doing here? At this hour?"

Then she looked past him, over his shoulder, to the door gaping open, its glass panes broken and scattered on the floor.

To the basket of food and money knocked on its side on the doorstep.

It was him. Him and Enyon. How had she not pieced it together before? He was always up until dawn, so of course he was the one to come here in those too-early-or-too-late hours to leave her supplies. He was the one to pen a note about maidens and chivalry.

He was the one to help in such a way that it left her dignity intact. Because that was Bram Sinclair.

Her gaze tangled with his, and she lifted a hand to rest against his face. His jaw was stubbled, his eyes so achingly blue-green and fierce. Fierce on her behalf, not in anger with her. "Bram." She didn't even try to make her voice work above a whisper. A whisper was all she needed. "My knight in shining armor."

He gave the smallest shake of his head. "You don't need a knight, Emily. Just someone to stand beside you."

She wasn't so sure. She'd felt pretty helpless with Nigel's hand around her throat, and even with Tristan's distraction, how long would it have taken for her brother to give him a kick that would have hurt him or worse? He was still just a puppy.

But that was Bram, too, always ascribing strength to her where she couldn't see any in herself. Just one of the reasons her heart had taken to squeezing every time she thought of him. "However you describe it . . . *you're* what I need."

The words were too bare, too honest, too forward. Mother would have gasped in horror, and were Emily's blood not still gushing to and from her head in a flood, she probably would have had the sense not to say such words aloud.

But she couldn't exactly regret it when Bram's gaze dropped to her mouth a second before his lips followed its trajectory. It was a soft touch, gentle and tentative, a question more than a kiss. Because he would be keenly aware even now of the bruises her brother had inflicted, of how powerless she had felt in Nigel's hands, and he wouldn't want her to feel the same now.

She felt the opposite. With his arms around her, she felt strong and bold, cherished and capable. She felt like a princess worthy of the valiant knight's devotion. She felt so full that it all brimmed over and spilled back into him with her kiss, hungry and confident.

He pulled her closer, the kiss going from a question to a desire, perhaps even to a need. Her head swam with it, soared with it, swelled with it. She could live in this moment forever, she was certain. Just here, with his arms around her and his lips on hers and this certainty pulsing through her that said this was what life was supposed to be, this was what it meant to belong, this was what her heart had always craved. Not just a kiss or a man, but *this* kiss, *this* man—the one who always made her stronger instead of telling her she was weak. The one who built her up instead of tearing her down. The one who made her glad to be who she was.

"Oh, gracious me! What has happened? Is everyone all right?"

Mrs. Gilligan's voice came from outside, directly followed by the sound of her feet running up the stairs. Emily and Bram had just enough time to pull away and for him to help her to her feet before her landlady appeared in the broken doorway, horror on her face. "I heard shouting. Breaking glass. I came as fast as I could."

Bram's hand still rested on the small of her back, protective and warm. "Enyon and I were dropping off something that Mrs. Dawe sent over," he said with a nod toward the abandoned basket, "and we found the lady's brother strangling her, her maid unconscious. Call for the constable if you would, Mrs. Gilligan."

The woman's hand flew to her mouth. She rushed into the room instead of back down the stairs. "My poor girl! You've bruises on your neck. Your own brother, you say?"

She could feel his fingers around her throat again. Practically hear his hiss in her ear, and her father's. If she backed up that claim, if she called the authorities on her own brother, there would be no going back to them. Ever.

The door hung there, open. A threshold she'd approached before, that she'd leaned across when she chose the Tremaynes two months ago. But she'd not fully crossed through it. Not like Bram was asking her to do now.

Her mouth was dry as a desert. But Tristan was a bundle of barely contained energy at her feet and Bram's hand was warm and still trembling her back. Funny how his shaking could make her steady.

She nodded. "He kicked Tommie in the head—Enyon has just carried her to her bed. We'll need a physician too. If you would be so good, Mrs. Gilligan?"

"Anything you need, my lady, anything at all!" Then she shocked Emily—and likely Bram—by stretching up and smacking a kiss to his cheek. "Praise God you and Enny were here! He must have sent you, my lord, to protect these girls."

His larynx bobbed. "I do believe you're right, madame."

"Let me peek in on dear Thomasina first, then I'll be dreckly off." She bustled down the corridor, clucking her tongue as she side-stepped the odds and ends that had ended up broken on the floor in the scuffle.

"I'll have everything replaced," Bram said. "And the door repaired

278

straightaway. You rest easy, madame. Though I think it best if the lady and her maid remove themselves to Tresco for the time being." He slanted a glance down at Emily, though it was less to ask permission, she suspected, than to make it clear this was not up for debate. "At least until this place can be fortified a bit."

By the time *that* was accomplished, her lease would be up anyway. And really, she wasn't certain either she or Tommie would feel safe here again. "I think I forgot to lock the door. When I came in this morning."

"Even if you had, I doubt it would have stopped him. It wasn't exactly the sturdiest lock in the world."

She shivered and pressed a little closer to his side as Mrs. Gilligan vanished into Tommie's room. "All the threats Nigel made, all the things he's done . . . he's never raised a hand to me. Not until we came here." She touched a finger to her cheek and found it tender.

Bram made a little noise of protest and turned her face toward the light now coming through her open door. "I hadn't seen that one."

"It will heal." But the rift between her and her brother, between her and all her family? Every step she took today was going to make it wider. The weight of that settled on her like an island of granite. Her eyes slid shut.

Bram pressed a kiss to the top of her head. "Libby would say I'm being overbearing, making decisions for you. Maybe I am, but I'm not going to apologize for it. I can't. You can't stay here alone anymore, sweetheart."

As if she had any desire to argue that right now. "Bear away, Bram. I don't mind."

His chuckle sounded tired. "I'll remind you of that when you're so fed up with my protectiveness that you threaten to lock me in a tower."

A sigh slipped out. "I can't imagine ever growing tired of protectiveness."

"You will, once I've convinced you that you don't need it."

She couldn't help but laugh. And lean her head against his shoulder. And thank the Lord that He'd sent Bram to her rescue.

———————○———————

Tommie blinked against pain and light, her mind a muddle as she tried to piece together those two things. She felt the familiar mattress and blankets of her bed beneath her, heard Emily's familiar voice from somewhere, smelled the familiar scent of bacon frying. But none of it was *right*. Emily shouldn't be making food . . . and Tommie shouldn't still be abed.

She hadn't been, had she? There was a memory there, blurred and cloudy, of Tristan's frantic barking, of leaping up, of . . . Nigel. Nigel here, in their flat, with his hands around Emily's throat.

She sucked in a gasp and tried to sit up, urgency in every nerve ending even as those current familiarities told her it was useless. If he were still here, Emily would not be talking to anyone and cooking bacon. Tristan would still be sounding an alarm.

"Easy, love. Your head must be pounding, and you'll only make it worse." Gentle hands urged her back to her pillow as her vision cleared. Enyon? What was he doing here? And with such a look on his face, all devastation and . . . something deeper. Something beautiful. Something she didn't dare try to name.

"Enyon?" She turned her head to better see him, but the light slashing in through the window struck her like a dinner gong and made her wince. "What happened?"

"You and Tristan saved the day when that monster went for his sister, that's what—though you're a little worse off for the heroics. The doctor's on his way; Mrs. Gilligan went to fetch him." He took one of her hands between both of his and lifted it to his lips. Kissed her knuckles. Held it there against his mouth. "You scared a decade off my life, Thomasina. When I came in and saw you on the floor like that—I thought I'd lost you. And without you knowing how much you mean to me."

Presumably Emily was all right—she heard her laughter, strained but audible, in the other room. Which meant she was free to focus on that "*how much you mean to me*," if she had the courage for it. Perhaps she would, once the thumping in her head subsided a wee bit. "But what are you *doing* here?"

He held her gaze for a long moment, darted a glance through the open door, and then sighed. "I've been ferrying Telford over to bring the food and money. It was his idea, mind," he added quickly, as if afraid she might give him too much credit. "And certainly his cash."

But Enyon had helped. She smiled a bit at the thought of those two—unlikely friends as they were—slipping out before dawn to help them. Darlings, both of them. "I wouldn't have guessed it was him. There were never any sweets in the basket."

Enyon chuckled. "He debated. Would have given him away, he said. Or else he wanted to keep them all for himself."

She let her eyes slide closed again for a minute, but she curled her fingers around the hand that held them. Let her mind drift back. "I'm thinking it was a good thing you were making another delivery this morning, or things could have ended very differently. You may say Tristan and I rushed to the rescue, but clearly Nigel dispatched us without too much trouble."

But she'd faced him—that counted for something. She'd not only faced him, she'd found the courage to rush forward, to defend Emily.

"We'll credit the Lord for that timing, and I'm grateful for it. But standing up to him as you did, after what *he* did—that took gumption. I'm proud of you. And, Thomasina . . . will you look at me? Please?"

She peeled her eyes open again at his tone, so humble and heavy with emotion. Never mind how the light hurt. Never mind the aches and pains. Any discomfort in the world was worth it to see him looking at her as he was doing.

He kissed her fingers again. "I realize there are depths to your wounds that I can't know. That you may not even know, but which will likely come up as time goes by. I realize that there may be times that I inadvertently remind you of him, though that's the last thing in the world I'd ever want to do. I realize you will naturally hesitate to trust me. But I pray you'll give me a chance, dearover. Give me a chance to prove I'm different. To prove that I can love you like you need to be loved, like you *deserve* to be loved, if you'll but let me."

Love? Deserve? Her mouth went dry even as incredulous joy flooded her heart. How could he speak so easily of love when he knew all he did of her? But then she remembered her own words to Ailla, and Senara's words from last night.

It had taken courage, yes, to rush at Nigel so she could help her friend. But this took even more. Stepping out into the future, trusting this earnest man beside her to care for her heart, trusting that God could have something better for her . . .

This was the true test. The true challenge. The true quest. This was where she proved herself either a coward or a heroine.

She pulled his hands toward her and rested her cheek against them. It wouldn't be easy—but the best things never were. "I'll let you."

Bram must have a veritable thunderhead on his face, the way everyone scuttled out of his path as he strode beside Enyon toward the docks. But he couldn't convince his countenance to relax so much as a smidgeon.

Nigel had hurt her. That monster had struck her. Strangled her. Kicked poor Briggs in the head hard enough to send her into next Tuesday. And all for information on what Vandermeer was doing?

He'd come unhinged, that was what. And that made him even more dangerous than he'd been before.

Bram's hands had curled into fists when he left Emily in the care of a passel of Scillonian mothers bent on seeing to Briggs and helping them pack, and they hadn't come unclenched since. Not when he and Enyon banged on the door of a carpenter who promised he could fix the smashed door, not when he sat in the constable's office and walked the man through the events of the morning, and not when Enyon convinced him they'd better return to Tresco so they could trade his small sloop for the larger *Adelle* if they meant to transfer the girls' belongings along with them.

Not that Enyon chided him for the scowls and fisted hands. He was flashing plenty of lightning of his own.

Bram didn't know whether to be annoyed or relieved when he saw Millicent and Vandermeer hurrying toward them at the quay. On the one hand, he needed to let Sheridan's sisters know that Emily would be leaving St. Mary's and advise them to hire a bit of protection for themselves as well—who was to say who Nigel would target next? On the other hand, he wasn't certain he could handle any of the American's cheerful jabs at the moment.

But Vandermeer wasn't smiling. He looked worried, in fact, as they met in the sand. "What's going on? Nigel came tearing through an hour ago, absconded with the *Victoria*, and his father stormed after him in the other yacht."

Bram folded his arms over his chest. "I suggest you press charges for the theft of your yacht, then. We just filed a report ourselves, given that he broke into Emily's flat and attacked both her and her maid."

He expected the explosion of reactions from both of them. What took him by surprise was the hand Millicent set on Vandermeer's arm, and the troubled look in her eyes when she said, "Enough is enough, Donald. For whatever reason, he's decided to focus on your involvement in all this. It's time for you to return to America."

"And leave the rest of you to parry the danger? Don't be an idiot, Millie." But he covered her fingers with his. "I'm not going any-where, not unless the lot of you are coming with me." He angled a brow at Bram. "Game? Trip to America for everyone?"

"Tempting." The thought of Emily and Libby both in danger was enough to make him twitchy. "But my mother's en route even now, and I somehow can't imagine the Tremaynes agreeing to leave. I'm frankly not certain Mamm-wynn's strong enough for a trip, though she'd argue if I said so."

"Then that settles it. We stay, and we stop him." Vandermeer jerked his head toward the hotel. "Lord Scofield may be a powerful man, but he's not going to cover up his son's crimes. Among the rest of us, I daresay there's influence enough to counteract his."

They did have his earldom, Sher's marquessate, and an American with more money than sense—not to mention the insider knowledge and community of the islanders, and the imagination of Gibson and his family. More, they had something Nigel surely wasn't counting on—a sister who knew him far better than he gave her credit for.

Bram nodded. "He doesn't stand a chance."

Millicent reached over and rested her free hand on Bram's arm. Those eyes of hers, the ones always so quick to spot a problem, whether it was hers to solve or not, sparked. "I know well it wouldn't have been Emily's idea to go to the authorities. You know what you're asking of her, don't you? Her family may never forgive her for this."

His throat felt dry as he swallowed. He'd sworn to Sheridan not eight hours ago that liking her didn't mean being ready to propose. That he wasn't ready to proclaim his undying love.

But that was before he'd seen her brother's hand choking off her air, the way her eyes bulged before she crumpled to the ground when he released her. That was before he feared, for one terrible second, that he'd lost her.

Forget slow courtships and testing the waters—there'd been no doubt in that moment. He loved her as surely as he did Libby or Edith or Mother or Mamm-wynn, and that meant he'd sooner die himself than see her hurt again.

"She can mourn their loss—she has the heart for it. But I'll see she's never without a family to surround her."

Millicent's lips turned up, and she blinked a few rapid times, squeezing his arm. "Our lads, all grown up. She'll be good for you, and you for her."

He nodded. "We need to get back to Tresco and get the *Adelle* so we can transport them and their trunks to the Tremaynes'. You and Abbie should probably add a few guards to your employ too."

Vandermeer straightened. "We'll take care of that." He didn't look the least bit sorry to hear Telford all but proclaim he was going to marry Emily—but then, it wasn't exactly disinterest in his eyes as he watched Millicent, now, was it? Nor rivalry.

Interesting. Sheridan would get a kick out of this one.

Sheridan—blast, they still had to let everyone else know what was going on. To think that everyone on Tresco was still peacefully slumbering, having no clue what had transpired here over the last hour. The thought lit urgency in his stomach anew, and he stepped around them. "Thanks. We'll see you later."

A few minutes more and he and Enyon were under sail, the waters rushing beneath them, making him keenly aware of the growing distance between him and Emily. He had a feeling Enyon was feeling the same about Briggs.

He let himself sag a bit, braced his elbows on his knees, and held his head in his hands. *Father God*. He wasn't exactly an expert at praying. But the doubts he had once entertained had been burned out of him this summer. First with Libby's logic, then with Oliver's certainty. With Sheridan's new perspectives, with that too-insightful note from Morgan . . . and with Emily's boundless heart. He'd wondered how to reconcile God's love and mercy with His justice—but not anymore.

He could see it so clearly in her. They'd mingled in her spirit in equal parts, clear as day as she'd answered the constable's questions.

How did mercy and justice meet? With pain and sacrifice. And beauty beyond anything he'd ever seen.

Father God, only you can see the best path through this. Show us your ways, I beg you. And help us to follow them to where you want us to be.

21

Tommie ambled along the shores of Tresco, darting a glance to her side, where Ailla had cast her eyes. Toward St. Agnes? Or beyond, to the mainland?

Nigel hadn't been seen on the islands since Saturday morning, but it was difficult to relax in that knowledge, given that a team of Scofield's lawyers, barristers, and who-knew-what-else *had* arrived on the first ferry of the morning, according to Enyon, and they were setting St. Mary's abuzz already. They were claiming that Nigel had not *attacked* anyone. That he had startled some other burglar from his sister's flat, and Emily and Tommie's poor female brains were simply scrambled from the fright of it all. And he had not *stolen* Vandermeer's yacht, merely borrowed it to give chase to the aforementioned scoundrel. He ought to be heralded as a hero, they'd claimed.

She'd asked Enyon how they meant to negate the fact that both he and Lord Telford had witnessed Nigel throttling his sister, but he had shrugged. Apparently Nigel hadn't told them that bit. They'd get to watch them fumble and scramble later that day when he and Telford showed up again to enlighten them.

Part of her wanted to see it—and to add her own accusations to the mix. Part of her wanted to stay far clear. All this effort wasn't, she suspected, just to get charges dropped. No, Nigel wouldn't be content to just leave the area and cut his losses. Not with the museum still excavating Gugh, the Arthurian artifact still unfound, and Vandermeer still here. He wanted to come back. He wanted to find Ron. He wanted *his* name attached to the discovery, and it must be eating at him that his glory was threatened because his sister hadn't kept her mouth shut.

He'd want revenge for that. And on Tommie too. And, she feared, on Ailla for good measure, since Nigel couldn't be sure that she wouldn't add her own accusations to the collection of them, now that the law was involved.

Perhaps the girl knew it too. Perhaps that was why she'd looked so worried all through the hour-long conversation she and her mother and Tommie had just had with Oliver Tremayne. His words had offered endless comfort when it came to how God looked upon them.

But he couldn't exactly promise safety from the monster if he returned.

Tommie looked over her shoulder when Ailla did, to where Mr. Tremayne and Mrs. Marrack strolled behind them, too far away for their words to be audible over the surf and the wind. The topic now was Ailla's father. And Mrs. Marrack was clearly distressed. Mr. Tremayne had her by the arm, working what Mabena Moon called his "elbow magic." Peering into her soul, digging out her fears and hopes.

Tommie faced forward again. "His suggestion wasn't a bad one, Ailla. I imagine your brother would be glad to see you, and it would be far easier to disappear and avoid Nigel on the mainland. We just can't trust that he won't come back here. Not yet."

Ailla sighed. "I know. We'll write to Luke and see what he says. But part of me feels like if I run, if I hide out of sight until he leaves, then I'm letting him win. That's not what you did, is it? You came at him the other day with a frying pan."

For all the good it did. She had to look away from Ailla and the water beyond her even now, because the glare made her head pound. "I'm no one to emulate."

Ailla's fingers toyed with the end of her braid, which hung over her shoulder and reached down to her waist. "That's not the way I see it. You've survived. You've kept going. And you even have Enyon, who knows what happened and loves you anyway."

"*. . . loves you anyway.*" Tommie jolted a bit at the phrase, spilling so easily from Ailla's lips. It was one thing for the two of them to talk about loving and letting someone love you. But what did anyone else know about it? Couldn't it just be theirs right now, while they sorted through it all? Not that she was going to argue with Ailla, of all people. "Certainly imitate surviving and even finding a future, but fighting back . . ." She shook her head softly because the ache hadn't fully left it yet. "Better to let the law do its work and keep yourself safe."

"But you said before that the law would never catch him up!"

"That was before he raised a hand to his sister and Lord Telford witnessed it. I heard his lordship saying he meant to push for attempted murder charges, and he's still so fired up about it, I think he may have a chance of making it stick."

It shouldn't be different just because this time he attacked a noblewoman instead of a servant or a common girl. But it was.

Ailla pursed her lips, a stubborn glint in her eyes.

Tommie sighed. "Why do I get the feeling that you take after your tas?"

For the first time in their weeklong acquaintance, Ailla smiled. "Drives poor Mam to distraction. One or the other of us always blustering about as we do."

"Well, bluster yourself to the mainland, Ailla, and out of his reach. Please. Win by moving on and flourishing."

Ailla grunted. "I'll do whatever they tell me to. But in the meantime, I'll help you all in any way I can. Anything to put the screws to him."

She didn't know what help the girl could really offer, but she wasn't about to say so. "Thank you. I'll pass that along to the others. In the meantime—"

"Stay safe, yes, I know." She spun around to watch her mother and the vicar for a long moment, frowning. "What do you think they're deciding? About telling Tas?"

Tommie could only shrug. "Mr. Tremayne is in general a fan of honesty—but he's *not* a fan of violence, and if he fears your father may resort to it . . . well, he could at least advocate for waiting until the Scofields have left the islands for good. But I really don't know."

"Is it cowardly of me to hope that if they decide to, Mam will do it? Preferably when I'm at Luke's?" She shook her head and faced forward again. "I don't want to see the disappointment in his eyes. The shame."

How well Tommie could understand that. Hadn't she thought the same in regard to her mam? But maybe she wasn't giving her mother enough credit. "Sounds as though your father adores you. He wouldn't blame you for it."

"Maybe not. But it would still change everything, wouldn't it?"

Tommie could only shrug. "Perhaps. But perhaps . . . 'changed' could be better. You can be sure Mr. Tremayne will be praying about it. And I will be too."

Ailla linked their arms together. "I'm glad Enny's found you. It'll be nice having you for a neighbor after you marry. Knowing there's someone else in the Scillies, anyway, who understands."

Her cheeks felt red as the apples Mrs. Dawe was cooking with today. "Now, there's been no talk of marriage."

But Ailla laughed. "Oh, Tommie—*everyone's* talking of it. His mam's planning a Christmas wedding."

What? Her cheeks felt hot as flames. "Do you think they'll remember to consult me on the matter?" She heard the sparks in her words, too, the frustration.

Ailla must not have. She was still chuckling. "Probably hasn't crossed their minds. If you have an objection, you'd better make it now."

Tommie pressed her lips together. She didn't know if she had an objection or not to the idea itself—but she certainly had one to the entire island chain deciding on her future before she could.

She'd had enough of other people deciding her fate for her.

———————◦———————

Rain had been pattering down all through their sail from Tresco and showed no signs of letting up. Emily gripped her umbrella in one hand and kept ahold of Bram's arm with the other, trying to tell herself there was no reason to be nervous as they watched the ferry dock and passengers begin to come down the gangway. His mother was sure to be a delightful woman. And hadn't Emily been raised to impress a gentleman's mother? No need for the acrobats in her stomach at all.

On Bram's other side, Libby pressed a hand to her own abdomen— apparently the acrobats were performing there too. "I'm going to be sick."

Bram sighed. "For the last time, Lib, Mother will adore the Tremaynes and happily bless your engagement. You have nothing to worry about."

"Edith could have rubbed off on her. She could be ready to deem anything I do or think or want improper."

"Stop. Worrying."

"Why didn't you let Oliver come, then?"

Bram sighed. And touched his hand to Emily's. "Suggesting he wait for us at the hotel is not the same as not letting him come. It's merely giving me a chance to make sure Mother is in the right frame of mind before the introductions."

Libby frowned at him from under her own umbrella. "Then why did you insist Emily come?"

The very question she'd been wondering herself.

Bram, however, just chuckled. "Think about it, Lib. What could possibly put Mother in a better frame of mind than seeing me with Em?"

Libby moved her mouth for a moment without replying, then smiled. "Sometimes I forget what a wonderful big brother you are. When you aren't conniving and controlling and trying to protect me from every stray sunbeam."

His only answer was to nudge Emily's umbrella a bit higher when the spines bumped his hat.

"Sorry." She moved it a bit to the left, too, because if it was hitting his hat, it was also probably leaving his whole left side exposed to the rain.

"Oh—there she is!"

At Libby's cry, Emily began scanning the passengers making their way up the dock, though she had no idea what their mother looked like. Had she seen her before in London at some event or another? Probably, but she couldn't match a face to the name, so instead she simply searched for someone who bore a resemblance to the siblings beside her. Blond hair, perhaps. Elegant, surely. She found herself looking for a woman who held herself with that bearing that they all learned from birth, and her eyes snagged on just the right sort of posture, clothed in a pristine blue traveling suit.

But the woman's hair wasn't blond. It was red. And the face entirely familiar.

Emily thrust the umbrella into Bram's hand. "Mother?" Hope surged up, had her lunging forward. And then the cold rain splashed fear into her soul and brought her just as quickly to a halt.

She wouldn't be here to see Emily. She'd be here because Father told her to come and gather his belongings, perhaps, or to wait for his return. Perhaps Father was even on the ferry, too, lagging behind a bit.

She should turn again. Dip her head. Hide in the crowd. Better to be unseen by her mother than ignored by her one more time. Or, worse, to be told in person to take her brother's side.

"Emily!"

Too late. Mother had spotted her and was hurrying her way, face beaming. *Beaming*. Emily blinked, certain the rain was simply

291

blurring her vision, but Bram had joined her with the umbrella again, so it couldn't be that.

Before she could think up any other explanations, Mother was before her. Mother's arms were around her. Mother was half-laughing, half-sobbing into her hair. "My sweet girl. Finally. Did you get any of my letters at all? When I realized they were being intercepted by one of your father's men and not sent—but I hope the last ones made it at least."

"I . . ." Emily returned the embrace because she needed to, as desperately as she needed to breathe. But it didn't quiet all the questions. "Letters? No. I only got that one telegram telling me not to anger Nigel. Mother, what are you doing here?"

Her mother pulled back, though she didn't let her go. She kept one hand locked on her shoulder and lifted the other to brush the tears from her own cheeks. Her gaze moved over Emily's face, down to her neck and the bruises she hadn't been able to hide. "I was so afraid he'd hurt you—and he has, hasn't he? I never thought . . . I knew he said horrible things to you, but I never dreamed he would turn to violence. Not until I mustered up the courage to go through your father's files. The things I found, Emily—the things he covered up for him . . ."

Mother shook her head, tears spilling onto her cheeks. "That was when I found all my letters to you too. I don't know which of the servants had been holding them, but I am certain it was at your father's command. Here all this time I had been writing instead of sending you telegrams, thinking you would appreciate the more personal touch. I'm so sorry. You must have thought I didn't even care."

Exactly what she *had* thought, because Mother had always taken Nigel's side. But she could understand that, a bit. A mother's un-willingness to see her firstborn child's cruel streak. Still, to realize that Mother hadn't intended to be silent all these weeks, and that as soon as she realized what was happening she must have taken steps to come here herself . . . that changed everything. Everything.

And that telegram—had it been warning, then, not command? It must have been.

Grateful that Bram was holding the umbrella over them, and only peripherally aware of another woman hugging Libby a few feet away, Emily gripped her mother's wrist. "But if that had all been on Father's orders, aren't you taking a risk by coming here? Won't he be angry?"

"Let him be. It is high time he realize what his actions have done." She sniffed, straightened, and looked more like Emily expected her to—elegant and unflappable. "I apologize that it took me so long to make my way here, but my solicitor was on holiday and then there was the research you'd asked me to do, and then when I bumped into Augusta at the tearoom one day—well, that was providence, without question! I knew Lords Telford and Sheridan were here, and when Augusta said she was coming to join her children, we decided it only made sense to travel together."

Augusta? Emily followed the flutter of Mother's hand and really saw for the first time the lovely lady who stood under Libby's umbrella with her, an arm around her daughter's waist. Lady Telford was watching them unabashedly, a smile on her face.

And her son was standing fully in the rain while he sacrificed their umbrella to Emily and her mother. "Oh! Bram, you're getting soaked!"

He gave her a soul-warming grin. "Believe it or not, I'm not made of sugar. I won't melt."

His mother chuckled. "Even so, moving this reunion to the hotel wouldn't go amiss. I instructed the stevedores to haul all your trunks there, too, darling. Is that all right?"

All *his* trunks?

"Ah." He pushed the umbrella back into Emily's hands. "We'll just have to load them on the *Adelle*, so there's no point. I'll go and intercept them and be right back."

Emily stared after him, then glanced again at Lady Telford before finally settling her gaze on her own mother. Her brain was still buzzing with it all, sorting it out in bits and pieces. Mother was *here*. Not at Father's behest, but for *her*. And . . . "Wait. Solicitors? And what research?"

"Into King Arthur, dear." Mother grinned. "I had quite a bit of fun going through all the most obscure texts to be found in the museum. Spent a whole week in the King's Library as a matter of fact—which your brother certainly hadn't done. He tore in and out in his usual fashion and missed absolutely everything worthwhile."

Lady Telford laughed and gestured toward Bram's retreating back. "The question will be whether you found anything my son doesn't already know."

"Doubtful," Libby said dryly. "Highly, highly doubtful." She grinned when her mother leaned over and pressed another kiss to her cheek. "I've missed you, Mama."

"And I you! I can hardly wait to meet this young man of yours. I've never heard your brother praise anyone so highly. Is he not here?"

"Bram made him wait at the hotel so he could sound out your mood." She sent Emily a dimpled smile. "And sweeten it if necessary by letting you see the absolutely perfect young lady he's chosen."

Before, Emily could convince herself that Lady Telford was watching *them*, not *her*. No such comfort was possible now as the lady stepped closer and held out a hand. Emily took it, praying her own wasn't shaking as badly as it felt to her.

The countess squeezed her fingers and said, "I am so looking forward to making your acquaintance, Lady Emily. If both Bram and Libby like you, then you must be a special young lady indeed."

Her cheeks went hot. "I don't know about that, but I'm certainly blessed to count them both as friends."

"Ah, your mother was right. Your sweet spirit is visible in a glance." With one more squeeze of her fingers, Lady Telford released her again and turned back to Libby. "And now I think we ought to leave Lady Scofield and her daughter to their reunion so that I can meet this Mr. Tremayne, my dear. You say he shares your love of botany?"

"He knows all the Latin names. And he's a vicar, even though after poor Morgan passed away he also inherited Truro Hall, and . . ."

The Sinclairs moved away, leaving Emily alone with her mother, if one discounted the crowd of ferry passengers paying them no heed. She met the familiar eyes again and drew in a ragged breath. "You've really been spending these last weeks trying to help me?"

"And succeeding, I hope. With the help of my solicitors, I've managed to have all your funds—both your dowry and what you stood to inherit from my parents upon your twenty-first birthday—transferred into an account that you can access now. It was only six months early, after all."

"An inheritance?" She could only blink at her mother. She scarcely remembered her maternal grandparents—they had died when she was five—and had never heard a word about any funds held in trust for her.

"You don't think they forgot you, do you? You were their little darling. They tried to warn me about Nigel, but he was only thirteen when they died. I thought he would grow out of his behavior. I didn't see what they saw so clearly even then. And I was rather angry with them, I'll admit it, for leaving him so little and you so much. But I see their wisdom now."

Her mind was whirling. "They . . . does he know that?"

"Yes. He was allowed in for the reading of the will." Mother frowned at her. "Don't you remember, dear? That's why he locked you in the wardrobe the next day. I'd told him to play with you—you were so upset at losing them both so suddenly. I never dreamed he would do something so cruel, Emily, but I had so much to attend to in the wake of their deaths, and I wasn't at home to realize you hadn't been found. . . ."

Emily's vision blurred. How could she have forgotten that? It came back to her now. The sorrow that had dampened her days and made her so sullen. The sudden hope when the brother who never paid her any attention said he would play hide-and-seek with her. The knowledge behind the fear when he locked her in—that

Mother was gone, that Father didn't care, that no one would think to look for her.

Mother slid an arm around her. "Have you been all right? I've been so worried that you'd run out of pocket money before I could get here, and I knew your father wouldn't relent."

"I did. But I've been all right. Lord Telford saw to that."

Mother's smile shifted, looking nearly conspiratorial. "He's a fine-looking young man. All the ladies in London have been trying to get their husbands to introduce their daughters, but he's been aloof since his father's death. Quite a catch, though, without doubt."

"He's so much more than that, Mother." She couldn't help but look down the dock, toward where he stood with a stevedore and a pile of trunks that made her eyes go wide. "Did his mother say those are *his*?" Of their own accord, her feet pointed her in his direction.

Her mother laughed and fell in beside her, their arms linked. "He asked her to bring a few books. He apparently has quite an impressive library on King Arthur."

A *few*? Sheridan's sisters had arrived with a *few* of his things. It looked like Lady Telford had brought an entire library, if all those trunks were filled with books. She paused at Bram's side, unable to hold back a smile at the frown he was directing at the pile. "Think the *Adelle* can hold them all?"

"No. But this isn't my fault—I sent a list. There were no more than forty books on it. It seems they only got my request for my Arthur books, not the particular ones I wanted." He glanced down at her, looking more sheepish than she'd ever seen him.

She lifted her brows, knowing well her amusement was all over her face. "Your Arthur books."

"I . . . may have a bit of an . . . interest. In the legends."

She smiled at the way his neck went red. "An interest."

"One might even term it a *fascination*." Perhaps his neck was as hot as it was red. He lifted a hand to it and rubbed.

"I see." There were no fewer than twelve trunks. There really was no way the *Adelle* could haul it all back to Tresco—nor room in the Tremaynes' house for them all. "Are you certain the word you're looking for isn't *obsession*?"

His face screwed up into an expression she'd never seen on him before, but which brought mirth bubbling up. "You still have time to run away."

Laughter slipped out. "I do appreciate the consideration, but no thank you. Though I think you'd better take your mother's advice and have them sent to the hotel. You can take a room for them and then pluck out that mere *forty* that you wanted to show us."

His embarrassment seemed to be turning into amusement, at least. "And I'll tell Oliver he has to cart them all back. Just to see the look on his face."

She laughed again and then turned back to her mother. Her mother—here, for her. Her heart was so full she could scarcely keep it in her chest. "I imagine you're ready to get to the hotel as well."

"I *could* use a chance to tidy up. Don't you have a flat nearby? I was hoping to stay with you."

"Oh." Emily shook her head. "I mean, I do, for a little bit longer, but after Nigel smashed the door on Saturday—"

"He what?"

She nodded. "Broke the glass panes and damaged the hinges on his way out. It's been replaced, but we thought it best I transfer to Beth's house on Tresco."

Mother's face darkened. "In case he comes back, you mean." She stood straighter, chin up. "I rather hope he does. I have a few things to say to that boy. I'll stay in your flat, even if you're with Beth. I'd just as soon not be in the same hotel as your father just now."

Emily had a hard time swallowing. Her family had never been what Beth's was, but it seemed now it was fracturing straight down the middle. She'd never wanted that. But she had no idea how to mend it.

22

Bram had compromised and brought only a dozen of his books to Tresco with him today—after entertaining himself with watching Oliver go bug-eyed and speechless upon seeing the carts roll in with his trunks—but he wasn't currently looking at any of them.

The rain was still pattering against the rooftop, and from the drawing room he could hear laughter drifting down the corridor as Mother got to know Mamm-wynn and the man who had won her daughter's heart. He'd stayed with them long enough to be certain that she had been far quicker than he had to see that the Tremaynes, though scorned by the elite in London, were as fine a family as ever tread England's soil, and Libby would be happy here. More than happy.

How could Mother be anything but content?

Bram had left them once talk had turned to which season would provide the most beautiful wedding in the Abbey Gardens, tucking his smile behind a roll of his eyes. He wouldn't be surprised if, by the time evening fell, Mother had agreed to an autumn wedding. He could hear Mamm-wynn even now insisting that the end of October was still beautiful here, and really, they didn't even have a winter to speak of and the gardens were in bloom even in January.

They may not have much of a winter, but today certainly felt like autumn with the cool rain that hadn't let up. Oliver had relented to the weather and lit a fire in the library's grate an hour ago. Which made it rather cozy as the puppy slept in front of the hearth and Bram pored over the manuscript carefully laid out on the table.

No, not just a manuscript—a treasure. It was old, the parchment fragile and crumbling around the edges, and he had no idea how Lady Scofield had managed to convince the British Museum to entrust it to her care. But here it was, unrolled before him. An Arthur story he'd never read before—or rather, not quite like this. It was a variation of a familiar tale, but with a few interesting diversions from the traditional telling.

Emily moved to his side and rested her hand on his shoulder. "How's it coming, O Wise Translator?"

He smiled up into her face, beautiful despite the bruise on her cheek. "I can't believe no one else wanted to tackle the Old English."

From the sofa behind him, Sheridan snorted. "Your turn, that's all. To shine."

"And you call yourself an Englishman." But he didn't at all mind having the parchment to himself. He turned his attention back to Emily. "Your mother is a gem."

"As is the chap in charge of the old documents, who assured her this really was about King Arthur." Emily leaned over his shoulder to take another look but shook her head. A red curl tickled his nose, smelling delightfully of rain and roses.

Since the only other ones in the Tremayne library were Beth and Sheridan, he didn't mind grumbling, "If you're trying to distract me, sweetheart, it's working."

It was so easy—and so rewarding—to bring a blush to her cheeks. She looked down, her uncertainty finally settling into a grin. "Actually, I came to offer sustenance." She lifted her other hand to show him a paper-lined basket of Mrs. Dawe's taffy.

"You're a gem too. Join me?"

She pulled out the chair beside him and slid into it while he unwrapped one of the sweets and bit off a chewy hunk. "Here." He slid a few sheets of paper over to her that he'd already written on, and a few fresh ones too. "Let's see if you can decipher my scrawl and turn it into something legible for the others."

She took up a pen. "Is this some sort of test? A proof of my noble blood? 'For only the worthy can read the wizard's hand . . .'"

He couldn't quite resist leaning over and stealing a quick kiss at that. She was just so perfect.

"Saw that."

Bram blindly lobbed a wad of rejected paper over his shoulder at Sheridan. "Don't care."

The paper came soaring back a moment later and bounced off the back of his head.

Beth sighed. "I have a feeling we're going to be dealing with such antics for the rest of our lives, Em."

Emily flushed again and darted a look at him that said she wasn't quite as willing to speak of the rest of their lives as Beth was. Or was afraid to, perhaps. He sent her a wink that would hopefully reassure her. "You'll get used to it."

Sheridan snapped his fingers. "Future later. Back to shining. Chop-chop."

It must be driving his friend mad not to be the one working through this new puzzle, but Sher had always been rubbish at Old English. "Perhaps I need a break. A walk. A meal. A—"

"I will hurt you."

He chuckled and turned back to the text before Sheridan pretended to know karate too. He only had another page to work through and was rather eager to get back to it, truth be told.

Emily got to work, too, writing carefully where he'd just been scrawling. After a few minutes, she paused. "Isn't this just the story of Arthur's final battle with Mordred? But we know that already."

She sounded disappointed, which he had been, too, at first, when it seemed that this "undiscovered" tale was in fact a well-known one. Bram shook his head and tapped a bit lower on the page. "It starts as the familiar story. But look. Every one I've ever read has him dying at a lake and insisting that either Sir Bedivere or Sir Griflet return Excalibur to its waters."

She read through his transcription, her eyes lighting up when she got to the single word that had lit his excitement. "This one has it as Sir Tristan?"

"It does." Which would make as much sense as it being any other knight, if the rest of the story were the same—that as King Arthur lay dying, he knew that the magical sword must be returned to the Lady of the Lake, from whom it had come. That no matter how noble a knight followed him on the throne, the power of the sword could not be theirs, for no one was that noble. That worthy. That able to wield the power.

In most of the stories, whichever knight was given this final command hesitated in its fulfillment, only pretending to toss the blade into the nearby waters—thereby proving even the best knights unworthy, guilty of secret greed.

But after a second order from the king, Sir Bedivere or Griflet finally threw the blade as far out into the lake as he could, and a hand reached up. Caught it. Brandished it three times and then sank with it into the waters.

This one was different, though. Because it was Sir Tristan to whom he handed the blade as he lay dying, yes. But the king didn't then just motion toward whatever random lake was nearby—it had never made sense to Bram that Arthur would just expect the Lady to be there at Camlann, but there were so many variations on who the Lady even was. No, he handed it to Tristan and told him that his last quest must be to restore the sword to the Lady directly.

Which was the part of the story Bram was at now, and he let his brow furrow as he pieced together the archaic words. Tristan was doubting his ability to find the Lady and insisting that they must focus instead on getting the king himself to Avalon, where he could be healed of his wounds.

But Arthur kept insisting. The sword must be returned to the very hand of the Lady, and Tristan must not rest until he found her.

And if I cannot? Bram scratched Tristan's question onto the page and looked back at the manuscript to see the king's answer.

Then protect it until you do. Take it far from England's shores. She will find you over the waters.

Was that right? Over the waters? Bram tried a few other ways to arrange the words, tried to think of similar-looking ones that this could mean instead, but he kept coming back to that as the most likely phrase. *She will find you over the waters.*

Far from England's shores.

Bram sat back in his chair, not exactly surprised when Sheridan pulled out the one on his other side, his eyes wide. "Well? Finished?"

"Nearly." Enough that he could look his best friend in the eye and say, "It isn't Ron—it isn't a spear or a lance at all. It's Excalibur. The artifact is Excalibur."

Sheridan snatched the latest page of his scrawl from in front of him. "Explain. You're certain?"

"It has to be. He gave it to Tristan with express orders to return it directly to the hand of the Lady of the Lake, and if he couldn't find her, then to take it 'far from England's shores' and wait for her to find him 'over the waters.'"

"Over the waters." Sheridan hunched over the page. "Lyonesse. Could be, anyway. As logical as any legend, don't you think?"

"And far more logical than a spear having survived unbroken in this weather," Emily added. "My brother was wrong. He's been searching for the wrong thing all this time, which means looking, perhaps, in the wrong places."

"Praise the Lord for that." It set enough of a buzzing through Bram's system that he had to stand up to pace. "So, Tristan, obedient to his king, took the sword far from England—to his own kingdom, Lyonesse." Upon hearing his name, the pup lifted his head, wagged his tail twice, and then gave up and went back to sleep. Bram had to grin. "But the Lady never found him to ask it of him, so he never considered the quest complete."

Sheridan tapped a finger to his lips. "It *was*, at that. A symbol of nobility, I mean, from the later story."

"Exactly. A symbol that he would have considered it his duty to protect above all, and to honor—and to keep out of England, honestly. He would have passed it to his heir with that warning. That it was a symbol of nobility and honor, and that it wasn't to be held by an unworthy people."

Emily had stood, too, her eyes alight. "When the people of Lyonesse fell into sin and didn't repent, Trevelyan, aware of the legend, would have considered the tidal wave to be the Lady demanding its return."

Beth clapped her hands together. "So he hid it! Returning it to her." She turned to Sheridan. "Does that mean we're looking for a sea cave rather than a cairn's burial chamber? A place where there's water?"

"Maybe. Or not—I mean, who's to say? What was or wasn't underwater in that day?"

True. The waters could have receded or gone up more since then. How were they to know?

But it was Excalibur—that much Bram felt as certain about as one possibly could when one was dealing with legend. Or at the very least, he felt certain that Elizabeth Mucknell was certain. He glanced over at Emily.

Her always-fair cheeks had washed paler still, and she stared at them glassy eyed, lips parted. "Em?" His excitement turned to alarm. He hurried back to her side and eased her down into her chair again with a hand on her shoulder, sitting back in his along with her.

She blinked and drew in a ragged breath. Her eyes refocused, finally. But she looked no less distraught. "Don't you know what this means?"

He'd thought so, but her reaction certainly didn't align with his. He darted a glance at Sheridan. Sheridan gave him a shrug that seemed to say *women are baffling* and looked to Beth. Beth hissed out a breath and moved over to stand behind Emily's chair. "Your family?"

Drat. And blast. He was an idiot.

Emily nodded, her eyes awash with tears despite rapid blinking. "As mad as hunting for the spear has made Nigel, the stories about Ron are rather obscure. If he or my father gets wind of this—if there is really a sword buried somewhere on these islands that Lizza found, that *she* believed was Excalibur—if there is record of this story elsewhere, as clearly there is for her to have known it, and they have that as provenance—if they can convince others that it's true—"

"What greater fame could an Englishman seek than finding Excalibur?" Beth sighed and squeezed the shoulder Bram wasn't already bracing. "They would do anything to have that discovery to their name."

"Anything." Emily pressed a hand to her chest. "I thought I knew before how Lizza felt, but I had only a hint. This—*this*." She bit her lip, clearly struggling to keep her emotions contained, but it was a losing battle. A few tears broke free with her next blink. "It would destroy them. Because there would be no line they wouldn't cross. My brother has already proven himself at his breaking point—he would kill for this. Literally kill for it. I know he would."

Seeing those twin droplets roll down her cheeks did the strangest thing to Bram's heart. He'd always hated seeing his mother or sisters cry, and he'd been more than a little grateful that Libby, at least, wasn't prone to tears. But these were entirely different from the ones Edith tended toward, over catty insults from friends or a denial of a new hat she wanted. They weren't just the tears of grief and mourning that even he had shed when Father died two years ago.

These were a liquid glimpse of her soul, and were he a knight in some ancient tale of chivalry, he had a feeling he could have caught them, bottled them, and used them to heal mortal wounds or break enchantresses' spells or save a kingdom. These were tears of a selfless heart breaking over someone else's sin. These were the tears of a sister who would do anything to save her brother from destruction, even when he didn't deserve the sacrifice.

Especially when he didn't.

For a moment, Bram could scarcely breathe. He'd never paused to ask what sacrifice really was, why it really mattered, but now he saw the answer to the question he hadn't entertained. This was the sort of love that set worlds in motion. This was the sort of love that led God to give up His precious Son for a people who had turned away. This was the love that propelled that Son to a vile death so others might live.

Nigel would do anything to claim the discovery of Excalibur. Emily would do anything to save Nigel from himself. And Bram . . . Bram would do anything to protect Emily's beautiful heart.

He reached up and caught one of her tears, thumbed away its path with as gentle a touch as he could. And he imagined, as the droplet spread over his skin, that it was something like a baptism, helping to wash away the stains of selfishness in his own heart. As she tilted her face into his palm and closed her eyes, he prayed that God would forgive him for being focused for so long on his own thoughts, his own desires, his own strength. He begged the Lord, as Emily drew in a shaking breath, that He would help him be worthy of this young woman who demonstrated Him so clearly.

Beth reached for Sheridan's hand, and Sher dropped his other to Bram's shoulder, sealing the circle. "Two options, then," his friend murmured, voice low and reverent.

Beth nodded. "We either destroy all evidence of this and let Nigel and your father go on thinking it the spear they're looking for, which they'll never find . . ."

Emily sighed. "But he could find the sword accidentally while he's searching for Ron. We can't risk that. We have to find it first and then somehow decide what to do with it." Her brows drew together. "My instinct is to hide it again as Elizabeth did—but that isn't fair to the rest of you. You deserve to find the treasure."

For once, Sheridan didn't return with a joke or even crack a smile.

"In a perfect world, maybe. This isn't, though. And really—" He looked at Beth. "We have, haven't we? Found treasure enough, I mean. For a lifetime."

"For two of them." She smiled at him and then down at Emily. "We'll not be insisting on this charge into battle, Em. This one is your call. If you say bury it, we'll not only find it first, we'll then make certain he never can."

Emily drew in another long breath and looked at Bram. "What do you think? King Arthur is your passion—you must want this."

"King Arthur is a story from which I draw inspiration. And what's the point of it all if I'm not inspired to make the right decisions in the here and now?" Bram shook his head and let his thumb caress her cheek again. "You're more important than any legend, Emily. What could I possibly need with Excalibur or the Holy Grail or the very crown that rested on his brow when I have you?"

Beth's "Awww" was, thankfully, interrupted by the opening and slamming of the front door. Bram expected to hear Gibson's shout of greeting, or perhaps Enyon calling out a hello, but instead hurried steps sounded down the corridor, pausing only briefly at the drawing room door. A moment later, the rain-bedraggled figures of Vandermeer, Millicent, and Abbie burst into the room.

Bram could only stare. Never in his life had he seen Sheridan's two sisters both looking like this—men's mackintoshes thrown on over their fine day dresses, whose hems were muddy and dragging, their once-exquisite hats soggy and dripping with rain, their hair coming unpinned beneath them. Even Vandermeer looked strange, with a fisherman's hat and coat on over his fine worsted wool.

The American huffed like he'd run the whole way up the hill into town, and the Howes' chests were heaving too. "We have a problem," he wheezed.

Bram's stomach turned to a stone. He pushed to his feet, Emily rising with him. Beth and Sheridan both took a step away to give them room. Only once he was standing and the newcomers had come a few more steps inside did he even spot Lady Scofield behind the sisters, similarly soaked and as pale as Emily.

"What is it?" he asked, since he apparently regained his faculties before the others, who were still staring.

"It was my fault," Lady Scofield gasped out, as those from the drawing room came to join them in the library. "I thought I'd paid him enough to keep quiet, but . . ."

"The archivist reported to Lord Scofield on what he delivered to his wife." Vandermeer braced himself on the chair at the end of the long library table and dragged in a huge breath, shaking his head. "Blast, but I'm not as young as I used to be."

Bram's stone-for-a-stomach dropped a little lower. "So Lord Scofield knows we're looking for Excalibur."

He'd have put the pieces together as quickly as they just had. Because Sir Tristan meant Lyonesse, and Lyonesse meant the Scillies.

Emily's shoulders sagged. "And if Father knows, he'll realize it's what Nigel has been looking for, and they'll have compared notes. They could both be searching now."

Sheridan held up a hand. "How do we know? This, I mean? That he reported to Scofield?"

Vandermeer managed a half-smile at that one. "Well, I admitted already I'd been paying one clerk to report to me. You don't think I'd not have another up my sleeve, do you?"

Beth looked from Vandermeer to Emily. "But surely your brother wouldn't dare come back here—not now, with the law looking for him."

Abbie's lips had that thin, pressed look they always got when she found a particular truth distasteful. "We spoke to the constable just moments before we left St. Mary's. He'd received a wire from the magistrate in Cornwall, ordering him to allow the Scofields to proceed with their task on the islands unhindered."

"What?" The explosion came, it seemed, from half the room, Bram included.

Abbie jerked her head in a nod. "They presented some story

that painted him the victim of his sister's madness and her suitor's jealousy-inspired vindictiveness. Which was enough—"

"At least when combined with a handsome bribe," Millicent interjected.

"—to get him a free pass for a few days, anyway."

Millicent pulled her ruined hat from her head. "They're on their way back. That was the long and short of what Donald's sources sent."

It felt as though someone had sucked all the air out of the room. The Scofields were on their way back. And they knew that the search wasn't for a spear, but for Excalibur. They knew that Elizabeth Mucknell had found it once already and rehidden it. The only thing they didn't know was the local story about Trevelyan, but how could that even help them when it didn't give them any direction as to where he'd buried it?

Wait. Bram turned his gaze back on Vandermeer. "That list you gave us the other day, of the locations Eben listed in his deposition. Are you certain they don't have that?"

"One hundred percent." Then he frowned. "Ninety percent. Eighty? I'm *fairly* certain."

Sheridan sighed and rubbed at the bridge of his nose. "We clearly have no time to lose. We need to redouble our search."

When Emily wavered a bit, Bram slid an arm around her. Not that he expected her to faint or anything—she was made of sterner stuff than that—but he didn't mind the excuse. "I'm sorry," he murmured into the side of her head. "I wanted the choice to be yours."

Her shrug felt solid. Resigned. "The choice was always the Lord's. Lizza Mucknell managed to keep her husband from finding it, but it didn't spare his life. And as for Nigel . . . we can only extend the hand of mercy. We cannot make him take it." She angled her head to meet his gaze. "But we'll do what we can."

Millicent cleared her throat. "There is one other—"

"Very minor." A nervous-sounding Abbie.

"—complication." Millicent sent an apologetic look to Sheridan. "George is on his way too."

Sheridan muttered a few syllables that must have been in Druidean or something, because Bram couldn't make it out. He understood the sentiment, though, and echoed it.

Lady Scofield looked confused. "George?" she asked.

Abbie offered a tight smile. "*Prince* George. We invited him a month ago."

"To see Theo's finds."

"Because they're his—the prince's. He's the Duke of Cornwall. He owns all salvage rights in the islands."

"But he hadn't been able to get away until now." Millicent wilted a bit. "Impeccable timing, isn't it?"

Sheridan scrubbed a hand over his face. "So then. Had better collect the treasure all up again. While we're hunting for Excalibur."

Blast. It was going to be far too eventful a week.

23

WEDNESDAY, 19 SEPTEMBER

Perhaps on the surface, they looked like an ordinary couple out for a stroll on an abandoned island, Emily mused as she walked slowly over Samson's heathered knoll. She with her hand in the crook of Bram's arm, Tristan running circles around them, tail wagging madly and yipping at every new find. The sun shining down on them and bringing with it a reminder of the summer just past, though the wind was still cool as it danced over the hill. Just an ordinary couple. An ordinary day.

If one ignored the basket on her wrist with its packet of pirate treasure under the food yet again, and the list in Bram's pocket of places they'd been assigned to search today.

She couldn't keep her eyes from tracking, yet again, toward the bumps in the distance that were St. Agnes and Gugh. Were her father and Nigel back yet? Had they arrived under cover of darkness last night? All day yesterday she'd waited for the knock on the door, the whisper that they were spotted. She'd expected it while the rain pattered itself out in the morning, and she'd expected to see it with her own eyes in the afternoon, when they'd gone out with the return of the sun.

She'd certainly expected it when she and Bram sat with her

mother and his in the hotel dining room. Every person who entered through the doors she thought was Father or Nigel. Her throat had ached so badly at the memory of Nigel's hand closed around it that she'd barely been able to eat a bite.

She hated this. Hated the fear, hated not knowing where they were or when they would descend upon the islands again, hated the thought of Mother alone in the flat above Mrs. Gilligan's shop, with no one but her maid and a few paid guards who could probably either be bribed or dispatched far too easily.

"Worrying again, sweetheart?"

Emily sighed and shifted the basket a little higher on her wrist. "Sorry. There's just so much to worry over."

"Mm." He brought them to a halt when Tristan stopped at what must be a particularly interesting flower, and Bram grinned down at her. "I can distract you, if you like." He leaned closer, head tilted down, that glint in his eyes that made her heart race. "Purely out of the goodness of my heart, of course. In the interest of your peace of mind."

Kissing him didn't exactly result in *peace*—that was entirely the wrong word, given the way electricity seemed to sizzle and zap all over her skin at his touch, and her mind filled with a million bright lights at the first brush of his lips over hers. But as distractions went, this had quickly become her favorite. Smiling, she angled her face toward his. "I can hardly deny you a chance to be so noble."

And she could still hardly believe that this had somehow become real—that he really looked at her as he'd been doing, that he'd been letting Sheridan and Beth joke about the future. That when their mothers hinted at dinner yesterday about a spring wedding, he'd neither bolted for the door nor immediately changed the subject. He'd merely chuckled and told his mother she should probably focus on Libby's wedding before she began planning the next one.

The next one. Had he meant that? The question had swirled through her head last night as she was trying to fall asleep. Not helped any by Beth's giggles and far-too-pointed questions of *"Do you love him? Is he the one, Em?"*

It seemed odd to put such words to this. They seemed almost too . . . ordinary. All she knew was that when his arms came around her as they did now, when his lips caressed hers, she felt like a princess who had somehow caught the attention of the most valiant knight in the land. It didn't feel quite real—and yet at the same time, it felt like all her life had been leading her here, to him, to this exact moment in time when their hearts could meet.

Had they been introduced in London, would they even have spared each other a moment's thought? She couldn't be certain. But now she couldn't imagine traveling this path forward with anyone else at her side.

He pulled away, his hand cupping her cheek, and made a show of examining her face. Then shook his head. "No. You're still thinking far too much."

He leaned down again as she laughed, though he paused when Tristan gave his "I see a friend!" bark, effectively drawing their attention back to the little path they'd been following down to the shoreline.

Tommie and Enyon were hiking toward them, both of them smiling. They'd been armed with a basket and a map, too, and had retrieved a parcel of their own after dropping Emily and Bram here on Samson.

"Ready?" Enyon called up the hill.

Bram winked at her. "We will continue this distraction later." Then louder said, "Coming!"

Tommie had a lovely flush to her cheeks, and Emily suspected it was more thanks to Enyon than the warm sunshine. It was so good to see her friend happy, vibrant, smiling. So good to see her eyes without the shadows in them that Emily hadn't even realized were there until they were gone.

According to Beth, all the locals had Enyon and Tommie's wedding more or less planned, and the mams and mamm-wynns were "secretly" plotting quilts to sew and recipes to copy and other household essentials to bestow upon them. Tommie had gone stiff, though, when said gossip had reached them.

She'd come around. Emily would make certain of it—if anyone deserved a bright future, it was her. But, selfishly, she'd miss her. They'd only just become friends, and now, just as she'd feared, she'd lose her. Well, not *lose* her exactly, because she'd be able to visit her whenever she—they?—returned to the islands. But she wouldn't be there every day. Bittersweet, that.

And not something she'd breathe a word of aloud.

A few minutes later, they were on Enyon's little sloop, and soon enough they were back in the quay on Tresco. Then strolling up the street as if the baskets they carried didn't contain priceless treasure they'd soon be delivering to the prince.

Gracious. She still couldn't quite wrap her mind around that one.

There were voices coming from the back garden, which pulled their feet in that direction. Emily wasn't surprised to see Ladies Abbie and Millicent there, nor Vandermeer. But she was a bit surprised to see Mother had come over again.

And none of them looked happy.

Mother surged forward, hands outstretched, the moment they rounded the corner. Emily handed the basket to Bram and released his arm so she could take her mother's gloved hands in her own. "What is it?"

Mother held her gaze steadily. "They just returned with Mr. Vandermeer's yacht. They hastened directly to Gugh, presumably for their equipment. I don't think they're even aware yet that I'm here, but we hurried over straightaway to tell you."

"At least I have the *Victoria* back." Vandermeer looked angrier than she'd ever seen him. "Your brother had the gall to claim that I'd given him permission to use it 'whenever he pleased.' And that buffoon of a magistrate on the mainland tried to tell me that if I hadn't ever once used those words, then clearly the poor boy just misunderstood."

Millicent patted his arm in a comforting gesture. Which was strange, wasn't it? And Vandermeer took her hand in his in the next moment.

Knowing her confusion was on her face, Emily looked to Abbie, who was drifting their way. Abbie sighed—though her eyes were sparkling. "I do believe there's something in the air here. Perhaps all Theo's mutterings about love potions have more truth to them than I'd thought."

Millicent and Vandermeer. Well, she couldn't honestly think of a better match for the American—and she shuddered to consider the force they would pose in the world of antiquities if they combined their efforts instead of constantly butting heads. They'd probably be behind every single discovery of the next half century.

And she was likely fixating on those entertaining thoughts solely to avoid the actual purpose of their coming. She squeezed her mother's hands. "Are you certain you don't wish to stay here? You heard Mamm-wynn say her son Mark and his wife would be glad to have you stay with them."

"Quite certain, dearest." She lifted her chin and looked like the countess she was. "I am not afraid of your father's bluster, nor of your brother's temper."

Emily couldn't be quite so confident on either score, but they had plenty more to worry about. Like how to collect the rest of the Mucknell treasure without their noticing, now that they were back.

Not to mention finding an Arthurian needle in a Scillonian haystack.

Tommie edged backward, pulling Enyon along with her until they were out of sight of the ladies and gents. Then she turned to him and whispered, "We need to warn Ailla. Now."

Enyon nodded and kept pace with her as she took off. "And pray it isn't too late already. She may well know, I mean. Not that I think Nigel went straight after her or anything."

No, he couldn't have. Even he wasn't so brazen that he would attack a girl in broad daylight with her family and neighbors right there. At least, she prayed it was so.

"She won't know yet. She was spending the day on St. Thomas with her cousin, helping with her new baby."

Enyon slanted a smiling look down at her. "Know all the goings-on around here now, do you?" Then his smile went sober. "Then you'll have been hearing all the other gossip, too, about us—and that could well feel like a burden to you. Oh, Thomasina, I'm so sorry. I've tried to tell everyone to focus on Ollie and our lady and Mabena and Casek, but it's like they've all got wedding fever."

She took a long moment to just look at him. To see the distress in his eyes at the thought of *her* being distressed. To feel the warm press of his fingers around hers but to know that if she tugged her hand free, he'd let it go. To realize that he wanted only to protect her, to cherish her.

The islanders' assumptions *had* been a burden, it was true. Funny how simply by hearing him acknowledge that, the weight was lifted. She even tried on a grin. "Well, I can't blame them for wanting all their favorite lads to be happy."

"Wouldn't call myself a favorite." His mumble accompanied a flush, though. And then he pulled her to a halt under the trellis that marked where the Tremaynes' front garden let out onto the street. "But I admit to the happy part. Being with you, getting to know you this last month . . . it's the happiest I've ever been. You bring a light to my life, Thomasina."

Her throat went tight. "And you to mine, Enyon. More than you can know."

He darted a glance up but then looked down again. "I don't mean to rush you into any decisions. And I want you to know that I'll wait as long as you need—you're worth it. But it seems Lady Emily could soon be leaving the islands, and if . . . well, you said you intended to go home after. Which I don't begrudge you. But I want you to have a reason to come back. Or perhaps I want a reason to come and meet your mam and sisters. Regardless, the thought of not being together has made me think I ought to speak—but then I second-guess myself. What if you say no?"

Her throat eased, and a laugh tangled up in it. Was he going to ask her what she thought he was? A week ago, it may have panicked her. But today it felt right. Perfect. "I know one certain way to find out."

There, a bit of smile on his handsome face. "Thomasina, would you—no, wait." He dropped to one knee like some sort of fairy-tale hero, there under the still-blooming trellis. "Mam said the knee was a must."

She laughed again and blinked back tears too. "Just ask, you silly man."

He kissed her fingers first, each of them in turn, melting her heart more with each touch. Then he pulled out a simple silver ring with a small blue stone and held it up. "Will you marry me, dearover? Will you let me spend the rest of our days showing you how much I love you?"

"Yes!" The word burst forth on another laugh, and she had to bite back a thousand more yeses as he slid the ring onto her finger, then wait for him to stand again so she could wrap her arms around him. "And I'll spend them showing you the same."

No bashful looks now. No, now he was all grins as he framed her face in his hands. They shared a kiss to seal it, then started walking again, a bounce in both their steps. Frankly, Tommie was amazed she didn't float away, she felt so light and happy. "You know, *cariad*, you're going to have to teach me to sail. If I'm to be a Scillonian."

"Carry-what?"

She laughed again. "*Cariad*. You give me Cornish, and I'll parry with Welsh. It means *darling* or *my love*."

"Ah. I like it." He nodded, though then he frowned at the sea. "And of course I'll teach you—but it'd be best to wait for spring. Our weather may stay milder than most, but the surest sign of autumn is the currents getting nasty in those channels. If you have any spills

316

and tips, I'd as soon it be when you'll not get swept out to sea before I can dive in after you."

"Oh." She too looked out toward the water, as beautiful in its blues and greens as ever. But she could only see the surface. The shallows. She certainly couldn't argue about dangers that hid in the depths. "Spring or summer will be perfect. You'll just have to ferry me around in the meantime."

"Shame, that."

Indeed. They shared another smile and picked up their pace again. With a bit of luck, she'd be able to convince Ailla to spend a week or so with her cousin and the new little one on St. Thomas, or with her brother, Luke. Anywhere, Tommie prayed, that was well out of the way of Nigel Scofield.

24

This was why Bram had never been drawn into the world of archaeology like Sheridan. It wasn't just boring—it was frustrating. He reached as far as he could into the crevice, felt up and down and left and right, but there was nothing there. Just as there hadn't been anything there in Piper's Hole on St. Mary's. Or the one on Tresco. Or at any of the cairns that Sheridan had dragged him to. Or in any other crack or crevice in the islands or the whole of England or perhaps the entire blasted world.

At this point, he was ready to proclaim that every single thing to be found had been uncovered already, wash his hands, and stomp all the way home to Telford Hall, where he could turn a knob and chase away the darkness and forget for just two blasted minutes about the mists of the past.

A growl slipped out as he pried his arm out of this particular empty hole.

Sheridan, lantern held aloft, lifted his brows. "Well, you can't blame me. Not for this one. I mean—*you're* the Arthurian expert."

"The joy of studying King Arthur is that I've only ever had to do so from the comforts of my modern, electrified study." He pushed back to his feet, letting out an exasperated breath when he saw that he'd torn yet another seam on yet another shirt.

"Now. Not *ever*. That is—you only had the electricity installed two years ago." Sheridan held out a hand.

Bram slapped his into it and let his friend haul him up, wincing when a particularly ambitious wave crashed into the opening and soaked his foot before he could raise it back to the ledge. And perhaps growling a bit more too.

Sheridan chuckled. "I do hope Emily likes bears."

Bram made for the opening. "*You* get to feel around in the next empty crevice with the icy water."

"Promise?"

He couldn't hold back the laugh. "It isn't my fault my arms are longer."

"I'm spry. Flexible. And nicer. I'll lure it out with my charm and wit."

Bram winced as he stepped out into the sunlight—it had seemed weak and watery before they ducked into this tiny little carving-out in the rocks that was too slender to really be called a cave, but the light assaulted his eyes. He blinked against it and then thought to look down at the place on his hand still stinging from that latest blind exploration.

A few dots of blood bloomed to life on the scrape. He pulled his handkerchief from his pocket and dabbed at it.

Sheridan blew out the lantern and glanced at his hand. "Mortally wounded? I can call for Merlin."

His friend was having far too much fun with all this. "Hasten me to Avalon. Though I daresay it'll have to be amputated." There. The blood was barely even seeping out now, so he tucked the white linen back into his pocket. And pulled out two foil-wrapped toffees while he was in there. He held one out to Sher. "Hungry?"

Sheridan sighed. "Yes. And toffee is not really food." But he took it and unwrapped it and slipped it into his mouth all the same. "Why don't you have any lemon drops in there today? Or—better still, a nice sandwich."

That did sound better than sweets just now. "I had a dozen sandwiches. Ate them all when your back was turned."

"Vile fiend." With a sigh of his own, Sheridan eyed the rocks they'd climbed down to reach this opening. "We're sure this was the right spot?" His voice was strained.

It was no mystery why. They were running out of places on their lists, and neither burial chambers nor sea caves had revealed any swords, legendary or otherwise.

Telford put a hand on the cool granite, feeling for the mark his eyes had barely been able to discern after two-and-a-half centuries of tides and waves and weather. Was it really Mucknell's *M* with a circle around it, the same mark that had been on the original map Beth had found? Or had he merely wished it to be so? "I don't know. I think so."

He dropped his hand so Sheridan could feel for it one more time too. He traced the circle just where Bram had imagined it to be, and the *M* within it. "Blast. I really think it is."

"I know. I hate it when I'm right."

"Back up, then?"

"Unfortunately." Bram liked scaling cliffs about as much as reaching into black crevices. But the silver lining to this being the last place on their list was that now they got to go back to the Tremayne house and see what Mrs. Dawe had prepared for luncheon. They'd had a delectable roast beef last night that would make fine sandwiches. Or perhaps she'd done that magical thing with the chicken again. And made some sort of apple-something for dessert.

His stomach was growling by the time they safely reached the hilltop again, and they still had to row back to the larger island to rendezvous with the girls and sail to Tresco. He turned for where they'd tethered their boat and nearly took what would have been a disastrous step backward in his surprise.

Nigel Scofield stood there, up to his ankles in water, just lounging between their small rowboat and a larger craft that must be his—or which he'd stolen, anyway.

But the shock only lasted a second. Then, fingers curled into his palm, Bram darted forward, over the bare rocks.

Nigel was in that second boat before Bram was halfway to him, laughing as he pulled a small engine to life and roared away.

An engine—he certainly didn't steal that from anyone in the Scillies. And blast, but it meant the blighter could get around far too quickly. But at least not silently.

Sheridan came to a halt beside him at their boat, watching Scofield splash through the waves. He was heading away from the Eastern Isles, at least—not toward where the girls were. And why had they let them insist it was perfectly safe to separate for an hour? What if he *had* aimed for his sister and tried to toss her from the rocks or something?

"Beth would have shot him. Wouldn't have hesitated."

Bram let out his pent-up breath. "Excellent point." Even so, Sheridan looked just as shaken as Bram felt. And even so, he wouldn't feel better until he could be certain the girls were unharmed. He scrambled into the boat—checking first to make sure there weren't any Nigel-wrought leaks—and picked up his oars.

Sheridan followed suit, and an eternal ten minutes later their boat was bumping up against the hull of the *Naiad*, and the two most welcome faces in the world were greeting them.

"Praise God!" Emily offered a hand to help him into the sloop. "We saw Nigel. He circled us in some motorized monstrosity he must have acquired on the mainland and then took off toward where you were. He must have seen we were empty-handed."

"Same with us." Bram cleared the rail and folded Emily into a fierce embrace. "Gave me a scare, to think of you two here without us."

She held him just as tightly, he noted. "I had a few unpleasant moments myself. Did he say anything to you?"

"Nothing."

"Nor to us." Emily drew away enough to look him over, then glanced toward Sheridan too. "No swords, I see."

Bram shook his head. "And unless the others had better luck, we've run out of locations. I don't know where we'll search next."

"We'll start over." When Bram turned to glare at him, Sheridan just grinned. "What? You know it's true. Off by an inch—"

"Off by a mile," Beth finished for him. She was already unfurling the sail and motioning them to take their seats. "You're right, dearovim, we could have simply looked right over it at any one of those sites. And really, our luck of earlier in the summer couldn't continue. It's nothing short of miraculous that we found the silver within minutes of digging, and the chest within twelve hours."

Bram knew that. He'd seen Sheridan spend weeks at a site, months even, without finding more than a few shards of pottery. Hence his opinion on archaeology. But that didn't help them now, did it?

"That doesn't mean God won't grant us another miracle." That beautiful smile curved Emily's mouth and banished a good bit of his bad mood. The smile went teasing when she looked up at him. "After all, Bram has been rising by eight each day and speaking before nine. What more proof do we need that miracles are still happening?"

He laughed along with the others and tugged her playfully to his side, ready to punish with a well-aimed tickle.

"Do be careful!" Beth's voice, more urgent than he'd expected, snapped him back to seriousness. She offered an apologetic smile and motioned toward the water splashing the hull. "Not a good time of year to take a swim right here. I don't want anyone falling overboard."

Duly chastised, he slid a protective arm around Emily instead.

The others spoke as they sailed for Tresco, but they were only rehashing what he already knew—and musing about Vandermeer and Millicent—so he was content to ignore them and watch the water go by, the birds swoop overhead, and the way the weak autumn sunlight brushed liquid gold over Emily's face and hair.

She'd bloomed over these last few weeks, smiling and laughing and talking, even when Beth wasn't with her. She'd suffered, and she'd grown stronger. She'd gone without, and she'd made sacrifices.

And now, according to Mother, who had been spending most of her time with Lady Scofield on St. Mary's when she wasn't with him and Libby, the inheritance that had been held in trust for her, which she hadn't even realized was hers, was in her name. She was an independent woman, not reliant anymore on her father's humors.

Certainly not reliant on the bread and cheese Bram snuck from Mrs. Dawe's kitchen and paired with a few coins from his pockets.

She had a fortune of her own. Enough that Mother's eyes had fairly glowed when she pronounced it "the most handsome dowry, Bram. You couldn't do better."

He agreed with her there, but the dowry and inheritance had nothing to do with it. What they *did*, though, was give Emily an option that she certainly deserved to have. He'd joked about her still having time to run away, but it was true, wasn't it? However all this ended, whenever all this ended, she could just walk away if she wanted to do so. She could stretch her wings and consider, for the first time in her life, what *she* wanted to do.

What if what she wanted didn't include him? What if, when life resumed its normal pace and this mad summer of adventure and pirates and princes and legends was behind them, she found she *didn't* like his morning gruffness and night-owl tendencies and overprotective way of loving those who mattered most? What if she wanted her own quiet manor house instead of bringing laughter and light to his?

The thought sent an ache pulsing through him with every beat of his heart.

"Bram?" Her voice beckoned him out of those thoughts. She was standing, the quay at Tresco bobbing around her. Sher and Beth were already off the sloop. "Are you coming?"

Bram nodded but couldn't convince his legs to lever him up.

323

Emily slid back to her seat at his side and took his hand in hers. "What is it? What are you thinking?"

"That I love you." It wasn't how he'd planned to say it. No, actually, he hadn't planned how to say it at all. But if he'd had the sense to think it through, the first time he uttered those words probably would have involved flowers or moonlight or music or *something* other than the smell of fish and salt and the laughter of local sailors in the background.

But terrible setting aside, the words were true.

Emily looked as shocked by the admission as he'd been, lips parted but no words coming out.

Just the effect he wanted to have on a girl. He winced and ran his free hand through his wind-gnarled hair. "Sorry. That wasn't exactly a romantic way to say—"

"The way was—that's not . . ." Emily sighed and squeezed his hand. "You looked so unhappy. So serious. I expected you were thinking about Nigel or the futility of the hunt or . . ."

Then out he'd come with *that*, as if loving her upset him. Blast, could he bungle this any more? Probably. But in for a penny, in for a pound. "Not unhappy, not about you. Only . . . afraid, I suppose. That when we leave the islands, you'll realize you don't need me anymore. You'll—"

"Bram." *Beatific*, that was the word for the smile that touched her lips now, looking both tentative and strong, hesitant and bold. She reached up and touched a fingertip to his lips. "My darling. I don't love you because I need you—I need you because I love you."

On second thought, this was the perfect backdrop. Life was behind them. Life was before them. He kissed her fingertip, then kissed it again. "You do?"

She nodded and moved those fingers to trace his jaw. "I love you because you believe I'm strong. I love you because you call me worthy."

He turned his hand over on the seat so his fingers could tangle with hers. "You *are* strong. You are worthy. And I love you because your every virtue inspires me to be better. To try to deserve you."

She caught his free hand and wrapped hers around it, anchoring him. "I love you because you are noble, because you are a protector. Because you care fiercely and without reserve. And if I can truly count myself among the number of those you love, then I am blessed indeed."

They sat there for a long moment, the gulls crying overhead, the fishermen laughing on the sand, the *Naiad* rocking gently in her moorings. Then Bram smiled. "I *will* say it sometime with moonlight and flowers and music."

"And chocolate. I absolutely demand chocolate."

"I daresay that can be arranged." He inclined his head. "Shall we?"

"We'd better, before they come back for us."

Despite knowing Nigel was out there, ready to pounce the moment they found something—if ever they found something—he felt lighter as they strode up the hill, through the village, and toward the Tremayne home. At least until Emily came to an abrupt halt upon reaching the gate—or perhaps upon seeing Tommie Briggs standing there, deep in conversation with a dark-haired girl. He wasn't sure what made Emily suddenly hesitate, but he paused right along with her.

And silently thanked God that she seemed favorable toward letting him do just that for the rest of their lives.

Emily's breath came out in a whoosh when she saw Ailla Marrack standing there with Tommie, laughing and talking as if she were just an ordinary girl gossiping with a neighbor, her cheeks a healthy rose, her long black braid dancing as she gestured animatedly as she spoke.

Emily would probably ruin all that if she made her presence known, just as she'd done merely by walking along Old Lane nearly two weeks ago.

No, Ailla deserved better than a reminder of Nigel. Tommie had told her that the two of them had developed a rapport, that she and Enyon were doing all they could to keep her safe, that Oliver had been talking to her and her mother. She was glad of that, all of that. And if the only way she could help was to stay far removed from the young woman, then that was exactly what she'd do. Knowing Bram wouldn't question her yet, she pivoted away.

"Lady Emily! Where are you going? Come and meet Ailla properly." Tommie's voice sounded pleasant. Pleased, even. And she certainly wouldn't call out like that if the girl hadn't wanted her to . . . right?

Emily turned back around, clinging to Bram's hand. He'd know, once he heard Tommie say her companion's name, what was going on. He'd heard the name of the girl Nigel had attacked, and though no details had been shared, his imagination was as sound as her own. He squeezed her fingers back.

Stepping through the garden gate and passing under the trellis, Emily willed a smile onto her face as she approached. Once standing before the girl who had first greeted her with such horror, she held out a hand. "How do you do, Ailla?"

Ailla took her hand and pressed it between both of hers. "Better than I thought I'd be. And sorry, my lady, for assuming what I did of you." Her gaze fluttered down to Emily's throat. The bruises had faded, but they were still green at the edges and visible if one knew to look for them. "I heard what he did to you."

All the Scillies had by now, she imagined. "There was no lasting damage."

"I also heard . . ." Ailla released her hand and sent a look over her shoulder. To Tommie? Or beyond her? Then she leaned close and dropped her voice to a whisper. "No one's said much—it's clear you're all trying to be secretive. And no one wants *him* to hear a stray word from their lips. But is it true that you're checking all the places with Mucknell's mark? For whatever it is *he's* after now?"

Well, the gossip mill certainly was alive and well on the islands. But she had to admire their apparent restraint with it in this situation too. After a glance to Bram—he shrugged in a way that seemed to say, *Your call, sweetheart*—she nodded. "We have been, yes. We've a master list we've been working our way through."

When Ailla grinned like that, she looked more like a child than a woman. "And you're not afraid of Mucknell's curse, I take it."

At that, Emily lifted her brows. "Mucknell's curse?"

The girl laughed. "Not real, I know that now—but Old Man Gibson had us all convinced of it when we were children. Whenever we saw the circled *M* anywhere, we ran the other way screaming, certain his ghost was going to jump out and devour us whole."

That she could well conceive. Emily chuckled too. "I imagine he had some interesting tales about it."

"They gave me nightmares for weeks every time I heard one, but that never stopped me coming back for more." Ailla twirled the end of her braid around her wrist. "You checked the one on St. Agnes, then?"

"On St. Agnes?" Emily blinked and turned to Bram. She didn't recall one on St. Agnes, but perhaps it had ended up on someone else's list.

Bram was shaking his head too. "There was nothing listed there. Only the one on Gugh."

Ailla's high spirits seemed to bank a bit at that. "St. Agnes wasn't on there? But I'm certain it was his mark. Luke and I found it . . . gracious, eight years ago, I suppose. And the wind was wailing through the rocks, so at the time we were convinced it was Mucknell's spirit and we came running back home as fast as we could. I haven't been back since, but the mark was there. Deep but worn."

Emily gave what she hoped was a bolstering smile. "We don't doubt you, Ailla. It's just that one wasn't on the list."

"The list was of places Eben watched his master hide things," Bram explained to Ailla before pausing. "But not every place he considered." Bram squeezed Emily's fingers. "Maybe Mucknell never used that one—maybe that's why his wife did."

For a moment, the world seemed to pause. Then it pounded with extra vibrance. "Do you remember where it was, Ailla? Could you show us?"

Now Ailla beamed to rival the sun. "I could help? Truly? Yes, of course! I can take you right now, or any time you like."

Emily wanted to leap directly back onto the *Naiad* and fly over the waters to St. Agnes then and there.

But somewhere in those waters, her brother was circling like a shark, watching their every move. This was no time to proceed without a plan.

25

Who in the world ever would have thought that the Prince of Wales would make a perfect diversion?

Bram couldn't resist a grin as their plan was solidified, hinging on the news that Abbie, Millicent, and Vandermeer had just brought with them from St. Mary's—His Royal Highness and his wife would be arriving in Porthcressa Bay on a private sailing yacht at around three o'clock that afternoon, and they would like nothing more than to begin their three-day stay in the islands with a tour of the excavations on Gugh. It seemed that Dorrien-Smith, the Lord Proprietor, was in the royal company as well, and the entire party would be staying at Tresco Abbey.

Which accounted for the bustle outside the Tremayne home that rivaled the one within.

But it was perfect, really. Absolutely perfect. Sheridan's sisters and Vandermeer would, in typical fashion, absolutely take over and insist on being the ones to give the prince the tour on Gugh, despite the fact that it wasn't their dig. Their eyes positively gleamed in maniacal joy at the thought.

Because the Scofields—both young and old—would have to be on hand to defend their part in the discovery. There was no way that the fame-hungry Nigel wouldn't make certain he was there to expound on finding the cairn that he had only scorned, and there was certainly no way either he or his father would let Abbie and Millicent fill the prince's ears with *their* version of events.

"And you're certain you don't mind collecting the remaining two packets?" Oliver directed his question to his sister and Sheridan.

They'd had a bit of a challenge finding a good time to retrieve the last two parcels of treasure. Each time they'd attempted it, people had been swarming about.

Sher grinned. "Try and stop us. Or don't—that would be counter-productive."

Oliver smiled, too, and cast a glance at Libby, then swept it out to encompass Mabena, Casek, Ainsley, Senara, and Collins. "And we'll transport everything to the Abbey and set up our presentation for the prince." They all nodded along.

Oliver's deep gaze settled on Bram and Emily. "And you're certain you don't mind going alone with Ailla?"

"Hey." From the corner of the library, Enyon sent his best friend a good-natured glare. "Hardly *alone*."

Oliver grinned. "Well, the four of you will be alone with her. I'd frankly rather all of us be there to offer defense if this is really the spot, but that may garner undue attention."

"We'll be fine, Ollie. I'll have my hunting piece." Enyon couldn't possibly be as confident as he sounded, could he?

Bram wasn't. Nigel wasn't exactly known for his predictability. And in all likelihood, this *M*-marked crevasse on St. Agnes would be just another empty hole that Bram got to feel around in. He'd tear another shirt, earn a few more scratches, and they'd scurry back to Tresco empty-handed to present the prince with the treasure they *had* found.

Oliver was nodding, though. "I suppose that settles it, then. Everyone fetch what you need and we'll send ourselves off with a prayer. We haven't much time."

"Wait." Bram pushed away from the wall he'd been leaning against.

Oliver paused. "Have I forgotten something?"

"Well, I don't know. But we ought to ask, oughtn't we?" He turned to Mamm-wynn, who had been knitting in an armchair by the fire. She'd come in quietly with the rest of them and hadn't made a single peep throughout the planning. "Mamm-wynn, in many ways it was your insights that started us all on this path, and certainly that have guided us and kept us alive. If you've any new ones . . . ?"

She smiled at him in the exact way Father had done when Bram had finally mastered a hard-won skill. "I think you all have it well in hand. My only advice . . ." She tilted her head, as if listening to words the rest of them couldn't hear, and then looked Bram straight in the eye. "Choose mercy. Always choose mercy."

Less spectacular than her plan to appear in Piper's Hole and startle Lorne away from killing any of them, but if *mercy* was the word they needed, then he'd take it. She'd proven herself as apt a guide through their adventures as any Merlin or Lady of the Lake could ever have been.

Bram gave her a short bow. Oliver said a short prayer. And then they were off, their group splintering into the factions that would, he knew, be permanent. Oliver and Libby. Sheridan and Beth. Enyon and Tommie. Casek and Mabena. Even Ainsley and Senara had their arms linked as they prepared to help with the transport to the Abbey, Collins alongside them, flashing Bram a warning glance over his shoulder that shouted, *Be careful—I don't fancy finding a new position.*

Bram and Emily. He took her hand as the others filed out of the library, pausing for a moment when Tristan barked and tumbled around their feet, tail wagging. Bram sighed and stooped down. "Sorry, boy. I know you feel this is your adventure, too, given your namesake, but you're not quite big enough yet. And you've already done your part by biting the villain's ankle. Stay and guard Mamm-wynn today, all right?"

The puppy whimpered even as he plunked to a seat at the word *stay*. In her corner, Mamm-wynn chuckled. "We shall keep each other excellent company. Shan't we, Tristan? Come here. Come, now."

With one last soulful look at Bram, Tristan wagged his way over to the matriarch and contented himself with the bone Mrs. Dawe had given him.

Bram and Emily exchanged a smile and followed after Enyon, Tommie, and Ailla Marrack, who'd stood half behind Tommie through the entire planning session, her eyes wide.

The streets through the village were busier than usual, everyone having heard by now that they'd be in royal company by that evening. And though, yes, the Scillies were technically the property of the Prince of Wales, this particular title-bearer had yet to pay a visit to the islands. All about, rugs were being beaten, doorsteps tidied, flower boxes weeded, and laundry rushed in off the line. Tresco was turning itself out in style, it seemed. No one paid them much heed as they hurried back down to the quay.

Enyon soon had them under sail and gliding toward St. Agnes. Ailla was the only one who really spoke, chattering on about how she hoped to catch a glimpse of the prince and princess, how sweet her cousin's new baby boy had been, and recalling the adventure from all those years ago that had led her brother to put his hand just so on the rock that had borne the circled *M*.

Bram didn't mind the chatter—not until Enyon was dropping his anchor in the little harbor between St. Agnes and Gugh, alongside the *Victoria* and an even larger yacht that he'd never seen but had to assume had brought Prince George here.

Electricity seemed to gather in the air like a fist. Bram's eyes scanned the horizon. Usually when clouds moved in it was from the southwest, but that skyline was still clear and blue. To the northeast, however, black thunderheads were rolling over one another like an angry sea.

The hairs on the back of his neck stood on end. He glanced over at Enyon, who was staring at the sky with consternation etched on his face. "Did Jeremiah Moon's big toe predict a storm today, by chance?"

Enyon shook his head. Pressed his lips together.

Lightning forked down a few miles out at sea, and he imagined he could hear the sizzle as it struck water. "Has he ever missed one before?"

Enyon's lips pressed even tighter before he parted them. "Once, in my memory." He met Bram's gaze. "The one that killed Ollie and Beth's parents."

Bram bit back the words that wanted to spill from his lips and leaped into the surf, reaching up to swing Emily down. "We have to hurry."

Thunder punctuated his claim. And the next flash of lightning marked the last sight in the world he wanted to see—Nigel, appearing on the brow of the hill. Spotting them. Running toward the tombolo.

They hadn't much time.

The others scrambled off the sloop, too, Ailla's cheer now settled into hard determination as she waved for them to follow her and dashed up the beach, promising that she could get them to the spot well before Nigel could make his way to St. Agnes. Bram prayed so, but Nigel wasn't their only concern. He glanced over his shoulder at the storm clouds.

Sheridan and Beth were out there. On the water, darting about the islands after those last two blasted parcels of treasure. *Father God, protect them. Keep them safe.* He very nearly added, *Why didn't you warn us? Whisper in Mamm-wynn's ear or make Jeremiah Moon's toe throb?* But he stopped himself. The Lord always sent storms. Sometimes they stole life, sometimes they gave it. But always He was there, walking over the waters, waiting for His followers to shout for Him. Hadn't Oliver preached on that very thing in the sermon he'd nearly forgotten to write two weeks ago?

I'm shouting for you, Lord. Save us. Help us. Deliver us.

The sky darkened in what felt like half a minute, autumn sunshine swallowed up in sudden twilight. Ailla led them along the shore but out of the sand, into grass and green life. He heard cattle lowing somewhere nearby, alarm in their calls.

The last time he'd been to St. Agnes and Gugh, he'd admired the way slabs of granite cropped out of the land, slanted as though some giant hand had stabbed them into the earth and left them there to shatter. This time that imagery sent a shudder through him, given the lightning snaking down at the same angle as the fractured rocks. Water splashed up around the ones farther from shore, foaming over them until they vanished, treacherous weapons hidden in the waves.

His gaze scoured the landscape, wondering where their guide was leading them. A stone hedgerow cut across the land before them, separating them from the baleful calling of the cows. A wooden stile led up and over, but rather than climb those steps, Ailla darted to the left. The rock wall ended there in a tangle of vines and granite— granite that stretched up and then crowded all the way down to the sea in hunching shoulders of the same slanted, broken rock.

There were cracks everywhere. Crevasses. Footholds and tracks for water to run through and continue its breaking of the unbreakable. Places where a lad could put his hand and feel a circle carved into stone, an *M* within it. Spaces, perhaps, where a heartsick wife could stash a sword she feared would be her husband's ruin.

"This way!" Ailla had to shout to be heard over the wind that had come up and over the patter of rain in the leaves, moving ever toward them.

He took a moment to hope that the museum's tents held firm and could offer Abbie and Millicent and their high company some shelter. And to pray that Nigel Scofield hadn't been able to see where they were going as he made his mad dash toward the tombolo.

"Here!" Ailla had climbed up on the outcroppings, well out of the way of the highest tide, into a nook where several of the largest boulders met. From his vantage point, it looked like just one more corner of stone, one more fissure big enough only for water. But Ailla slid a hand into the darkness, and it swallowed her limb.

She felt around for something, her face brightening. She nodded. "There's the mark!"

She began to reach deeper inside, but her movements stopped when a faint shout echoed through the air. Not wind, not the rain beginning to dapple the rocks, not cows.

A man, screaming like someone had torn his heart in two.

Ailla's face looked just as agonized as the scream sounded. "Tas? No. Tas!" Without so much as a glance at them, she jumped back down to solid ground and tore back the way they'd come, toward the beach. Toward the tombolo. Toward Gugh.

Tommie followed her only a few steps before spinning back to them. "Her mother was telling her father today. About what happened. She couldn't have realized Nigel would be there now. He's been away from Gugh, chasing us around all week."

Bram shook his head and slapped palms to wet granite, hoisting himself up. "Follow if you must. But we have to hurry here." He didn't stop to see whether she stayed or left. He focused entirely on not losing his grip on the slippery rocks with his rain-soaked hands. The skies had opened in earnest, water pouring down, blinding him.

But he didn't have to see. He only had to feel. There, the etching that marked this place as Mucknell's. There, the cool, dry space between the rocks, protected somehow from all the weather raging about it.

There, the incongruous feel of . . . leather?

A crack split the air, thunder following.

"Bram, *hurry*!" Emily screamed up at him. "Get back down here, don't worry about what's there or not! We need to leave!"

But his fingertips had already brushed over the leather, around it. His hand had already closed around something solid within the wrapping. He pulled his arm back out of the hole, bringing with it something long. Something slender. Something with some sort of crosspiece near the top, making the leather bulge.

He jumped down, clutching his find in one hand and reaching for Emily with the other. Enyon had his own hand knotted with

Tommie's, and they were already running back for the beach. "The sloop! We have to stop Ailla—she's going after him!"

In the sloop, on the water, seemed like the last place in the world they should be right now—but he understood as soon as he could focus his eyes through the rain. A motorboat was racing away from the shores, and Ailla had leaped into another small craft, rigged with a single sail. She was screaming, looking for all the world like she'd fill those sails with her own breath to propel her, if she must.

On the tombolo, surrounded by an ever-growing crowd, he could just make out the prone figure of a man, his fisherman's boots splayed apart, legs at awkward angles. Ailla's father—it had to be. And if Nigel was the one racing away in his motorized craft, then Bram could only assume he and Marrack had had some sort of confrontation.

They all jumped back into Enyon's sloop, it occurring to Bram only when it was too late that they ought to have made Tommie and Emily stay ashore. The waves sloshing over the hull made that clear even as they rendered the point useless. The winds were already tugging them out into deeper waters.

Bram moved the leather-wrapped object from one hand to the other so that he could angle it into a safe place in the bottom of the boat and pull out an oar instead. The wind tore at the wrapping, tugging the top edge free.

Lightning flashed off steel and gold, seeming to echo the dragon fire said to have forged the sword of legend. He stared at it for one second, mesmerized. Then he stashed it under his seat.

"He saw." Emily gripped his arm, panic in both her voice and fingers.

Bram looked up again, gut clenching when he realized it was true. Nigel was turning his boat directly toward them, madness and menace in the lines of his shoulders even as rain obscured his face.

Enyon spilled the wind from their sail and grabbed the tiller, shouting at them all to get down.

Over the crashing of waves, Bram could barely hear the first pop, the hiss of bullet kissing water. But he was cruelly aware of the second one smacking into the hull, splintering well-loved wood. And of the third that blew a chunk off the rail far too near his head.

He pulled Emily and Tommie down, covered them both as best he could, and prayed with more urgency than he had ever prayed in his life.

Another crack, and chunks of wood sprayed him from the mast. One more, whose destination he couldn't tell. Then Enyon shouted, "He's out!"

But that didn't make him turn around. Bram peeked over the rail and saw the madman bearing down on them with all the speed his motor lent him. Enyon leaned hard into the tiller. The sloop fought against the waves, but it wasn't enough.

Nigel's boat crashed into theirs, knocking it into the next wave. Bram caught a glimpse of water coming through one bullet hole, of Ailla's sail not far away, then his entire focus centered on the man leaping aboard.

"Give it to me!"

Enyon couldn't let go of the tiller and lines or they'd be done for, and there wasn't much room to maneuver in the small space. Bram pushed upright, muttering for the women to stay down.

Nigel was upon him in the next second, seeming oblivious to the fact that the waves were stealing his motorboat away, stranding him here on Enyon's sloop. He threw punches left and right, which Bram ducked. At least he hadn't room on Enyon's boat to really use any of those nasty kicks and spins of his. Bram managed to block the next flying fist and even landed one of his own in Nigel's stomach.

Then the next flash of lightning glinted on steel. Not long and elegant and dragon-forged, but short and blunt and wicked in Scofield's hand. It sliced the air, his jacket, then his arm. A cry, part of rage and part of pain, tore from Bram's throat as he staggered back a step and down to his knee.

Nigel slashed again.

"No! Nigel, *stop*!" *Emily.*

Bram saw her from the corner of his eye and feared for a moment that she would throw herself at them, between them, that the blade would find her instead of him. *No.* He couldn't bear that. He'd rather die than see her hurt. The force of that was enough to bring him back to standing.

But she didn't throw herself between them. She swung a long, gleaming piece of legend through the air and brought it down with a crash on Nigel's arm.

Maybe it was the wind that sang like dragon's song. Maybe it was his own pain screaming in his ears. Or maybe it was the warning sizzle of electricity before the next flash of lightning. But it sounded to Bram as though it came from the sword in his beloved's hand, its beauty as blinding as the lightning.

She'd hit her brother's wrist with the flat of the blade, not the edge. His cry was surely more of surprise than pain. But his own blade clattered to the deck, and Bram lunged for it, his fingers closing around the handle just as another cry echoed—higher, from out in the water—and then another crash rocked the boat.

Ailla had arrived.

Enyon cursed and fought to keep ahold of his lines. Bram grabbed for Emily with one hand, his arm circling the air in search of her, while his other wrapped around the boom.

Nigel tottered at the impact, eyes flashing panic. For a moment he stood there suspended as the sloop crested a wave. Then it crashed, and he fell backward, his feet swept out from under him with the surge of water that pulled Ailla's boat away from them again.

Bram's fingers finally caught on Emily—or one end of the ribbon sash that encircled her waist, anyway. He tried to wrap his hand around the slick satin, and maybe he would have succeeded had she not deliberately lunged away from him in the same moment, the sword clattering to the deck as she grasped after Nigel, crying his name.

"Emily!" Kicking the sword aside so he had room to plant his feet, Bram lunged, too, arms out, ready to fold, to catch her.

338

They closed only on the splash of water as the siblings tumbled together over the rail.

Each heartbeat was a roar of thunder. Each blink a flash of lightning. Each second an eternity. It was as if he were watching from above himself as he doubled over the side, clamping his legs around a bench and leaning as far over the rail as he could, grabbing at those precious fair hands that were even now reaching for him. He grabbed her arms just above her elbows, pulling.

But it wasn't just Emily's weight, or even the tug of the sea. Nigel's hands were there, too, trying to climb his sister like a ladder. Nigel's face, pushing out of the water instead of Emily's.

For one moment, Bram looked down into that hateful face and felt all the rage that had been building for months, since this man first threatened Libby, since he first tossed Emily scornfully to the ground outside Piper's Hole. For one moment, he pictured himself doing exactly what he'd been saying for months he wanted to do and plowing his fist into the man's nose.

Then Bram crashed back in on himself, Mamm-wynn's voice joining the wind's in his ear. *"Choose mercy. Always choose mercy."*

Tommie was at the rail, too, reaching out to clasp Emily's hands.

Bram did what he had never imagined himself capable of doing. He held out a hand for Nigel.

26

Emily didn't know which way was up. She couldn't tell the difference between sea and wind, the crashing of the waves or of her brother's body. She didn't know whether the things wrapped around her wrists were hands pulling her up or seaweed dragging her down. She could only whisper in her soul, *I am yours, Father*, and go still. Stop fighting, before the last of the air burning in her lungs demanded release.

She sucked in again, expecting the new burn of saltwater, but it was air that filled her mouth, her chest. And definitely hands clamped around her wrists, wrists she counter-gripped with her own hands. She tried to blink vision back into her eyes, but it was all a swirl of blue and grey, wood and water.

There were hands at her waist, too, though. Pushing, tugging, trying to propel her down to propel themselves up. Her head went under again, just after she heard Bram shout, "You're drowning her—just take my hand, Nigel!"

Though her every instinct was to flail, she knew that if she did so, Tommie—for it was Tommie's capable hands wrapped around hers—would lose her grip. So instead she forced calm, forced stillness, and a moment later, her face broke the surface again.

"—pull you in! Just stop fighting me!"

Though Bram's voice sounded like life in her ears, beside her, Nigel was scrabbling, kicking, clawing at the side of the boat. Ignoring the arm outstretched toward him, set instead on climbing up over Emily and grabbing the rail for himself.

"Nigel." Water choked her, rising over her face again, back down. She spat it out and tried to see her brother through the spray.

She tried to see her brother through the monster who would kill her if it would save him. Who would kill her if it would *benefit* him. She tried to see the boy he once was, the person God loved so ferociously that He would sacrifice His Son for him.

Another wave crashed over her, and in the silence, in the dark, memory flashed before her eyes. Herself as a child, chasing a butterfly on a summer's day. The small pond on their country estate, the waters beckoning. She heard herself laugh as she chased the butterfly out onto the miniature dock. Heard herself scream as she got too close to the edge and slipped. For a moment, blackness and fear—and then hands pulled her up. And her brother's face, young and innocent, appeared before her. Fear in his eyes, but confidence, too, as he pulled her back onto the dock and wrapped his arms around her. *"It's all right, Em. I've got you."*

Real? Imagined? Memory or wish? As she sputtered water out again now, she didn't know. But it was the Nigel she had to believe existed, somewhere under this current version. The brother she knew how to love.

The brother she had to try to save, so that he could live to see how he truly needed saving. She knew heaven awaited her on the other side of the waters, but what would greet him if he succumbed to these waves?

She blinked her eyes clear and met Tommie's gaze. "Let me go."

"What?" Her friend's lips formed the words, though Emily's ears couldn't hear them over the rush of the blood in her veins and water around her and the wind whipping through the sail.

Instead of speaking the request again, Emily simply obeyed her own advice. She let go of Tommie's wrists. She let the next wave sweep her own wrists out of her friend's fingers. Her arm tangled with a line—she didn't know whether it was from Enyon's boat or if it was floating free and would be of no help at all, but she grabbed it anyway and wrapped it around her arm. Then, with the other hand, she gathered as much as she could of Nigel's shirt and pulled him toward her.

"Nigel." Their heads broke the surface again together, and he jerked around to face her. His eyes were wild. Blind to her. "Nigel, I'm here! Let me help you."

Above them, Bram's hand still stretched. "Nigel, take my hand!"

He shook his head, an elbow connecting with hers, and slapped Bram away.

Her own words from earlier came back to her. *"We can only extend the hand of mercy. We cannot make him take it."*

She wanted to. She tried to. She held onto his shirt as long as she could, but Enyon screamed a warning before a wall of water crashed over them, and then the world was dark and cold and wet again. She kept her hand fisted—kept her arm tangled in that line. But the boat rocked, the waves crashed . . . and then she felt the bite of the current gnawing on her feet.

She heard one gurgled scream in her ear from her brother's lips— and then he was snatched from her fingers, pulled away so hard and fast she could only grasp after him, screaming.

In the next moment, she saw a figure cutting an arc through the air above her, splashing into the waves behind her. "Bram—no!" The only thing that kept her from disentangling herself from the line and going after him was that she saw he'd tied a second line around his own waist.

Her shoulder was on fire, but the rope around her arm held steady. But it gave her no freedom to cut through the waves, letting the current take her toward her brother. "Bram!"

He swam with the current, each stroke bold and wide, even as the waves continued to crash over him. For a moment, one moment, she thought she saw a third arm—Nigel's—break the surface. She thought she saw Bram's hands grab at his. And she feared, even as she hoped, that he'd found him—feared it because even now she suspected Nigel would grab and claw and drown them both before they could get back to the boat.

Then Bram's line snapped taut, and she saw him jerk against it. If there had been a third arm, she didn't see it again. Only angry waves, thrashing and crashing and hissing, and Bram's gut-wrenching cry for her brother.

Her heart didn't know what to feel. But as those still in the boat began to reel them both back in, physical sensations took over for a few blessed minutes anyway. Her sleeve was torn and her skin bloodied, her wrenched shoulder screaming. But then she was tumbling onto the deck again, clutching the rail to see where Bram was, adding her dubious strength to his line to bring him back to her. Then he, too, was tumbling back over the rail, and strong arms were around her. Bram's heartbeat was beneath her ear.

But Nigel was gone. She could feel it in Bram's stillness, sense it in the angry lashing of the storm. Nigel wouldn't reach beyond his hatred long enough to grasp at love. He couldn't trust them enough to let them pull him in.

"I'm sorry." Bram whispered the words into her hair, held her tight against him, and rocked her as the storm raged on.

Emily sat on the beach, wet sand beneath her, a fire roaring before her, and a musty-smelling blanket wrapped around her shoulders. She had a tin mug of tea in hand but had only managed a few sips. Her throat was raw, from screaming or saltwater or both, and even the honey in the tea didn't soothe it.

Bram sat at her side, a matching musty blanket around his own shoulders . . . and shielding the length of gleaming metal hidden beneath their legs, wrapped once more in its centuries-old leather.

The storm had emptied itself as quickly as it had come upon them, the *Victoria* had towed them all back to shore, and fishermen had taken to their boats to go in search of the missing man who she suspected none of them really wanted to find. But they would search until they lost the light. They would search all day tomorrow.

It was what they did.

Someone had already had the fire blazing, blankets waiting, and tea ready, and though she'd known they could find better refuge in any of St. Agnes's houses, she hadn't the energy to go one more step and had collapsed here five minutes ago. Neither Bram nor their friends had argued, just flopped down with her.

Ailla trudged up to them, looking exhausted and spent. Tommie, on Emily's other side, sipping her tea, spoke before she could. "How's your father?"

"Awake. He's too hardheaded to stay unconscious for long, despite my fears." The girl offered a fleeting smile.

"Emily? Emily!" Mother's voice carried over the sand and the scrub, tugging Emily's gaze from the bedraggled Ailla. She looked up in time to see her mother splashing through the six inches of water covering the tombolo. She was soaked to the bone, her hat gone, but the relief on her face was palpable.

Emily braced herself. The relief would give way to grief when she realized that Emily had failed to save Nigel.

"Mother." She set her tea in the sand and stood, nudging the piece of driftwood that had been at her back to cover the sword.

Mother's arms enveloped her, but not before Emily caught sight of another figure stomping his way through the risen tide.

Father.

Her bones felt brittle as glass. One stray word, and she might just shatter. "Mother—I'm so sorry. I tried to save him. We tried to save him, Bram did all he could—but he wouldn't take our hands. And the current—"

"Shh. Hush, dearest." Though Mother's voice quavered, it still sounded like strength and love as her hand stroked Emily's hair. "We saw much of it from the shore. We know."

Emily squeezed her eyes shut and clung to her, letting the solace

344

of the embrace seep into her. She would need it, she knew, when she opened her eyes again and faced Father.

She heard his approach, sensed his presence, but he didn't speak. Maybe he was staring out at the sea, willing it to give him back his son. Maybe he was glaring at her, wishing he could trade her life for Nigel's.

Or maybe, she saw when she finally forced her eyes open and pulled away from Mother, he was too weary to do more than stand there, his shoulders slumped.

She swallowed, having no idea what she could possibly say to him that he would accept. But Bram had stood, too, and now eased up behind her, and simply feeling him there gave her strength to look her father in the eye.

For once, he didn't look away or straight through her, nor glare down at her. He simply drew in a long breath and asked, "Why?"

Her brows knit.

Father lifted his wrist a few inches from where it had been dangling beside his leg and flicked it toward the sea. "Why did you try to save him? Jump in after him as you did? He wouldn't have—didn't—try to do the same for you."

She swallowed once more, tasting again the salt and the fear for him. Nigel had not found it in himself to accept the hand they held out. Could their father? "Because mercy isn't for those who deserve it—it's for those who don't. I wanted him to have a chance to choose a better way."

Father shook his head, storms swirling in his eyes. "He hated you."

It was the truth, undeniably—but still it hurt. And yet it didn't change the other, beautiful side of the truth. "I know. But I loved him."

"He didn't deserve your love."

It was the first time in her life she'd ever heard that tone of her Father's—the one filled with derision, that he usually reserved for her—applied to Nigel. And it broke her heart. "Everyone deserves love. Everyone."

He didn't argue. Didn't agree. But his nostrils flared, and then he took those last four steps to join them, and he set a hand on her shoulder.

It was the closest thing she'd ever had to an embrace from him.

"Oh, thank God you're all right, all of you." A new voice rang out, more splashing footsteps sounded, and a whole swarm of people descended. At the front of them strode the owner of the voice—a man she recognized from photographs, though she'd never met him.

Emily dipped into a deep curtsy as Tommie and Ailla did the same, Bram and Enyon dropping into a bow. "Your Royal Highness," they all murmured in near unison.

He ignored the obeisance and hurried toward them, hand outstretched. "That was without question the foolhardiest thing I've ever seen, rushing after them like that." He shook Bram's hand, Enyon's too, greeted Tommie and Ailla, and then lifted Emily's hand to drop a polite kiss onto it. His eyes were sparkling. "And perhaps the bravest as well."

Bram settled a comforting hand on the small of her back. "We only regret that we failed to save the lady's brother."

"Yes." Prince George's gaze sobered at that. "But it is to your credit that you tried. Even jumping in!" He shook his head, eyes widening. "We couldn't see the line you'd tied around yourself at first, my lord, and we were certain you'd just jumped to your own death. You ought to have heard the cheering when we saw them reeling you back in."

Bram didn't look proud at the praise—if anything, humbled. He inclined his head and pressed just a bit closer to Emily. "I had to try anything I could, sir. I wish I'd been able to do more."

The prince measured him for a moment, then nodded and stepped back again, motioning behind him, to where Abbie stood arm-in-arm with his wife. "We are bound for Tresco, and Abbie tells us you will be too. Join us?"

They'd planned on returning with Enyon and Tommie, but their friends were grinning and edging away, so she suspected they wouldn't mind having an emptier sloop on their own return. Emily dipped her head even as Bram said, "Thank you, sir."

No one seemed to notice the leather-wrapped bundle Bram kept under his blanket as they boarded the royal yacht, but Emily was keenly aware of it during the entire half-hour trip to Tresco. She'd scarcely given any thought to the sword during the storm, but now she curled her fingers into her palm and remembered its feel there.

She'd held plenty of swords in her life—there was an entire armory at Scofield Hall that she'd explored often as a child. She'd hefted broadswords too heavy for her to lift above her head and fenced imaginary opponents with sabers as light as air.

This one hadn't been quite like any other. It was lighter than its size led her to think it would be, the pommel perfectly smooth in her hand.

Magical? She couldn't bring herself to say so. Legendary? Perhaps. Without question, it had belonged to some nobleman of centuries past, and it had been forged by a master bladesmith.

And also without question, it was the artifact Elizabeth Mucknell had hidden from her husband. Because *she*, at least, had believed it to be Excalibur. Delivered by a dying King Arthur to the hand of Sir Tristan . . . carried by Sir Tristan over the waters to Lyonesse . . . passed down until Trevelyan returned it to the Lady when his people proved themselves unworthy of its legacy.

She leaned against Bram's arm as the yacht dropped its anchor in the deeper waters off Tresco and the crew prepared smaller boats to row them ashore. Perhaps the people of Lyonesse were ignoble— but she'd found a man who would risk his own life to save someone who called himself an enemy. She couldn't think of anything nobler than that.

The rowboats took them to a private landing on Abbey grounds, and though she'd expected to bid the prince's party a temporary farewell and rush back to the Tremaynes' to change into dry clothes and tidy up, that plan was waylaid by the presence in the Abbey's Great Hall of all their friends.

All their friends, safe and well and dry and looking at her and Bram's bedraggled forms with wide eyes.

Dorrien-Smith laughed at their expressions and strode forward to clap Oliver on the shoulder. "I see you fared the storm better than your friends, Tremayne. Good! And His Royal Highness is very much looking forward to your presentation, I know."

His Royal Highness was shaking Sheridan's hand, laughing over something, and turning to be introduced to a madly blushing Beth.

Emily grinned and leaned close to Bram. "Well, look at that. Something *can* ruffle her."

A servant approached them with a deferential expression. "My lord, my lady—we have a fire built, if you would like to seek its warmth. And there is refreshment for you, and dry blankets."

Suddenly aware anew of how musty and ragged their current wraps were, Emily was happy enough to follow the servant into a grand drawing room and over to the crackling fire.

Before the enormous windows, the tables were set up with all they'd found this summer—the crate of silverware once belonging to Queen Elizabeth, liberated by a pirate for his wife, and then found again centuries later by the two other Elizabeths present in the room. And the chest's worth of treasure spread out with care and order—necklaces, diadems, rings, ingots, coins, loose gems.

Far more interesting just now was the tray of cakes and sandwiches, the bowl of steaming Bovril, and the pot of tea.

"I say—you all *have* been busy!"

Abbie laughed at the prince's observation. "Well, you know Theo, George. He never can sit still."

Emily shed the old blanket and accepted a fresh one from a servant, choosing a place close to the hearth as Sheridan took his cue and launched into the story of all their finds—his sisters and Beth interrupting him at least twice every sentence.

Bram handed her a plate filled with her favorites. And then held out his waterlogged handkerchief. When she tilted her head in question, he just leaned forward, a small smile on his face, and wiped at some smudge or another on her cheek. "There. Perfect."

"Doubtful. But thank you."

He tucked the square back into his equally soggy jacket. "You've never looked more beautiful, sweetheart. Not to my eyes."

She lifted a petit four to her lips and took a nibble. "I can't decide if that's sweet or insulting."

"Sweet. I promise."

She smiled, though it faded again when he turned back to the tray to fill a plate of his own. Her muscles ached, and exhaustion was setting in. She dreaded sleep, though. Dreaded closing her eyes and seeing her brother's face, feeling his hands clawing for purchase. Dreaded watching him, over and again, refuse to take what was offered and keep trying to steal salvation instead.

They could have saved him. They all could have returned, safe and whole, to St. Agnes. If only he would have let them help.

Bram's arm came around her, and his mouth moved to her ear. "I know what you're thinking—but you cannot, sweetheart. You cannot blame yourself. If we hadn't done all we could—if we hadn't sacrificed our own safety for his—then perhaps you could doubt. But it was, to the very last, his choice. And he chose his own strength rather than trusting us. He chose destruction over salvation."

Not so very unlike John Mucknell, who hadn't been willing to give up pirating just because his initial reason for it was null and his sovereign back on the throne. Some people, it seemed, would always seek their gain at the expense of their souls. Some people would seek fame itself above the nobility that ought rightfully to earn it.

At least she had the comfort of knowing her parents would let her mourn with them. It was a strange solace, but a real one nonetheless.

"Very impressive indeed." Prince George stood at the end of the table closest to Emily and Bram now, examining the last pieces of treasure. "And I must insist you all choose an item to keep—a finder's fee, if you will."

Sheridan grinned. "Generous of you, Your Majesty. For mine—

well. That site on Gugh. That is, if the museum is finished with it. Or when they are."

The prince laughed. "You *are* predictable, Theo. Of course. I'll have a word with the trustees. For that matter, as far as I'm concerned, you may excavate any Druid cairns you like in the empire."

Sheridan looked like he might give the prince a hug.

Bram cleared his throat and stepped forward, somehow looking like a valiant knight even with his wrinkled suit and a blanket for a cape. "Your Majesty, there is one more thing we need to show you."

The others all went still, their eyes widening when Bram bent down and stood with the leather-wrapped package he'd carried in with him. Obviously no one had noticed it, the prince included. He looked to Sheridan for explanation.

Sheridan held up a hand. "Not me. Not on this one. Telly—well, he's the foremost scholar on this subject, actually."

"This subject?"

"King Arthur." Bram unwrapped the sword. "And I don't know that I would call myself—"

"You are." Sheridan folded his arms over his chest and glared. "Trust me."

Apparently Bram decided it wasn't the right time to argue the point. "Well. Regardless, I can perhaps explain this." And so he did, with the blade resting on his palms. He told the prince about Elizabeth Mucknell and her journal, about the local legends of Sir Tristan's Lyonesse, about the noble Trevelyan. And then he held out the sword, an offering, to the prince. "I cannot say if this is truly Excalibur, Your Majesty. But it is without question yours."

"Excalibur." The prince stepped closer, but he kept his hands clasped behind his back as he surveyed the length of gleaming steel, the pommel and hilt of gold. "The Sword in the Stone."

"Well—no. That was a different sword, unnamed. Excalibur is said to have been forged by dragon's fire and delivered to Arthur by the Lady of the Lake in . . ." Bram cleared his throat at Prince

George's lifted brow. "But this is King Arthur's sword, the sword of legend. Or what some believe to be it, at any rate."

The prince reached out, more tentatively than she would have expected. He wrapped his hand around the hilt and lifted it, brandishing it so that the light from the fire behind her caught the steel and gold and made them flash.

Did he feel it, as she had? Did he hear, as he experimentally swung it in a circle away from them all, the same song as blade sliced through air?

Did he wonder, as he considered its possible heritage, whether the legends were true? That this blade, and the magic it was forged with, could unite an empire? Make him the most powerful monarch the land had known in centuries? Did it spark the same lust for power in his blood as it had in the knights of legend who would have fought and killed for it?

The prince turned back to Bram. "Do you believe it, Lord Telford? That this is Excalibur?"

Emily eased up a step, standing just behind Bram, to the side, as he'd done earlier for her. There, just in case he needed to feel her presence.

His shoulders straightened. "I don't know, sir. On the one hand, I *want* to believe it. Want to believe some bits of the legends are true, and that we can aspire to that nobility. But on the other hand . . . we've seen today what can happen to men thanks to greed and ambition and the lust for fame. Excalibur is, sadly, also a symbol of that. And that makes me hope that, if it's out there, it's *never* found."

"I see your point there." The prince nodded. "And agree with you. We cannot know whether this sword is the one of legend—even if I were to deliver it to the most esteemed historians, they could not tell us that. But the very question would arouse greed and stir hearts to violence." He squared himself up, lifted his chin, and leveled a strange look on Bram. "But regardless, it is a sword to rival any of my own. And given that it is in hand, there's something I feel called to do. I shall invoke my father's name for it—I don't think he'll mind when I tell him."

Then he smiled, and he pointed the sword toward Bram, but angled up. "I haven't the Investiture stool with me, so you'll simply have to kneel on the rug, Lord Telford."

For one moment, Bram was completely immobile—then he dropped to one knee, head bowed, shoulders rising as he drew in a deep breath.

Emily took the blanket from him, her own heart thrumming as his must be.

The prince's smile went serious. "I am no Arthur, and I have no Round Table to invite you to join. But today, Lord Telford, you have proven yourself noble in the truest sense of the word. And though without the usual ceremony, it is with the most heartfelt gratitude that I take this action today."

He touched the flat of the sword to Bram's right shoulder, then to his left. "I dub thee knight. Rise, Sir Bram."

Bram rose, and it seemed to Emily's eyes that he stood even taller than he had before. Yet somehow humbler too. And if she wasn't mistaken, his eyes were every bit as damp as her own. *She* had already dubbed him her knight in shining armor. But it was altogether different for the future king to recognize him as the same.

Prince George cleared his throat. "I haven't the usual insignia to offer you either, I'm afraid. So, this will have to do." He rested the sword on both palms, as Bram had done a few minutes before, and held it out.

Bram made no move to take it, and though Emily, still a step behind him, couldn't see his face, she could hear his confusion in his voice. "Sir?"

Something rippled over the prince's face. Something that made her certain he *had* heard the music in the blade. Had felt its power as surely as she had. He'd felt the tug.

And yet here he stood, holding it out. Did his hands tremble, or was it her vision wobbling?

The prince shook his head. "England is not ready for Excalibur, my lord—nor for the question of it. Mucknell's treasure we'll put on display, but the sword . . . no one must know of that. And so, as Arthur did, according to legend, to protect both it from his men and his men from it, I shall do too. I shall put it into the hands of a trusted knight and order him to see to it."

Bram hesitated one moment more, drew in another long breath. Then he reached for the sword. He held it upright for one long moment, that firelight dancing off its lines once again. And then he shrouded it once more in the leather that had been its home for centuries. "I will not let you down, Your Majesty."

The prince smiled again, a little brighter this time. "I have no doubt of it." He clapped a hand to Bram's shoulder and then turned away. "You'll find a good spot for it, I trust, Lord Telford. After all, you're the foremost scholar on the subject, I'm told."

As if a cord had snapped, conversation sprang up among the others, laughter and gestures and exclamations of wonder.

Sheridan and Beth, Libby and Oliver all hurried over to Bram and Emily. Sheridan, naturally, was the first to peek under the leather. "On your side, I'd say. What to do with it, I mean—wear it for all to see, and no one would question. *Sir Bram.*"

Bram snorted, but that adorable flush had crept up his neck again. "It would go so well with all my suits."

His sister poked him in the side. "It would blend in quite well with all the suits of armor in Telford Hall, though. Or hanging over the mantel in your study along with the sword with the family crest in the hilt."

Bram shook his head. Emily settled the blanket on his shoulders again.

"You could always bury it back on St. Agnes." Oliver shrugged. "Or toss it into the sea."

"He'll come up with something." Sheridan punched him in the shoulder. "Later. For now, put it down and come over with us. You can pick out a gift. For Emily, you know." He waggled his brows. "Engagement ring?"

"Oh, I already have one of those planned—it's just at Telford

Hall." Bram reached for her hand, his smile a warm, secret, wonderful thing. "She'll just have to choose something else today. Perhaps a crown for that ivory brow?"

Wonder rushed through her, filling her, lifting her. There would be no blending into the crowds at this man's side—and that was all right. Together, they could live whatever legend unfolded.

Epilogue

The night was perfect—warm and clear, awash in starlight, full of promise. A perfect night for a king to sally forth with his knights . . . or for an earl to walk through a neighbor's garden with the most beautiful woman in the world on his arm. Bram smiled down at Emily as she watched a star shoot across the heavens. The wonder on her face always made his heart squeeze, and then gallop.

Perhaps one of these days he would be used to the idea that she was his to love, to honor, to cherish, to protect. But not yet. Tonight, it was still as wonderous as a thousand shooting stars.

"Are you ready?"

She tilted her face down, but the stars had found a home in her eyes. "Are you?"

After all his careful planning, he had better be. He nodded, and with a last look over his shoulder at the ball in full swing at the castle, he tugged Emily with him into a hole in the hedge. They followed it, tripping and giggling in the darkness, until at last they came out at the place that was, as best as he could guess, the very tree under which he and Sher had camped that Midsummer night so long ago. The night Bram had become more of who he was meant

355

to be. The night he began to understand that it didn't matter if King Arthur ever lived or died or was going to ride out of Cadbury Castle or some other place that wanted to claim him. The legend itself was enough for him. Enough to live up to.

The legend itself would have to be enough for England too.

In the darkness, something wriggled, and a muted whimper sounded. The moonlight caught on the golden coat of Sir Tristan, who was still sitting exactly where Bram had told him to earlier in the evening, though he looked as though he may squirm out of his skin if he wasn't released from the "stay" command soon. With a chuckle, Bram patted his leg. "Come, boy. Good boy. Aren't you the best knight in the realm?"

With a happy yip, Tristan—fully grown but still a puppy at heart—launched himself at Bram with a lolling tongue.

"That's right. You've guarded the treasure as well as a dragon would, haven't you, boy?"

Tristan grinned up at him, moved over for a pat from Emily, and then trotted back to the bush where he'd been stationed before.

Bram followed him to it, reached into the underbrush, and pulled out the case he'd stashed there earlier, in the daylight. He could have just buried it then, it was true, rather than leaving his dog to guard it.

But he'd wanted the ceremony. He'd wanted midnight and Midsummer Eve and his lady fair at his side.

Emily stood beside Tristan, absently stroking his ears while he leaned into her, ever protective. "Where is this crypt you say you found?"

He chuckled and pointed a bit deeper into the forest. It likely wasn't a crypt, but he'd been convinced it was as a lad—more, that it was Arthur's. Hence why he and Sheridan had chosen this spot. With an adult's eyes, he thought it more likely to be a forgotten piece of an abandoned wall.

But then, who was to say?

Regardless, there was a section where it had collapsed and revealed a cavity deep in the earth behind it, stone-lined and perfectly sword-sized. With the sword in one hand and Emily's fingers in the other, their dog at their heels, he followed the path of moonlight to it.

It didn't look as though anyone else had been here since he last had, fifteen years ago. Perhaps no one would be again for another decade, or a century, or two. Until, perhaps, some other lad or girl or wizened old gent needed to stumble across it, tales of kings and knights and chivalry in their head. Someone, perhaps, who needed to believe in something noble and good.

He slid the sword into the opening, the case he'd carved with Old English letters protecting it from the scrape of stone. Then he reached for one of the tumbled rocks and fit it back into place.

Emily helped him—after first tugging off her long satin gloves— and a few minutes later, it was done. Moss-covered stones were shielding the sword, none but the moon and Sir Tristan as witnesses to where they'd put it.

"There." He stood back to survey their work, content. Perhaps it wasn't where the sword had begun its life, but it was where he had set out on his own path, anyway.

Emily wrapped her arms around his waist, and Tristan leaned into his opposite leg. "Do you believe?" she whispered. "That it's really Excalibur?"

A question he'd asked himself all through the winter, all through the spring. One always in the back of his mind as he watched his sister pledge her life to a man who loved her like none other under late-autumn foliage in the Abbey Gardens. As he stood beside his best friend in the chapel at Sheridan Castle before sending him and his new bride off on an archaeological honeymoon, looking for new Druid sites in Scandinavia.

As he'd stood beside Emily a month ago and promised her the best of himself for the rest of their days.

Were legends ever real? A sword? A king? He could only shake his head and tousle their dog's ears. "I don't know. But I *want* to believe it is. And that Arthur was."

"And that he'll sally forth tonight with his knights true? The 'once and coming king'?"

His lips turned up. "Well, that part I don't really need. We have a once and coming King already—you helped show Him to me. He is enough."

She came up on her toes, so he leaned down, caught her lips in a kiss both familiar and thrilling. The dog barked his demand for attention, and they pulled away with a laugh. Then Bram ordered Tristan to lead the way out, and they took to the path, back through the hedges, back into the well-tended gardens of the castle.

At another command, Tristan went galloping off toward their carriage and the treat that Collins and the driver had ready for him, leaving Bram and his lady and the looming, fairy-lit castle before them.

Flowers scented the air, the stars shimmered overhead, and music wafted out of the open windows of the ballroom, serenading them as they neared. "Ah. I owe you something." He halted them again at the base of the gardens, far from the other laughing couples, and reached into his pocket. He pulled out a small paper sack, unrolled the top, and shook it. "Chocolate drop?"

Emily laughed and selected one, popped it into her mouth. "You owe me chocolate?"

"And moonlight and flowers and music. And . . ." He swept her into his arms, into the steps of the waltz that spilled across the gardens, twirling her until she laughed from the joy of it and then leaning down to press a kiss to her chocolatey lips. "An I-love-you."

When she smiled at him like that, when she kissed him again, he couldn't help but think, *Yes.* He did believe. In legends and nobility and true love . . . and most assuredly in happily-ever-afters.

Especially when she whispered, "Well played."

Author's Note

There's always been something inside of me that wants to believe—in magic, in legends, in fairy tales. Something that makes me read the old stories with an eye to where truth and imagination may meet. A part of me that is no less thrilled when I realize that the true power isn't from sorcerers or enchantresses or dragons, but from a God of miracles. A God who did the impossible when He raised His Son. When I come to know, over and again, that it's His love that works the most amazing things in our world.

When I set out to write this trilogy, with its pirates and princes and buried treasures, I honestly had no idea I would end up drawing King Arthur into the mix. It wasn't until I finished *To Treasure an Heiress* and sat down to work out the summary for this book that I realized that Bram had been the one to name Abbie's pug Lancelot and that it was an indicator of a passion he kept secret—but the very one that fueled his protectiveness. When I peeled back the layers of this big brother who had made an ogre of himself in the first book but proven himself the truest sort of friend by the end of the second, I saw that he had a core of true nobility. And that nobility demanded a new sort of treasure—one that even Elizabeth Mucknell would have deemed ancient and full of legend.

I am by no means an expert on Arthurian tales, but I can tell you that there are innumerable legends about him and his knights from many different periods of history, and each era put their own flourish and slant to the stories. Is there a kernel of truth to the legend, a real king who ruled what is now England? Historians disagree. Some say yes. Some say there were many Arthurs, and their stories have combined into one legendary personage. Some say it's nothing but a fiction. I say, as Bram did, that it doesn't honestly matter, so long as we take the right inspiration from the tales. And, like Bram, that I *want* to believe.

The research I present on Lyonesse and the Isles of Scilly is indeed drawn from Cornish legends and beliefs, however. Experts do indeed disagree on the timing of the sinking, but what has been proven through underwater investigations is that sometime in the late eleventh century, there was a ferocious storm, and many islands off the coast of England vanished into waters that suddenly rose. They've found evidence of entire civilizations, buried and gone in the wink of an eye. Which one was Lyonesse? On that the experts don't agree. But I like to think that the Scillies really are its remains.

The stories of Trevelyan are as varied as the other legends but also rooted in the real Cornish tales; I decided it would be fun to put my own spin on them and introduce that "symbol of nobility" for him to have carried, though it's present in none of the actual stories. Inserting Excalibur into the tale was all my creation, and one I hope you enjoyed.

If you're curious about the letter that Morgan wrote before his death and Bram found, you can read the story about it in the free bonus chapter, "The Heart of His Brother," which you'll receive when you sign up for my newsletter. Just visit roseannamwhite.com for that signup and other resources for the story.

And finally, Emily. She, too, was a mystery to me when I first had her arrive in the Isles of Scilly near the end of *The Nature of a Lady*. I thought her a typical young woman eager to please her parents. I didn't realize until later how hard they were to please and how heavy the burden of the Scofield name weighed upon both her and her brother. But as I got to know her better, I realized that through her eyes I could explore a theme that had begun to weigh heavily on my heart: that those who need mercy most are those who deserve it least. That those most incapable of love are the ones we must love most selflessly. And that even our enemies are so valuable to God that He sent Christ to die for them. Yet, how often do we focus on stopping them for our sakes rather than their own? How often do we pray *about* them instead of *for* them?

I hope you enjoyed this adventure of my kindhearted lady, my noble-hearted lord, and the cast of characters who seemed to make the story and the islands burst at the seams. This whole series has been pure joy! And as you go about your daily life, I pray you remember the truths that those characters learned.

The Lord knows your name. He's given you wings. He sees you.

So, to bid you farewell as Morgan would do: Live the legacy, my friend. Walk worthy of His calling. Go forth boldly—and live.

Discussion Questions

1. Bram is a bit embarrassed by his long-standing fascination with the "childish" tales of King Arthur. Are there any loves you never outgrew—and are you proud of them or embarrassed? Do you find the King Arthur legends interesting?

2. The Scofield family has placed heavy expectations upon themselves and one another, and Nigel and Emily reacted very differently to them. Have you ever struggled under familial expectations? Did you have to "live up to" any ideas of your family?

3. Nigel is without question a villain. What do you think turned him into the person he became? Do you think anyone could have gotten through to him had the ending gone differently?

4. Emily comes to the conclusion through Elizabeth Mucknell's example that loving isn't a matter of whether people deserve it but is all the more needed when they don't. Do you agree? Is there anyone in your life you struggle to love as God does?

5. Tommie and Emily both struggle with feelings of worthlessness, even though outwardly their positions are so different. Have you ever felt like you weren't deserving of affection or friendship or a second chance? How did you overcome it?

6. Who is your favorite character? Your least favorite? Why?

7. In the end, Tommie's decision to reach out to Ailla provided them with the key clue. Would you have gone to St. Agnes in her position? Would you have warned people about Nigel sooner?

8. What do you think made Bram and Sheridan such good friends? What about Beth and Emily?

9. If you were to write a letter for a future inhabitant of your house or your room to find, what would it say?

10. If you've read through the entire SECRETS OF THE ISLES series, which was your favorite story? Is there anything you're still left wondering about? What do you think the future holds for our treasure hunters?

Roseanna M. White is a bestselling, Christy Award–winning author who has long claimed that words are the air she breathes. When not writing fiction, she's homeschooling her two kids, editing, designing book covers, and pretending her house will clean itself. Roseanna is the author of a slew of historical novels that span several continents and thousands of years. Spies and war and mayhem always seem to find their way into her books . . . to offset her real life, which is blessedly ordinary. You can learn more about her and her stories at roseannamwhite.com.

Sign Up for Roseanna's Newsletter

Keep up to date with Roseanna's news on book releases and events by signing up for her email list at roseannamwhite.com.

More from Roseanna M. White

When Beth Tremayne stumbles across an old map, she pursues the excitement she's always craved. But her only way to piece together the clues is through Lord Sheridan—a man she insists stole a prized possession. As they follow the clues, they uncover a story of piratical adventure, but the true treasure is the one they discover in each other.

To Treasure an Heiress • THE SECRETS OF THE ISLES #2

You May Also Like . . .

Fleeing to the beautiful Isles of Scilly, Lady Elizabeth Sinclair stumbles upon dangerous secrets left behind by her cottage's former occupant and agrees to help the missing girl's brother, Oliver Tremayne, find his sister. As the two work together, they uncover ancient legends, pirate wrecks, betrayal, and the most mysterious phenomenon of all: love.

The Nature of a Lady by Roseanna M. White
THE SECRETS OF THE ISLES #1
roseannamwhite.com

After receiving word that her sweetheart has been lost during a raid on a Yankee vessel, Cordelia Owens clings to hope. But Phineas Dunn finds nothing redemptive in the horrors of war, and when he returns, sure that he is not the hero Cordelia sees, they both must decide where the dreams of a new America will take them— and if they will go there together.

Dreams of Savannah by Roseanna M. White
roseannamwhite.com

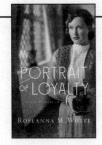

A skilled cryptographer, Zivon Marin fled Russia determined to offer his skills to the Brits. Lily Blackwell is recruited to the intelligence division to help the war with her unsurpassed camera skills. But when her photographs reveal Zivon is being followed, his loyalty is questioned and his enemies are discovered to be closer than he feared.

A Portrait of Loyalty by Roseanna M. White
THE CODEBREAKERS #3
roseannamwhite.com

◈ BETHANYHOUSE

More from Bethany House

When their father's death leaves them impoverished, the Summers sisters open their home to guests to provide for their ailing mother. But instead of the elderly invalids they expect, they find themselves hosting eligible gentlemen. Sarah must choose between her growing attraction to a mysterious widower, and Viola struggles to heal her deep-hidden scars.

The Sisters of Sea View by Julie Klassen
ON DEVONSHIRE SHORES #1
julieklassen.com

Captain Marcus Weatherford arrives in Russia on a secret mission with a ballerina posing as his fiancée, but his sense of duty battles his desire to return home to Clare. Clare Danner fears losing her daughter to the father's heartless family, but only Marcus can provide the critical proof to save her. Can she trust Marcus, or will he shatter her world yet again?

In Love's Time by Kate Breslin
katebreslin.com

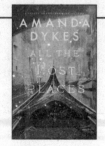

Discovered floating in a basket along the canals of Venice, Sebastien Trovato wrestles with questions of his origins. Decades later, on an assignment to translate a rare book, Daniel Goodman finds himself embroiled in a web of secrets carefully kept within the canals of the ancient city and the mystery of the man whose story the book does not finish: Sebastien.

All the Lost Places by Amanda Dykes
amandadykes.com

BETHANYHOUSE